ARIA TO DEATH

A Joseph Haydn Mystery

ALSO BY NUPUR TUSTIN

NOVELS
A Minor Deception: A Joseph Haydn Mystery, #1
Aria to Death: A Joseph Haydn Mystery, #2

SHORT STORIES
*A Whiff of Murder: A **FREE** Joseph Haydn Mystery*
The Evidence Never Lies
Mrs. Sutton's Project: A California Cozy

ANTHOLOGIES & MAGAZINES
The Baker's Boy: A Young Haydn Mystery
In ***Day of the Dark***, Edited by Kaye George

The Christmas Stalker
In ***Heater Magazine***, Vol. 4, #11

ARIA TO DEATH

A Joseph Haydn Mystery

Nupur Tustin

Foiled Plots Press

Aria to Death
A Joseph Haydn Mystery
Foiled Plots Press

First Trade Paperback Edition, 2017
Copyright © Nupur Tustin, 2017
Cover Design by Karen Phillips

This is a work of fiction. Names, characters, places, and incidents are
either a product of the author's imagination or are used fictitiously.
Any resemblance to actual persons, living or dead, business
establishments, events, or locales is entirely coincidental.

ISBN-13:978-0-9982430-3-0

Printed in the United States

ACKNOWLEDGMENTS

On the subject of music authentication, I am indebted to Beethoven scholar Jeffrey Kallberg, Associate Dean for Arts and Letters at the UPenn School of Arts and Sciences, and Monteverdi scholar Tim Carter, David G. Frey Distinguished Professor at the UNC Department of Music.

Rachel Bindman at the Venice-Abbot Kinney Memorial Branch Library and Solveigh Rumpf-Dorner of the Österreichische Nationalbibliothek provided invaluable information on funeral rites and death in Austria.

Craig Koslofsky, Professor of History at the University of Illinois, was generous in sharing his expertise on the differences between Lutheran and Catholic burial practices in Europe.

And, as always, I'm ever grateful to my husband, Matt, for providing me with the resources I need for every writing project.

CHAPTER ONE

Dusk was fast turning to night by the time Wilhelm Kaspar finally emerged from his uncle's doorway. He paused at the threshold, a bearded, slightly stooped figure silhouetted in the fading Vienna light, and peered into the evening gloom.

The carriage his colleague Albrecht had sent for waited in readiness on the street outside; the coachman springing down from his seat to hold open the door.

"Do you climb in and take your seat first, Albrecht." Wilhelm Kaspar turned toward the tall young man who had come up behind him. As he spoke, his brown eyes fell on the heavy wooden chest the young man carried in his arms.

The creases etched on Wilhelm Kaspar's forehead and running down his cheeks deepened. *God in heaven*! Could the old f—He pursed his lips with an imperceptible shake of the head.

"Here, let me take that from you." With a ponderous sigh, he grasped the ornate brass handles on either side of the chest. Onkel Dietrich had meant well, no doubt, but of what good was a set of dusty old scores to a man in need? The casket itself with its walnut wood and ivory inlay would, undoubtedly, fetch a larger sum than the music it contained.

"Take heart, Kaspar." Albrecht, seated within the carriage now, reached for the chest. "The music must be of some value. Why else would the good merchant bequeath them to you?" He regarded the older man with a sympathetic smile.

"Why else, indeed?" Wilhelm Kaspar attempted a smile as well but could manage no more than a feeble stretching of his lips. He would count himself fortunate if one of the many booksellers in town could be persuaded to give up a few kreutzers in exchange for the scores he had

1

just inherited.

"Herr Anwalt seems convinced of their worth," Albrecht persisted. "Is that not so, Herr Anwalt?" The young violinist raised his voice to address the middle-aged lawyer who appeared in the doorway.

The lawyer, a broad-shouldered man slightly above the medium in stature, came forward at the sound of his name. "Not carping at your bequest, are you, Kaspar?" he enquired as he approached the carriage.

"Never fear"—he clapped a hearty hand on Wilhelm Kaspar's stooped shoulders—"your uncle would not saddle you with a parcel of useless scores. Why, old Wilhelm Dietrich would have it they were worth as much or more than the rest of his estate! I have no doubt of it.

"But I question the wisdom of your traveling alone at this hour, Kaspar." The lawyer surveyed the near-empty street lined with tall buildings, his forehead puckering. "What with the robberies we have had of late."

"He is hardly alone," Albrecht called from within the carriage.

"Unprotected, then," Herr Anwalt accepted the correction easily. "I'll warrant neither one of you wields anything more dangerous than the bow of a violin." He turned to Wilhelm Kaspar. "Your uncle would never forgive me if anything were to befall those works"—he pointed to the small casket resting at Albrecht's side on the front seat—"I had best accompany you."

"I scarcely think it necessary, Herr Anwalt. But if you wish it—" Wilhelm Kaspar gave a slight shrug and proceeded to climb into the rear seat opposite Albrecht. He slid down to the far end to make room for the lawyer.

Through the window he saw the coachman raise his whip and heard its stinging crack as it landed across the horses' backs. He held onto the sill, bracing himself as the horses jolted into motion, their momentum pulling the carriage wheels forward across the cobblestone square.

The carriage sped away from the Carinthian Gate, but to Wilhelm Kaspar's despondent eyes, all twenty feet of it still loomed over the city. As relentless as the debts that dogged him, he thought, now that his hopes had come to naught.

A few gulden would have gone a long way. But what tradesman would accept a quantity of yellowing paper as payment for his goods? At what apothecary could he hope to procure medicaments for Amelie?

His expectations were, perhaps, greater than they should have been. But it was Onkel Dietrich himself who had raised them so high.

"Never fear, Kaspar!" the childless old man had wheezed, his wrinkled, old fingers grasping at Wilhelm Kaspar's wrist. "It will all be yours after I am gone. My life's treasure. All yours. You and your Amelie will lack for nothing, my boy. Your old uncle has seen to it."

Kaspar's fingers tightened on the windowsill. *God in heaven, what would become of him*? It was on the strength of this avuncular promise that he had thus far kept his debtors at bay. But now—

A sudden streak of light flared briefly in the darkness and a jolt as of lightning ran through his gaunt frame. *Good God, what was that*? Rough voices could be heard outside as the carriage came to an abrupt halt, the horses neighing loudly.

The carriage door burst open. A man in a black mask thrust his head in.

"What is the meaning of this?" Herr Anwalt's voice rang out in loud outrage. "Who are you? What—"

"Quiet, you old fool!" the masked robber cut him off. He turned toward Albrecht, his dagger pressing into the young violinist's arm. "The chest. Hand it over, my good man. Now!" he barked when Albrecht hesitated. A thin streak of blood slid onto the edge of the blade where it dug into the young man's arm.

Albrecht grimaced. "If it is money you want. . ." He attempted to reach for the purse fastened to his waist.

"Not so fast!" the masked man snapped, slicing so deep into the wound, Albrecht yelped out in pain, simultaneously clasping his arm to stem the blood that spurted forth from the gash.

The suddenness of the attack had stupefied Wilhelm Kaspar, but the sight of the blood gushing freely from his young friend's arm galvanized him. "Oh, give the man what he wants. It is pointless to resist," he cried, lunging forward to grasp the chest. "Take it, then! And much good may it do you."

He was about to push the heavy case toward the coach door when an explosive sound assailed his ears. Through the gray smoke he saw the bandit clutch his arm and fall back, cursing vociferously. He had barely grasped the situation when he felt the lawyer's hand thrusting him back into his seat.

3

Herr Anwalt drew forth a second pistol and surveyed the men outside. "Unhand the coachman or the next shot will be directed at your head." He opened his coat to reveal three more pistols in his belt. "And think not to persist in your dastardly act. I have lead aplenty for each of you."

Growled imprecations greeted the threat, but the ruffians fell back at once. Satisfied that they were gone, the lawyer resumed his seat.

"It is just as well I thought to accompany you," he continued once they were underway again.

"Indeed, it was." Wilhelm Kaspar was attempting in vain to staunch the blood still spurting from Albrecht's wound. "Who would have thought a parcel of old music would bring such trouble upon our heads?" He frowned down at the wound. "And it is your bowing arm, too, Albrecht."

"It is but a flesh wound, nothing more." Herr Anwalt's tone was reassuring. "This should help." He pulled the silk scarf off his neck and proceeded to knot the length of fabric above the wound on Albrecht's arm before attaching the loose ends to the barrel of his discharged pistol.

"The attack is not to be wondered at, Kaspar," he went on, applying the tourniquet as he spoke. "News of wealth such as you have inherited takes not long to reach the ears of those fiendish brigands."

"It seems to have taken no time at all," Albrecht murmured. "Why, it was only today that the will was read."

The lawyer nodded. "And until we searched the hiding place Wilhelm Dietrich indicated, even I had no idea what it was he had left you, Kaspar. God be thanked, those villains were not well armed. The fools!"

"Then. . ." Wilhelm Kaspar gazed first at his companions and then at the chest. Could the old man have been as good as his word? "I should not have doubted him," he murmured. He glanced up at the lawyer. "B-but, I know nothing of Italian music, Herr Anwalt. Did my uncle say nothing of what these pieces are valued at?"

The lawyer shook his head. "Not a precise amount, no." He applied the finishing touches to the tourniquet with a, "There. That will do for now," before turning toward Wilhelm Kaspar. "But what of it? You know just the person to evaluate the music."

Albrecht, nursing his injury, looked from Herr Anwalt to Wilhelm

4

Kaspar, a bewildered expression on his face. "Who—" he began only to be interrupted by the older musician.

"But he is no longer in Vienna, Herr Anwalt." Wilhelm Kaspar's brow had furrowed. "And I cannot hope His Serene Highness will give him leave to come here to attend to my paltry affairs. Still, I suppose it can do no harm to write to him."

<center>~~~</center>

The warm April sun streamed into the Rehearsal Room of the Esterházy Palace in Eisenstadt, creating a dappled pattern on the blue-and-gold marble floor. But for the balmy weather the small Hungarian town enjoyed, Haydn could have wished himself in Vienna.

Although, as matters stood at present, he thought with uncharacteristic bitterness, even a cold Vienna day was preferable to being in close proximity with the impossible Elisabeth Dichtler.

"That was not a trill, Frau Dichtler. I assure you, it was not." Haydn forced himself to smile at the soprano, who stood looking indignantly down at him from her position to the left of the harpsichord. "Merely a set of sixteenth notes, some of them alternating between the A and the G, but quite assuredly not a trill."

"Ah!" The singer's scarlet lips withdrew from the petulant pout into which they had been thrust and curved into a mollified smile. She cast a languid glance around at the orchestra before returning her gaze to Haydn. "I thought for a moment, Herr Kapellmeister, that you had—"

"Forgotten your aversion to ornamentation?" Haydn's eyes briefly flickered toward his Konzertmeister, Luigi Tomasini, who responded with a sympathetic shrug of his shoulder. "The Prince made your objections so clear to me when he first introduced us, I am unlikely to forget them even in my dotage, Frau Dichtler."

His Serene Highness, Prince Nikolaus Esterházy, had also made it quite clear that he would brook no objections to hiring Elisabeth Dichtler, even though her singing skills left much to be desired. Why, the woman could barely sing a note without the support of an instrument.

"Elisabeth, Herr Kapellmeister. Do call me Elisabeth," she murmured, coming closer to the harpsichord. "There is just one other thing." She bent low over the instrument, her bare bosom almost exploding out of her low-cut bodice to thrust itself provocatively out at

5

the Kapellmeister.

Haydn drew back hastily, but the soprano seemed quite oblivious to both his reaction and the chuckles it had elicited from the orchestra.

"Can you not play forte? I can barely hear the notes at present?" She leaned a little closer to the Kapellmeister, who slid so far down the bench he was in danger of falling off it. But Frau Dichtler was not to be deterred. She sat promptly down beside him and played a few notes on the lower keyboard before turning to gaze reproachfully at him.

"Oh! The manuals aren't coupled, Herr Kapellmeister! Now if only the upper manual were joined to the lower"—before Haydn could prevent her, the singer reached up to adjust one of the stops on the instrument—"we would have a much bigger sound." She sat down, played a few more notes, then turned toward Haydn with a brilliant smile. "There! What do you think?"

Haydn eyed the wretched woman for a space, too put out to trust himself to be courteous. "It is so loud, Madam," he said finally, "I fear I shall be at peril of drowning out both the orchestra and the beauty of your voice."

Frau Dichtler frowned, head tilted to one side as she contemplated the Kapellmeister's words. Haydn gazed steadily at her. Would to God, she would accept his explanation.

The orchestra could in truth have played over the harpsichord even with both keyboards playing together. And as for Frau Dichtler, what her voice lacked in skill, it more than made up for in volume.

The selfsame objections must have occurred to the singer herself. "I don't see why—" she was beginning to say when there was a fortunate intercession from the Konzertmeister.

"The Kapellmeister is quite right, Frau Dichtler." Luigi approached the fortepiano, his limpid gaze resting steadfastly on the singer's pouting face. "The comely Grilletta would never roar out her lines in a lusty fortissimo. It is entirely out of character."

"Ye-es, I suppose it is!" Frau Dichtler appeared none too happy at having this irrefutable aspect of the matter pointed out to her. "Well, the fortepiano, then! Can we not use that?" She turned toward Haydn with a determined air.

"The fortepiano?" Haydn chewed on his lower lip.

Luigi must have been aware of his hesitation, for he said rather quickly: "Now that may not be such a bad plan, Joseph." The Konzertmeister's handsome features crinkled into a smile. "We would have fewer interruptions in our practice if Frau Dichtler could but hear her part clearly enough to sing it correctly."

Haydn continued to hesitate, unsure of the wisdom of calling attention to Frau Dichtler's singing deficiencies in so pronounced a manner. The softer harpsichord might leave some room for doubt. But even the most casual listener would hear the doubling of the vocal part on the fortepiano.

"And Grilletta has but two arias," the Konzertmeister pressed his point.

"Very well." Haydn rose from his seat to ring for a footman. But his Schantz fortepiano had barely been dragged from its usual place in the Music Room into the Rehearsal Room when a sound at the window claimed Frau Dichtler's attention.

"Oh, it is the mail coach!" she cried. "There will be letters for me from Vienna, I am sure." She turned toward Haydn with a pout. "Oh, you cannot expect me to stay on and rehearse that dull old aria yet again, Herr Kapellmeister! Do let me go. There is always tomorrow."

Haydn, looking forward to his own correspondence and glad of this heaven-sent opportunity to be momentarily rid of the singer's presence, was about to agree. But Frau Dichtler was at the door and out of it before he could utter a word.

CHAPTER TWO

In the Esterházy kitchen downstairs, the sound of the mail coach lumbering into the inner courtyard held no excitement for Rosalie Szabó, the palace maid. There would in all likelihood be another letter from Rohrau.

The thought made the corners of her mouth droop, and for a moment she remained where she was: on tiptoe, fingertips still touching the last of the rose-and-gold china cups she had been putting away.

She slowly dropped back to her feet. Letter or no letter, she had best get on with it. Herr Haydn would be wanting his mail. He must, if Rosalie knew him, be awaiting it quite eagerly.

She stepped out of the kitchen and cast a quick look around the hallway. The thought of her own correspondence filled her with such dread, she would gladly have entrusted the task of receiving the Kapellmeister's mail to Greta or one of the other maids. But no one was around.

Reluctantly, she took her place behind Her Serene Highness's maid, Frau Schwann. A footman had already begin sorting the letters into neat piles on a table near the entryway. *God forbid, there should be a letter from Mama—*

The sudden loud clatter of a woman's heels jolted Rosalie's mind away from the dreadful possibility. She glanced over her shoulder, violet eyes widening at the sight of Elisabeth Dichtler.

The soprano swept past the waiting maids and came to a halt beside the footman, her satin gown cascading to the floor behind her in soft crimson folds. *Good heavens, what did the woman think she was doing?*

"Are there any letters for me?" Frau Dichtler stared at the visibly disconcerted footman. Without waiting for a response, she snatched the

8

stack of correspondence out of his startled hands and began impatiently sifting through it.

"The impertinence of that woman knows no bounds," Frau Schwann muttered to Rosalie. "Why Her Serene Highness tolerates her, I shall never know." The lady's maid drew herself up, her shoulders set in a disapproving line

Rosalie was about to whisper a response when her attention was drawn back to the soprano.

"Is this all there is?" Frau Dichtler's voice rose to a pitch so unpleasantly strident, the footman flinched, shying nervously back a pace. Oblivious to the movement, the soprano drew an envelope from the stack in her hands, tossed the rest onto the table in an untidy heap, and surveyed the table and marble floor around it. "Are there no packets for me?"

She turned to stare at the footman, who seemed able to do little more than gaze haplessly around. His apologetic expression did nothing to appease the soprano, who whirled around with a little snort of disgust. She tore into her letter, an unbecoming shade of purple suffusing her cheeks as she cast her eyes over the thin sheet.

". . .*unfortunate venture. . .no gains.* . ." Rosalie heard her mutter as she walked past. ". . . *hadn't bargained for.* . ." Frau Dichtler flung her head up at the ceiling. "Is the man a fool?" she demanded of no one in particular. "I shall have to provide for myself at this rate." She clattered down the hallway, grumbling to herself.

Frau Schwann watched her go, her lips pursed. "Really! How many men does that woman expect to provide for her? His Serene Highness pays handsomely enough to keep her in spirits, not to mention that no-good husband of hers."

"Most strange," Rosalie agreed, her troubles temporarily forgotten. She twisted around to gaze after the singer. She thought she heard the faintly uttered words: ". . .promises me the score of. . ." as the singer went out of sight.

Had Frau Dichtler been expecting a new singing part? "Do you suppose that's what she's in such a pother over? A singing part that never arrived?" Rosalie asked Frau Schwann, even though it seemed unlikely.

The lady's maid harrumphed. "I can't imagine why. It's as much as Herr Haydn can do to keep her in the Rehearsal Room."

It was with no little concern that Haydn watched Rosalie leave the Music Room. She had delivered the mail with something close to her usual manner. But her attempt at a smile had been wan and her features still seemed pale and pinched. Her despondent air had struck Luigi as well, for the Konzertmeister remarked upon it almost as soon as she pulled the door shut.

"Still grieving, I see, poor child!" He contemplated the door through narrowed eyes.

"And still being made to bear her mother's recriminations, if I mistake not," Haydn replied with an imperceptible shake of his head. "There was a letter poking out of her apron pocket. From Rohrau, no doubt.

"It was in vain that I explained it was as much my fault as anyone else's. The boy would have come to no harm had I not hired him." He pursed his lips, the corners of his mouth drawing down. Engaging Rosalie's brother had caused more trouble than it was worth. He had managed to avert the worst of it, but it was not a decision he could be proud of.

"You blame yourself needlessly, Joseph. How could you have known he would be so lacking in judgment?" Luigi demanded.

Haydn shook his head, unable to so easily deny his own culpability in the matter. "I was too blind to see it. If I had, I might have saved him from death."

Letting out a heavy breath, the Kapellmeister rose from the little lacquer table at which they sat and walked the few paces toward his desk. He was about to retrieve his correspondence when a knock on the door interrupted him.

"Johann?" The Kapellmeister's eyebrows were raised, but he was not overly surprised to see the slight form of his youngest brother at the door. "Herr Porta is eager for news of our progress, I suppose."

The Prince's ardent desire to open the opera house at his newly renovated hunting lodge in Eszterháza had lent an urgency to Herr Porta's efforts. That Johann had been pressed into service was no surprise. The Opera Director relied upon him. But Herr Porta had gone so far as to recruit every church singer in the Esterházy troupe as well.

"It is only to appease His Serene Highness." Johann walked into the room, an amused smile brightening his pale, thin cheeks. "He has no more desire to leave for Eszterháza than any of the rest of us."

"Who can blame him? Eisenstadt is positively cosmopolitan in comparison," Luigi exclaimed as a spasm of distaste flitted across Haydn's face.

Eszterháza was even smaller than Eisenstadt. A rude Hungarian village, devoid of any Germans, untouched by civilization. Who would want to hasten there? Worse still, if the Prince had his way, there would be no returning until the end of summer.

Every fiber of Haydn's being recoiled at the thought. Not even Satan had the power to make a heaven of that particular hell.

"At any event," Johann's voice intruded upon his thoughts, "Frau Dichtler affords us all a welcome respite. And Herr Porta is well aware of it." Johann drew up a chair to the rose-patterned black lacquer table at which Luigi remained seated and, with a smile, sat down next to him.

He glanced over his shoulder. "He is more eager to know whether you have received your copy of the *Wienerisches Diarium*. He sent me up as soon as he heard the mail coach arrive."

He looked expectantly at the Kapellmeister. "Have you?"

"It would appear not." A mild note of bewilderment colored Haydn's disappointment as he rifled through his letters. The back issues of the court newspaper he received from his bookseller in Wiener Neustadt were his sole connection to the musical center of the world.

He searched through his correspondence again, growing more puzzled. Herr Weisenstein's brain might be as jumbled as the contents of the drawers beneath the counters in his bookstore, but he had never once forgotten to send an issue. He was well aware just how much Haydn enjoyed reading the *Diarium's* accounts of the musical happenings in Vienna.

He walked slowly back toward his seat by the window, still sifting through his correspondence. One envelope caught his eye this time, and he paused to inspect the postmark. "From Vienna," he said in some surprise, carefully breaking the seal.

"From Vienna!" Luigi repeated, his eyes lighting up. "Who is it from?"

Haydn turned the letter over, his eyes briefly scanned the closely written page before coming to rest on the signature. "Wilhelm Kaspar. He wishes me to come to him." He peered over the top of the sheet at the two men seated before him. "It is a matter of some urgency, he says."

———

Rosalie glanced up from her letter, glad of the quiet pervading the Servants' Hall. How her mother contrived to turn every phrase into an indirect reproach!

"My dear daughter," Frau Szabó had concluded her letter, *"I pray you may never know what it is like to see a child you have watched over with such care led astray!"*

Rosalie folded the letter with a frustrated sigh and stuffed it into her apron pocket. If she took exception to the words, Mama would reply in pained resignation that she was only expressing her grief. That it was Rosalie's own guilty mind making her imagine Mama held her to blame.

She sighed again. "She will learn to forgive me in time, no doubt."

She was prevented from dwelling any further on the matter by a commotion outside the window. She twisted around on the oak settee. Through the open window she saw Frau Dichtler walking agitatedly around the bergamot planters in the herb garden, berating her husband.

Her curiosity piqued, Rosalie leant closer to the open window. A rapid stream of words emerged from the soprano's lips, but Rosalie could hear only the sound of her high-pitched voice. An expression of sullen resentment descended over Herr Dichtler's handsome features as his wife spoke.

"What can that awful woman's husband have done for her to take on so?" Greta's loud whisper caused Rosalie to nearly jump out of her skin.

"It is not her husband," Rosalie whispered back, pointing to the letter Frau Dichtler was thrusting at her husband's chest. "It's that letter that has put her in such a state." She related what she had overheard while waiting for the Kapellmeister's correspondence.

"Gambled her money on some dodgy scheme, has he? And without her knowledge, I'll wager." Greta's plump cheeks puffed out as she voiced the opinion. She knelt on the settee and pushed the long stalks of marigold out of her way for a better view. "Put her in quite a tizzy, it has, hasn't it? Small wonder, too!"

Rosalie shook her head. "Whatever it was, she must have known of it. Something to do with—"

"You must go procure it, Fritz!" Frau Dichtler's penetrating tones invaded their ears. "Are we to lose the opportunity of a lifetime because of this. . .this—" She jabbed at the letter, apparently at a loss for words, then turned on her heels.

"But the money, Elsa?" They heard Fritz Dichtler protest as he followed behind.

"What can those two be after?" Greta peered out of the window, her eyes following the Dichtlers.

"Something to do with music—a new singing role," Rosalie hazarded. "She was expecting a score in the mail. I heard her say so," she continued at the skeptical expression on Greta's plump features. "Although, if it is that, how she can have lost money, I don't know."

Greta shrugged. "Neither do I. All I do know is that those two"—she pointed a dimpled hand in the direction the Dichtlers had gone—"are up to no good. No good at all!"

"Herr Anwalt is confident the works will prove to be the operas of the great Claudio Monteverdi. In the maestro's hand, no less! Only consider their worth, if that is true."

Johann raised his head from the letter he had been reading aloud. "Monteverdi's operas! All of them!" His voice rose in incredulity as he glanced first at the Konzertmeister and then at Haydn. "It scarcely seems plausible, does it, brother?"

But Haydn, rapt in a study of the undulating landscape visible through the window and the sandstone farmhouses dotting the richly verdant country, made no reply. It was Luigi who spoke.

"It is not entirely impossible, I suppose. The old merchant traveled often enough to Italy." The Konzertmeister paused to scratch contemplatively at his beard. "You know, he recounted the most unusual tale to me when I was in Vienna.

"Something about an old monk who took such exception to Monteverdi's music, he dispatched some men to steal it. Every score would have been destroyed. But one of the thieves, enchanted by the music, kept the original and gave the monk a copy."

Luigi's remarks had drawn the Kapellmeister's attention. He twisted around in his armchair, his eyes narrowed. "And the originals passed in some fashion, I take it, to Kaspar's old uncle?"

Luigi shrugged, spreading his hands wide. "So, old Wilhelm Dietrich claimed. He said he had met the great-grandson of the brigand in question, a printer in Cremona."

"And it is *that* tale that forms the basis of poor Kaspar's hopes?" Johann stared at the Konzertmeister. "It is an amusing anecdote to be sure, but. . ." His eyes drifted toward his brother. "Can it be true?"

Haydn considered the question, chin cupped in his hand. "The more important question," he finally replied, voicing the thought in a pensive adagio, "is whether the scores contain the music Monteverdi wrote for his operas."

"And that cannot be determined until you have examined them." Luigi reached for the letter Johann had placed on the table between them. "Why Kaspar did not enclose them with his letter, I cannot understand. His Serene Highness is hardly likely to grant you a leave of absence at this time."

"After that first attempt on them, how could he not be wary of entrusting them to the mail coach?" Haydn murmured, his gaze fixed upon the pink roses painted on the table before him.

"But—" Luigi began, then stopped. His hazel eyes, misting over in confusion, slid toward Johann in an unspoken question. Johann shook his head and turned toward his brother, about to ask a question when Haydn spoke again.

"Re-read the section about the robbery, if you please, Johann." He leaned back in his chair, bringing his fingertips together, elbows resting on either armrest.

"Ah!" he said when Johann had finished reading the passage. "So someone must have been convinced the bequest was valuable. Those ruffians appear to have known exactly what they were after."

"That is not to be wondered at, Joseph." Luigi leaned forward. "All of Vienna knew Kaspar would receive a substantial bequest upon his uncle's death." He turned toward Johann. "The old man had no children and Kaspar was his only nephew."

Johann nodded, clearly in agreement with the Konzertmeister. "Besides," he added, "Kaspar says Vienna is grown so unsafe, a man had better carry some additional florins in his purse for just such a mischance as he encountered."

"And yet it was not money the thieves wanted," Haydn replied. "It was the casket. Had he inherited money or precious stones, would he have been foolish enough to carry them so openly? At night no less? No! But a parcel of old, apparently worthless music, why even Herr Anwalt must have seen no harm in—"

He stopped abruptly, his brow furrowed. "Why. . ." he murmured, then shook his head.

"Well, it was fortunate the thieves were not well armed." Luigi broke the silence that had fallen upon them. "It is odd that they were not. But they could not have been expecting much resistance."

"An odd fact, indeed." A troubled expression descended upon the Kapellmeister's features. "There can only be one reason for it, I fear."

"You mean that it was a deliberate attempt?" Johann ventured, sounding unconvinced. "But that would mean—"

"That someone knew exactly what the bequest consisted of," Haydn completed his brother's thought, his tone somber.

"But who?" Luigi wanted to know.

"Who indeed?" Haydn replied quietly.

CHAPTER THREE

The day's events fled briefly from Haydn's mind that evening, dispelled by the bowl of chicken and dumplings his wife placed before him.

"Paprika," he muttered, eyeing the telltale flecks of red in his broth. "Surely there was no need to ruin a perfectly good stew with it! It is all we shall be having before long."

Even the steam arising from the bowl reeked of its unpleasant odor, he thought, wrinkling his nose in distaste.

"Then, you had best get accustomed to it, husband," Maria Anna retorted. "Why we must remove to the swamplands of Eszterháza, I am sure I don't know," she grumbled on as she ladled out a second bowl of stew for Johann.

"It is a most dreadful inconvenience." She set the bowl before her brother-in-law. "Papa was expecting us in Vienna."

"Was he indeed?" Haydn stared at his wife. The Kellers were well aware His Serene Highness never set foot in Vienna between the months of April and November if he could help it. There was certainly no question of the musicians venturing out to the capital on their own.

"Therese is in Vienna." Maria Anna sat across the kitchen table from her husband and gazed straight into his eyes.

"As she has been these several years. What of it?" Haydn replied, determined to remain impassive. He lowered his head to his meal, somehow unable to meet his wife's eyes. A small, painful flutter arising within his breast made him wince.

Indigestion. From the wretched paprika, no doubt. What else could it be?

It was ten years, or more, since he had last set eyes on his sister-in-law.

"I meant that she is home from the convent," Maria Anna snapped.

The words brought Haydn's head up with a jolt. He was still trying to frame a response when Johann fortunately spoke: "And you naturally wish to see your sister, do you not, sister-in-law?"

He cast Haydn a quick glance of sympathy. "It will be some months before the Prince moves to Eszterháza. Should you wish to travel to Vienna in the meantime, sister-in-law, I am sure it can be arranged."

It took Haydn a moment to comprehend. He nodded slowly, grateful for the suggestion. For Kaspar's sake, he would have hastened to Vienna, but the prospect of traveling to the capital seemed far less pleasing now. He had no desire to encounter his sister-in-law.

But if Maria Anna would consent to go on her own, he might still be of service to Kaspar without—He turned to his wife as another painful flutter afflicted his chest.

"Her Serene Highness will be traveling back to Vienna before long. She will not object to your accompanying her."

"Go on my own! Unaccompanied by my husband!" Maria Anna rose to her feet, her hands on her hips. "What harm have I ever caused you that you would wish to humiliate me so, husband?"

"It was not to offend you that we made the suggestion, sister-in-law." Johann seemed just as taken aback by Maria Anna's outburst as Haydn. "Your going, you see, could also benefit a friend of ours. Kaspar—"

"Yes, Papa did mention his recent bereavement." Maria Anna sat down again. "But the funeral is over." She snorted. "Do not tell me Kaspar wanted you to travel all the way to Vienna to attend his uncle's funeral? He might have known it would not be possible."

"He wanted no such thing—" Haydn began, only to be interrupted.

"Poor man!" Maria Anna shook her head. "To have his expectations thwarted so."

"But his inheritance?" Johann protested. "Why, the music his uncle bequeathed him—"

"Is unlikely to be of any value." Maria Anna settled herself back against the wooden spindles of her chair and folded her hands on her lap. "Papa said so himself. The old merchant was forever going on about some old operas he had discovered. Always in his cups, mind you. The lost operas of Monteverdi! Whatever next?"

"Fabrizzio?" Wilhelm Kaspar rose hesitantly from his seat to greet his unexpected visitor. "You say you knew Onkel Dietrich?" He gestured toward the shabby emerald-green armchair in front of the porcelain stove. It was a chilly day and his visitor, rather too warmly clad for a Viennese spring, might be more comfortable seated near the fire.

"You met him, I suppose, on his travels to Italy," he continued once his visitor had settled himself against the worn embroidered cushions on his chair.

"My father counted Wilhelm Dietrich a good friend," Fabrizzio replied. To Wilhelm Kaspar's tired eyes, he seemed like a young Hercules, basking in the radiance of his youth. "They were more than just business associates," his visitor continued with a discreet glance at his surroundings.

Wilhelm Kaspar's eyes followed his, noticing anew the damp patches against the ceiling, the faded floral design on the walls, the threadbare carpet. What must Fabrizzio, in his silk shirt, with ruffles all the way down to the edge, and gold waistcoat, think of this poor apartment?

He stifled a sigh. The money from the music, if there was any left once Amelie's baths and medicaments had been paid for, might allow for something to be done.

Fabrizzio's eyes returned to Wilhelm Kaspar's features. "I had hoped to renew my acquaintance with your uncle, but. . ." He spread his hands wide.

Wilhelm Kaspar inclined his head at this gesture of condolence. A brief period of silence prevailed. He cleared his throat and began to speak again: "Your father—"

"I regret to say is no more." Fabrizzio pulled himself forward, his long fingers clasping the ends of the armrests. "It was some years back. He spoke often of your uncle on his deathbed, recalling their shared interest in music."

Wilhelm Kaspar's eyes widened. "Your father collected music?" he repeated slowly. *God in heaven, could there be something after all to the strange tale his uncle had so readily believed*? "Why, it must have been he who introduced my uncle to the printer who sold him Monteverdi's music!"

"Ah, that!" Fabrizzio's thumb gently stroked the short glossy tuft of beard on his chin, his gaze fixed on the carpet. "There was a printer, yes."

He continued to regard the worn carpet. "Father often recounted the tale to us, but"—he raised his eyes—"it was Wilhelm Dietrich who introduced the man to him."

He leant back, holding Wilhelm Kaspar's eyes in a pensive stare. "Whether Father set any store by the tale, I don't know. I suppose if he had, he would have bought the music himself."

Wilhelm Kaspar paled. "Then, the bequest. . ." Was it so completely without value? But how could that be? The attempt on the chest suggested otherwise, surely? Besides, Herr Anwalt himself was convinced of its value.

"Forgive me! I should not have spoken so plainly. Your aunt did mention your bequest to me." Fabrizzio looked contrite. "Wilhelm Dietrich must have had the music authenticated," he continued in a rush. "What man of the world could fail to do otherwise?"

"I. . .er. . ." Wilhelm Kaspar's voice faltered. Onkel Dietrich had done no such thing as far as he was aware. What could have possessed the old man to buy such a parcel of old scores? And what must he have paid for it?

Fabrizzio propelled himself forward again and looked earnestly into his host's eyes. "I would be happy to authenticate the works for you myself, if it has not yet been done. The possibility of your bequest containing the lost operas of the great master are very slim. But there may be some merit in the music, nonetheless."

He gazed out at the overcast skies and yellow building visible through the parlor window. "I must confess as a music scholar, it quite intrigues me. This possibility of re-discovering works long held to be lost. But no. . ." He shook his head ruefully. "It is unlikely to be the case."

He turned from the window. "There is news of the Empress having procured two such works herself. You will have heard of it, no doubt."

Wilhelm Kaspar nodded wordlessly, his expectations ruptured. He had, until this moment, been counting on selling the works to no less a personage himself. He attempted to buoy himself up again.

"If two such works have been discovered, why should not the rest come to light?"

"Ah, yes!" Fabrizzio steepled the fingertips of his hands together. "But Her Majesty's source claims to have unearthed them all." He paused before continuing. "Still, there may be hope yet. If you will but allow me to examine the works." His eyes searched the room, coming to rest upon an old bureau standing near the small clavichord.

Wilhelm Kaspar hesitated. Perhaps, Fabrizzio meant no harm. But how could he entrust his inheritance to a man he had just met? A man so adamant the bequest was without value; yet so eager to examine it?

His fingers closed nervously upon the edge of his seat. If only he had heeded Herr Anwalt's advice to put the music in safekeeping. The lawyer had warned him another attempt might be made upon it.

"The scores are not here," Wilhelm Kaspar uttered the lie hastily. "My lawyer has charge of them and has already arranged for them to be authenticated." *Would to God, Haydn could come to him*!

"*Oh!*" A flash of annoyance seemed to flicker across Fabrizzio's features. He shrugged lightly. "Well, it had best be done soon, then." His dark eyes bore into Wilhelm Kaspar's. "Before Her Majesty acquires the same works from another source."

"Her Majesty harbors some doubt as to their authenticity, then?" Haydn twisted his head to one side. The green silk curtains had been drawn aside and the glare of the late morning sun streaming into the comfortably furnished alcove was making him squint.

The Kapellmeister had come prepared to broach the rather delicate matter of a leave of absence to his employer, only to be informed the Empress required his presence in the capital.

Prince Nikolaus Esterházy shrugged, his eyes still on the thick white notepaper in his hand. "She appears to have bought the music on a whim." He glanced up, his hand falling to his lap to reveal a glimpse of the imperial crest embossed in gold on the paper. "Her Majesty likes the arias well enough. If it were just for herself, it would matter little if the music turned out to be penned by some lesser-known composer."

"But her source claims these works were authored by no less a personage than Monteverdi?" Haydn's mind was still struggling to grasp the situation. The implications for poor Kaspar did not bear thinking of.

The Prince shrugged again. "A cursory examination has excited no suspicions as to that fact. But the man claims to have several more such works, and His Imperial Majesty, Archduke Joseph, is naturally reluctant to expend any more gold on them without verifying his claim. Her

Majesty could think of no one more qualified than you, Haydn, to undertake the task."

"*Ach so.*" Haydn nodded. His eyes drifted toward the cypress trees laid out along the paths of the palace gardens behind them. It was only to satisfy her son, the Emperor, that Her Majesty was calling upon his services, then?

Would it be wise to mention Kaspar's inheritance? He had intended to do so, certain the prospect of acquiring the works of an old master would hold sufficient appeal for his employer to allow him to travel all the way to Vienna to examine the bequest. But in the light of this unexpected development—

"We shall remove to Vienna at once, Haydn. The entire household must prepare to go."

"*The entire household?*" Haydn's voice rose. Was there to be no respite from Elisabeth Dichtler?

"All the musicians, the singers, even Frau Dichtler," the Prince hastened to clarify, evidently mistaking the look of consternation Haydn directed at him. "Your presence in Vienna need not disrupt your preparations for Eszterháza."

"No. Indeed not." Haydn's eyes were drawn toward the window again. He thought he had caught a glimpse of the soprano herself. Frau Dichtler, clinging to the Estates Director's arm, appeared from one of the broad avenues. Haydn lips tightened. He averted his gaze.

"Her Majesty has expressed a desire to see the works performed if they should prove to be genuine." The Prince was still speaking. "Under your direction, I might add. And that being the case, it should not be too difficult to arrange for the Esterházy troupe to be a part of the production."

"It would be an honor indeed," Haydn murmured. He could still see the soprano and the Estates Director out of the corner of his eyes.

The Prince looked at him curiously, then twisted his head over his shoulder to glance out the window.

"If she can satisfy the Empress with her performance, it may well be our opportunity to rid ourselves of that woman." His tone was so enthusiastic, Haydn stared at him, scarcely able to credit his ears.

Haydn was about to make his way to the West Wing staircase when the arched oak-paneled door leading to the palace grounds opened behind him. The Estates Director entered the hallway with Frau Dichtler's slender form draped around him.

"You will give my proposition some thought, won't you, my dear Peter?" the singer pleaded through pouting lips.

The Estates Director must have noticed the Kapellmeister staring at him for he struggled to disentangle himself from the soprano. He need not have troubled himself. The singer, turning her head to follow the direction of his gaze, released her hold on him as soon as she espied Haydn.

She swept up to the Kapellmeister and regarded him, head tilted to one side. "Did you come down in search of me, Herr Kapellmeister? Well, I *am* flattered. Here"—she offered Haydn her arm—"You may escort me up to the Rehearsal Room."

Haydn ignored the proffered arm. "I was on my way to the Music Room, Frau Dichtler," he said somewhat stiffly. "But Luigi—Herr Tomasini—and the orchestra await you in the Rehearsal Room."

The Estates Director cleared his throat noisily. "Now that the Kapellmeister is here, I would like a word with him myself. In my office, if you please," he added when Haydn looked his way in surprise.

"Oh!" Frau Dichtler regarded the two men for a moment, then gathered up her skirts and flounced off with a toss off her head.

"What was it you wished to see me about?" Haydn enquired once they were in Rahier's office. He would ordinarily have resented this unexpected intrusion upon his time, but the Estates Director's request had at least saved him from having to endure Frau Dichtler's presence.

Rahier drummed his fingers on his cherry wood desk, appearing to have trouble meeting the Kapellmeister's eyes.

"It is about Herr Dichtler," he said finally. "Would it be possible to spare him—only for a few days, you understand? He is needed in Vienna—"

"Is this the proposition Frau Dichtler asked you to consider, Herr Rahier?" Haydn was outraged. It was not the first time the Estates Director had presumed to tread upon areas that were by rights within the Kapellmeister's purview. "Were you to secure a leave of absence for her husband? Why—"

"Herr Kapellmeister!" Rahier held up his hand. "It is on my account that Herr Dichtler will be traveling to the capital. There are some important business matters that must be attended to," he explained in response to Haydn's questioning frown.

"And you would charge Herr Dichtler, a mere singer, with these matters?" Haydn raised an eyebrow. Did the Estates Director take him for a fool?

Rahier inspected his desk with pursed lips for a moment before raising his head at last. "An opportunity to purchase some items of considerable value has come into my hands. The gentleman in question"—he waved a hand in the direction of the open window— "is reluctant to let them out of his sight without receiving a substantial assurance.

"Herr Dichtler has offered to examine the items on my behalf and procure them should they prove to have any merit."

"He possesses the ability to assess the value of such items?" Haydn allowed his skepticism to ring through.

The Estates Director's pale cheeks turned crimson. "I would imagine a singer might know something of music."

"*You* have an interest in collecting music?" Haydn's jaw nearly dropped at the revelation.

"Well if you must know, it is for His Serene Highness." Rahier sounded irritable. "I hope to present them for his collection if the items are of any worth."

"Indeed!" Haydn rose to leave. "You may count yourself fortunate, then, Herr Rahier. His Serene Highness wishes the entire household to move to Vienna. You may still have the opportunity to peruse *these items*"—he could not help emphasizing the words—"for yourself."

CHAPTER FOUR

"The entire household to go to Vienna!" Luigi followed Haydn into the Music Room. "What could you have said to His Serene Highness to persuade him to that course of action?"

"It was not I—" Haydn began to say, but his Konzertmeister, bent over the fortepiano in the middle of the room, continued to speak.

"It is a welcome opportunity to be sure, but hardly necessary, Joseph." With his long fingers, Luigi executed a rapid tremolo on the keyboard before turning to face the Kapellmeister.

"I would gladly have taken over all your tasks in the interim. With Johann here, it would have been no trouble, I assure you. As for Frau Dichtler"—the Konzertmeister's hand swept through the air—"Why, all she needs is a firm, guiding hand."

A shadow fell over Haydn's face at the soprano's name. "Were it my decision, I would happily have left her in your care. But His Serene Highness's mind was already made up. Prompted no doubt by Her Majesty's request for my presence in the capital."

He gestured toward the silk-covered armchairs embroidered with pale pink hyacinths that stood near the window. When they were both seated, he briefly imparted the substance of his conversation with the Prince.

"Her Majesty's interest bodes well for our Kaspar, wouldn't you say?" Luigi gently stroked the long brown hairs of his beard with his thumb.

"Does it?" Haydn pursed his lips, his eyes staring vacantly at the petals of the embroidered hyacinth on his Konzertmeister's armrest. His gaze shifted abruptly up to Luigi's face. "Where was it that you met the old merchant?"

"In a tavern the court musicians often frequent. Why—"

"The wine had loosened his tongue, then, when he told you his unusual story? About the monk," Haydn explained, noticing the befuddled expression on Luigi's face.

"On the contrary, he seemed quite sober." The Konzertmeister appeared to be trying without much success to make sense of Haydn's questions. "The illness that took him was already upon him. He could have drunk no more than one glass of wine."

"He did not appear to be. . ." Haydn frowned. What was it Papa Keller had said in his letter to Maria Anna? "It was no idle boast, then?"

"An idle boast?" Luigi stared at Haydn.

"To impress you. A musician connected with the Esterházy family, temporarily in the employ of the Archduke Joseph."

Luigi's eyes widened. "Surely you do not believe Wilhelm Dietrich would knowingly leave his only nephew an assortment of music with no value, Joseph? Why, he was quite concerned about poor Kaspar's predicament!"

"Then why not simply leave him money?" Haydn murmured. He turned toward the window. A pleasantly warm breeze blew in, redolent with the fragrance of just-ripened peaches and the heady scent of the cherry blossoms from the trees dotting the slopes of the Leitha Mountains.

"Well. . ." Luigi shrugged, apparently at a loss for words.

"And he spoke quite freely of it—this music he possessed?" Haydn's head slowly pivoted to where Luigi sat. "In a tavern where all could hear?"

"I doubt anyone heard us speak," Luigi dismissed the suggestion. "The old man spoke in such muffled tones, I had trouble hearing him myself though I sat not more than two paces from him."

"Hmmm. . ." Haydn drummed his fingers restively on his armrest.

Luigi leaned forward. "It was not through him that anyone learnt of Kaspar's bequest, Joseph."

"Yes, but it was not the first time he had spoken of it," Haydn pointed out. "And always in a tavern," he continued, recalling his father-in-law's words.

"Always in his cups, you mean?" The Konzertmeister spoke slowly, the corners of his eyes crinkling in surprise.

Haydn nodded. *Could the bequest be genuine, after all?* Old Wilhelm Dietrich, it appeared, had only spoken of it when inebriated, keeping his own counsel at other times. *Still. . .*

He glanced up sharply, struck by a thought. "How strange that he should speak of it so openly with you, a man he had just met, but refer to it in such veiled terms in his will."

<hr/>

"I might have known you would wheedle His Serene Highness into a trip to Vienna."

Maria Anna stood at the parlor door, wiping her hands on her apron. It was a room rarely used, but Haydn and Johann had been banished to it that evening; the kitchen out of bounds until the evening meal had been prepared.

Haydn glanced up from the fortepiano but said nothing. It would be in vain, he knew, to protest that their impending visit to Vienna had nothing to do with him.

Maria Anna appeared not to have noticed his silence. "We have barely returned to Eisenstadt," she grumbled, coming into the room, "and now I must gather together all our possessions once again that you may satisfy your desire to see Therese."

His desire to see Therese? Haydn swiveled around on the leather bench, quite unaware of the note he was forcefully holding down. He released it, recalled to the fact by his younger brother's pained expression directed at the keyboard.

"It is at Her Majesty's request and His Serene Highness's express command that I travel to Vienna, Maria Anna." Did his wife's contrariness know no bounds? It was but yesterday she had wished herself in Vienna.

"We do not travel until the day after tomorrow, sister-in-law," Johann gently reminded her. "I would be quite happy to help with your preparations. And I am sure brother Joseph will do all he can to ease your task as well."

Maria Anna sniffed. "Well, I am glad of it. It is not that I would not like to see Therese myself." She stood near Johann, her slim form and dark curls reminding Haydn of her younger sister. "And any opportunity to go beyond the confines of this little town is not to be scoffed at."

She sat down with another sniff. "Still, I can only hope you will remember that she is married to the Lord now."

"And that I am married to her sister," Haydn muttered, oblivious to his wife's feelings. "It is not something any man could easily forget." He would not have uttered the words had she not goaded him so.

Maria Anna frowned, but Johann interjected to soften the dissonance between them before she could respond: "Frau Dichtler was none too happy at the prospect of traveling to Vienna. She must have thought your absence would excuse her from rehearsals."

"Ah, yes! The idea seems to have irked her more than one could imagine." Haydn's lips stretched into a broad smile at the recollection. "She had hoped, in truth, to send her husband out of the way to enjoy a dalliance with the Estates Director."

Maria Anna, about to leave the room, turned back. "Why would she need her husband out of the way just for that purpose? His presence never seems to deter her from throwing herself at every man she sees. His own behavior is just as reprehensible.

"Why you hired the pair of them, I shall never know." She left the room, head held high.

"A dalliance with the Estates Director?" Johann remarked once Maria Anna had left the room. "Surely Rahier—"

"He approached me himself this morning to beg a leave of absence for her husband. It is ostensibly to allow Fritz Dichtler to evaluate some music Rahier wishes to purchase."

An amused twinkle appeared in Johann's eyes. "He might have come up with a story more plausible than that. I would not have thought anyone quite so hard-headed as the Estates Director would allow himself to be played for a fool in that manner."

Rosalie huddled within the warmth of her loden cape and peered out into the darkness. The carriage was turning off Wienerstrasse onto Himbergerstrasse, the coachman prodding the horses into a quick trot. They had been on the road for more hours than she could count, plodding down roads that were little more than potholed tracks of mud after the previous night's downpour.

Beside her, Greta stirred. "When do we get to Vienna?" she mumbled, brushing away a strand of blond hair from her eyes.

"We are in Leopoldsdorf," Rosalie whispered, casting a guarded glance at Her Serene Highness's maid sitting opposite her, head lolling back; the low, steady rumble of her snore punctuating the silence that reigned within the carriage.

"In a little over an hour, then." Greta stretched out her pudgy arms. "Thank heaven for that! My limbs are sore from sitting for so long." She glanced out the window. "Rustenfeldgasse? We are not lost, are we?"

Rosalie shook her head. "The horses can go no farther. And His Serene Highness thinks it unsafe to continue on in the dark. We are to stop at the Gasthof Obermayr, and resume our journey tomorrow."

The carriage turned onto Gärtnergasse and slowed to a halt before the large wooden gates of an inn. The Princess's coach had driven through and was standing in the courtyard.

"Frau Schwann. Clara!" Rosalie reached over to nudge the Princess's maid. When the woman failed to stir, Rosalie shook her more vigorously. "Wake up, Frau Schwann!"

"She sleeps like the dead, our Clara." Frau Dichtler's ringing tones at the carriage window startled both maids. "It doesn't surprise me. She would insist on adding an entire packet of sleeping powder to her decoction of valerian root at our last stop."

She turned toward the maids with a dazzling smile. "Well, I shall simply have to take Clara's place tonight. Her Serene Highness is in need of her headache powders. You will help me, won't you?"

Rosalie exchanged a glance with Greta. "There's no need for you to trouble yourself, Madam," she began, fumbling at the carriage door. But Frau Dichtler had already stepped around to the back of the carriage where the Princess's belongings and her own were secured.

"A-A-Ah!" Frau Dichtler's piercing screech reached the maids' ears, startling them both.

"What is it?" Rosalie cried, hurrying toward the back of the carriage with Greta following on her heels.

Frau Dichtler stood before an untidy heap of boxes and cases loosely secured with rope. One hand pressed a handkerchief to her lips, while the other held up the frayed edges of the rope.

"My enamel trinket box! It is gone. And small wonder. Just look at this!" She held the rope out toward Rosalie. "What was Clara thinking to have allowed the boy to use such an old, worn length of rope?"

Rosalie quietly took the rope and inspected it.

"And where is Her Serene Highness's walnut medicine case?" the singer continued. "Fallen by the wayside, too, by the looks of it."

Greta frowned. "Well, that is odd! Frau Schwann examined the rope herself at our last stop. It was stout enough, then. And it was under her careful eye that the stable boy secured the cases."

Rosalie pulled out what remained of the rope and stuffed it in her apron pocket. "It still seems stout enough for the most part." She pointed to the brown fibers of hemp still clinging to some of the travel cases on the outside of the pile. "It cannot have frayed too long ago."

The soprano's face lit up. "Then, there is still hope for my little trinket box! Oh, do take a lantern"—she gestured to the innkeeper, who stood waiting hesitantly, to come forward— "and see if you can find it. With any luck, the wretched thing frayed just as we were making our way to the inn.

"Your lamp, if you please, my good man," she continued, taking the lantern from the innkeeper's hands and giving it to Greta.

Greta's fingers closed reluctantly around the brass lantern handle.

"I suppose we can look around for a bit." She sounded disgruntled. "I don't see as there's much hope of us finding anything. Still, no harm in looking. Not as though we had anything better to do," she muttered under her breath.

Haydn sat at the small walnut wood secretary in the larger of the two rooms assigned to him at the Gasthof Obermayr. Maria Anna, complaining of a headache, had already retired to bed. He read over the note he had hastily scribbled to Wilhelm Kaspar, sealed it, and hurried down the stairs in search of the mail coach.

The yellow-and-black carriage with its team of four horses harnessed for departure was visible through the stable doors. Haydn stepped inside and looked curiously around. But the postilion who had promised to ride over to the Esterházy city palace on Wallnerstrasse and to Kaspar's residence in the Kohlmarkt was nowhere to be found.

Hearing muted voices, he squeezed past the coach only to find the postilion leaning against one of the stalls with Frau Dichtler's form pressed close to his muscular frame. Haydn rolled his eyes. *God in heaven! Was no man safe from the woman's attentions?*

He was about to turn around, but his foot rustled against the straw strewn on the stone floor, causing the singer to turn sharply around.

"Herr Haydn!" Frau Dichtler appeared none too pleased to see the Kapellmeister. "I was just delivering His Serene Highness's letter to this good man, here." She glided up to him. "But what brings you here?" Her lips curved into a smile. "*Away* from your wife?"

"An errand very similar to yours," Haydn replied, reaching beyond her to hand the letter and two guldens to the young postilion. "It is the gray building beyond the fountain. Third floor," he continued, relieved to see Frau Dichtler pick up her skirts to leave.

She was waiting beside Her Serene Highness's carriage, her back to the stable, when he returned to the courtyard. He quietly hurried into the inn, head bent low, hoping she would not turn around.

CHAPTER FIVE

Shortly afterward, Haydn stepped out into the inn garden where his brother and Konzertmeister awaited him. He stood near the door, a mug of fine ale in his hand, allowing his eyes to adjust to the evening gloom as he inhaled deeply. The air, damp and agreeably cool against his cheeks, savored so strongly of Vienna, he smiled.

The aroma of coffee mingled pleasantly with the fumes of wines and beers. The faint, appetizing smell of sausages, cooked hours earlier, still hung in the air. He could even detect the stench of steaming horses, always slow to dissipate in the close city atmosphere.

He spotted Luigi and Johann at last, seated on gnarled tree stumps around a wooden table, and made his way over to them.

Luigi grinned up at him as he approached. "You have the persecuted look of one who has just met our lovely soprano!"

"She was in the stables," Haydn replied with a shudder. "Favoring the mail-coach postilion with her attentions."

"We are to meet Kaspar tomorrow, then?" Johann enquired as Haydn lowered himself onto the tree stump next to him.

Haydn nodded. "At the Seizerkeller. If Frau Dichtler allows the mail coach to leave on time, Kaspar will receive my letter within the hour."

"The Seizerkeller!" Luigi's face had brightened at the mention of the wine tavern situated on the Tuchlauben. "You could not have chosen a better place, Joseph. The wine there is the finest in all of Vienna. Besides, that is where I met Kaspar's uncle."

"When he recounted that improbable story to you?" Johann took a sip of his ale and wiped the foam off his mouth with the back of his hand.

"It may not be so very improbable after all. The few hours I spent at the Prince's library before we set out convinced me of that." Haydn contemplated the clear amber fluid in his mug.

"Cremona was the great master's birthplace. There was indeed a monk—a canon of the Congregation of San Salvatore—Giovanni Artusi, who took great exception to the new musical style Monteverdi favored."

"To the extent that he had the great master's manuscripts stolen?" Johann's voice rose to such a degree of skepticism, Haydn found himself doubting the veracity of what he had read.

He raised his head. "Monteverdi *was* waylaid on one of his journeys to Venice. Attacked by brigands." The journals His Serene Highness's grandfather had kept of his travels in Italy, and the memoirs he had acquired, had been most instructive.

"Like Kaspar?" Luigi asked.

Haydn nodded. "What I cannot understand," he continued, his mind returning to a detail that continued to perplex him, "is why the old merchant should have chosen to speak so freely on the subject to you, Luigi."

"*You* knew of Kaspar's bequest, then?" Johann turned toward Luigi, curiosity lending his voice a sharper edge.

"He said nothing of his intention to bequeath the music to Kaspar." Luigi's gaze drifted toward the hydrangea tree in the middle of the garden and rested contemplatively on its white blooms. "The topic of the music itself came up quite casually as I recall. I had mentioned my travels in Italy—Cremona, in particular. Naturally, the conversation turned to Monteverdi."

The Konzertmeister looked at Haydn, his hands spread wide. "I cannot recall very much more than what I have already told you, Joseph. It had been a long evening. The wine was particularly excellent. And by the time we spoke, I had indulged myself a little too freely in it."

"But you believed his story?" Haydn persisted.

"To tell you the truth, no! What man could believe it? That a monk, no less, would arrange to have all of his rival's music stolen?" Luigi threw his hands up in the air, turning from Haydn to Johann.

"But when I said as much, Wilhelm Dietrich informed me he had met the great-grandson of the very brigand who had stolen the music at gunpoint. That he had seen the scores with his very own eyes."

"But not that he had bought them?" Haydn leaned forward.

The question appeared to startle Luigi. "Well, not in so many words.

. ." He frowned. "I suppose not. I must have assumed he had when we learned of Kaspar's bequest." He stared at Haydn. "But surely, it is just a detail, Joseph."

Haydn flushed, conscious of the inquisitive stares his companions were directing at him. "It occurred to me. . ."

He paused. It was such an unlikely supposition, it would be ridiculous to share it. Besides it was pointless to speculate until he had examined the music for himself. If anything, what he had learnt simply confirmed it was genuine.

"It is nothing. I was merely curious, that is all."

"Just as I thought," Greta grumbled, holding the lamp high. "There is nothing to be found here."

The maids had retraced their path as far back as Himbergerstrasse, scrutinizing every bump and pothole on the road leading to the inn but had found no trace of either a trinket box or a medicine case.

"Let us turn back," Greta said again, but Rosalie took no notice. She continued on a few paces down Himbergerstrasse instead, head turning right and left as she slowly made her way down the road.

"Whatever possessed you to tell that woman the rope had been recently torn?" Greta reluctantly followed her friend down the road.

She held the lamp grudgingly before her, illuminating the dark puddles of water, the ruts worn deep into the surface of the road, and the muddied impressions of horses' hooves and coach wheels that Rosalie was intent on inspecting.

"We would not be on this fool's errand, if you had not mentioned it."

Rosalie turned around. "The rope did not fray on its own, Greta." She took the cord out of her pocket and held it out. "See how neatly torn the edge is."

Greta frowned, turning the rope over in her hand. "Deliberately cut, then. But when and by whom? We may not have been going above six miles, but no one could have climbed on to the back of the carriage to cut the rope. And for a medicine case, no less."

Rosalie shrugged. "Or, someone may have cut through some of the fibers, knowing the rope would eventually give way. And the smaller cases would fall to the roadside for anyone to find. We know not what else might be missing."

"Well in that case, let us go on a little farther and see what we can find." Greta led the way down the street. But when they had gone a mile down the road and still found nothing, she was forced to admit defeat. "I suppose we had best turn back then. It is too far to walk all the way to Wienerstrasse."

The yellow-and-black mail coach was just setting out from the inn when Rosalie and Greta returned. They stood by to let it trundle past. The coachman, a heavily bearded, ruffianly-looking chap winked broadly at them as he drove past.

Frau Dichtler was still standing by their carriage when they entered the courtyard, arms crossed, left foot impatiently tapping the cobblestones.

"Ah, there you are!" The soprano came forward. "Where could you have been this entire time?"

Rosalie and Greta exchanged a glance. "Your trinket box and the medicine case. . ." Rosalie began.

The singer waved an airy hand in the general direction of the carriage. "All here. Nothing is missing. You were not looking for those trifles all this time were you?"

She led the way to the back of the carriage. "Well, come along then. We must carry Her Serene Highness's things up to her room. I can't do it all by myself, you know."

The next hour was spent carrying boxes and cases of varying sizes up a wide red-carpeted staircase under Frau Dichtler's direction. Two stable boys had already dragged the Princess's heavily built, still-slumbering maid, Clara, up the back stairs to her room. Rosalie and Greta were carrying the last of the travel cases down the hallway toward Her Serene Highness's room when Frau Dichtler burst out of it.

"Her Serene Highness's trinket box!" she gasped. "You haven't seen it, have you?" She glanced at each maid in turn. "An enamel-coated box painted with delicate blue flowers?"

"It is the exact replica of the one Elsa—Frau Dichtler— has," Her Serene Highness called from within the room. "Not lost, is it?"

"It had better not be," the soprano hissed at the maids. "It contained the sapphire-and-diamond necklace His Serene Highness gave the

Princess for her name day."

—————

Wilhelm Kaspar raised his head from the letter he had been reading. It was written in a crabbed hand and his eyes felt weary from the effort of deciphering it.

The offer his correspondent presented was a tempting one—so tempting indeed, that his hand had in the past few minutes reached forward several times for the writing materials stacked in the pigeonholes of his old, scratched mahogany bureau.

The chill wind entering through the cracks of the window forced him to turn his attention to the stove. He picked up a poker and began absently stoking the dying embers, his mind still on the letter he had received.

Amelie's fever, though mild, boded no good, he feared. The Peruvian bark he had been giving her in a cordial mixed with tincture of rose had done nothing to dispel it. If only he could send her to Baden. *And there—* he glanced over his shoulder at the letter on his bureau—*is the very opportunity to do it!* But to give over—

"Wilhelm Kaspar!" The voice at the door startled him out of his thoughts. "I trust I have not come at an inopportune moment." Fabrizzio entered the dimly lit parlor.

"No—er, not at all." The young man was the last person Wilhelm Kaspar wanted to see, but he rose politely enough to greet his visitor by the hand.

"An acquaintance of mine"—Fabrizzio's eyes scanned his surroundings as he spoke—"has expressed an interest in your unusual bequest. Has it been assessed already?"

"It is being done as we speak." It was no lie. Haydn was on his way to the city, if not already in it. "A possible buyer, you say." Wilhelm Kaspar gestured toward the green chaise by the stove. It was the most comfortable seat in the parlor.

"He has made no firm offer." Fabrizzio inspected the seat before lowering himself into it. "But he wishes to examine it. The sooner he is able to do so the better. He is a capricious man, and his interest in it may soon wane." The young man paused and looked intently at his host. "Not to mention the other sources of such music in the city."

"I would be happy—"

"I had hoped you might have a score or two available for him to peruse," Fabrizzio continued to speak.

He glanced around the room again, his gaze lingering on the sheet of paper on the open writing flap of the bureau. "Opportunities such as this are so rare"—his brown eyes met Wilhelm Kaspar's—"the wise man does not hesitate to seize them when they come."

Wilhelm Kaspar regarded his young visitor in silence. There was a curious persistence in his manner that he did not much like. Nor did he particularly care for Fabrizzio's pointed insinuation that his bequest was not genuine. After all, from what Haydn had said, the Empress was not so very sure of her own source.

And if all else failed, he could still fall back on the offer he had just received.

"I will be sure to consider it—this opportunity you speak of," he said, leading the way to the door. When Fabrizzio made no move to rise from his seat, Wilhelm Kaspar opened the door, and held it wide open.

"My age does not permit me to keep long hours. We will meet again soon, I hope. Until then. . ." He inclined his head toward the passageway outside.

"It is not to be wondered at." Her Serene Highness, Princess Marie Elisabeth, was sitting up in her bed, the satin coverlets drawn up to her chest. She took a sip from the small bowl of broth on the tray before her. "Clara would insist on having it tied to the rest of the travel cases at the back. She said no highwayman would think to look for it there."

She glanced up at the maids standing mutely by the doorway. "The rope was frayed, you say? It is not like Clara to be so careless, but. . ." She shrugged, turning her attention to her broth.

"Well, there is nothing for it!" Frau Dichtler turned toward Rosalie and Greta, her hands on her hips. "You must go out again and look for it. How could you not have seen anything? God knows, you were out wandering the streets long enough!"

Rosalie glanced at Greta, noticing the mulish look on her friend's face with misgiving. The soprano must have noticed it too for she took a few steps toward them, her voice taking on an ear-piercing shrill tone.

"Well, go on. Don't just stand there!"

"No, no!" Her Serene Highness gestured impatiently with her silver soup spoon. "There's no need to send the girls out at this hour, Elsa. The trinket box must be long gone by now. And who knows where it might have fallen."

"But your necklace—"

"I knew something of the sort would happen." Her Serene Highness brushed aside the soprano's objections. "Didn't I say so? Clara is most astonishingly stubborn." She shook her head mournfully. "It is a pity about the trinket box, though. Such a pretty little thing. I shall miss it. It was just like the one you have, Elsa."

CHAPTER SIX

"It is a generous offer, is it not?" Wilhelm Kaspar had to raise his voice to make himself heard. All of Vienna seemed to be crowded into the cavernous depths of the wine cellar and its vaulted brick roof reverberated with the buzz and murmur of their voices.

He took a nervous bite of the pumpernickel bread he had wrapped around a small vinegar-marinated sausage, peered anxiously at Haydn and then cast a quick glance at Luigi and Johann as though seeking reassurance.

"A little too generous, in my opinion." Haydn glanced up from the letter Wilhelm Kaspar had handed him shortly after their arrival at the Seizerkeller.

He set the paper on the oak wine barrel that served them for a table. "All of Amelie's medicaments and bath cures at his expense in return for a chestful of scores that are yet to be authenticated! What can he hope to gain by it?"

"It is for his niece, he says." The lines on Wilhelm Kaspar's forehead moved to form a slow furrow of bewilderment. "What can he gain other than that? Why, nothing, I suppose—"

"Unless the music be so valuable," Luigi interjected, "that the amount he would forego in treating Amelie at his own expense would be a trifle compared with the riches he expects to gain through a judicious sale."

Johann took a small sip of his wine. "Who is this physician, Kaspar? And where did you come by him? He is either generous to a fault or, as is more likely, a charlatan of the worst kind. What think you, brother?"

But Haydn, his eyes fixed on a dapper little gentleman with a dark

38

goatee who stood leaning against the stone counter, made no response.

"I know nothing more of him than you do, gentlemen." Wilhelm Kaspar fingered the note unhappily. "This letter here is the first I heard of him." He raised his head. "I assumed he had heard of my needs through Herr Anwalt."

"Herr Anwalt!" The mention of the lawyer drew Haydn's attention back to Wilhelm Kaspar.

"He promised to make a few enquiries on my behalf. He said a few well-placed words might contrive to raise sufficient interest in the collection for us to make a quick sale of it once you had examined it."

"It was he, was it not, who suggested that the works might belong"—Haydn lowered his voice, aware of the bearded gentleman's dark eyes darting curiously toward them yet again—"to Monteverdi?"

"Yes, indeed! Onkel Dietrich must have mentioned his collection to him."

"But you yourself had no reason to suspect—" Haydn paused abruptly. Why had the old merchant confided in his lawyer but not his only nephew?

"How could he have?" Johann began before Wilhelm Kaspar could reply. "It is not as though old Wilhelm Dietrich spoke of it other than—" He cleared his throat, but appeared unable to ward off a desperate fit of coughing.

Haydn bit his lip. Johann's words had brought a niggling doubt in his mind to the fore. *Had the wine loosened the old merchant's tongue or had*—? He shook his head. Most likely it was the former.

"Your uncle must have trusted his lawyer unreservedly to make him his confidante," he remarked, turning toward Wilhelm Kaspar.

The musician shrugged. "No reason not to. Herr Anwalt has taken care of Onkel Dietrich's affairs for as long as I can remember. A more honest man, you could not find. Truly, if he had not the forethought to be armed, I should have lost my bequest the very day I inherited it."

Luigi grinned broadly. "A man after my own heart!" He gulped down his wine and hailed the bartender for another bottle. "It is quite the best way to deal with ruffians such as the ones you encountered. It was fortuitous they were not as well armed as he."

"And fortunate, indeed, then that *he* himself was," Haydn commented dryly. "In what other ways has he been of service to you?"

Johann turned toward his brother, his eyebrows raised in mild surprise. But Wilhelm Kaspar showed no signs of having noticed anything amiss. He took a deep draught of his wine, and continued: "Why, it was he who suggested I write to you, Joseph."

He tipped his wine glass to his lips again. "I only wish I had taken his advice to entrust the scores into his keeping. They would have been safer in his chambers. There is a music scholar—a most persistent fellow—who keeps coming around to the house. Claims his father knew Onkel Dietrich. I do not—"

"Herr Anwalt *suggested* you entrust your bequest to him?" Haydn straightened up in his chair, his voice rising to a crescendo that attracted the attention of the sprucely attired gentleman, who still stood by the counter.

He made an effort to lower his voice. "The music is still in your keeping, I trust, Kaspar."

When Wilhelm Kaspar nodded, he leaned forward, his voice urgent. "Be sure not to let it out of your hands until I have had an opportunity to examine it. I shall do it directly I return from Schönbrunn."

"But surely, Herr Anwalt—"

"The music will be safer in your house than in his chambers. And as for this physician of yours"—Haydn reached into his pocket for some banknotes and thrust them into his friend's hands—"I trust fifty gulden will suffice for Amelie's bath cure. Tell the doctor you prefer to have the music authenticated before you consider any offers for it."

"But. . ." Wilhelm Kaspar looked down at the bank notes in his hands in bewilderment. "This is much too generous, Joseph. I cannot—"

"It is much the best way, my friend," Haydn murmured, his eyes moving from the bar counter to the arched wooden door. The bearded little man in his elegant suit of black velvet was gone. *A foreigner*? How much of their conversation had he overheard, Haydn wondered. And what interest could he possibly have in their affairs?

"I shall have to examine the works, Your Majesty." Haydn opened one of the vellum-bound scores the Empress Maria Theresa had handed him and perused the pages curiously.

He and Johann had accompanied the Prince to Schönbrunn that

afternoon and now sat in the Empress's white-and gold-receiving chambers in the west wing of the summer palace.

"But at a casual glance"—Haydn raised his eyes—"they appear authentic enough."

He gently rubbed his right thumb over the paper. It felt thick and strong under his fingers. He turned his attention to the binding. The cream-colored vellum was unusually soft and the gold trim exceptionally fine.

Johann reached for the second score the Empress had placed upon a gold stool upholstered in rich crimson and read the dedication within. "The hand appears to be that of a copyist, brother." He turned toward the Empress, who was still seated at the harpsichord. "As would be quite natural under the circumstances, Your Majesty."

The Empress's finely shaped eyebrows drew together into a frown. "I hope you are mistaken, Master Johann. Dr. Goretti swore to me those works were in the composer's own hand. I have no reason to doubt his sincerity."

"And yet you would have Haydn authenticate them," His Serene Highness murmured. His eyes drifted toward the portrait of His Imperial Majesty, Archduke Joseph, set into a panel on the wall behind the Empress.

Haydn suppressed a smile, having glanced up in time to catch the movement in the ornate gilt-framed mirror hanging opposite him. The Prince had complained often enough, as had his Konzertmeister Luigi, of the stinginess of the Archduke's purse.

"It is the composer's identity rather than his hand that I desire your Kapellmeister to authenticate, Esterházy!" The Empress's tone was sharp, her heavy jowls quivering in exasperation.

"If I may be so bold as to ask," Haydn interjected gently, "how much did Your Majesty pay for the scores?" No doubt the purchase had caused a rift between the Empress and her son and co-regent.

"Pay for the scores!" Her Majesty's lips protruded into a startled round, blowing her cheeks out. "Why no more than a hundred ducats apiece. But—"

Haydn hastily withdrew his eyes from the portrait looming over the Empress only to find her large blue eyes inspecting him closely.

"I am still Empress, gentlemen." She fingered the gold lace on her mourning gown of black velvet, her tone even. "But in this instance, I am in complete agreement with my son. It was not entirely for my own pleasure that I bought the music."

"Her Majesty intends to initiate a revival of opera seria in the capital with the great works of Monteverdi," the Prince explained without much enthusiasm, his own tastes running to the lighter opera buffa style.

"Among other things." The Empress's eyes were veiled. "And too much rests upon it for me to take the word of the good physician who brought it to me."

"It was a physician who brought these works to you, then, Your Majesty?" Johann leaned forward, his voice rising a little.

The Empress nodded, the skin under her jaw forming loose, fleshy folds under her chin. "Giacomo Goretti. A fine physician, in my opinion, although van Swieten"— she gestured with a well-fleshed but shapely hand in the direction of the ante-chamber where her imperial physician waited —"would have it otherwise."

"An Italian?" Haydn enquired, his eyes meeting Johann's. "And he was only able to bring you these two works, Your Majesty?"

"With the promise of more, as I am sure Esterházy will have mentioned to you." The Empress shifted her bulk in the direction of the Prince, who nodded wordlessly. "If these prove to be authentic, we shall purchase the entire collection. They will be more valuable still in the great composer's own hand."

"And he discovered them, I presume, in Venice," Haydn hazarded. It was where the great master had ended his days, having left the Mantuan court to assume the position of Kapellmeister at the Basilica of San Marco in the city-state.

"On the contrary. It was here in Vienna that he found them."

"And what is your opinion, Herr Haydn?" Baron Gerard van Swieten's faded blue eyes studied Haydn's features. "Is the music genuine?"

"It is too early to tell." Haydn strolled slowly between his brother and the imperial physician, enjoying the pleasantly cool air within the pergola in the privy garden.

"It is quite possible, I suppose," he continued, admiring the purple flowers on the trellis. "But one wonders how the works of an Italian master, in his own hand, no less"—he turned to face the Dutchman—"could have made their way to Vienna."

The imperial physician snorted. "Stolen, the Mantuan historians would have it, by the imperial family and their soldiers."

"But that is preposterous!" Johann exclaimed. "Surely the Empress does not believe that claptrap?"

"And when would they have had any opportunity to steal it?" Haydn had come to a halt in the middle of the pergola.

Van Swieten rolled his eyes. "About a hundred years ago, apparently, when the imperial army besieged the city. It is arrant nonsense, of course!"

His blue eyes held Haydn's gaze steadily. "I have found no evidence that any music from the Gonzaga court ever made its way back to Vienna when the Emperor Ferdinand attempted to oust Charles of Nevers from Mantua."

Haydn nodded. "And, if it had, there would be no reason for it to have left the imperial library, would there?"

"Not without my knowledge." A worried expression clouded the Dutchman's rounded features. "If there is any truth to the story, it would mean the scores had been stolen from our possession." He straightened his back. "If that is the case, I am prepared to resign from my position as chief librarian."

"They could have been removed at any time in the course of these hundred years." Johann's tone was gentle. "There is no reason to suppose the theft occurred under your watch."

The Dutchman shook his head. "Very few people beside the imperial family have access to the imperial library. No, Master Johann! The implications of such a supposition do not bear thinking of." He regarded the brothers earnestly. "Besides, I am convinced Dr. Goretti will prove to be a charlatan of the worst order."

"Indeed!" Haydn raised an eyebrow.

"Medically speaking, he is a quack, gentlemen. An utter quack!" The imperial physician stood before them, hands behind his back, chest puffed out in indignation.

"His ideas on smallpox are irresponsible to say the least. Rub the infected pus from smallpox victims into the wounds of the healthy, indeed! Why, we would have an epidemic on our hands in no time at all."

"And the Empress would wish herself so treated?" Johann sounded incredulous.

"That it is a remedy the illiterate Turks take recourse to does give her pause." Van Swieten's tone was wry. "I have heard of some cases of success with it, gentlemen. But there have been just as many incidents of virulent illness and death as a result. And Dr. Goretti has no satisfactory explanation on the subject."

"But rather than let nature choose her victims"—Haydn shuddered—"he would expose us all to his untried remedy." In a crowded city like Vienna, the consequences of such a thoughtless action would be disastrous. Far better to chance the disease as he had and trust in the restorative powers of margrave powder and barley tea!

The Dutchman pulled the corners of his mouth into a grimace. "And his knowledge of music is equally deficient, according to Kapellmeister Reutter!"

Haydn's eyes drifted toward Johann. His old teacher could be quite pigheaded in his views. Was there any truth to his impressions? He turned toward van Swieten.

"How came he by these scores, then?"

The imperial physician spread his hands. "It is a question I have often asked myself. At best, it is a chance occurrence that he seeks to capitalize upon. At worst. . ." he shook his head. "I would take you to him, but he is nowhere to be found. For a man who seeks a position at the imperial court, he spends very little time here!"

CHAPTER SEVEN

L uigi glugged down the last of the wine and plonked the bottle unsteadily on the oak barrel between them.

"Joseph was right, then?" The Konzertmeister retained his grip on the wine bottle. The close, stale air within the Seizerkeller, the vast quantity of wine he had consumed, and the heady fumes of wine and smoke were beginning to tell on him. "About that physician of yours being a no-good charlatan?"

He enunciated his words with care, but his voice, even to his own ears, sounded slurred and slow.

". . . Such a vast sum of money! I was sorely tempted, I can tell you that." Wilhelm Kaspar was speaking again. Luigi opened his hazel eyes wide, forcing himself to pay attention.

"If it were not for the man's desperation—why, he was quite ready to set down the money then and there in exchange for the entire parcel of scores—I might've been persuaded. . ."

Luigi's eyes flew open, jolted to alertness by a hand shaking him.

"Are you quite all right?" Wilhelm Kaspar's brown eyes gazed anxiously into his own. "It may be time for us to leave, my friend."

Luigi staggered to his feet. "Best get back to my lodgings," he mumbled.

It was the pounding at his door that aroused him the next morning. "Herr Tomasini!"

Luigi buried his head in his pillow, willing the ruckus to go away.

"Herr Tomasini!" The urgency of his landlady's summons, reflected in the sharp rising of her voice, dispelled the last mists of slumber. He forced himself out of bed and opened the door.

"What's amiss?" Luigi frowned down at the plump woman who stood at the door, a tray of coffee in one hand, the other, clenched into a fist, ready to strike at the door again.

It was the man-servant behind her, vaguely familiar to Luigi, who responded.

"It is my master, Herr Tomasini." He thrust a card into Luigi's bewildered hands. "He is gone!"

"Kaspar!" Luigi stared down at the card. "Kaspar is gone, you say?"

"Did your master not return home at all after—" Luigi frowned as he strode down the street. Had Kaspar accompanied him to his lodgings or had they parted ways at the Seizerkeller?

"He set out early in the evening for the Seizerkeller—" Wilhelm Kaspar's aged servant scurried after Luigi, sounding breathless.

"Yes, we met at the wine-cellar." Luigi slackened his stride to allow the servant to catch up to him. If only he had not indulged so freely last night, but an entire day with the infuriating La Dichtler was enough to drive a man to drink! Even the tavern had barely provided an adequate refuge from her presence.

"Master returned home late, Herr Tomasini. Barely an hour before he was to have retired for the night. It must have been the message that sent him rushing out again—"

"Message? What message?" Luigi stopped short. Kaspar had made no mention of a message, had he?

Kaspar's servant swallowed a few gulps of air before responding. The streets had been washed that morning as always, but the dust was already rising from them. Luigi resisted the urge to press a sleeve to his nostrils.

"It was delivered shortly after my master came home. He had no sooner read it than he set out again. Told me not to wait up for him. But I was to keep the door unlatched, so he could let himself in."

Luigi frowned. "The message was delivered after he returned home from the wine cellar, then?" The coffee he had hastily gulped down—lukewarm by the time his landlady had served it to him—had done much toward reviving his senses. But he still felt lightheaded.

"What did it say? Who was it from?" he demanded when the servant nodded.

Wilhelm Kaspar's man-servant scratched sheepishly at his thinning gray head. "Master did not say, Herr Tomasini. And even if I could read, I wouldn't know. He scrunched the note up and put it in his pocket as soon as he'd read it."

He peered anxiously at Luigi, who was tugging at his beard pensively. "It is not like him to be out all hours of the night, Herr Tomasini. Not like him at all." He paused, then continued in a rush, "I would not have troubled you had I not feared for his safety. But Herr Haydn was not at Wallnerstrasse, and they told me there—"

"It is quite all right, Rudi." Luigi set off down the street toward the Tuchlauben at a brisk pace. A police guard would have to be found and the night watchmen questioned. Where could Kaspar have gone so late last night?

A commotion down the road attracted his attention. He was about to head down one of the side streets on the left toward the Graben, and thence to Kohlmarkt, when he caught a glimpse of a white uniform trimmed with blue

"There appears to be some trouble up ahead," he murmured. "But no doubt one of the police guards can be persuaded to help us."

"The street was blocked this morning." Rudi panted heavily from the exertion of keeping pace with Luigi. The servant drew a deep breath. "I had to go past Petersplatz to get to your lodgings."

The crowd milling around the Seizerkeller had begun to disperse by the time Luigi and Kaspar's man-servant arrived at the wine cellar, sent firmly about their business by two of the police guards. A third supervised two watchmen as they carefully began to hoist a makeshift litter carrying the supine body of a man onto their shoulders.

"Beaten and left to die, poor soul," a stout woman observed to Luigi. "By robbers, the guards think." The woman sighed. "It is a common enough occurrence, I fear," she added, evidently in response to Luigi's horror-struck gaze.

The Konzertmeister found himself unable to tear his gaze away from the man on the litter, his plain brown suit of clothing scuffed and torn, his arms and neck covered in lacerations, and his brown-gray hair matted with blood. His mouth felt parched. He attempted to shield the aged servant behind him from the grim sight, but Rudi's dim eyes were already widening in horrified recognition.

"It is my master!" He turned a stricken face toward the

Konzertmeister. "But why would anyone harm him? Poor man! He had nothing worth stealing."

———

"Do you know this man?" The servant's strangled cry had caught the police guard's attention. Holding up a peremptory hand to halt the watchmen, he turned from Rudi to Luigi, his sharp blue eyes scrutinizing both men.

Luigi swallowed. "Wilhelm Kaspar—he is a violinist." He swallowed again. His throat felt hoarse, and he cleared it noisily before beginning again: "At St. Michael's Church, but he plays on occasion at the Kärntnertor Theater and at the Hofburg."

"One of Her Majesty's musicians, then?" The police guard appeared perturbed at the thought.

"On occasion, yes." Luigi nodded. "He fills in when asked to. But it is at the church that he is employed." His eyes were drawn toward the litter again. Through Kaspar's torn clothing, he could make out the gaping tears in his skin and the red-tinged flesh. Kaspar's nose appeared to be smashed in; and his eyes. . . A wave of nausea overcame Luigi and he averted his eyes.

"Such brutality!" he murmured, more to himself than to the police guard. "Who could have done such a thing?"

"Who else but the thieves that plague this city? We found this purse discarded by the way side." The police guard held out a small, scuffed leather purse in his hands.

"That is Master's purse!" the servant cried. "But he had little enough money to carry in it, poor man."

The police guard shrugged. "Had he a little more, his life may have been spared."

The callously uttered words enraged Luigi. "Are the thieves here grown so desperate that they would fall upon a man not rich enough to steal from? Are they so bold that they would kill a man for being too poor to have more than a few florins in his purse? Look at his clothes, man! Did he look like a man worth stealing from?"

He had, quite without thought, taken a step toward the police guard, his fists clenched. It was a mistake. The two guards who had been dispersing the crowd moved forward, rifles at the ready.

"Then, perhaps, he was a thief himself and received his just deserts." The first police guard's tone had hardened. Old Rudi, Kaspar's servant, was shaking his head vehemently, but the guard continued on relentlessly. "Or, was it the wine"—he threw a contemptuous glance at the wine cellar—"that drove him to violence? A drunken quarrel between friends that took his life?"

"For shame! Would you sully a dead man's name? Master never stole a kreutzer in all his life; nor ever drunk himself into a stupor."

One of the other police guards thrust himself in front of the first guard. "Poldi meant no disrespect, did you now, eh Poldi?" He frowned at his colleague. "But when a man is found beaten to death, his purse emptied of its contents and tossed to the ground. . ." He lifted his shoulders and spread his palms out in an eloquent gesture. "Did he have nothing worth stealing, then?"

Luigi tugged at his beard. "Only a snuffbox," he said, remembering the box inlaid with precious stones Kaspar had been twiddling with the previous evening. "A tiny thing of rare beauty, but still. . ."

"Then that was what they were after, my good sir," Poldi's colleague asserted. He gestured in the direction of the litter. "See those bruises and tears on his wrists? He must have resisted them." He shook his head. "A mistake our good citizens too often make."

"No, no. . ." Luigi could feel a vein in his head throbbing painfully. There was something very wrong here, but the police guards seemed blind to it. If only Haydn were here.

"You had best come with us to the police station," Poldi said in a gruff voice. "If you have any knowledge of this matter, the Herr Inspektor will wish to be informed of it."

Luigi nodded mutely. He withdrew a pen from his pocket and a sheet of paper, scribbled a hasty note, then pressed it into old Rudi's hands. "Take this to Wallnerstrasse and have someone send it to Herr Haydn. Tell them it is most urgent. I will go to Baden myself, once my business at the police station is concluded, and convey your mistress back to town."

"What an unusual collection of portraits! This one is particularly striking, Johann." Haydn drew his brother's attention to an exquisite pastel of a child clutching a doll to her breast. It was, like all the drawings

49

in the room, by the Genevan artist, Jean-Étienne Liotard.

Johann, studying a portrait of a young boy in profile, was about to respond when the door behind them opened.

"Gentlemen!" The imperial physician leaned briefly against the door to regain his breath. "I am sorry to have kept you waiting," he said at last, "but I am not as limber as I used to be." He entered the room followed by a tall young man whose left arm hung stiffly by his side.

"I had hoped Kapellmeister Reutter would be able to place one of his more experienced musicians at your disposal, but"—he gestured toward his companion's bandaged arm—"without the use of his bowing arm, Albrecht here is no good to the orchestra, and the Kapellmeister is hard pressed to spare any of his men at present."

"I am sure he will do admirably, Your Lordship." Johann directed an encouraging smile at the young musician standing, head bowed, at Baron van Swieten's side.

"How came you by your injury, young man?" he continued, once the Baron, having made his introductions, had left.

"A knife wound from a brigand, I am afraid." Albrecht shrugged ruefully, seating himself at the gold-upholstered chaise Johann had indicated with a brief motion of his hand. "They were after my friend's inheritance, although how they could have known anything about it when the will had just been read, I will never understand. If it were not for the lawyer who rode with us. . ." he shrugged again.

"This friend of yours—" Haydn scanned the young man's narrow face. It was scarcely possible, he thought, for two men to have experienced the same sort of robbery. "This friend would not happen to be a man by the name of Wilhelm Kaspar, would he?"

Albrecht's hooded eyes opened a little wider. "The very same! I had no conception Kaspar was acquainted with a man so eminent as yourself. Why, it must have been you Herr Anwalt was referring to when he suggested Kaspar have his bequest evaluated." He hesitated briefly.

"If I may be so bold as to ask, are the scores genuine?" His eyes darted eagerly from Haydn to Johann.

"It is too early to tell," Haydn responded lightly. Albrecht, he feared, was too young to be discreet, and Kaspar's inheritance had already attracted quite enough attention. "The will had *just* been read, you say?" The words had caught his attention. He frowned, trying to recall whether

Kaspar had made mention of the fact in his letter.

Albrecht nodded. "That very evening. Why, even Herr Anwalt knew not what Kaspar's bequest consisted of. That is why it was so odd—"

"Odd indeed!" Haydn's lips had tightened. The entire circumstance was so odd, he would have to pay a visit to the lawyer once they were back in town.

Johann's cough drew his attention back to Albrecht. The young man was staring at him in open curiosity.

"Dr. Goretti, I take it—" Haydn began.

"Is still in town, no doubt." Albrecht looked apologetic. "Baron van Swieten takes great exception to his prolonged absences, but they are for an entirely worthy cause."

"Indeed?" Johann's eyebrows were raised.

"He lends his services at the hospital run by the Brothers of Mercy. There is not much he can do here—" The young man's eyes slid to the floor, intent on the red carpet at their feet. "His views are. . ." he shifted uncomfortably in his seat, apparently still having trouble raising his eyes.

"You are in agreement with his views, then?" Johann directed an amused glance at Haydn

Albrecht turned red. "I am no medical man, of course," he said hurriedly. "But if there is a way of preventing, even eradicating, a disease as fatal as small pox, I think. . . that is to say. . . well, it is worth a try."

"And what of his musical abilities?" Haydn could not help probing. The Italian doctor appeared to have made quite an impression on young Albrecht. Had he been equally successful in bamboozling the young violinist as to his musical abilities?

But a sharp rat-a-tat sounded at the door before Albrecht could respond. The imperial physician rushed into the room, a folded piece of paper in his outstretched hands.

"An urgent summons from the city, Herr Haydn." He held the note out. "The servant who brought it seemed so distraught, I thought it best to deliver it myself." He peered anxiously at Haydn. "Not ill news, I hope. . .Your wife. . ."

"What is it, brother?" Johann asked when Haydn glanced up from the note, his usually nut-brown cheeks a sickly shade of gray.

"It is Kaspar. He was. . ." He rose to his feet. "We must return to the city at once, Johann."

CHAPTER EIGHT

"Beaten to death," Johann repeated in a low, shock-dampened tone. He looked up from the note delivered to them not above a half hour ago. His eyes, like his brother's, had drifted toward the carriage window.

Haydn swallowed hard, attempted speech, but the words he sought had trouble moving past the lump in his throat. In the end, he could do no more than nod mutely.

How could Kaspar be dead? Who had killed him? And in so brutal a fashion? A misty, tear-moistened image of the fountains in the Court of Honor rolled before his eyes. The carriage sped through the main gate. Before he knew it, they were traveling across the drawbridge over the River Wien.

Out of the corner of his eyes, he saw his younger brother's gaze return to the note Luigi had sent them.

"A squabble outside the wine cellar?" Johann said. The pianissimo of doubt swelled to a crescendo of disbelief. "But who could pick a quarrel with a man so mild as Kaspar?" He raised his eyes and squinted anxiously at the Kapellmeister. "You don't suppose it had anything to do with his bequest, do you?"

Haydn's fingers tightened on the windowsill. It was what he had supposed from the moment he had read his Konzertmeister's message.

"I am afraid it is the only conclusion that can be drawn," he said quietly, turning to his brother. "If there was a dispute, it was over his bequest—quite obviously valuable judging by the interest it has garnered since he inherited it. If he was set upon by thieves, it could only have been the very same who attacked his carriage."

On the very the day the will was read, he murmured to himself.

But Johann nevertheless caught the words. "Your suspicions seem to be drawn toward the old merchant's lawyer, brother. But—"

"I am more than ever convinced the robbery was staged, Johann. The will was read that very day. The men who attacked Kaspar's carriage knew what to get their hands on. And Herr Anwalt appears to have used the attempted theft to persuade Kaspar to entrust the music into his own hands."

"Yes, brother, but Herr Anwalt had no more idea than anyone else what Kaspar's bequest consisted of. Kaspar told us so himself. Besides, what reason could there be to distrust a man so well acquainted with the family? Surely, you are—" Johann checked himself abruptly.

"Surely, I am allowing my suspicions to run away with me," Haydn completed the thought with a faint smile. His brother looked mortified. It would not be the first time, but there had been reason enough when he had suspected his violinist of a nefarious act. And there was reason enough now.

"Then allow me to explain. My suspicions are not entirely groundless. Herr Anwalt appears to have been the only person old Wilhelm Dietrich knew who was convinced he possessed all of Monteverdi's operatic music, even those long held to be lost. Quite likely he guessed at the nature of the bequest. And he knew, in all likelihood, where the scores were kept—in a chest of walnut wood inlaid with ivory."

"And his motive in all this?" Johann still sounded skeptical.

Haydn lifted his palms up. "It was the attempted robbery that convinced Kaspar his bequest was valuable—dangerously so, in fact. So dangerous that he was, when we met him, still considering entrusting them to his lawyer.

"At that point, what could be easier than for Herr Anwalt to take the original scores and replace them with an assortment of old music of relatively little value? My examination would merely have confirmed what everyone suspected: that the old merchant was mistaken in the worth of the scores he had been duped into buying."

Johann frowned. "The robbery was never meant to succeed, then?"

"Precisely so. The robbers were most inadequately armed; and the lawyer quite suspiciously well-prepared."

"But Herr Anwalt does not appear to be the only person desirous of getting his hands on Kaspar's bequest. That physician he mentioned—

when the Empress informed us her source was a man of medicine too, I could not but wonder whether it was the same person who had approached Kaspar."

Haydn nodded gravely. "And there is the music scholar," he mused. "The only question is whether they are working alone or in concert with the lawyer. For all my suspicions, it never occurred to me that one of them might be desperate enough to commit murder." He shook his head, clenching and unclenching his fists. "If it had, Kaspar might still be alive now."

"Recriminations serve no purpose, brother." Johann's voice was gentle. "It is not your fault he is dead." He leaned forward, clasping his brother's hand for a brief moment before letting go. "Once the Police Inspector is informed of the facts, Kaspar's killer will soon be brought to justice. And as for the music, at least Amelie will want for nothing."

———

Rosalie laced her arms firmly through the stout handles of her heavy shopping baskets and began to carefully weave her way out of the Neuer Markt. The cobblestone square was lined with stalls, forcing her to move at snail's pace.

"What can the police guards be thinking of to allow such goings-on?" A woman under one of the brightly colored awnings was gesticulating fiercely, the loaf of bread in her hands swinging up and down in a wide arc that almost hit Rosalie on the head.

The maid stepped adroitly aside, swinging her baskets out of the way. God forbid the eggs she had just bought should break or the cream spill over. But the mention of the police had caught her attention, and she slowed down even further to hear what she could.

"And the Hofburg not over a mile away," the fishmonger in the next stall agreed with the first woman, her voice carrying over the hubbub of people haggling over vegetables, meat, and cheese.

Rosalie drew her baskets closer to her side. It was to avoid talk such as this that she had decided against going to the Hoher Markt or the Bauern Markt, but news of the killing must have spread all the way to this part of town. She wondered again who the murdered man was.

The household had already been in uproar. The discovery that there were barely enough eggs for the chocolate torte ordered for the evening meal, not to mention the delicate concoctions of orange-scented cream Her Serene Highness favored had put the head steward in quite a state.

But the news of a murder—of a member of the orchestra, no doubt, or why had Herr Haydn been sent for? And where was Herr Tomasini, for that matter?—so close to the fashionable district had alarmed both the musicians and the servants to no small degree.

Rosalie edged past the carriages and carts crowding the streets leading into the market. Why, even the usually stolid Clara Schwann had balked at the idea of crossing the Kohlmarkt to get to Her Serene Highness's bank. Only Frau Dichtler, appearing oddly run-down and irritable, was unaffected by the news.

"Oh, for heavens' sake! What is there to fear—in broad daylight and in my presence, no less? It is not as though any one of us is in the habit of consorting with persons of ill-repute and frequenting wine taverns at all hours of the night. Do get a move on, Clara!"

"CLARA!"

Rosalie was almost near the Graben when an ear-piercing screech assailed her ears. Recognizing Frau Dichtler's voice, she pushed her way through the throng. The singer stood at the head of the road, a petrified Clara by her side.

"What is it?" Rosalie gasped, pushing her way toward Her Serene Highness's maid. "What has happened?"

A police guard with bristly brown hair had come up to the women and was asking the same question.

"Th-the Princess's jewels—" Clara gestured helplessly toward a boy in a threadbare shirt fleeing past the crowd in the direction of the markets to the north.

"Snatched right out of our hands." Frau Dichtler stood with her hands on her hips. "Run after the rogue, Clara. You cannot expect me to do it in my gown."

"Here, let me." Rosalie began to set her baskets on the ground, but the police guard, having spotted the boy, was already giving chase. He soon returned with both the boy and the jewelry case.

"Hand it back! Now!" He issued a hard cuff to the young thief's ear. "It is all in order, I hope, Madam?" The guard turned toward Frau Dichtler, inclining his head solicitously.

The singer opened the case and briefly inspected its contents before thrusting it into Clara's hands. "It is indeed, Officer—?" She arched a playful eyebrow in his direction.

"Poldi at your service, Madam!" the police guard responded with a slight bow.

"Well, we had best be off to the bank, then, Clara"—the singer began to march forward, not deigning to glance back at the maid—"now that we have dilly-dallied to your heart's content."

"But Her Serene Highness's necklace, it was stolen in Leopoldsdorf, wasn't it, Frau Schwann?" Rosalie tugged at the other maid's arm.

"No it was not." Clara whispered back to Rosalie's surprise and pulled her arm free.

<hr/>

It was late morning by the time Haydn and his brother were ushered into the Police Inspector's office: a large, sunny room, far more cheerfully decorated than one would expect of a guard house with a prison. The Inspector, a man of medium height, rose from behind a capacious walnut wood desk and surveyed his visitors through piercing blue-gray eyes.

"I take it you knew the man found in the Tuchlauben this morning, Herr Haydn." The Inspector indicated the comfortable chairs upholstered in the same shade of Prussian blue as the intricate pattern on the soft tufted carpet.

"Wilhelm Kaspar, a violinist," he pronounced, glancing down at a slim dossier on his desk. "We cannot release the body, you understand. The cause of death is plainly evident, but"—he shrugged apologetically—"under the rules, the circumstances in which the dead man was found necessitate a full postmortem."

Haydn glanced at Johann, unsure how to broach the subject now that he was in the Inspector's presence. "The police guards, we are told, suspect nothing more sinister than a casual robbery."

The Police Inspector drummed his fingers on his desk. "Your Konzertmeister did make his suspicions known to us."

He sighed.

"I hardly know where to begin, Herr Haydn. Your friend was bludgeoned to death, a manner of attack usual among the thieves that beset this city at night. The pistols they carry only serve to frighten. They would scarcely risk the noise of a shot. The blast of the discharge would reverberate through the streets. Besides, what common thief would know enough about music to want to steal a bundle of old scores?"

"The very same thieves who attacked his carriage the night Kaspar inherited his bequest," Haydn replied, his tone grim. "They were not after money, but—"

"The chest. Yes, your Konzertmeister did mention it." The Police Inspector ran a harried hand through his brown hair. "But only consider, gentlemen, chests such as those commonly hold precious jewels and bank notes. What thief would want a few paltry gulden when faced with a treasure such as one would expect to find in a chest?"

Johann leaned forward. "There is sufficient evidence to suggest the thieves knew both the nature of the bequest and of its considerable value."

"No matter how valuable your friend's bequest, whom could they sell it to? What pawnshop does traffic in old manuscripts?" The Inspector clapped his hand on the dossier. "The facts speak for themselves, gentlemen."

"True enough." Haydn had not considered the difficulty the thieves would face fencing the scores. But then he had never thought the thieves were acting on their own behalf. "They must have been hired by someone."

"Someone who could just as easily have ordered them to break into your friend's house," the Inspector retorted. He began to drum his fingers on his desk again. "If the attack on him was intentional, it can only have been by someone known to him."

He pulled a cord hanging from the wall behind him. "The dead man's effects, if you please," he barked at the guard who entered the office.

"We found a note in your friend's pocket—crumpled and mostly torn, but the words we could decipher along with his servant's testimony indicate they were sent by someone he knew well."

Haydn stared at the Inspector. They were at least in agreement that the thieves had been hired to attack Kaspar. Whether by a friend or a more casual acquaintance only time would tell. "Then, you will investigate the possibility—"

"No, Herr Haydn." The Inspector shook his head emphatically. "I have not the resources to investigate that aspect of the matter. The Emperor wishes the robbers brought to heel. Our efforts must be concentrated on that task, although I greatly doubt we will succeed. I can promise nothing more than this: If the robbers are apprehended, you may question them yourself regarding this affair."

CHAPTER NINE

"What is the matter, Frau Schwann?" Rosalie's violet eyes, shrouded in concern, rested on the sturdily built lady's maid. Every member of the palace staff had risen to go about their work, but Clara Schwann still sat slouched over her meal at the servants' dining table.

If she had heard Rosalie, she gave no sign of it, staring morosely into her bowl of beef noodle soup instead. She had barely touched it. What could be so amiss?

Something to do with Frau Dichtler, Rosalie was willing to wager. The singer had stomped into the palace shortly before the afternoon meal. And Frau Schwann, looking oddly deflated, had trailed despondently behind her.

"The necklace. . ." Rosalie hazarded. How it could be that, she did not know. But what else could it be?

"Colored glass and paste, according to the bank manager." Clara raised a pair of dull gray eyes toward her. "So cleverly fashioned, it fooled us all. Why, the clerk even held the necklace up to the light, and the stones blazed as though they were genuine sapphires and diamonds. But Herr Strasser had only to touch them to know they were paste."

"He could have been mistaken?" Rosalie hoped for Clara's sake that was the case, but it was unlikely the bank manager would have been mistaken about such a thing.

Clara shook her head. "Herr Strasser says paste feels warmer to the touch than real gemstones. He even tried rubbing an edge of one of the stones against a glass case. It made not a single scratch."

Rosalie brushed a lock of dark hair out of her eyes. "It was never lost in Leopoldsdorf, then, was it?" Frau Dichtler might have mentioned that.

After all the fuss she'd made over the matter, too. Sending them out into the cold like that!

"Yes, it was." Clara nodded miserably. "That is why I was so surprised to see it back. But when I examined the stones, there was no doubt about it. Each stone had the tiny black mark Her Serene Highness had the jeweler place on it."

"B-but you said. . ." Rosalie's eyes crinkled in confusion. She took a deep breath. "But you said just this morning the necklace wasn't stolen." She tried to prevent an accusatory tone creeping into her voice, but it swelled in indignation, nevertheless.

"It was the fake necklace that was lost. Her Serene Highness insisted on carrying the real thing herself—concealed in her foot warmer. A trick she learned from an English lady at court this past winter."

"*Ach so!*" Rosalie's eyes widened in appreciation at this strategy. "I did think it odd that Her Serene Highness should be so unconcerned about the necklace. She was more put out at losing her trinket box. But"—she frowned—"when was it exchanged for the original, then?"

"When that little ragamuffin stole it from me this morning," Clara declared, thrusting her lips out defiantly. "It was genuine enough when I set out this morning with Frau Dichtler. I examined it myself. Her Serene Highness has taught me how to recognize the marks the jeweler inscribed on the paste stones."

"But the little rascal had no opportunity to open the case," Rosalie objected. "Why, the police guard took off after him almost as soon as he snatched the case out of your hand."

"Well, I had no opportunity to take it either, if that is what you're implying." Clara glared at Rosalie. "And, why would I? I have been with Her Serene Highness from the time she was married."

"It isn't what I was suggesting at all, Frau Schwann," Rosalie cried, mortified at having unwittingly offended the lady's maid.

"Well, it is what that dratted Frau Dichtler has been suggesting! I have never seen Her Serene Highness look so displeased. First, the paste necklace in Leopoldsdorf. Now this. If anything else goes missing, I can say goodbye to my post!"

The gray building just past the enormous fountain of yellow marble that stood in the middle of the Kohlmarkt was in desperate need of a fresh coat of paint. Haydn gave the brass numbers above the door a fleeting glance before he pushed it open to let himself and Johann in.

A steep, narrow staircase led them up to Kaspar's apartment on the third floor, high enough to escape the dust that constantly rose from the city's streets, but too close to the attic to be entirely desirable.

The black paneled door stood slightly ajar. Through it Haydn could see beyond the hallway into the parlor where the distraught widow was seated by the fireplace. His fingers closed on the heavy brass door handle and lifted it, but before he could let it fall, a slim male figure standing with his back to the door turned around.

"It is Herr Haydn!" Albrecht rushed to greet them. "Is...?" Albrecht's voice rising in question, faltered. He looked beyond Johann's shoulder toward the staircase.

"Unfortunately not." Johann had divined the substance of the young man's question. "We were able to retrieve his effects"—he followed the young man into the parlor—"but until a thorough postmortem is conducted—"

"It is a mere formality, nothing more," Haydn interjected hastily, seeing Amelie's tear-filled, wide eyes staring at them in consternation.

Kaspar's widow nodded silently, her lips tightly compressed. A much-wrinkled handkerchief of gray cambric, clutched between nervous, white fingers, lay across her knees.

"We have his purse," Johann began, holding out a small pouch of scuffed black leather. "And the—"

"It is unfortunately empty." Haydn stared at his brother, imperceptibly shaking his head. Far kinder to allow Amelie to think her husband's death was an accident rather than a deliberate attempt on his life. Besides, he wished to examine the note more closely.

Amelie reached out for the purse, her fingers mechanically smoothening out the faded leather.

"His keys." She cleared her throat and twisted her neck to look up at Haydn. "He would not have left without them."

"His keys?" Haydn repeated, his eyes fixed on the widow. Her beauty had never been striking, but traces of it still remained in her smooth, unlined features. Their excessive pallor was the only mark her illness had left on her. "Do you mean the keys to the apartment?" There was surely no reason for the thieves to take those, unless—

"And the ones to his bureau." Amelie's eyes gravitated toward where Albrecht stood by the mahogany bureau, tugging at the ornate handles of its drawers. "Kaspar insisted on keeping them close at hand."

Albrecht had by now succeeded in pulling the writing flap down. "It is unlocked!" His forehead creased into a puzzled furrow. "Could Kaspar have been in such a hurry that he forgot to lock the flap? The drawers are open, too."

"No." Amelie shook her head vehemently. "No, Kaspar would never forget to lock his bureau. It is quite unlike him." She pushed herself forward in her agitation, turning to look at each of the three men in turn. "Quite unlike him!" she repeated. "What can it mean?"

Haydn gripped the marble mantelpiece, unwilling to let his mind dwell on precisely what the unlocked bureau meant. From where he stood he could see the tiny marks around the lock on the writing flap. The thieves had wasted no time. No time at all!

"There is a locksmith down the road." Albrecht came forward. "It might be best—"

"Yes, indeed," Haydn agreed, feeling in his coat pocket for a few gulden to cover the young man's expenses. He followed Albrecht to the door.

"But surely it is quite unnecessary." Amelie dabbed the corners of her mouth with her wrinkled handkerchief, her bewildered gaze following Haydn. She gestured vaguely around the room. "There is nothing here to tempt a thief."

"It is a mere precaution, that is all." Johann gave the widow a reassuring smile. "And you will need a new set of keys now that Kaspar's are lost. I take it you have no spare?" When the widow shook her head, he continued: "Then, a fresh set of locks must be made as well."

Haydn returned to the room. "The purse was found discarded on the street near"—he took a deep breath—"near the wine cellar where Kaspar. . .where he was found, Amelie.

"In all likelihood, the thieves rid themselves of his keys somewhere along their way. It would be too much to expect the guards to conduct a search for something quite so trivial and. . ." He lifted his hands in a gesture of mild apology.

"I quite understand." Amelie gave them a faint smile. "But the keys—

the ones to the bureau, at any rate—were of some value. They were made of gold; each one embedded with a tiny diamond and hanging from a slender gold ring."

She smiled again. "I suppose that is why Kaspar kept them so close. That and his snuff box and the gold band he wore on his finger were the only things of value we possessed."

Haydn allowed his eyes to drift toward Johann. "Then, I suppose that is why they were stolen." It was not a supposition he was inclined to believe himself, but there was no reason to alarm Amelie. And the new locks Albrecht was having made would keep the thieves at bay.

He turned his gaze upon the bureau, his eyes searching its scratched surface. Nothing appeared to be disturbed. Had the thieves merely contented themselves with trying the locks? Quite possibly they had not had sufficient time to do very much more than that.

"Still, it would be as well to look through his papers to ensure all is in order," he suggested. The task of sifting through the contents of her husband's bureau would, at least, keep Amelie occupied.

<hr />

Not more than an hour had elapsed since her conversation with Her Serene Highness's maid when Rosalie was startled to hear a commotion in the inner courtyard. This was soon followed by a sharp knocking on the enormous paneled doors at the entryway.

Wiping her hands on her apron, she went out into the hallway, arriving just in time to see a footman opening one of the double doors.

A uniformed palace guard stood outside. He frowned at the sight of the footman. "There is a police guard here," he announced. "Insists Her Serene Highness sent for him to report a theft."

"And so she did!" A tall man in the blue-trimmed white uniform of a police guard thrust himself forward. "Would you stand in the way of justice?" The guard had by this time wedged himself through the doorway, forcing the footman to step aside.

Rosalie's eyes narrowed. The brusque voice had seemed familiar enough. But there was no mistaking the bristly brown hair. It was Poldi, the police guard who had introduced himself to Frau Dichtler on Singerstrasse that morning. Had Her Serene Highness really sent for him? But why? Surely, she didn't suspect her own maid.

"What does a police guard want with us?" Rosalie heard Greta's voice behind her, pitched too low for anyone else to hear. She winced slightly as her friend's plump hand sank heavily down on her shoulder.

"Something to do with the necklace stolen this morning and Frau Schwann, I'll warrant." She regarded the men arguing in the doorway. "It doesn't bode well for her, I fear."

She was about to push Greta back into the kitchen when Poldi's sharp blue eyes, scanning the hallway, espied her. "Hey du, you there! You were there this morning, weren't you, lass?" A peremptory forefinger beckoned her forward.

Rosalie had to fight down her trepidation as she reluctantly obeyed the summons. "I was."

She forced herself to keep her gaze on Poldi as she spoke, then turned toward the bewildered footman and the frowning palace guard. "A street urchin filched a necklace from Frau Schwann this morning, it is true. But this officer was fortunately able to retrieve it."

She was determined not to admit to anything more. Poor Frau Schwann was in enough trouble as it stood. "I know of nothing else that has been stolen since then."

"Oh, but it has!" Frau Dichtler's strident voice loudly contradicted Rosalie. She swept past the maid. "For heaven's sake, let the man in!" She pulled Poldi by the arm into the hallway, motioning the footman and the palace guard out of the way with an urgent flick of her wrist.

"It was a paste necklace in the case you retrieved, my dear Officer," she continued, leading Poldi down the hallway once both servants had departed.

Rosalie followed the pair down the wide passage. Clara Schwann—an expression of utter dismay on her face—stood beside Greta now; drawn out, most likely, by the sound of raised voices.

"The guttersnipe who snatched it must have substituted a fake for the original, or. . ." The soprano allowed her voice to trail off as her palm moved eloquently through the air in the direction of the lady's maid.

"At any rate, I thought it best to call you back to question all who were present at the scene before"—Frau Dichtler's dark eyes went unerringly toward Clara, lingering upon her stout person—"the trail grows any colder."

Rosalie's forehead puckered in annoyance. "That woman seems to be trying very hard to make Frau Schwann lose her position," she whispered to Greta as the soprano led the police guard and Her Serene Highness's maid into the servant's hall.

CHAPTER TEN

"What trouble can Therese be in?" Haydn shifted restlessly in his carriage seat, his fingers drumming an anxious beat on the windowsill. "And what can Maria Anna expect me to do about it?"

He glanced down at the note clenched in his fist, his frustration mounting at the deliberate vagueness of the message. *When could she expect him to grace her parents' home with his presence*? Maria Anna had enquired. Her younger sister was in dire need of his help.

It had apparently not occurred to her to elaborate any further on the circumstances.

"We shall know soon enough, I suppose," Johann replied. "Although, what predicament a nun leading a sheltered life could have gotten herself into, I hardly know. Could my sister-in-law have been exaggerating the circumstances?"

"Who can tell?" Haydn moved uneasily in his seat again. "The woman delights in being cryptic."

But for the mention of Therese, he might have been tempted to ignore his wife's summons. Kaspar's death and his widow's well-being were problems of sufficiently great moment to risk Maria Anna's displeasure. But if Therese were in distress. . .

He thrust his head out the window. "We should have gone past the Michaelerplatz instead of taking this circuitous route."

The Keller house, in the suburb of Landstrasse just beyond the city gates at Stubentor, was not above a few miles distant. Their journey should have taken no more than twenty minutes. Yet, here they were, still on Dorotheergasse, marking a slow progress past the carriages and people thronging the narrow streets of Vienna.

He turned toward Johann. "She can scarcely be in need of money or of means to support herself, can she?"

Johann considered the question, then slowly shook his head. "It is unlikely." He gazed pensively out into the streets. They appeared to have made their way beyond the city center. "Most likely the convent needs some help with a quandary of its own—something that requires your connections or your expertise in music, no doubt.

"The Archduke Joseph has been chafing at the bit—ever since he was made co-regent, according to Papa Keller—to close down every cloister and monastery in the city that serves no useful purpose."

Haydn pursed his lips. "And in his mind, I suppose, none of them do!" He hoped it was nothing more than that. A scandal—or even the suspicion of one—could result in a nun being dismissed in disgrace. But surely Therese would not—He shook his head. Best not to even consider the possibility.

But the prospect of meeting Therese again after all these years still unnerved him, and it was with tremendous reluctance that he forced himself to climb down from the carriage outside the doors of 51 Raabengasse where Maria Anna's father, the imperial wigmaker, Peter Keller, made his home.

"Ah, there you are, husband!" To Haydn's relief it was Maria Anna who responded to his uncertain rap on the door. "I was beginning to think you had quite forgotten the purpose of our visit—to see Therese and my family, of course," she continued in response to his blank stare.

Johann's eyes met Haydn's, the corners of his mouth twitching slightly. "Then your sister is not in any grave trouble, I take it." He followed her across the spacious courtyard, a mild note of enquiry in his voice.

Maria Anna spun around. "I have promised her your assistance, husband." Her chin jutted out defiantly. "You will *not* let me down!" She turned on her heels.

Haydn was about to enquire further into the matter when she called over her shoulder: "What took you so long, anyway?"

"It was Kaspar—"

"What about him?" Maria Anna sounded impatient. "What ails him that you must neglect your own family to help him?"

"He is dead, Maria Anna."

"Dead!" Maria Anna swung around to face him, then turned toward her brother-in-law.

"He was found this morning in the Tuchlauben," Johann explained. He glanced at his brother before continuing. "Attacked by robbers, the police guards think."

Maria Anna seemed shaken by the news. "And what of Amelie?" she asked, turning toward Haydn with a frown. "The bequest"—she glanced down at Haydn's empty hands—"have you examined it?"

"No—" A mortified blush darkened Haydn's nut-brown cheeks. Amelie had still been sifting through Kaspar's papers when he and Johann had abruptly left her husband's house. "There was not enough time—" He broke off, unwilling to give voice to his thoughts.

But Maria Anna seemed to have divined his unspoken words. "Well, I should have known the least mention of Therese would bring you scurrying here." She pushed open the door, head held high as she stepped over the threshold.

"Peregrin di lido in lido."

It was not a song he was familiar with, but the words sung in Therese's rich, dulcet voice brought a smile to Haydn's face. Left alone for no more than the few minutes it had taken Maria Anna to greet them at the door, Therese must have gravitated, as she was wont to, to the small clavichord that stood by the parlor window.

"Che del ver cherch'il. . ." Still singing, she was about to seat herself at the instrument when Maria Anna pushed open the door.

Haydn could have wished the song to continue, but Maria Anna's brusque, "He is here, Therese," brought her sister's singing to an abrupt end.

Therese—Sister Josepha, as she was now called—turned, lips stretching into a beatific smile. She was at the door in an instant, arms outstretched in greeting. "Joseph, how well you look! Why, it has been—" The skin visible under her wimple corrugated in an effort to compute the intervening years.

"A decade, at the very least," Haydn replied, feeling the strain from the past few hours melting away under the warmth that shone from his sister-in-law's sapphire-blue eyes.

Therese's smile widened, threatening to dissolve the hard knot of resentment he had carried with him from the day he had learned she was abandoning him for the Lord.

She turned to greet Johann. "You were a boy still in Rohrau when Joseph lodged with us, but Maria Anna speaks so frequently of you in her letters, I feel I am meeting an old friend."

"They came as soon as they could." Maria Anna led the way into the parlor.

Sun streamed in from the window, casting bright patches of light on the dark wood of the clavichord and the damask roses on the cream upholstery and rug. "His friend was—" Maria Anna turned a sickly shade of gray.

"Poor man," she muttered. "What is the world coming to?"

Therese turned toward Haydn, eyes filled with such compassion and concern, he felt anew his guilt at failing Kaspar. He explained the situation as delicately as he could. "Amelie is as well as circumstances will allow, for the moment. But you have troubles of your own, I hear. Maria Anna—"

A carmine flush suffused Therese's features. "You did not rush here on my account, I hope?" At Haydn's nod, she turned a reproachful glance toward Maria Anna. "Oh, sister, you should not have—" She turned back to Haydn. "Besides, I know not how you can be of any help, Joseph.

"And with your friend gone, surely his poor widow's straitened circumstances must take precedence over—"

"Well, now that he is here, you may as well entrust the matter to him." An undercurrent of impatience, mingled with irritability, harmonized Maria Anna's words. She bustled toward the serving girl who had just entered, nearly snatched the tray of coffee out of her arms, and set it down on the parlor table.

"Whatever you may say about the man"—she glared at Haydn over the coffee pot—"he is resourceful enough. I am sure some means can be found."

Therese sighed. "I hardly know where to begin." She carefully extended a steaming cup in Haydn's direction. "Although the task Reverend Mother Catherine has set me is so onerous, any assistance would be welcome."

"It is this task that brings you out of your convent, then?" Johann asked, reaching out to receive his cup from the nun.

Therese nodded. "Ordinarily the Kellermeisterin would have been sent out. It was she who noticed that our vellum and our handmade paper had been used. And she who made the subsequent discovery that vast quantities were missing from our supplies." Therese wrung her hands.

"But the convent library, in particular the music it contains, are under my charge . . ." She wrung her hands again. "The Reverend Mother wishes me to make enquiries at every bookseller within the city and within a mile outside its gates."

"To what end? To track down quantities of vellum and paper?" Haydn burst out. "But that is a fool's errand, Therese!"

"She is not tasked with tracking down the convent's writing supplies, husband!" Maria Anna rolled her eyes "Her Abbess wishes her to look for manuscripts that might have made their way out of the convent to the booksellers."

"Stolen?" Haydn was aghast. *From a community of devout women lacking any contact with the outside world?* Surely, that was impossible! How could anyone have spirited anything out?

Therese bit her lip. "It is a possibility that must be considered"—she hesitated—"although nothing is missing that we know of."

Haydn glanced swiftly at Johann. Had Therese, cloistered all these years at St. Nikolai, picked up her sister's habit of speaking in riddles?

"What then?" he asked, returning his gaze to her.

"Some months ago, we employed a scribe—a male scribe, the female usually assigned to us being unavailable for the purpose. It was quite urgent, you see." Therese gazed at them earnestly, hands clasped together. "Her Majesty has asked for some of our papers—old papers entrusted to the convent upon our founder the Empress Eleonora's death.

"Reverend Mother Catherine thought it would be wise to make copies for Her Majesty rather than let the original documents out of the convent."

"To what purpose?" Johann's voice reflected Haydn's own bewilderment. The Abbess could hardly be so jealous of the convent's possessions that even Her Majesty's handling of them might be cause for concern.

The corners of Therese's mouth twitched. "It was not Her Majesty's request for the papers that caused the Reverend Mother any concern. The manuscripts are so ancient, we feared they might be damaged beyond repair if carelessly handled."

Her mouth twitched again at Haydn's look of utter surprise. "Old vellum turns brittle, you see. The ink may fade or flake off entirely. It is for this reason that we keep a quantity of vellum and handmade paper— that our oldest documents may be preserved in a state as close to the original as possible. The scribe even attempts to copy the precise details of the hand that penned the original.

"And it was clear, the papers were of great significance to Her Majesty. It would have been no great trouble to hire a scribe from one of the other convents, but when a man presented himself to us, bearing a letter from the Hofburg, naturally we hired him directly."

"He was sent by Her Majesty, then?" Haydn enquired.

"So the Reverend Mother thought. But, now it would seem. . . That is to say. . ." Therese's voice warbled with uncertainty. "Her Majesty may have misjudged the man, of course."

It took a moment for Haydn to comprehend her concern. Then his eyes widened as the reason for it began to dawn upon him. "If the man was sent by the Empress, you will need concrete evidence of theft before leveling any accusations against him."

Therese nodded vigorously. "There is always the possibility that he deceived us, but . . ."

"But were the Reverend Mother to admit the possibility, it would expose her to a charge of carelessness." Johann's voice was soft.

"Precisely." Therese nodded again. "The matter must be handled with the utmost discretion."

Haydn stared vacantly at the cherry tree outside the window, pondering the issue. The missing vellum and paper were an odd detail. Yet if the convent's possessions appeared to be in order . . . He was about to put the question to Therese when the door opened and a servant announced the serving of the afternoon meal.

CHAPTER ELEVEN

Clara Schwann and her escorts were nowhere to be seen when Rosalie and Greta followed them into the short passage leading to the kitchen area of the palace. But the gruff tones of the police guard's voice soon drew them to the small parlor the head steward shared with the housekeeper.

The soprano had left the door slightly ajar, and through the narrow crack, the maids could see Clara sitting opposite her interrogators, her head held low. Rosalie pressed her ear to the crack.

"A previous attempt was made on the necklace?" Poldi's voice rose, outrage competing with disbelief. "This very necklace?"

Clara merely nodded, but Frau Dichtler leaned forward, tapping a slender finger urgently on the low table between herself and the maid. "The very same, Officer. The very same, I am afraid." She paused to look at the maid before turning back to the police guard.

"By great good fortune, Her Serene Highness had the forethought not to entrust the genuine article to her maid. So the item stolen was a fake. It fell by the wayside"—the soprano glanced at the maid again—"or so we are led to believe."

She briefly recounted the circumstances to the police guard. "But the maids I sent out to retrieve it found nothing."

"Or so they said!"

Rosalie straightened up, barely able to restrain the gasp of indignation that threatened to explode from her lips at the police officer's remark.

Greta, impatient as always, was not quite so cautious. "Of all the—" But Rosalie hurriedly stuffed a handkerchief into her friend's mouth to stifle the furiously muttered words. She shook her head, holding a forefinger to her lips. It would never do for them to be discovered before they'd even had an opportunity to hear the entire conversation.

"All three acting together, I am sure," Poldi continued, fortunately oblivious to the consternation his earlier remark had caused. "She"—he jerked his chin toward Clara—"could hardly have stolen the necklace if she was asleep the whole time."

"So sound asleep, the devil himself could not have woken her!" The soprano gave a disapproving shake of her head.

"Why would I steal a fake necklace?" Clara asked in a heated tone, raising her head. Her eyes began to widen at the sight of the two maids at the door. But at a signal from Rosalie, she hastily withdrew her gaze before either Poldi or Frau Dichtler could detect anything amiss.

"Who else knew about the fake necklace?" Poldi's voice was stern.

"There was no reason for anyone but Her Serene Highness and myself to know of it." Clara kept her head held high, then threw the soprano a pointed glance before continuing: "So you see, *I* could not have stolen it."

"No?" Poldi enquired softly, drawing out the syllable. "And did Her Serene Highness examine the necklace as carefully as you did every time she took it out to wear it?"

Clara looked puzzled. "No. Why should she? She knows I am as capable as she of examining the marks on it. She taught me herself."

"Trusts you as much as that, does she, then?" Poldi murmured.

"B-b-but," Frau Dichtler stammered, turning from the police guard to the maid, "it makes no sense. What possible reason could she have to purloin an item she knew to be fake?"

Poldi leaned back against the wide chintz-covered splat of his chair. "What her reasons might be, I cannot say, Madam. But to make a second attempt on the necklace, the thief, or thieves, would have had to know of the existence of the genuine article. How else could they have come by that knowledge?"

"Oh!" Frau Dichtler clapped a slender hand to her mouth.

"To plan the event, moreover, there would have had to know to whom the necklace belonged. How could some stranger, chancing upon a trinket along the wayside, have obtained this information? How could such a person have been privy to the exact day and time you would set out for the bank with the original?"

Clara had turned whiter than the finest flour at the police guard's relentless recital.

"Indeed!" Frau Dichtler kept her hand pressed over her mouth. "And how," she continued in a hurry, "could they have known to which bank we were going? It was on Singerstrasse that the street urchin waylaid us. Oh, yes"—she sounded almost relieved at the explanation—"I see now." She turned toward Clara. "It all points to—"

"The involvement of someone on the inside." Poldi stared at Clara, whose cheeks had crumpled by this time. "The facts speak for themselves, Madam."

Rosalie retreated from the parlor door. "It doesn't look too good for our Frau Schwann, does it?"

Greta snorted. "*The involvement of someone on the inside,* that numbskull says. Why, it could have been anyone. We all know where Her Serene Highness banks, and it is no secret that Frau Schwann was to accompany that wretched woman to the bank with that very necklace."

"Yes, but only Frau Schwann knew the necklace stolen in Leopoldsdorf was a paste replica of the real thing." She reached out to grasp Greta's plump hands. "They could arrest her, Greta—the mere suspicion of having staged a robbery would be grounds enough!"

The afternoon meal over, Papa Keller led Haydn and Johann into the parlor again. A luscious bowl of sun-ripened cherries and a steaming pot of coffee awaited them.

"From the tree you and our Therese were so fond of, Joseph," Papa Keller said as the maid proffered the bowl to his guests. Drawing on his pipe, he turned toward Johann. "Oh, you should have seen them sitting together! How they would sing their lungs out!"

Haydn smiled, the memory drawing his gaze toward the open parlor window and the ancient cherry tree beyond. Rich burgundy clusters of fruit weighed down its boughs. A wooden bench stood against the scarred tree trunk. There Therese would sit, singing from the scores he procured for her from the bookseller at the Michaelerplatz while he played the simple obbligato accompaniment on his violin.

He reined his wandering mind in, forcing it to return to the present. The conversation had turned to Wilhelm Kaspar. The manner of his death had profoundly shocked the old gentleman.

"Killed for his bequest, you say." Papa Keller drew deeply from his pipe, his heavy brows gathering together into a thick, stormy line of disquiet. "It was a parcel of music, was it not?" At Johann's nod, he continued: "God help us all, it may be just as you say."

Haydn was surprised. "Your opinion of its value has undergone a change, then?"

Papa Keller shook his head, still troubled. "No. But someone in this city seems to be intent on stealing music." He tugged at the drooping ends of his walrus moustache before continuing. "Kaspar was set upon by thieves, you say. And of all the valuable manuscripts that scoundrel of a scribe could have taken from St. Nikolai, he chose to take an old work of music."

Haydn looked up sharply. "It was a work of music that was stolen from Therese's convent, but"—he glanced at Johann—"Therese made no mention of the fact."

"Said nothing about it, you say!" The old gentleman looked astounded. "What in the name of heaven was she gabbing about then all this while? Was it for nothing that we had to content ourselves with cold fowl this afternoon?"

"In truth," Johann intervened upon this tirade, "Sister Josepha had no opportunity to finish her tale. She was interrupted by the maid announcing the afternoon meal. And—"

"And here I am prattling away, while she waits." Papa Keller rose to his feet. "I will bring her in directly."

"I thought Therese said nothing was stolen," Haydn mused as Papa Keller left the room.

Johann nodded. "Yet there was some suspicion of theft. Although"— his fingers fanned out, as though searching for any detail that could illuminate the matter—"on what grounds, if nothing was missing, I cannot fathom."

"It was the very question I was about to put to her when the servant interrupted our conversation," Haydn replied. Although, now quite another question occupied his mind.

What inexplicable traffic in music was causing the city's thieves to direct their efforts toward procuring scores?

The sun was slightly past its zenith when Luigi eventually found himself at Wallnerstrasse. He had traveled to Baden and back, forced to break the unwelcome news of Kaspar's demise to his widow. A task no man should have to deal with.

He could have dealt with a flood of tears, but Amelie's pale, quiet reception of the news had unnerved him. He had desperately sought for words of comfort. But what words could ease the plight of a woman made destitute by her husband's death? To offer money—the only thing that could help—seemed sordid.

Despite his discomfort, Luigi would have waited the entire day with her at the Kohlmarkt. But the fortuitous arrival of Kaspar's young colleague, Albrecht, had relieved the Konzertmeister of his vigil. He had been most glad to return to his duties at the palace.

The musicians, to his relief, were still at their afternoon meal. He hurried up to the Music Room. Frau Dichtler had found Monteverdi's *Lament of Ariadne* in a Book of Madrigals in the Prince's library, and, much to Luigi's dismay, insisted upon performing it for Her Serene Highness's guests that evening.

What had stimulated this sudden interest in the great master's madrigals, the Konzertmeister knew not. Ordinarily, he would have cursed the impulse that had led to it. The madrigal certainly could not be sung in its present form. And without Haydn or Johann to help, the task of modifying the work fell entirely upon him.

But now, seated at Haydn's desk, dipping his pen into the silver inkwell to make the changes needed, Luigi welcomed the respite it afforded from the day's events. It was not just that the five-part texture had to be reduced to a solo with basso continuo—He would have Niklas, the cellist, play the bass line while he himself improvised on the harpsichord. It would be much the easiest way of proceeding.

The lament had originally been written for Caterina Martinelli, a singer whose capabilities far exceeded Frau Dichtler's. The piece would have to be greatly simplified to suit La Dichtler's limited talents. He hoped to complete his work before Frau Dichtler burst through the door in her usual impetuous, hurricane-like manner.

But an hour later, Frau Dichtler, to his great astonishment, had still not shown her face. He waited a few more minutes, beginning to get annoyed. Where in the name of heaven was the blighted woman? He had succeeded in paring down the music to its barest essence, but the lament would not sing itself.

None of the musicians in the Rehearsal Room had seen her either.

"She went out this morning with Her Serene Highness's maid," Niklas, the cellist, offered.

"But she was back within the hour," Lorenzo, the second violinist, said. "She has been known to spend time with the Estates Director"—Lorenzo's eyes slid slyly over to where the Estates Director's nephew sat—"Herr Rahier may perchance know of her whereabouts."

Rahier's nephew scowled at the other musician's sly insinuation, but otherwise remained silent.

Luigi searched the room, brows drawn together, as though expecting La Dichtler to walk out of one of the closets. Finally, he closed the door and went down the stairs. The commotion in the circular entryway drew his eyes, but he curbed his curiosity and made his way down the hall toward the Estates Director's rooms.

Frau Dichtler would have to be found if the evening's entertainment had any hope of success. And from what Haydn had told him a few days back, the woman was most likely to be found in Herr Rahier's arms.

The door to the Estates Director's office was ajar, but there was no answer when Luigi rapped his knuckles on it. He waited a few minutes and knocked again. He put his ear to the door, but hearing no sound from within, gently pushed it open.

The room was empty. The Estates Director's private rooms were just beyond the office. Luigi considered knocking on the door in the back wall, but the thought of seeing La Dichtler and Herr Rahier together was so distasteful, he turned back.

He edged past the Estates Director's desk, holding a hand out to prevent the stack of papers precariously balanced on its edge from falling when his eye fell on the rolled newssheet at the top.

It was a copy of the *Wienerisches Diarium*. He reached out for it, turning it over in his hands as he inspected it. A name was scrawled in a sprawling hand across a small piece of paper rudely affixed to one corner.

Joseph Haydn!

What was the Estates Director doing with Haydn's copy of the court newspaper?

Luigi unrolled the newspaper. The remnants of the seal on the wrapper indicated it had been sent from Haydn's bookseller at Wiener Neustadt to the palace in Eisenstadt.

Was this the copy of the newspaper that had ostensibly never been delivered? Luigi stared blankly at the *Diarium*, his mission quite forgotten. Had Herr Rahier stolen Haydn's newspaper? Why, in the name of heaven, had he done a thing like that?

CHAPTER TWELVE

T hey had been waiting for no more than a few minutes when Papa Keller ushered Therese into the room with a gruff: "Your sister has no need of your help, child. She has managed well enough without it these ten years."

Therese allowed herself to be steered toward a parlor chair. She lowered herself onto the silk-embroidered seat, gently protesting all the while. "That it was a work of music is of no consequence, Papa. It would have been no better had it been a treatise of some sort."

Smoothening the folds of her black habit, she turned toward Haydn. "The scores were entrusted to us by the nuns of St. Jakob auf der Hülben. Were the matter to become common knowledge, St. Nikolai would be accused of abject carelessness, at best; of engaging in commerce, at worst."

She wrinkled her nose ruefully. "And I am afraid the Emperor, if he ever hears of the affair, will put the worst interpretation on it."

"But why would the Emperor think your convent was engaging in commerce?" Johann enquired at the same time as Haydn asked: "Has the Abbess of St. Jakob threatened to make the matter known to the Emperor?"

"*Ach*, child! The devil could not have foxed two men more than you have Joseph and his brother with the telling of your tale," Papa Keller admonished his offspring. "Start at the beginning, and be not so scatterbrained!"

Therese sighed, fingering her habit. When she spoke again, however, it was to respond to Haydn's question. "The Abbess has made no threats, Joseph. She knows nothing of the matter. We ourselves had no knowledge of it until the bookseller we have regular dealings with brought us some music. Among the works were the songs from St. Jakob."

"A work of some value, I take it?" Haydn interrupted the narrative. The nuns frequently composed their own music. But why, despite the rich polyphony of their compositions, should they hold any attraction for a thief?

"Not to the rest of the world, perhaps." Therese's slender shoulders lifted in a delicate shrug. "But to the nuns of St. Jakob, they hold some importance. They were written some seventy years ago by their Chormeisterin, Sister Mariana von Raschenau."

She turned to smile at Johann. "It was a song from one of her works that I was singing when you arrived."

"A most beautiful piece." Johann returned her smile. "But why was her music sent to St. Nikolai?"

Haydn leaned forward, eager to hear Therese's reply. What profit could there be, after all, in stealing the music of an obscure Chormeisterin? The scores were unlikely to even contain her name, the nuns being unwilling to claim authorship of music they considered to have been called forth from the Lord.

"We asked for them," Therese said simply."Reverend Mother Catherine thought it would please Her Majesty to hear the works again when she came to St. Nikolai to offer prayers in memory of her beloved husband."

Her eyes blazed briefly, illuminated by a quick sparkle of amusement. "The Emperor Francis, God rest his soul, was so enchanted by Sister Mariana's music, the nuns at St. Jakob were compelled to perform it at every service he attended."

A decade ago, Haydn would have been bewitched by the beauty of those sapphire eyes. Now his mind spun with innumerable questions.

"If the works were so important, how could they not have been missed? When does Reverend Mother Catherine intend to inform the Abbess of St. Jakob of this unfortunate incident?"

Therese hesitated. "The works are not missing, Joseph." She raised a hand to prevent Papa Keller, who was impatiently harrumphing, interrupting her. "They were never missing. The songs were rewritten to accommodate our abilities—"

"And it was this arrangement that was stolen and eventually found its way back to the convent via your bookseller?" The rising tones of Johann's voice reflected Haydn's own incredulity. Who would trouble with an obscure work, much less steal an arrangement of it?

"Not our arrangement," Therese clarified. "Merely a copy of it. Had it not made its way back to the convent, we would have suspected nothing." She hesitated again, then a troubled stream of words bubbled out of her: "There is no knowing what else might have been copied, Joseph. What other manuscripts have been taken out of the convent to be hawked like common wares in the market?"

"If it was the scribe, the manuscripts he was set to copy might give us some clue," Haydn murmured absentmindedly, head bowed deep in thought. *An arrangement. Not the work itself, but an arrangement!* What possible reason could the thief have had? . . . *Unless* . . .

He raised his head. "How greatly modified were the works?"

Therese wrinkled her nose ever so slightly as she considered the question. That it puzzled her was clear. But she sought no further explanation. "Well, our arrangement of it differed very little from the original. We have no bass voices or female tenors, accordingly Sister Agnes eliminated those voices. And the prolonged melismas are quite beyond the capabilities of any of our altos. So those parts were altered as well . . ." She paused.

"Although," she began again slowly, "now that I think about it, there was one curious detail." She contemplated the clavichord, head tilted to one side. "The hand resembles Sister Mariana's so closely, you would have thought she had penned the arrangement herself."

"*Ach so!*" Haydn murmured. He frowned, attempting to grasp a barely-formed thought as it stirred in his brain. But it sank into the depths of his mind before he could seize it.

⚬⚬⚬

What greater evidence could there be of Her Majesty's goodwill toward her subjects in Mantua?

Luigi's eyes drifted down to read the article the Estates Director had circled in the *Wienerisches Diarium*. Still reading, he moved towards Herr Rahier's chair, an imposing fawn-colored wingback.

To soothe their ruffled feelings, she intends to dedicate the opening of the new concert hall, the finest in the modern world, to the city's greatest son since Virgil: the musician, Claudio Monteverdi.

Why was Herr Rahier so interested in the construction of a concert hall at the Royal Academy of Science and Fine Arts in Mantua? Luigi sank into the lush depths of the fine calfskin that covered the chair. Had he not been so preoccupied, he would have luxuriated in its softness.

We are informed that the Empress has even committed herself to restoring to the city the works of its beloved composer. Most of these are reputed to have been lost when Mantua was attacked by her great-great-grandfather, the Emperor Ferdinand II.

A brief comment followed on the impossibility of the task Her Majesty had set herself. The Konzertmeister quickly perused it before lingering on the final sentence.

Anyone who finds the works will doubtless earn Her Majesty's eternal gratitude.

The words "eternal gratitude" were heavily underscored. Luigi put the newspaper down and considered the panels of polished walnut on the doors of the cabinet opposite him. Somewhere in the depths of his mind, a faint memory stirred.

When Joseph had jested about it a few days ago, the Estates Director's interest in acquiring works of music had seemed implausible.

But now that he thought about it—Luigi's gaze dropped down to the article in the court newspaper—it seemed plausible enough. Rahier would do anything to curry favor with the imperial family. Why, it was not above six months ago that he himself had been loaned to the Emperor's household for just such a reason!

He perused the brief article for a second time, his eyes lingering on the great master's name. Was it a collection of his works that Rahier had wanted Fritz Dichtler to examine? The Estates Director knew nothing of music. Of course, it was unlikely that Fritz Dichtler, a passable tenor at best, could do much more than read it. Luigi very much doubted Fritz would be able to even recognize, much less authenticate, Monteverdi's music.

Still, Rahier must believe he had found the great master's operas. It would account for La Dichtler's sudden desire to sing the *Lament of Ariadne.* She was angling for a role, no doubt. Luigi's lips stretched into a wide grin at the thought of La Dichtler in a Monteverdi opera.

Why, even recitatives like that of Ottavia's in the *Coronation of*

Poppea required a range of ornamentation and depth of character that were quite beyond La Dichtler. Or, perhaps the woman saw herself in the more promiscuous role of Poppea!

A brief expression of distaste passed over his features. He found La Dichtler's supreme confidence in her ability to seduce profoundly irritating.

His mind returned to the present. *Who* was Rahier's source, he wondered.

Kaspar?

Surely, Kaspar would have said something if that were the case.

Besides, where would the Estates Director have learned of Kaspar's bequest?

From Herr Anwalt, Kaspar's lawyer.

The thought made Luigi uneasy. He drummed his fingers rapidly on the table. But Herr Rahier could not—would not, surely—have arranged for—

He shook his head, too disturbed to allow his mind to complete the thought.

———

Luigi was still contemplating the court newspaper in the Estates Director's office when a staccato burst of outrage interrupted his thoughts.

"I will not have my maid accused of theft, Elsa. I simply will not have it!"

Luigi frowned, recognizing Her Serene Highness's voice. Wrath had sharpened her usually pleasant alto tones to an ear-piercing treble. What could La Dichtler have done to infuriate her patroness?

He stepped out of Rahier's office in time to see Her Serene Highness sweeping down the hallway with her right arm outstretched, forefinger pointing. "You! Out of my house. Out, now!"

A police guard scurried before her advancing form. Frau Dichtler hurried along behind the Princess.

"Who else but Clara could have taken your necklace? She was the only person to know it was a mere replica of the genuine article."

The Princess paused to turn upon the soprano. "And why, Elsa, would Clara have stolen a necklace she knew to be a fake?"

83

"To...er...to—" La Dichtler to Luigi's surprise was stuttering. "Why, to substitute it for the real thing when we went to the bank this morning. It was an ingenious plan. And if the bank manager had not thought to inspect the necklace, the paste replica would have reposed in your safe. And you would have been none the wiser."

Her Serene Highness's beautiful dark gray eyes had narrowed. She regarded Frau Dichtler in silence. "An unnecessarily elaborate plan, if you ask me," she remarked eventually. "Why not simply steal it and be done with it?"

"To prevent the discovery of its theft until it was too late, Your Serene Highness." The police guard wheeled around to face the Princess.

"*Poldi!*" The guard's features were instantly familiar to Luigi. Their encounter that morning had been so unpleasant, he doubted he would ever forget them: the flat, hard cheeks dropping precipitously down to a square chin; the eyes sharply appraising. "What business does that dolt have here?"

"You know him?"

Luigi nearly bit his tongue at the sound of Rosalie's astonished voice at his elbow.

He twisted his head around to glance down at the maid. "He was one of the guards who found Kaspar's"—he swallowed—"Kaspar, the man found murdered near the Seizerkeller." He angled his chin at the police guard. "But what is he doing here?"

"Frau Dichtler sent for him. He helped to retrieve Her Serene Highness's necklace this morning," Rosalie explained. "But not before the ragamuffin who snatched it from Frau Schwann's hands had substituted a paste replica for the original."

"How fortuitous that he had a fake to substitute," Luigi remarked quietly, his eyes returning to the scene ahead of him.

"I will not have her arrested. Clara is no thief," Her Serene Highness's tone had sharpened again. "I will stake my life upon it."

"And our Poldi was there, you say?" Luigi asked softly, without turning around.

Rosalie nodded, although it was doubtful the Konzertmeister saw her.

"There must be a shortage of police guards in the city," he muttered to himself, "if Poldi is to be found at every sign of trouble."

84

CHAPTER THIRTEEN

It was late evening. The Kellers had retired for the night, leaving Haydn and Johann to mull over the day's events in the small room that served as Papa Keller's study and library.

A fire blazed in the porcelain stove directly in front of the comfortable green leather armchairs in which the brothers were ensconced. They were quietly contemplating the flames when Johann spoke.

"Could Papa Keller be correct in his assumption?" he asked, still staring at the fire.

"That the entire affair was engineered by the Emperor as a ploy to close down the convent?" Haydn took a sip of the excellent cherry wine that Papa Keller had left with them as he considered the question.

It was no secret that the Archduke Joseph had no use for either convents or monasteries. But to instruct a scribe to make unauthorized copies of manuscripts? And to attempt to sell them in such a clumsy fashion that the attempt must be discovered, thus calling into question the convent's renunciation of all things worldly?

It was a scheme of such diabolical proportions as to be plausible only in Papa Keller's fevered imagination.

"It would not be unlike His Majesty," Johann persisted. "If Papa Keller's tales of his officious nature are anything to go by."

Haydn nodded, recalling his father-in-law's account of the fire the Archduke Joseph had set in the middle of town to see if the city's firefighters would respond in time. They had apparently not, leaving the Emperor to put out a fire he had set himself.

It was a miracle any long-lasting damage had been averted, but the Emperor's anger at the "incompetence" of the city officials had known no bounds. And now new employees to the fire department were to be interviewed by His Majesty himself before being confirmed to their appointment.

Haydn set his wine glass on the walnut table that stood between his chair and Johann's. "I have no doubt of his desire to close down the convent by any means at hand. But whether he would actually resort to so foolish a strategy to do so"—Haydn shook his head—"why, that is another matter altogether."

He studied the curlicues of leaves and vines that ran around the edge of the table, forming an ornate border. "Such a thing would be discovered immediately. A simple investigation would bring the matter to light. And the Empress—" He shook his head again. "His Majesty can do nothing without his mother's consent. She may have loosened her hold on the reins of power, but she has not resigned it completely."

The thought of the Empress recalled him to the task she had charged him with. He retrieved one of the hand-bound scores Her Majesty had given him from his leather music case.

"I had best get to these," he said, unfurling the protective wrapping that encased the fine vellum manuscript. "There is nothing more we can do tonight for the Convent of St. Nikolai."

Luigi surveyed the Rehearsal Room one last time. The instruments had been put away and the scores returned to the Music Library. The rest of the orchestra had departed. He was the last to leave. Satisfied that all was in order, he took the cone-shaped extinguisher from the shelf behind the door and began putting out the candles in the elegant silver sconces around the room.

It was a job for one of the maids, and one of them would be up to do it, no doubt. But Luigi had been a servant long before his elevation to a position in the Esterházy orchestra. And old habits from his days of servitude prevailed. He allowed the candles in the sconces by the door to remain lit. The maids would need the light to inspect the room before they extinguished the candles.

The evening's entertainment, to his relief, had gone remarkably well. Despite her distracted air at their brief rehearsal, La Dichtler had acquitted herself well enough to attract more than a few compliments for her rendition of *Ariadne's Lament*. Her Serene Highness, indeed, had gone so far as to present her with a sapphire ring of dazzling proportions and a small bag of gold.

He hurried toward the staircase, tucking the court newspaper he had retrieved from the Estates Director's office securely within his overcoat. Haydn, he hoped, would return on the morrow from whatever business it was that had taken him to the suburb of Landstrasse.

Luigi could fathom no reason for Rahier to have filched Haydn's newspaper. *No good reason, that is,* he corrected himself. And as for the Estates Director's interest in the great master's operas, Luigi could not bring himself to believe it was mere coincidence.

Deep in thought, he sped down the stairs, his eyes on the gold floral pattern on the blue carpet covering the treads. He had barely reached the last step when a voice startled him out of his reverie.

"Am I to believe they simply took themselves off?"

The Estates Director's icy tones carried past the hallway, penetrating his ears so sharply, Luigi's eardrums were still vibrating long after Rahier had spoken.

Curiosity drew the Konzertmeister beyond the circular area at the foot of the stairs and down the hall toward the Estates Director's office.

Rahier, his hands behind his back, towered over a group of palace maids huddled before his door. He was without his wig, and strands of his blond hair glistened under the bright candlelight that illuminated the area.

"Well, which one of you was it then?" Rahier surveyed the group before him.

A wall of silence greeted him. Luigi looked on, fascinated. It took very little to arouse the Estates Director's ire, and he wondered what had occurred to arouse it tonight. He stepped forward, but Rahier, intent upon interrogating the maids, was oblivious to his presence.

"Who was assigned the task of cleaning my rooms today?"

One of the maids stepped forward, chin jutting out at a defiant angle. Luigi recognized Greta's buxom form.

"It was I," she said, tossing her head to shake a strand of blond hair out of her eyes.

Rahier snorted.

"But I took not so much as a shred of paper outside the room."

Greta's voice had risen to an indignant forte. "Why should I?"

Rahier snorted a second time. "If you had indeed troubled to do your job, my dear girl, my desk would not be in the utter disarray I found it in. Papers strewn about." The Estates Director's arm circled through the air to illustrate his point. "Documents missing. And I must ask again: Am I to believe they simply took themselves off?"

Luigi grinned. Rahier must have noticed the disappearance of the copy of the *Diarium* he had stolen from Haydn.

———

"What is the matter?" he asked, his tone innocent. "Lost something, have you?"

Rahier's pale cheeks seemed to turn even paler as he regarded Luigi. "An important document, as it happens, Herr Konzertmeister. Although it is no business of yours."

"It would not"—Luigi unbuttoned his overcoat and withdrew the copy of the *Diarium* concealed within it—"be this, would it?" He held the court newspaper out in front of him.

A flash of anger glinted in Rahier's pale blue eyes. "What—" He swallowed, suddenly aware of the palace maids regarding him with open curiosity. "That will be all," he snapped as he motioned Luigi toward his office.

"What, Herr Konzertmeister," he began when they were inside the room, "were you doing inside my office? Trespassing, I might add."

"What were you doing with the Kapellmeister's copy of the *Diarium*?" Luigi countered.

"I merely borrowed it for a time." Rahier looked annoyed. "And I would have returned it to the Kapellmeister had he but chosen to grace us with his presence. Where is he, by the way?"

"Occupied on a matter of some urgency. For Her Majesty, as you well know."

Rahier seemed surprised. Luigi shrugged. If the Prince had chosen not to take the Estates Director into his confidence that was no concern of his.

"Chasing imaginary assassins again, no doubt," Rahier muttered under his breath.

Luigi ignored the comment. Rahier was as well aware as the next person that the assassins in question were no imaginary foes. Had it not been for Haydn's intervention, the Empress may well have lost her life.

He opened the newspaper to the article Rahier had circled and pretended to look closely at it.

The Estates Director's eyes narrowed as his gaze fell on the newspaper, and Luigi heard his sharp intake of breath. He raised his head, turning the newspaper so Rahier could see his thumb pointing to the article about the great master.

"Since when have you been interested in opera, Herr Rahier? And in such old works at that?" The Estates Director never attended an opera if he could help it. Luigi allowed his thumb to gently tap the article. "Those works of music you were so interested in acquiring, they would not happen to be opera scores, would they?"

Rahier turned so pale, his features took on a bluish tinge. "You forget yourself, Herr Konzertmeister. I am not answerable to you nor do I owe you any explanations." He stretched out his arm toward the newspaper. "Now, if I may—"

Luigi quickly moved it out of reach. "Now, now, Herr Rahier. This is not yours to have, as you well know." He tucked the newspaper into his overcoat and turned on his heels.

At the door, he glanced over his shoulder. Rahier was glaring at him.

"There are no assassins this time that I am aware of, Herr Rahier." Luigi grinned, unable to resist needling the Estates Director a little more. "But I imagine Joseph does have something of great value to offer Her Majesty."

Haydn pursed his lips and looked up, his eyes swiveling toward Johann. He was in need of his brother's counsel. But Johann, sitting with his chin resting on his chest, seemed unaware of the glance Haydn cast in his direction. He was either sound asleep or deeply engrossed in the book that lay open on his knees.

Repressing a heavy sigh of resignation, Haydn returned to his perusal of the score the Empress had entrusted to him. If this was a forgery, he thought, it was an extraordinarily good one. Try as he might, he could find nothing amiss.

He turned toward the title page. *L'Orfeo*, it read in an ornate script,

A Musical Fable. The words below the composer's name, "Rappresentato in Mantova," indicated that the score had been prepared after it had premiered at the Gonzaga court in Mantua. A work prepared before the actual performance would contain the words, "da rappresentare."

There was nothing unusual in this. Musical plays were a Florentine invention, never before seen in Mantua. Francesco Gonzaga must have been inordinately proud of staging an opera that easily surpassed the best Florence had to offer. There was every reason in the world to record the event.

The next page listed the cast of characters and instruments, rich and varied as befitted a lavish production sponsored by a noble family of means.

And if that were not all, the setting of the libretto showed signs of the great master's hand. Frequent rests punctuated lines, forcing the singer to pause where no pause might have been anticipated.

Why here, where a lesser composer might have set Orfeo's "you are dead" to a single, flowing musical phrase, Monteverdi had inserted a rest after the very first word. And then repeated the phrase.

You have departed from me, you have departed from me, never, never to return.

Haydn hummed the lines assigned to Orfeo under his breath. The repeated words and phrases beautifully conveyed the demigod's anguish at the news of his beloved Euridice's death. But they utterly undermined the poetic form.

The great master was so well known for changing the texts of his librettists that one of them had been heard to comment that he scarcely recognized his own work when he saw it on the stage. The madrigals he had set shared the selfsame characteristic.

"*T'amo, mia vita. I love you, my life,*" Johann murmured, giving Haydn a start. He must have been speaking aloud for his younger brother to have referred to one of the better-known madrigals.

Johann sat up and rubbed his eyes. "He uses the opening line of the poem as a refrain that the soprano interjects through the madrigal." He gestured toward the score in Haydn's hands. "The work must be genuine, if you see repetitions where there should be none."

"Y-e-es." Haydn nodded begrudgingly. He ran a finger lightly over the soft vellum cover. There was something not quite right about the manuscript. If only he could put his finger on it. But from the ornate script, the firm, sure hand that had formed each diamond-shaped notehead, to the instrumentation and the setting of the words, he saw nothing to fault.

His gaze fell on the cast of characters. He jerked his head up.

"Francesco Rasi!" At Johann's stare of utter astonishment, he continued more slowly: "It was Rasi who sang the role of Orfeo."

Johann nodded. "A singer with an unusual vocal range. Five semitones below the normal range of a tenor on the lower side, giving him baritone capabilities. Naturally, the lead role took advantage of his unusual abilities. What of it?"

Haydn jabbed at the cast of characters with growing excitement. "The same troupe of singers would have sung the madrigals. Other than hiring a castrati or two, the Gonzagas would have made use of their regular singers for all their musical plays."

Johann's eyes, a mirror image of Haydn's own dark pupils, stared back at him like gray pools of blank impassivity.

"Do you not see? I could compare the vocal ranges in the Empress's scores and Kaspar's bequest against the ranges in the madrigals. What composer could resist taking advantage of the talents of the best of his singers, while compensating for the limitations of the worst." His mind went briefly to Frau Dichtler, and he winced. "No forger, however skilled, would think to replicate the vocal ranges."

"Ah!" A glimmer of understanding brightened Johann's eyes. He straightened up and leant forward. "A burdensome task, but worth undertaking. And I could certainly help you and ease your load in some regard."

"Yes, yes." The Kapellmeister set the score down on the walnut table next to him with an air of satisfaction. "There is hope yet."

He reached into his jacket pocket for a pen to make a note of his plan, when his fingers rustled against a crumpled sheet of paper. He drew it forth, his eyes widening.

"It is the message that sent Kaspar out to his death," he said. "I had quite forgotten it in the press of the day's events."

CHAPTER FOURTEEN

I *have news concerning your bequest.*

The words from the torn note that had been retrieved from Kaspar's body rang repeatedly in Haydn's ears. What news, he wondered as his mind ran over the details.

The message had been written on coarse brown paper. If there had ever been a signature on it, it had been torn off leaving only the remnants of a name. The letters "lt" were all he had been able to decipher.

There could only be one person to send such a note. Only one person Kaspar would consent to meet so late at night. And Haydn and Johann were about to meet him as soon as their carriage fought its way through the early morning traffic on the Graben.

Herr Anwalt.

Haydn brought his silver timepiece out of his coat pocket and glanced impatiently at it. It was too early for the lawyer to be out on business, but nevertheless he wondered whether he should send Johann on to the Kohlmarkt. The widowed Amelie would need to be warned to keep her husband's bequest away from his lawyer.

But they were already driving past the Plague Column—a gilded representation of the Trinity sitting amidst angels atop a bank of clouds. And Herr Anwalt's offices were located but a few buildings past the enormous column that towered over the Graben.

Just past the column, the carriage stopped briefly again, the horses impatiently neighing and stamping their feet on the cobblestones as they waited for the road ahead to clear.

"At this rate, it would be easier to walk the few yards that remain," Haydn muttered. He leant out of the window to survey the busy street. He was about to climb down from the carriage when his eye caught sight of a familiar figure ambling down the other side of the street. He followed its progress with an annoyed frown.

Fritz Dichtler, assigned the role of Mengone in *The Apothecary*, the opera that would open the season at Eszterháza, should have been at the castle rehearsing his part. Instead, here he was sauntering down the Graben, gawking at the sights like a tourist. Haydn's eyes narrowed as the tenor smiled flirtatiously at a pretty woman who passed him by and stopped to talk with another, his hand sliding down her bustle in a manner that was altogether too familiar.

He turned to his brother. "I want a word with that young man. I shall be back directly."

Johann seemed startled, but Haydn was too irked to bother with explanations. He turned around, struggling to push open the carriage door. He had just succeeded when Fritz Dichtler happened to turn around. The tenor's jaw dropped open, and his hand dropped from its resting place on his companion's bustle.

Haydn climbed down from the carriage and began bearing down toward the young man. "What in God's name are you doing here, Fritz?" he demanded furiously.

"Noth—nothing," the tenor bleated, a stricken expression on his face. "What are you doing here, Herr Kapellmeister? Taking in the sights, are you?"

Haydn's brows drew together. "Have you permission to miss a rehearsal session?"

"Yes—No, no." Fritz Dichtler looked around as though searching for inspiration. "Best be getting along, then." His lips stretched into a weak smile. "Wouldn't do to be late now, would it, Herr Kapellmeister? How would that look?"

He had been edging away from Haydn as he spoke. And now, before Haydn could respond, he pivoted on his heels and fled, disappearing into the crowd.

The Kapellmeister returned to his carriage, which had driven past the Plague Column and pulled to the side of the street.

"Maria Anna was right," he fumed as he climbed back in. "Fritz Dichtler's behavior is as deplorable as his wife's. And he is just as irresponsible. It will be a miracle if that opera is anything but an unmitigated disaster."

The Music Room in the Esterházy Palace on Wallnerstrasse was not nearly as large or as grand as the one in Eisenstadt. There was no fortepiano. The harpsichord, painted a bright orange with a floral pattern in black, was small and light enough not to require two sturdy footmen to move it out of the way.

But the room was large enough to make plenty of work for two, Rosalie thought as she pushed open the window overlooking the street. Greta stood behind her, vigorously polishing the Kapellmeister's desk. She removed an untouched copy of the previous day's court newspaper from the desk and added it to the growing stack in the closet.

"Look at all these newspapers! Unread, untouched." She fingered the stack longingly. "There is enough here for a month's supply of curlers. If I took one—just one of these—"

"Herr Haydn would know." Rosalie smiled as she began to scrub the window panes. Greta's tightly curled hair needed the frequent aid of curlers. Without them, the thick blond strands became wavy and hung limply down to her shoulders.

"He didn't miss the one that Herr Rahier filched," Greta pointed out. Her plump cheeks puffed out the way they usually did when she was annoyed. She tried to conceal it by tightly pursing her lips. "He assumed it hadn't been delivered."

"That was because I thought it hadn't." Rosalie paused in her task and looked over her shoulder. "The footman was still sorting through the mail when I took my place behind Frau Schwann. And Herr Rahier didn't come out of his office in all that time. I don't see how could he have laid his hands on it."

"He must have—" Greta clapped her hand to her mouth. "Oh! I was going to say he must have swiped it from the Music Room, but—"

"It never made its way to the Music Room. I never saw it, and I delivered Herr Haydn's mail to him that day. I waited to see if you were around to do it because. . ." The corners of Rosalie's mouth tightened as they invariably did these days at the thought of Mama and her constant recriminations.

"It wasn't your fault." Greta came over to her and gently squeezed her hand. An awkward moment of silence followed, then Greta cleared her throat. "Well, this is quite a mystery! How do you think Herr Rahier did it, then?"

It was not a particularly important question, but Rosalie was grateful for the distraction. She thought back to the day. It had been the last mail delivery before they set out for the city.

"Either the footman made a mistake," Greta went on. "Or someone must have gone up to the table before he finished sorting the mail."

"Yes, but no one did." Rosalie was beginning to shake her head when the vivid image of someone sweeping down the hallway invaded her mind. "Frau Dichtler!"

"What about her?" Rosalie's startled cry had taken Greta aback.

"She insisted upon looking through all the mail herself before it had been sorted. And when she came away. . ."

"It could've been her," Greta said. "She is friendly enough with Herr Rahier. I wonder what his wife thinks of that!"

Rosalie barely paid attention. She concentrated on the image in her mind, her violet eyes almost squinting from the effort. Had there been anything tucked under the singer's arm?

"But what could either of them want with an old copy of the *Wienerisches Diarium*?" Greta babbled on.

Rosalie shook her head. She had no explanation for it herself, but it worried her nevertheless. "That woman is always to be found wherever there's trouble of any kind," she muttered.

A solidly built, ruddy-complexioned man opened the door to Haydn and Johann. He was slightly above middle age and dressed in a plain black suit.

"Herr Anwalt's chambers?" Haydn enquired, not sure who the man was. The suit was of a cut far beyond the means of a mere assistant. But a lawyer would not answer his own door. Much less allow a client to do it.

The other gazed earnestly at them before lowering his eyes to the card Haydn had handed him.

"Herr Haydn!" He opened the door wider and gestured toward the interior. "I have long been expecting you, my dear sir."

"Herr Anwalt, I presume," Haydn said, following him into an antechamber furnished with chairs surrounding a low table.

The lawyer nodded in response as he led the way into a larger chamber dominated by an enormous desk cluttered with papers. "My assistant is out on an errand, leaving me to answer the door. Please—" He gestured toward the chairs covered in burgundy leather.

He waited for his visitors to be comfortably seated. "Kaspar . . . You have heard the news?" His eyes moved tentatively from Haydn to Johann, coming to rest eventually upon the Kapellmeister's features.

Haydn nodded. "You saw him on the day of the unfortunate incident, I believe."

"Saw him?" The lawyer looked surprised. "I have not seen Kaspar since the day Wilhelm Dietrich's will was read."

"Not even once since that day?" Johann sounded skeptical.

Herr Anwalt shook his head, a perplexed expression beginning to form on his features.

"You did not send for him on the night he was killed?" Haydn's tone was stern. The lawyer's befuddlement seemed genuine enough, but the message Kaspar had been carrying could only have come from Herr Anwalt.

The lawyer shook his head again. "What is this about, gentlemen?"

"A message was found on Kaspar's person," Johann explained as Haydn reached into his pocket only to bite back an oath. He had been wearing a different jacket on the day before. And, in his haste to leave the Keller house that morning, he had entirely omitted to retrieve the crumpled bit of paper from its pockets.

God forbid, Maria Anna should forget to turn his pockets out before putting the jacket in the wash! It was an important bit of evidence. Now, thanks to his carelessness, it was all but lost.

Haydn swallowed his consternation. "The writer claimed to have some news regarding Kaspar's bequest. And, apparently, asked to meet him at the Seizerkeller."

Was it his imagination or had the lawyer turned pale? He pressed home his point.

"Who else but you could have any information regarding his inheritance, Herr Anwalt?"

The lawyer pushed some papers around on his desk, then, clearing his throat, looked up. "I assure you I sent him no message. If I had any news to convey, I would have had him meet me here in my chambers.

During my hours of business."

He pursed his lips for a space.

"I do not frequent wine taverns," he finished at last with a defiant tilt of his head.

Haydn exchanged a glance with Johann. He wished he had the note with him. He was at a singular disadvantage without it. He turned back to the lawyer.

"Who else could have sent it?"

"The signature was torn off," Johann enunciated slowly, beginning to realize Haydn was not carrying the evidence with him. "But the last two letters of it were clearly visible: 'l' and 't.' How many people does Kaspar know other than yourself whose names end with those letters?"

"That I cannot tell." The lawyer rose from his seat, his fists clenched at his side. "But I can tell you this much: I have known Kaspar for as long as I have known his uncle, Wilhelm Dietrich. I would not harm a hair on his head."

He walked around his desk, coming to stand before Haydn. "I have been approached by several interested buyers, Herr Haydn. The sooner you can examine the scores, the better. You will be doing his poor widow a favor."

"Yes, of course." Haydn tore his eyes away from a document on the lawyer's desk that had attracted his attention. "Is—"

"It is not here." Herr Anwalt's tone was curt. "Kaspar chose not to entrust it in my care. He may have lived, if he had."

It was not what Haydn had meant to ask, but the lawyer's words caught his attention nevertheless. His eyes narrowed. He opened his mouth to speak, but a furious knocking at the door interrupted him. The lawyer's assistant must have returned to his post, for the sound of the door opening came to their ears.

"Oh, come quick! We have been set upon by thieves again." Rudi, Kaspar's old servant, burst in through the door and gazed at each of them in turn. "Mistress is at her wit's end. Come quick, good sirs!"

CHAPTER FIFTEEN

Haydn stepped gingerly across the worn parlor carpet in Kaspar's apartment. He kept his eyes riveted on its faded colors, chary of stepping on any broken bits of glass that might still be embedded in its nap.

"You have cleaned the place well, Rudi." He turned toward the servant. "There is not a single fragment of glass on the carpet." He inspected the carpet again but failed to detect the least glint on its surface. It was just as well, he thought. The identity of the perpetrator could hardly be read in a heap of broken shards.

"There appear to be none on the windowsill either." Johann rubbed a finger carefully along the length of the inner sill and turned it over to inspect the tip. A smattering of dust stained the fleshy pad. He glanced up to smile reassuringly at Kaspar's old servant.

But Rudi lowered his head, embarrassed. "Mistress was in so agitated a state this morning, no thought of sweeping floors or dusting mantles entered my mind."

"Then. . .?" Haydn peered down at the floor, his forehead corrugating into a slow pucker. A strange revelation was beginning to unfold in his mind, gradually releasing its significance.

"The parlor is as we found it this morning." Rudi tilted his chin to indicate a teardrop-shaped vase with swirls of emerald near the base. "Had the thief broken the right pane instead of the left, that would have shattered as well."

"How considerate of him to have weighed the consequences of his actions," the Kapellmeister replied, quite certain now of what had happened. He used his hands to brace himself against the sill and leant as far as he could over it. *Ah yes, just as he had suspected.*

A few large shards of glass lay scattered on the narrow ledge below the sill, with several more on the one beneath it.

Pulling himself back in, he turned around to face the parlor. Amelie was deep in conversation with Herr Anwalt. Haydn stared closely at her. Her cheeks appeared fuller than they had yesterday, the complexion less sallow.

His gaze wandered around the room. Were the papers littering the surface of the bureau a result of her inspection? Or had the thief rifled through its contents again?

The low murmuration of Johann's voice mingling with Rudi's penetrated his consciousness, drawing his attention back.

"Has such a thing happened before?" Johann was asking Rudi.

Rudi hesitated. "I heard noises on the day Master was killed. A scuffling as of a key being jiggled in the lock. I thought it was Master returning home. But if his keys were stolen . . ." He swallowed, clearly stricken by the implication.

"They must have been quite desperate to have made a second attempt," Johann ventured. His gaze shifted toward Haydn; the words he left unspoken, easily divined. *It said something about the importance of Kaspar's bequest, surely?*

"Someone was desperate," Haydn agreed softly. His eyes returned to where Kaspar's widow sat with the lawyer. She twisted and untwisted her slender hands ceaselessly as she peered up at Herr Anwalt, but whether from agitation or eager anticipation, Haydn could not tell.

<hr />

Rosalie cursed herself as she hurried into the kitchen. If only she hadn't dawdled over her chores that morning. Goodness gracious, she was late! Already the musicians could be heard descending from the Rehearsal Room like a horde of hungry Turks. And she had only just gotten the warmers going in the Officers' Mess.

Good thing it was summer. It had taken no time at all.

She uttered another curse as the kitchen door slammed shut behind her. The soup and the boiled beef had been carried in. But four more dishes still remained. The roast pork was on a silver platter so heavy, she would have to come back for the dumplings that went with it. Then there were the vegetables. And the *kipferl*, sweet crescent-shaped rolls covered in cherry marzipan and chocolate.

"Greta will have to come back for those," Rosalie muttered, hefting the platter of roast pork with an ill-suppressed grunt and maneuvering her way out of the kitchen door.

She trudged down the hallway, the weight of the platter slowing her down when a light patter of footsteps caught her ears. *Who was it,* she wondered. Her feet itched to turn around, but the musicians were already at their meal and the roast pork would not convey itself to the Officers' Mess.

She willed herself forward. But the relentless tap-tapping behind her was making the hairs on the nape of her neck rise. She found her steps lagging. Was it her imagination or were the footsteps behind her slowing down, too?

Good heavens! Whoever it was, was right behind her. Rosalie whirled around.

The platter she held came into contact with a slight, apron-clad figure, catching the woman in her midriff.

"I beg your pardon!" the woman said breathlessly. "I didn't. . .that is to say. . ."

"Who are you?" Rosalie demanded. "Why were you following me?"

She planted herself on the marble floor, determined not to move until she had received an answer. The musicians would just have to wait.

"I. . .er. . ." A strand of brown hair escaped from its pins and fell over the woman's eyes. She swept it back impatiently. "I am the new maid."

"The new maid!" Rosalie repeated. She could not recall anyone mentioning a new maid. But then she had been so preoccupied with the events of the previous day, she had barely remembered to serve the midday meal.

"I was sent for," the woman continued. "Frau Dichtler—"

"Frau Dichtler!" What did that infernal woman mean by hiring a new maid? Rosalie had half a mind to send the stranger packing. Her eyes swept over the newcomer's form. She looked a bit long in the tooth to be a kitchen maid. And that hat—a rakish red affair with all those feathers! Most unsuitable for a maid.

She was about to say as much when she recalled Greta's gossip. Had the Estates Director become so intimate with the soprano that he now allowed her a share in his prerogatives? She had best keep her mouth shut if that were the case. She didn't want to get in any trouble.

And now that she thought about it, a new maid would be most welcome. She could certainly do with an extra pair of hands.

Rosalie regarded the woman, head tilted to one side. "Are you supposed to start today?"

"At once. So I was given to understand."

"Very well." Rosalie bit her lip. Should she be issuing orders to the newcomer? On the other hand, it would soon be time to serve the pork with its dumplings and vegetables. She tipped her chin in the direction of the kitchen. "Go in there, get the bowl of dumplings and the vegetables, and follow me."

The woman frowned. "But. . . Are you sure? That is to say. . . I don't know if that is it to be one of my duties, you know."

"It most certainly is." Rosalie stared at the girl for a space. "*So I was given to understand*," she added. She could always claim to have been mistaken. "Well, go on. You don't want to keep the musicians waiting, do you? And take off your hat!"

Really! Where had Frau Dichtler found the woman? Strolling up and down the Graben or the Kohlmarkt of an evening as she plied her godless trade? Rosalie had never seen anyone who looked less like a maid and more like one of those shameless creatures of the night.

"It was but yesterday that the locks were changed." Johann carefully picked up a fragment of glass from the ledge outside the window and dropped it onto the piece of paper Haydn was holding between his hands. "Not a moment too soon, in my opinion."

Haydn nodded but with a tentative air, more than a little surprised that Johann had noticed nothing amiss. If the window *had* been broken from the outside, there would be some fragments of glass on the parlor carpet. Yet they had detected none. The window itself was set far enough back from the ledge that the larger pieces of glass would inevitably have fallen inside the parlor.

Johann was still speaking. "Who would have thought the thieves would strike again so shortly after their first attempt? What can have gone through their minds when they found the locks changed?" The thought elicited a good-humored chuckle.

But Haydn was not amused. "If they were unable to walk through the door, they would have had to climb up, Johann." He leant over the windowsill again. They were well above the street. "It is either a very brave man or a very desperate one who would climb all the way up to the third floor."

He turned to face his brother. "Does it not strike you as strange that all the glass is outside the room?"

Johann's smile faded. He stared at his brother, then turned toward the window. "Well, perhaps. . ." He tried the left sash. It opened inward. "No, it would be the same even if the window had been open—" he checked himself and turned back to his brother. "Not that there would be any need to break the panes, if that were the case."

"None at all." Haydn pointed to the teardrop-shaped vase in front of the right sash. "No object of any beauty is damaged at all, save the panes on the left." He swiveled around, facing the room. "No part of the room is in any disarray save those papers on Kaspar's bureau. What thief would be so loath to leave disorder in his wake?"

Haydn's eyes came to rest on Kaspar's widow.

Johann followed his gaze. "Why, what reason could she have, brother?"

"Who can tell?" Haydn replied. He had not known Amelie long enough or well enough to be sure of her character. "To negotiate a quick sale, perhaps. Every attempt makes the bequest appear more valuable."

He started toward the widow. A question had occurred to him. He was quite sure he knew what the answer was, but to hear it in Amelie's own words would be helpful. Rudi returned just as he was making his way across the room. He dropped the paper with its collection of glass shards into Rudi's dustpan and emitted a low cough to attract Amelie's attention.

She smiled up at him. "How can I thank you, Joseph? Were it not for the precaution you advised yesterday"—she gestured around the room—"Kaspar's bequest would be gone."

"It is safe, then?"

"Oh yes!" Amelie tipped her chin at the litter of papers on the bureau. "Those are merely old papers I meant to throw away. I left them in a neat stack on the bureau, but, as you can see, they have been rifled through."

"Kaspar mentioned some buyers who were interested in the scores, Amelie. Did any one of them happen to come by after Johann and I left yesterday?" Haydn watched her closely as he asked the question.

Amelie's eyebrows lifted. "Why, yes! A visitor from Italy. A physician, I believe. He was most interested. Why—"

"Did he make you an offer?"

Amelie wrinkled her nose. "It was not as much as Kaspar hoped to get for it. Still, I was quite tempted, but"—her eyes swiveled to the lawyer, then back toward Haydn—"when he offered twice as much if I could offer solid proof the scores were as valuable as we thought they were, I thought it best to wait. . ."

She glanced up at Haydn. "But what greater evidence could there be of its value than this?" She motioned toward the window.

Herr Anwalt harrumphed. "Well, be that as it may, the music is clearly not safe here. What think you, Herr Haydn?" He turned toward Amelie without waiting for a response. "Nor you, my dear, while it remains here."

"Brother and I can take it with us," Johann interjected quickly. "It will have to be examined, and—"

"An ingenious notion," Haydn agreed readily. "To sell it to the first buyer without knowing its true value would be a fool's choice, Amelie."

"Very well." Amelie nodded obediently, but the corners of her mouth puckered in discontent. She rose heavily.

"Come with me," she said, leading them out of the parlor.

<hr />

"Kaspar thought it would be secure here." Amelie stepped into a small room.

Herr Anwalt was following close on her heels, but stopped short a few paces past the threshold. He cleared his throat and looked around him, apparently dismayed to find himself in a bedchamber.

The coverlet had been flung aside, exposing the wrinkled sheets to view. Haydn averted his eyes, as embarrassed as the lawyer and Johann, who stared straight ahead, his features expressionless. Amelie must have risen in haste that morning.

She was at the closet now, a large affair with doors of painted green and panels decorated with flowers. She opened first one door, cast her eyes down past the shelves, then threw open the other.

"It is not here," she cried, whirling around in disbelief.

Dresses and overcoats hung on pegs attached to the doors, and a number of garments lay neatly folded on the shelves. But from where he stood at the doorway, Haydn could see nothing resembling a sheaf of papers.

"Are you certain—" he began. If only he had thought to take the bequest with him yesterday.

"It was here. In a small walnut chest. The thieves must have stolen into the room"—Amelie's eyes opened wide—"while I lay sleeping." She turned toward Haydn, stricken. "But I heard not a sound."

With her hands clasped tightly together, she surveyed the room as though fearful an intruder lurked somewhere within, undetected. "Something—a noise, perhaps—aroused me this morning. But I sensed nothing amiss. I would have known, would I not, if a stranger were in the room?"

The lawyer shook his head gravely. "If only Kaspar had heeded my advice. The music would have been safer in my chambers. To conceal it in his bedchamber! What could Kaspar have been thinking?" He shook his head again. "A man who will break into another's home knows neither shame nor modesty."

He went toward Amelie, gently lowering her into one of the chairs by the window. "You are fortunate, indeed, in having come to no harm, my dear."

Johann rang the bell for Rudi. "Your mistress has had a tremendous shock," he explained when the old servant appeared at last in response to the summons. "A little brandy will do much to alleviate it."

Haydn glanced around the bedchamber, listening absently as Johann explained the situation briefly to Rudi. Amelie's distress seemed genuine enough. She had clearly not expected to find the music gone. But when had it been taken?

Rudi was apparently having trouble comprehending the situation. "But what has been stolen? God knows, we have little worth taking."

"A small walnut chest containing manuscripts of some importance," Johann repeated. "I presume nothing else has been taken."

"It is Master's bequest, Rudi," Amelie cried, rousing herself. "The thieves have taken it."

Rudi's face cleared. "Master's bequest! Is it Master's bequest you are worried about? Why, no thief will have found that!"

"But they have. It is gone. Gone, I tell you!" Amelie pointed an agitated finger at the closet.

"No, no, Mistress. Master's bequest is quite safe, never fear." He smiled at Johann and Haydn. "Master could not have found a better hiding place for it."

CHAPTER SIXTEEN

Frau Dichtler stood with her hands on her hips and glared at Rosalie and Greta. "What were you two thinking?" she demanded. Her voice bore relentlessly into Rosalie's ears— like the piercing cry of an alphorn driving cattle to pasture.

Rosalie cringed, violet eyes sliding over to Greta, who stood beside her, head bowed, plump hands clasped over her midriff.

"It was my mistake, Madam. Greta had nothing to do with it." She spoke quickly, not wanting to get Greta into any more trouble.

The Estates Director, left infuriated by his encounter with Master Luigi, had already taken a gulden out of Greta's wages the previous evening. He had even threatened a second fine if he received so much as a whisper of a complaint against her.

It would be just like Frau Dichtler, Rosalie thought, to go running to the old stick-in-the-mud grousing about this matter.

The singer had swept into the Officers' Mess, late as always— behavior that Herr Rahier allowed no other musician to get away with— and was sauntering over to her seat when her eyes fell on the new maid. Why the sight of the woman serving dumplings should have caused her so much fury, Rosalie had no idea. But it had.

"I thought—" she began only to be interrupted.

"Thought!" the soprano screeched, eyes blazing. "Why would you think at all? Leave the thinking to your betters. Since when have you been paid to think?"

Greta's head came up defiantly. "What was she supposed to think? Your friend did say she was the new maid."

"Nonsense! Why would she say that?" But Frau Dichtler's voice trembled ever so slightly.

"She said you had sent for her," Greta pressed her advantage. "She didn't say anything about wanting to be a lady's maid. Not then, she didn't. Besides, why would we have need of one when we already have Frau Schwann?"

A frown rippled over the smooth whiteness of the soprano's forehead. "Why would my friend want to be a lady's maid? That is utter nonsense!"

"But that is what she said when she saw you. We both heard her." Greta indicated Rosalie with a wave of her plump hand. "She said you had sent for her—"

"You must have misheard her," Frau Dichtler said briskly. The frown had disappeared, and she appeared to have recovered her equanimity. "I sent for her to. . . to. . . Well never you mind why I sent for her. It was most reprehensible of you to have compelled her to serve as a kitchen maid.

"But I see it was all a mistake now," she continued. "I should not have lost my temper. Here"—she opened the purse hanging at her waist and brought out a gold gulden—"I trust this will make it up to you."

Rosalie stared as Greta reached for the coin and, out of force of habit, bit into it. Frau Dichtler was not one to apologize for her words or actions. In the brief time they had known her, not a single word of regret had passed her lips. What had brought it on this time? And a gold gulden, as well?

"I see no need to mention this little misunderstanding to anyone, do you?" Frau Dichtler surveyed the maids. "Very well, then." With that, she swept down the corridor.

Greta, who was still inspecting the coin, barely acknowledged the soprano's remarks. "It is real," she said once the singer had left. "What shall we do with it? We could treat ourselves to some of that delicious blackberry-flavored ice the vendors on the Graben sell. Or have a meal at the Seizerkeller—"

"That was a bribe," Rosalie interrupted her friend.

"What!"

"I think she just tried to buy our silence with that gold coin." Rosalie turned to face Greta. "That friend of hers—or whatever she chooses to call her—came expecting to be hired as a lady's maid. Just as she said. Neither one of us misheard that."

Greta looked at Rosalie as though she had lost her mind. "Yes, I know. But we already have a lady's maid—"

"Only because Her Serene Highness refused to dismiss Frau Schwann and let that horrible police guard arrest her."

"You mean—" Greta's eyes turned round with horror. "But why? How does it profit her?"

"I don't know. But I intend to find out." If the soprano had been trying to cost Clara Schwann her job, she was hardly likely to stop now.

"No thief would think to look for it here, Master said."

Rudi opened a door at the back of the kitchen and stepped aside to allow his mistress and her visitors a view into a narrow pantry. White painted shelves stacked with jars ran around three of the walls. On the floor underneath the shelves stood a number of tall white ceramic barrels.

Flour, sugar, and noodles, no doubt, Haydn thought as he poked his head around the door. Maria Anna kept her stock of the selfsame items in just such jars, although hers were painted with a delicate floral design.

"But where. . .?" he began when he caught sight of a chest of walnut wood just behind one of the barrels. "I see it now." He smiled. "It is indeed a good hiding place."

No intruder, however determined, would have thought to enter the pantry in search of the scores. The chest itself, moreover, was not immediately visible when the door was opened.

"The scores were safe enough in our bedchamber," the widow said. "Why Kaspar felt the need to put them in with my spices, I shall never know!" Her face was beginning to look a little pinched.

"He had not told you of his decision, I take it." Johann stepped forward to help Haydn move the ceramic jars aside.

That Kaspar had not confided in his wife was evident. But the Kapellmeister knew his brother had asked the question merely to gauge Amelie's reaction. He saw her lips tighten as she curtly shook her head in response.

"He must not have wanted to trouble you, my dear," Herr Anwalt sought to reassure her. It may well have been the truth, but seeing Amelie's face, Haydn wondered whether that was the sole reason for

Kaspar's reticence.

The lawyer glanced back the way they had come and continued in a grudging tone. "It was wisely done, I must admit. Especially if the intruder entered your bedchamber, Amelie.

"Although now"—Herr Anwalt's head pivoted around just as Haydn moved the last of the barrels out of the way and tugged the chest toward himself—"it would be best to get the chest and its troublesome contents out of your house."

"Besides, the scores still need to be authenticated," Haydn said. "And I promised Kaspar I would examine them." He was determined not to brook any argument on the subject. The music had caused quite enough trouble already. It would be best to trust no one at this point. "I assure you they will be quite safe with me, Amelie."

The sound of the door knocker beating upon the front door prevented the widow from responding. She turned her head, gathering up her skirts to leave. "I will see who it is."

Herr Anwalt followed her out of the kitchen. "I had best be leaving myself. If Herr Haydn promises to take charge of the music, there remains little for me to do at the present time."

"I trust it is not another prospective buyer," Haydn whispered to Johann, not relishing the prospect of having to run the gauntlet between Amelie's impatience and the visitor's equally keen desire to procure the music, if it were.

"It is that young man Master found so annoying," Rudi said before Johann could respond. "I will lay my life on it." He craned his neck out, although little could be seen of the hallway from his position near the pantry door. "He always comes when he is least wanted."

"What young man, Rudi?" Johann voiced the question before Haydn could, but the Kapellmeister was quite sure he knew who it was. Kaspar had not been dead for more than a day, and already the vultures had started swarming around.

"A scholar, he said he was," Rudi replied. "Something to do with music. Master liked him not at all, I can tell you that. Why, it was after his second visit late one night that Master decided to keep the chest here."

Haydn was about to push the chest back into the pantry when he heard the newcomer's loud ejaculation: "What! Another theft? How is that possible?"

It was a voice he recognized, and it belonged to no music scholar.

———

"It is only Albrecht," Johann said to Rudi. "He is a violinist like your master and works for the imperial court."

He grasped one of the brass handles of the chest as Haydn edged it toward the door. It was not so heavy as to require two people to convey it, but Haydn was grateful for the help, nevertheless.

They could still hear Albrecht speaking. He had been coming up to ensure all was well with the widow when he had encountered a police guard. Sent by the Police Inspector, apparently, to inform Amelie that the medical examiner had concluded his examination and the dead body could be released for burial. It was a fortuitous circumstance, was it not. . .

Haydn listened with half a mind, his thoughts elsewhere. He had no doubt the scholar would be by before too long. If he had not come thus far, it could only be because he had not heard of Kaspar's death, or the brutal manner in which he had been despatched.

Although now that he considered the matter, how in the name of heaven had the doctor, Kaspar's other buyer? Haydn's grip tightened on the brass handle. Johann, peering over his shoulder as he retreated out of the kitchen into the narrow hallway, appeared to be unaware anything was amiss.

Haydn followed, his mind churning. Not many people could know the man found dead in the streets was Kaspar. And nothing Amelie had said suggested she was the source of the physician's information. The doctor, he had gathered, had been an unexpected visitor.

They were approaching the parlor. Johann peered over his shoulder again, slowly edging past the doorway into the room.

The reason for the visit may have been entirely innocent, of course. The man had seemed quite desperate to gain possession of the scores.

But what if it was not?

It would be as well to enquire more closely into the matter, Haydn decided as he in his turn entered the parlor.

———

The lawyer had already left, but Albrecht was attempting to persuade a bristly-haired guard with a bored expression on his face to take a report of the theft. He stopped mid-sentence when he saw Haydn and Johann enter the parlor carrying the chest between them.

"That is what the thieves were after!" he cried, pointing to it.

The police guard turned lazily in the direction of his pointing finger. "And yet here it is, still within the house."

"Yes, b-but. . ." Albrecht sputtered.

"Besides," the guard continued, speaking over Albrecht, "what crime has been committed when nothing was taken?"

"But the window!" Albrecht pointed to it. "Someone broke into the house. That *is* a crime."

The guard shrugged. "Most likely the work of some careless servant girl."

"I employ no servant girls as you can see." A frown of displeasure settled on Amelie's face. "I certainly hope you are not suggesting that I or anyone connected with my household had anything to do with it."

Haydn exchanged a glance with Johann as they set the chest down beside the bureau. Now why had Amelie's mind gone straight to that supposition? The police guard had said nothing to elicit such a remark.

The guard shrugged again but said nothing.

"My husband was robbed of his keys on the day he was killed. The house was broken into that very night. The thieves must have made a second attempt and, finding the locks changed—"

"The locks have been changed, have they?" The information appeared to have sparked the guard's interest.

"Yes," Amelie replied shortly.

"And it is that wooden chest, the thieves are after?"

"Yes." Amelie hands, Haydn could see, were balled into fists.

"Well, well. A pretty pickle we have here, then. You have changed the locks, and that has been no help. Nothing has been taken, so there is no crime to investigate." The guard stroked his face. "All I can do to help, meine Dame, is to suggest that the chest be taken out of the house. I will be quite happy to take charge of it, if you will allow me."

"That is quite all right," Amelie said at the same time as Haydn spoke up: "Your offices will be quite unnecessary. I intend to take charge of the music myself."

"It is just as you wish, good sir. And now, which one of you gentlemen will accompany me to the police station to take charge of the dead man?"

CHAPTER SEVENTEEN

Greta swirled her tongue over the mound of blackberry ice the vendor on the Graben had handed her. "Umm. . ." She slurped up a small quantity of the dark purple slush and swallowed. "To think we have Frau Dichtler to thank for this! I can't say I like the woman, but it *was* nice of her to arrange for us to have a half-day."

"I wonder why," Rosalie mumbled indistinctly as she bent her head over her cherry ice. She let her tongue linger on the treat, savoring the cold sweetness of it as it dissolved in her mouth in a burst of flavor.

At any other time she would have enjoyed the sights, but she was too preoccupied now to care where they were going. Her feet simply kept step with Greta as they sauntered down the Graben.

"I wouldn't have thought she had it in her," Greta said, taking another lick of her ice. "But she must be feeling quite sorry for yelling at us like that." She gazed around at the shop windows with their displays of fine porcelain, perfumes, jewelry, and silks.

The Graben was bustling with life even though most of the nobility had by this time left Vienna for their country estates. Carriages rolled slowly past, their wheels rattling on the cobblestones. Elegantly dressed men and women promenaded the street, enjoying the balmy spring air.

"She's up to something, I'm sure of it," Rosalie muttered. The gold gulden the soprano had given them was a generous enough gift. There had really been no need for a half-day as well. "She must be trying to get rid of us for some reason."

"What!" Greta thrust the ice away from her. "You mean she tricked us into taking a half-day we haven't earned?" She tugged at Rosalie's arm, trying to swing her around in the other direction. "We had better hurry back. We'll get the boot if Herr Rahier finds out. That old stick-in-the-mud won't content himself with just a gulden out of our wages for this. You know he won't."

"It is quite all right, Greta. We won't get in any trouble. It was the head steward who told me we could take the afternoon off. He said we had Frau Dichtler to thank for it."

"Are you sure?" Greta's plump frame slowly pivoted back a few inches. She clung to Rosalie's elbow, her gaze dwelling longingly upon the shop fronts. It was not every day that they received an unexpected half-day, or money for that matter. It would be a shame to turn back before they'd even had time to enjoy it all.

"Yes." Rosalie smiled, easing her friend's fingers off her arm. "But I still think Frau Dichtler wants us out of the way for a while."

Greta turned back to face her. "Why? So, she can get rid of Frau Schwann? Whatever for?" Her tongue lapped anxiously at her melting blackberry ice, desperately trying to prevent the sweet black-purple rivulets from dribbling down the side.

"I wonder if Her Serene Highness's necklace has anything to do with all of this." Rosalie frowned, pushing her finger up against the side of her treat to collect the melting ice.

She lowered her mouth to it, but raised it again sharply as another thought occurred to her. "What if she was using the necklace, Greta? To get rid of Frau Schwann." Melted cherry ice dribbled, unnoticed, through her fingers.

"That makes no sense," Greta mumbled, licking her ice. "She would have had to steal the necklace herself for that to work."

"What if she did?" An image of a frayed piece of rope arose in Rosalie's mind. Someone had quite deliberately cut it. Had it been Frau Dichtler?

"I trust Albrecht will have the forethought to ask the medical examiner for his report," Haydn said after they had taken their leave of Kaspar's widow. "It surprises me that he can have concluded his examination so soon. It has been but a day."

He wrapped his arm firmly over the walnut casket and clasped it close to his chest as he navigated the steep stairs. It was an uncomfortable way of bearing the article, but the stairs were so narrow they would have impeded the passage of any passerby had he allowed Johann to help.

Johann pulled Kaspar's door shut and followed his brother down the stairs. "If the medical examiner's report reveals nothing of interest, the undertaker may be of help. If I mistake not, it is the same man who arranged Wilhelm Dietrich's funeral. Kaspar said the man was a barber-surgeon, but left his practice for the more lucrative trade of arranging funerals."

Albrecht had, at Johann's suggestion, accompanied the police guard to the medical examiner's rooms where Kaspar's body would be released to him.

It was a task Haydn would have preferred to undertake himself, but the wisdom of Johann's advice could hardly be refuted. The thieves had already made two attempts to appropriate the music. Who was to say there would not be a third—in full view of the city at that?

A dapper man with a trimmed, pointed beard was making his way up the narrow stairs. He glanced up and had no sooner set eyes on Haydn than he pressed himself against the wall to allow the Kapellmeister to pass. Haydn nodded briefly at him over the top of the chest and, murmuring his thanks, hurried past.

"I will be glad to finally have an opportunity to peruse the contents of this chest, Johann," he said in a low voice as they made their way down. "It appears to exert an unnatural fascination upon everyone who hears of it."

"That it does. It must contain something of value. The doctor has been by already. The young music scholar will not, I suppose, be too far behind."

Haydn paused at the landing and glanced over his shoulder. "It occurred to me that he may not have heard the news. If Kaspar distrusted him as greatly as Rudi says he did, he would have rebuffed any offer he made. Having been spurned twice, I doubt he would come by a third time."

"I would think men like that are quite hardened against the most persistent repudiations, brother. Why, Kaspar's rejection of the doctor's offers were no less resounding. Yet he was by just yesterday."

"To offer his condolences, according to Amelie, along with a more material offer. He appears to have known of Kaspar's demise even though it was but yesterday that the discovery was made."

"What can you be implying?" Haydn heard Johann come to a halt behind him. "That the doctor—"

Haydn looked over his shoulder into his brother's eyes. "I can think of no other explanation unless Amelie sent word to him."

"She said she did not, but. . ." Johann looked troubled.

———

"I thought the only person who could've stolen the necklace was someone who knew it was a paste replica of the original." The corners of Greta's eyes crinkled as she gazed at Rosalie.

They were sitting on the stone steps encircling the enormous granite basin of Leopold's Fountain in the Graben. The imposing figure of St. Leopold, the Empire's patron saint, stared impassively down at them, its sightless bronze eyes appearing to hold the same question.

Rosalie glanced away, drawing a deep breath. "Frau Schwann could have taken the necklace—the genuine thing—at any time. After all, she is the sole person in charge of Her Serene Highness's wardrobe."

"If she had, suspicion would've fallen immediately upon her," Greta pointed out, licking the sticky residue of blackberry ice from her fingers. "She'd be a fool to simply take it."

Rosalie nodded, taking another deep breath. It had all made sense in her head, but now that she was giving utterance to her thoughts, the different threads she had woven were in danger of becoming a tangled mess. "So, if Frau Schwann had wanted to take the necklace, she would have had to concoct an elaborate plan, wouldn't she?"

Greta pondered this for a moment before slowly inclining her head. "I suppose a plan like the one that police guard, Poldi, mentioned would work. Steal the fake and then substitute it for the original at some point. Or have someone else do it. Didn't you say a ragamuffin snatched the case out of Frau Schwann's hands?"

Rosalie nodded again. "And Poldi gave chase and brought the case back."

"Hmmm. . ." Greta tapped a rhythm on the cobblestones. "Either the ragamuffin was very quick or Poldi was in on it." She raised her head sharply. "Poldi and Frau Schwann acting together? Impossible!"

She shook her head doubtfully. "But I don't see how it could have been Frau Dichtler, either. For one thing, when did she ever have an opportunity to take the fake?"

That was a question Rosalie could answer. "At Leopoldsdorf," she replied simply. "Do you recall how she sent us on a chase—"

Greta snorted. "A wild goose chase. Her jewelry case and the Princess's medicaments were where they were supposed to be. And you and I spent a good half hour traipsing around in the cold looking for them."

"Yes, but do you recall the rope?" Rosalie turned to face her friend. "I knew someone had deliberately cut it."

A small furrow appeared on Greta's brow. "You think Frau Dichtler cut it?"

"She was at the back of the carriage before either one of us was even out of it," Rosalie reminded her. Why was her friend, usually so wont to believe the very worst of Frau Dichtler, being so skeptical?

But Greta was convinced now. "So she was!" she gasped. "And she screamed blue murder about the rope being cut."

Rosalie bent forward. "She had plenty of time to take the necklace when she sent us off on our errand. Of course, she didn't know at the time that it was a fake. No one did except Frau Schwann and Her Serene Highness."

Greta's blond curls bounced as she bobbed her head up and down. "She either found out later that it was a fake or—"

"Or Her Serene Highness mentioned it to her," Rosalie said. "They are quite friendly. Frau Dichtler seems to have won her confidence, who knows how? Why, Frau Schwann was worried she might be dismissed. And she has served the Princess since her marriage to the Prince."

"It is likely enough." Greta regarded the gray cobblestones, dragging her foot forward and back against them. She glanced up after a few moments. "There is just one problem, you know?"

"What?" Rosalie wanted to know. Hadn't she explained it all clearly enough?

"We have no evidence, and no one will believe us without it."

"Oh!" Rosalie's shoulders drooped. She hadn't considered this aspect of the matter. All she had wanted to do was prevent that horrid soprano from costing Frau Schwann her job.

"No need to get all downcast." Greta reached over to pat her hand.

"We just have to find the necklace."

"Easier said than done," Rosalie said gloomily.

"Never fear. My cousin works at a pawnshop." Greta leaned over and continued in a whisper, "Sometimes, someone will come in with stolen goods and try to palm them off. The pawnshops aren't supposed to take items like that, but some of them do it anyway. Otto knows all the shops in the city. The ones that will accept stolen items. The ones that won't even consider it. If he can't help us, no one can."

CHAPTER EIGHTEEN

"Let us rest here a while." Haydn stepped onto the second-floor landing and eased the weight of Kaspar's chest onto his bent left knee, glad to momentarily relieve his arms of their burden.

"Shall I carry it the rest of the way down?" Johann enquired, coming up behind him.

Haydn shook his head. "There is no need. I require but a moment to catch my breath."

A few moments later, he hefted the chest up again, preparing to descend the last flight of stairs when he felt his progress barred. He peered over the top of the chest. Who had so rudely thrust a walking stick at him? It had struck him lightly against the shin. He could see no one but still felt the stick pressing firmly against his leg.

"Who are you and what business do you have here?" To Haydn's ears the voice sounded like the dry crackling of an autumn leaf.

He moved the chest to one side and found himself staring into a pair of age-dimmed, blue-gray eyes surrounded by innumerable wrinkles of brown, shriveled skin. They held his gaze with an unmistakable air of authority.

He gazed back, unable to tear his eyes away. A vague impression of an excessively thin figure seated in a wheelchair seeped into his mind. A woman, judging by her plain, black gown.

"I am Joseph Haydn," he replied, too startled by the encounter to take exception to her imperious manner. "Kapellmeister to His Serene Highness, Prince Nikolaus Esterházy." He indicated his brother behind him. "My younger brother Johann, also in the Prince's employ."

"Haydn?" She squinted up at him, uttering the name as though she knew him. There was something familiar about her person, although

Haydn had no recollection of ever having met her. "Joseph Haydn," she said again. "The boy who croaks out his solos?" She cackled.

The sound brought out a harried-looking middle-aged servant from the apartment behind her. "Oh there you are, Your Grace! It is time for your nap. I have your medicines all ready." She looked up at Haydn. "Her Grace—"

"Is the Countess of Kuenberg," Haydn said, recalling the woman whose complaints about his singing had resulted in all his solos being given to his brother Michael. There had been a shrewish quality about her even then, when she had served as the Empress's lady-in-waiting, and it appeared not to have improved with age.

"Her Grace means you no harm, sirs. She is old and takes every little change as cause for alarm. Let these gentlemen pass, Your Grace. They must be here to offer their condolences to the poor widow upstairs."

"Oh stop fussing, Katherl," Her Grace said sharply, but she withdrew her walking stick. "It is not young Joseph here who scares me. It is the ruffian and that scandalous woman who have me fearing for my life. Is not the musician who lives above us dead?"

"Wilhelm Kaspar?" Haydn enquired, interested despite himself. The Countess's sharp tongue had always been accompanied by equally sharp ears and eyes. "He was killed, Your Grace. It happened just outside a wine tavern."

The Countess grunted. "Well then, I suppose it could not have been those two. Although, I tell you, I have yet to see a more ruffianly pair. They acted brazen enough, but I saw the way they were looking over their shoulders."

"Looking over their shoulders?" Haydn repeated. Had someone really attempted to break into Kaspar's apartment, then? There would have been no reason to be furtive had they simply intended to pay the widow a visit. Yet all the evidence pointed to the robbery having been staged.

"Yes, looking over their shoulders." The Countess's dry croak broke into his thoughts. "Isn't that what I said? Clean the wax out of your ears, boy!"

"When did you see them?" Johann asked, speaking for the first time.

"I doubt she saw anyone at all," Katherl, the maid, murmured. "She is often restless at night. The pain keeps her from sleeping, and the numerous potions make her imagine things."

"I imagine nothing." The Countess banged her stick on the floor. "I saw those two, I tell you! Why, it was just last night. Long after every decent soul was abed." With a grunt, she turned her chair around and began to wheel herself back into her apartment. "I am tired now. Leave me alone."

"Last night?" Haydn repeated. It would have been impossible to enter through the door last night. The keys stolen from Kaspar's person would not have opened the new locks. Had someone—Amelie, perhaps—let the strange couple in?

It was an unsavory thought, and he chose not to dwell on it.

Katherl was still standing before him. She waited until her employer had gone indoors before turning to him.

"Last night," she began in a low voice, "was one of the few nights Her Grace slept well. She was in such pain, I mixed some opium in her hot chocolate. She fell into a deep sleep from which she only awoke this morning. I did hear steps late at night, but it must have been one of the young men in the garret, returning home after a serenade."

Haydn nodded. It was not an uncommon means of earning a few kreutzers for an impoverished young man. He had done it himself, there being no dearth of patrons willing to pay generously to have a young musician serenade a wife or daughter on her name day. But the information did nothing to ease his qualms.

***

Rosalie was quite out of breath by the time she reached Wallnerstrasse. She had barely paused to catch her breath under the stone portico of the building at the corner when she caught sight of a familiar figure in a silk-lined straw hat making its way down the street.

The wide brim sweeping around the hat shielded the wearer's features, but there was no mistaking the provocative swaying of Frau Dichtler's hips as she swept down the street.

She had made it back not a moment too soon, and just as she suspected, the soprano was on her way somewhere. Greta had insisted the necklace was already at a pawn store. They would be wasting precious time if they foolishly returned to the palace.

And who knew when another unforeseen half-day would present itself for them to retrieve the necklace? Better do it right now.

Good thing, she hadn't given in to Greta. She would still be traipsing the city in search of that necklace instead of simply letting Frau Dichtler lead her to it.

The soprano's visitor from earlier that afternoon followed close behind, still wearing her scarlet hat with its raised crown and dyed ostrich feathers. She hurried to keep pace with the singer, for Frau Dichtler, despite the care she took to sway her hips from side to side, managed to set up a tremendous pace.

Rosalie shrank back against the wall as the woman's head turned this way and that to scan her surroundings, but she needn't have worried. The marble columns that surrounded the portico, running from ground to ceiling, sheltered her from the woman's wary gaze.

Rosalie watched the women go past, then waited a while before poking her head out from under the portico. She crept out and began walking after them. She could walk as fast or faster than Frau Dichtler, dressed as she was in a simple dirndl. But God forbid, the woman should consider hailing the many cabs that slowed down as they coaxed their horses past the two well-dressed ladies walking briskly on.

And God forbid that either one of them should turn back and see her, she thought, as the soprano's friend began to twist her head around. Rosalie quickly stepped under the colorful awning of a stall selling bonnets, capes, and ribbons to avoid her gaze.

"The lace shawl," she said to the hat-woman whose eyes had brightened at seeing what looked like a possible customer. "I feel a slight chill, and it will do nicely enough for a day such as this." She pointed to the garment in question. It would also do very well to conceal her person from prying eyes, she thought.

She waited impatiently while the hat-woman brought down the shawl. Her eyes slid anxiously toward the swiftly-receding bustles of Frau Dichtler and her friend.

"No need to wrap it." She slapped a few coins down on the wooden counter. "I intend to wear it."

Frau Dichtler and her friend were almost out of sight by the time Rosalie had draped the shawl over her head and pushed her way through the crowded streets. It was late afternoon, and all of Vienna seemed to be out enjoying the fine day.

She followed the two women around twisting alleys and lanes, too intent on keeping them in sight to pay attention to where she was going. She fervently hoped Frau Dichtler intended to return to the castle after her errand. It would take her hours to find her way back to Wallnerstrasse on her own.

A couple of turns later, she caught sight of the two women disappearing through the door on the left of the main entrance of a building. She paused to take stock of her surroundings. There would be time enough to scout out the establishment Frau Dichtler and her friend had entered.

Beyond the buildings that lined the street on either side, she could see the twenty-foot- high walls of the city and the arched opening of the Carinthian Gate culminating in a triangular roof. Why, it was not above a week that they had entered the city through those very gates.

Rosalie frowned. What business could Frau Dichtler possibly have in this quarter of Vienna, so far from the palace?

"I doubt marriage would have improved her disposition," Haydn said, recalling his old teacher Reutter's observation regarding the Countess of Kuenberg. He stepped out from the dim interior of Kaspar's building into the bright warmth of the afternoon sun. His eyes blinked several times in rapid succession as they adjusted to the glare.

It had been several years since he had seen the Countess of Kuenberg, but the effect of his unexpected encounter with her, all these years after his dismissal from St. Stephen's, remained the same. She still chafed every fiber of his being like a garment of horsehair.

"I suppose not." Johann came up to stand next to him. "She was always a sour-tempered woman. But why let thoughts of her spoil your temper now, brother? She is an old woman, barely in control of her faculties."

"She seemed to know what she was talking about," Haydn replied. He stepped out from under the portico and glanced up. The sight that met his eyes made him draw in his breath in a quick, sharp hiss.

"Can Amelie be so lost to all sense of propriety that she allows a stranger to treat her with such familiarity?"

The man he and his brother had passed on their way down stood close behind Kaspar's widow by the broken window. The couple seemed oblivious to the world below them. Haydn watched in disgust as the man lightly brushed a wayward strand of hair from the widow's cheek, his fingers lingering against her skin.

"He may not be a stranger," Johann said, looking up just at that moment. "A cousin, perhaps, consoling her in her time of grief."

Haydn shook his head. For all his wisdom, his brother tended to be remarkably guileless when it came to relations between men and women. "There was nothing cousinly about his touch or her response. I could have sworn her lips parted. In a wanton desire she should not feel," he continued to mutter, "when her husband is barely cold in his grave.

"Why, he is not yet in his grave." He straightened up as he recalled the bitter, hard fact.

"Let us not be so quick to judge, brother," Johann admonished him. He gestured toward the chest Haydn was gripping hard against himself. "And let us hasten to the palace. It cannot be safe to be standing around in this crowded place with an object of as much value as this appears to be."

Haydn allowed himself to be propelled down the busy street. It was but a short walk to the Esterházy palace on Wallnerstrasse. Still, he wished they were in his carriage rather than being pushed and jostled by the coaches and people thronging around them.

But he had offered Albrecht the use of his vehicle to convey Kaspar's body to the undertaker. And who knew how long it would be before Albrecht returned?

Haydn's thoughts returned to Amelie's visitor. There was something familiar about the dapper figure in his coat of brown velvet. He said as much to Johann.

"It is as I said, brother. He is a relative, no doubt, of either Kaspar or Amelie. You must have seen him at their house."

But although Haydn could have sworn he had encountered the man before, he was quite sure it had never been at Kaspar's apartment. Nor, for that matter, had he seen the man on any prior visit to the city. His mind dwelt on the stranger's dark beard, trimmed to a neat point; his large, lustrous brown eyes, far too beautiful to belong in a man's face. Where had he seen those features before?

It had not been too long ago, he was sure of that. In his mind's eye, he vividly saw those eyes staring at him, darting away every time they caught him looking back.

It was only when they arrived at the palace that he remembered.

"It was at the wine tavern, Johann!"

"What?" Johann stopped, turning slowly to look at him.

"The Seizerkeller. That is where I first saw him. His eyes seemed to be drawn toward us. He was staring at Kaspar the way a spider contemplates the fly it wishes to feast upon."

CHAPTER NINETEEN

Johann regarded him for a space. "The tavern was dimly lit. Can you be certain it was the selfsame man you saw?"

"I could not help but notice him. His behavior struck me as most suspicious. He seemed to be doing his utmost to listen to our conversation."

"And Kaspar was talking about his bequest at the time." Johann frowned. His eyes wandered sightlessly around the inner courtyard. A thought must have struck him as he contemplated the facts, for his eyes opened wider and he turned sharply toward Haydn.

"How did Amelie come to make his acquaintance, then? If the man were known to Kaspar, surely he would have approached us."

Haydn gnawed pensively at his lower lip. "I should have drawn Kaspar's attention to him. He was seated between Luigi and myself and had only to turn his head a few degrees to see the man."

"Then most likely they were not acquainted." Johann must have seen something in Haydn's features, for he concluded the assertion on a tenuous warble. "Surely you are not suggesting that they were?" he demanded when the Kapellmeister remained silent.

Haydn continued to gnaw at his lip, not sure himself what he was suggesting.

"Most likely they were not," he conceded. "Kaspar could hardly have spent the entire evening without turning his head. And if he had, he would not have failed to see the man."

He strode briskly toward the palace doors as though the matter were satisfactorily settled. Yet his mind refused to dismiss it so easily. Something about the stranger's manner had suggested he had no desire to call attention to himself. Would a man unacquainted with Kaspar have any need to be so furtive?

Johann fell into step beside him. "Then however Amelie came to know him, it cannot have been through Kaspar."

"Most likely not," Haydn agreed. Now, why did he have no trouble believing that? If there was a possibility that Kaspar knew the man, why should he not have introduced him to his wife. Unless. . .

Haydn stiffened. *Unless he were a business connection, a man interested in acquiring Kaspar's bequest.* Even so—

"Who could have made Amelie known to him?" Johann's words echoed the question ringing in Haydn's mind.

"And more importantly," he replied quietly, "when did she make his acquaintance? After Kaspar's death?" *God forbid that it should have been before!*

<hr />

Rosalie slowly approached the building the soprano had entered with her friend. As she drew closer, she noticed the large glass windows on either side of the narrow door and the colorful displays of hats, jeweled pins, silken scarves, and lace stoles all draped over swathes of crimson velvet cloth.

A millinery?

It seemed fashionable enough, but what woman of society, accustomed to frequenting establishments on the Graben and the Kohlmarkt, would come all the way here?

The milliner—Madame Chapeau, read the sign above the door—also sold small items of jewelry. Beautiful brooches in jeweled colors lay nestled among the silks and laces on display.

Rosalie forced her eyes away from the dazzling array. Frau Dichtler was leaning over the counter, deep in conversation with a middle-aged woman.

The Madame herself, no doubt, Rosalie thought, taking in the woman's large green eyes and the glossy ebony curls that fell upon her bare shoulders, framing a face that was still beautiful. Frau Dichtler's friend stood behind the counter, arranging bolts of fabric on the shelves behind her.

Where was the necklace? Try as she might, Rosalie could see nothing. What should she do now? Rosalie had not stopped to consider the question when she followed Frau Dichtler. For all she knew, the woman was doing nothing more dubious than discussing the latest styles.

There was no question of entering the establishment. Everything in it was beyond the means of a maid such as herself. And she could scarcely pretend Her Serene Highness had sent her. The Princess was unlikely to patronize an establishment so far from the fashionable center of town.

Still, standing out here on the street was doing her no good. She edged closer to the door. Would it be possible to open it just a crack? She would have to do it very carefully so as not to make the bell above the door ring.

But if she could overhear some parts of the conversation. . . Well, who knew what that might yield. She was at the door now. She looked over her shoulder. No one seemed to be taking any notice of her.

She stretched out her hand, about to reach for the handle when she noticed the tiniest crack between the door jamb and the frame. Ah! What a bit of luck. The door wasn't closed all the way. She slowly inserted her finger in the crack, letting it widen until the sound of voices came to her ears.

"It turns out Herr Rahier's interest in acquiring music wasn't feigned." Luigi tapped the encircled article in the newspaper in Haydn's hands. "I found your missing copy of the *Diarium* in his office." He stood by the harpsichord, hazel eyes searching the Kapellmeister's features for a response.

But Haydn, who had just entered the Music Room with Johann, was still perusing the article his Konzertmeister had indicated.

"The operas of Monteverdi?" Johann took a quick peek over Haydn's shoulder before going over to his brother's desk with the ivory-inlaid chest containing Kaspar's bequest. "That cannot be a coincidence," he remarked, setting the chest down.

He returned to his brother's side, stretching the stiffness out of his fingers and wrists. "And to think we assumed he was only sending Fritz Dichtler away—" He broke off just as Haydn's head jerked up. "Why, then—" he turned to his brother.

Haydn nodded. "It was not to take in the sights that Fritz Dichtler was on the Graben this morning. We were on our way to see Kaspar's lawyer when we saw him sauntering along," he explained to Luigi. "Not above a yard from Herr Anwalt's chambers. One of the prospective buyers Herr Anwalt mentioned to us, no doubt."

Luigi's gaze had been swiveling back and forth between Haydn and Johann. "Then it was Kaspar's bequest that Herr Rahier was interested in all along? But how could he have known of it? Kaspar cannot have mentioned it to him."

"Herr Anwalt, I suppose," Johann said, although his faltering voice as he made the suggestion expressed his own doubts on the matter.

"It is a possibility," Haydn murmured as he glanced down at the newspaper. But as he cast his mind over his conversation with the Estates Director, a few more details churned up to the surface. And now quite another possibility was beginning to occur to him.

He turned the paper over, aware of his brother and his Konzertmeister staring at him.

"It seems to be the only possibility," Luigi said at last. "Unless you have thought of something else, Joseph."

"Have you, brother?" Johann wanted to know.

"Maybe," Haydn said, turning the paper over again. "I can see why he kept it. But I don't see why he took it," he muttered. "And this article, marked as it is. . ."

Luigi peered over the top of the paper. "It must have caught his attention." His voice rose to a question, and he frowned, clearly unable to fathom why the fact required any explanation at all.

"Precisely." Haydn raised his head. "But that means he wasn't expecting to see it."

"Yes, it is already here." Rosalie saw the milliner wave her hand dismissively as she spoke, her voice so low Rosalie had to strain her ears to hear the words.

What was Madame Chapeau referring to? The necklace? Caught up in her own thoughts, she missed most of the milliner's next words. ". . .arrangement for Sabina?"

The soprano had been leaning over the counter, but Rosalie saw her straighten up as soon as she heard the name, glancing over to where her friend stood arranging bolts of silk.

"You should have waited until you received my message?" The soprano sounded furious, but she tempered her normally strident tone to an angry hiss before continuing. "Do you trust me so little?"

"She was supposed to be gone by now, Elsa." Overtones of suppressed rage vibrated in the milliner's low voice. "We agreed to that. Or have you already forgotten."

"Well it is no fault of mine that she remains," the soprano hissed back with a quick glance over her shoulder. Rosalie withdrew from the door, pressing herself against the section of wall between the doorway and the glass window. "God knows, I have tried hard enough to rid myself of her."

What Frau Dichtler said next, Rosalie could not quite hear, but Madame Chapeau's words were unmistakable.

"Oh yes, the money! That is all you think of, Elsa."

Rosalie peeked through the window just in time to see Frau Dichtler tucking her reticule under her arm. "I will do what I can, Anna, but I make no promises." The soprano turned toward the door, a small smirk of satisfaction on her face. "You still have me. Let that suffice."

A narrow cobblestone alley ran down the side of the building. Rosalie hastily turned onto it and concealed herself under a sheltered doorway. A covered rack wagon stood behind her, the horse's harness jingling at intervals.

The soprano was not likely to spare the dingy little alley a single glance, but Rosalie didn't want to chance being seen. She had heard little that warranted her following the singer. There was no sign of the necklace. And yet. . .

She saw the soprano sweep past the alley. Frau Dichtler's friend was nowhere in sight, although Rosalie was beginning to suspect she was no friend at all. She decided to wait a few minutes before venturing out of the alley.

She was about to come out of her hiding place when a sharp tap on her shoulder made her jump. She would have shrieked out had she not bitten her tongue.

"What business do you have here, then?"

CHAPTER TWENTY

Rosalie turned slowly around and found herself staring at a brown button. Her gaze traveled up the coat to which it was attached, past a muscular neck and a firm mouth, straight into the intense blue depths of Gerhard Heindl's eyes.

"What business do you?" she retorted. Why he should make her feel so guilty, she couldn't fathom. The tavern keeper was expected at the Wallnerstrasse wine cellar with a delivery of wine from Eisenstadt. What was *he* doing loitering around in an alley at the outer limits of the city?

The corners of Gerhard's mouth twitched. Then a smile spread slowly across his handsome features. "It is not to commit any murders, I assure you. I have deliveries to make here. At the Karlskirche and the civic hospital beyond"—he tipped his chin toward the city walls—"and a few other establishments as well. I usually do them before driving to Wallnerstrasse."

Rosalie's cheeks burned. Word of her suspicions of him during the past winter had somehow gotten around all of Eisenstadt and even spread to Kleinhöflein where Gerhard had his wine tavern. She had barely time to recover her composure when he directed a few more questions at her.

"But what brings you here? And so far from the palace, too?"

Rosalie scarcely knew how to respond. After his teasing remarks, telling him the truth was quite out of the question. Fortunately, he continued to speak, saving her the trouble of a lie.

"Is it to chase rumors of poor Madame Chapeau, the milliner, being a fence?"

"What?" Rosalie's eyes widened. "Is she really?"

Gerhard's smile grew broader. "Your ears perk up at such talk, don't they? But that is all it is, talk. Her very success seems to breed it. As though a milliner could not thrive so far from the fashionable enter of town without being a fence."

Rosalie frowned. "But how *does* she thrive? Her wares must cost more than anyone who shops here could afford."

Gerhard rolled his eyes. "What I said was in jest, but I see I should have held my tongue. Madame Chapeau does well because she caters to every sort of person. A maid like you could get outfitted there just as well as could the Empress herself."

The rattling of a bolt being drawn back gave Rosalie a start. "That will be Sabina," Gerhard said. "Come to take delivery of Madame Chapeau's wine."

"Ah, Herr Kapellmeister! It has been a while since I last saw you," Rahier said as soon as Haydn entered the vast chamber that served as the Estates Director's office.

The veiled insinuation was typical of the Estates Director, but Haydn brushed it off with a smile. "I suppose it has."

It was information he was after. Allowing Rahier's jabs to nettle him would yield no good.

The Estates Director's expression had soured at Haydn's response, his lips compressing into a thin line as Haydn approached his cluttered desk and gestured toward one of the ornate wood chairs in front of it. "May I?"

"If you must, Herr Kapellmeister." Rahier leaned back in his chair, crossed his arms, and allowed a ponderous sigh to pass through his pursed lips. A martyr nailed to the cross could not have looked more put upon.

Haydn lowered himself into the blue velvet-covered seat and reached within his coat for the copy of the *Diarium* Luigi had discovered in Rahier's possession.

"We may have had our differences, Herr Rahier," he began as he spread the paper out on the desk, carefully smoothening the wrinkles out. "But if you wished to read my copy of the court newspaper, all you had to do was ask."

A pinkish tinge suffused Rahier's pale cheeks. His ice-blue eyes met

Haydn's briefly, then flickered away. "As I explained to your Konzertmeister, I merely meant to borrow it," he said at last. "That it was not returned sooner was an unfortunate oversight on my part."

"And I see you marked an article here." Haydn turned the page over to the article describing the Empress's interest in the great master's operas and slid the paper across the table toward the Estates Director.

Rahier withdrew his hand as the paper touched it, barely deigning to glance down. "It was something that caught my attention. Yes." He uttered the words in clipped tones.

Haydn suppressed a smile. The Estates Director had so carefully concealed the object of his interest, he could not be pleased at being found out. And by someone he regarded as his rival. It was most fortuitous that Luigi had discovered the *Diarium*, or Haydn would never have known of the matter.

"I thought it might have," he said lightly. "Learning of the Empress's interest in the works you were about to acquire must only have piqued your own interest. It *was* a collection of Monteverdi's operas, was it not? What stimulated your interest in such old works, I wonder. How did you even hear of them?"

Rahier's lips tightened even further. His hands were resting on the table. He leaned forward, shifting his weight on them. "I have my sources, Herr Kapellmeister. I see no reason to reveal them to you."

"No need at all, Herr Rahier. I saw Fritz Dichtler on the Graben, and—"

Rahier sat back in his chair. "You think to procure those works yourself, I suppose. I have long known of your interest in them."

"My interest in them?" Haydn began, but was interrupted before he could say any more.

The Estates Director held up his hand. "You may have them. Although I doubt you have the means, any more than I do, to pay the substantial assurance the owner seeks for a potential buyer to so much as look at the works."

"The owner seeks a substantial assurance?" Was the Estates Director referring to Kaspar's widow? Or was it Herr Anwalt who had imposed such an audacious stricture? The lawyer, most likely. Amelie was too eager to see the works sold to wait until they had been examined.

The Estates Director's mouth crinkled up in the slightest hint of a smirk. "You were not aware of that condition, were you, Herr Haydn."

Haydn regarded him with a frown. Was Herr Anwalt really the sort of man to keep potential buyers dangling? "It was to negotiate that condition, then, that you sent Fritz Dichtler to the Graben?" It was such an outrageous condition, he did not have the heart to berate the Estates Director for sending one of his men out without permission.

"What made you bolt like that?" Gerhard urged his horse forward with a gentle prod in the ribs, then turned his head to give Rosalie a quick look. "I could've acquainted you with Sabina."

"Whatever for?" Rosalie wanted to know, inwardly thanking the Lord it had not come to that.

She had caught no more than a glimpse of Sabina, struggling to open the ancient door—with its wood panels swollen and warped from long exposure to the elements—at the millinery's side entrance. But it was long enough for Rosalie to recognize the woman who had presented herself as Frau Dichtler's friend, and she had instantly fled from the alley.

The thought of what might have happened had the milliner's assistant seen her, much less been introduced to her, made her quail.

"I thought you might want to take a look around. Madame Chapeau allows Sabina to make her own sales from the surplus she stocks in the cellar. And if something in there caught your eye—a brooch, a fancy pin, a bit of lace or ribbon—Sabina would have cut her usual prices."

"Why would she do that?" Rosalie asked, cursing herself for not staying on. To scour the milliner's premises unfettered, and all in the guise of looking for some fancy bauble. No opportunity could be more heaven-sent! And she had foolishly lost it.

And now that she considered the matter, Gerhard's presence might even have afforded her a degree of safety. After all, Sabina could scarcely accuse her of following Frau Dichtler without admitting to her own presence at the palace.

But Gerhard was speaking, and she had not heard a word he had said. "Wine?" she said, repeating the first thing she heard.

He smiled down at her. "Yes. A discount on the wine. It is all I have to offer, but the wine is of excellent quality and just expensive enough for it to be worth it to Sabina. Oh, I take care not to make a loss on the deal.

And I am sure Sabina does the same. It is a common enough practice among tradesfolk."

"Oh," said Rosalie, feeling more confused than ever. Gerhard Heindl, the tavern keeper, would've offered Sabina a discount on his wine so that she could get a discount on the milliner's wares? Now, why would he do something like that?

"It was *not* at Herr Rahier's behest that Fritz Dichtler went to the Graben this morning?" Johann watched as Haydn, seated across from him in the carriage, sorted through several volumes of madrigals borrowed from His Serene Highness's library. "Did he tell you that in so many words?"

He was seated as close as he could get to the carriage window to accommodate the volumes the Kapellmeister had stacked next to him. Now, as Haydn reached across to add another volume to the pile, he edged himself still closer to the window.

"He was quite adamant on the subject." Haydn leaned back in his seat and raised his eyes toward his brother. "And to tell you the truth, the more I think on it, the less trouble I have believing it."

He turned toward the window, attempting to marshal his thoughts. It was late afternoon, and all of Vienna seemed to have congregated on the streets to bask in the golden warmth of the midday sun.

He gazed out at the multitude of carriages and people thronging the streets, his mind gathering up the numerous threads that made up the tapestry of his conviction. "Frau Dichtler was hanging onto the Estates Director, beseeching him to consider some proposition or other the day he sought my permission for a leave of absence for her husband."

"I recall your mentioning it," Johann uttered the words carefully, like an unskilled musician attempting to decipher a piece at sight. "It was the reason for our thinking he was after some sort of dalliance with her. Was it not?"

Haydn drummed his fingers on the windowsill. "The promise of something of the kind must have induced a man as cautious as Herr Rahier to even consider the proposal." He continued to stare out the window. "Quite naturally, he would have no desire to part with his money without examining the items. And Fritz, of course, could have no recourse to the items without first purchasing them."

He patted the chest beside him as he turned to face Johann. "Even Kaspar would not have let these out of his sight on the mere likelihood of a purchase."

Johann stared back at him for a space, brows slowly gathering together. The dizzying buzz of innumerable conversations and the steady clip-clop of horses' hooves on the cobblestones outside pervaded the carriage.

"The Dichtlers are paid far more than they deserve, but I doubt they have the means to make a substantial purchase on their own account, brother," he said after a while.

"They do not." Haydn untied the silk tassels gathering the heavy brocade drapes together on either side of the window. As they fell across the window, the interminable noise from the streets muted to a dull drone.

"But what better means," he continued, "to wheedle the money out of the Estates Director than to make him feel he would be losing out on a tremendous opportunity unless he acted immediately? That was likely their reason for taking the *Diarium*."

Rahier had inadvertently pointed the finger at the Dichtlers for that particular crime.

"I knew it was none of his doing," Haydn said. "It is too petty an offense even for him and completely out of character. It must have been Fritz who mentioned my apparent desire to acquire the music. I had no sooner mentioned his name than the Estates Director said he knew of *my* interest in the works."

Evidently, the couple had played skillfully upon Rahier's ambitions, stimulating an unlikely interest in the great master's music. To what end, Haydn knew not. He hoped his brother might furnish an answer.

But the furrow on Johann's forehead only deepened. "That would mean the Dichtlers knew of the bequest even before we did. That is surely not possible." He regarded Haydn with his head tilted to one side.

"I cannot tell how they obtained their information, but I am convinced they must have known. Herr Rahier, I am certain, was expecting the scores in the mail. The necessity of dispatching Fritz to Vienna only arose because the seller was apparently loath to part with them. Unless that was a ruse. Perhaps Fritz never intended Rahier should get too close to the scores."

Haydn paused, taking a breath before continuing. "Still, how the Estates Director can have believed anyone would be foolish enough to entrust items of such value to the mail coach, I don't know. Further evidence of that infernal woman's influence upon him."

Johann's face broke into a smile. "Then our venturing out to Vienna must have completely foiled the Dichtlers' plans."

Haydn smiled back. "And the outrageous story that it necessitated appears to have utterly spoiled Herr Rahier's appetite for the music." His smile faded as he continued. "What I would like to know is why Fritz Dichtler is so eager to get his hands on the music. Although now that we have it, I suppose that question does not need an answer quite so urgently."

CHAPTER TWENTY-ONE

"Whyever did you let him go?" Greta wailed, casting a longing look at Gerhard's departing wagon. "You may not have wanted a ride back. But I did. My legs are sore from walking all over town."

Rosalie bit her lip. Why had she insisted they could walk the distance back to Wallnerstrasse? There had been room enough in Gerhard's wagon for them both, and he had seemed willing enough. Even so, it would be imposing on the poor man, wouldn't it? And she had done nothing to earn any favors from him.

"There were things I wanted to tell you," she told her friend. It was not entirely a lie. "And I couldn't have done it in his presence."

"Oh!" Greta's face brightened immediately. She leaned forward, lips parted, eager as always for a bit of gossip. "What did you find out?" She linked arms with Rosalie. "Tell me everything. It will ease the pain of having to walk all the way to Wallnerstrasse."

"The woman who came to meet our Frau Dichtler is no maid," Rosalie began, as she slowed her pace to match Greta's. "And she has no need of a position." She paused, twisting her head to meet Greta's gaze.

Greta's eyes widened, urging her to continue.

"She works for a milliner—"

"Do not tell me it is Madame Chapeau?"

Rosalie stopped. "You have heard of her?" Greta had not been with the Esterházys very much longer than Rosalie. Could she really know so much more of Vienna?

"This very afternoon when I met my cousin. But her establishment is near the Kärntnertor. I wasn't looking forward to that walk, I can tell you. Although I would've done it, if it would help our Frau Schwann.

"But then I saw you, and Gerhard looked as though he would have driven you to the ends of the earth if you'd asked him to. . ." Greta's pupils sidled over to the corner of her eyes, and she looked up at Rosalie through a thicket of curling lashes.

Rosalie ignored both the insinuation and the glance. It was not above six months ago that Gerhard had wanted to marry his barmaid, Marlene, despite her betrayal of him and the child that quickened in her womb as a result. She had refused him. But surely it took more than a mere six months to recover from a love as deep as that?

"What else did your cousin say?" she asked as much for the information itself as to divert Greta.

She smiled when she saw Greta's eyes light up again. There were few things her plump, rosy-cheeked friend liked more than sharing gossip.

With a quick, furtive glance around her, Greta leaned in toward Rosalie and began in a conspiratorial whisper: "You remember I said there would only be a handful of places that do any trade in stolen jewelry as valuable as Her Serene Highness's necklace?" She paused, looking at Rosalie from under arched eyebrows.

At Rosalie's nod, she went on breathlessly, "Turns out there is only one shop in the entire city that will traffic in goods such as that."

"Madame Chapeau's establishment?" Rosalie murmured, a heavy leaden sensation filling the depths of her stomach at the news. It was what she had suspected, but. . . She took a deep breath. Why had Gerhard insisted it was all talk, then? Could he. . .?

She shook her head, not wanting to consider the thought. *Gerhard was a man of integrity, wasn't he?*

The undertaker the Kapellmeister and his brother were going to meet had his establishment near the Carinthian Gate. Haydn peered through the brocade drapes that covered the carriage window and then glanced restively at his timepiece. The streets at this late hour were so crowded, he had little expectation of arriving at Herr Moserle's establishment much before an hour.

His fingers began to drum an impatient rhythm on the windowpane. In Eisenstadt a journey of this short distance would have taken no more than a quarter of an hour. But here in Vienna, more time was wasted journeying to and fro than in accomplishing anything useful.

A man could walk faster than they were traveling, although with all the people swarming the streets, he doubted they would make any more progress than they were now.

"Chafing at the time never made it go any faster, brother"—Haydn turned to see Johann regarding him with an amused smile—"But it may seem faster if we allow ourselves a glimpse of those scores." Johann gestured toward the chest sitting next to Haydn. "They have caused so much trouble, I am quite curious to see them."

"As am I!" Haydn's face broke into a delighted smile. Why had he not thought of it himself? He drew the chest closer toward him. The brass hasp lifted up quite easily. Haydn peered into the dark interior, almost afraid to draw breath.

The yellowing scores within were organized into several loosely bound bundles. He put a hand out reverently, fingering the sheets with the gentlest touch. But the paper itself, rough-textured like a dense bit of pumice stone, seemed strong enough. *And very familiar*. As he touched it, images from his days as a choirboy swept over his senses.

"Handmade linen paper," he remarked to Johann as he handed him one of the bundles. "Like the old scores Reutter would have us study."

How they had loved to pore over those ancient sheets, the music serving in place of the lessons in theory that were rarely forthcoming from the perpetually busy choirmaster.

But as he ran his thumb over the pages, he was aware of a faint stirring in his brain. The shadow it cast grew stronger, but the notion itself, whatever it was, persisted in hiding within the deepest recesses of his mind.

He leafed through the music, his misgivings growing. He glanced up to see how Johann was faring and saw, reflected on his brother's features, his own confusion.

Johann must have felt the Kapellmeister's eyes on him. "If this music was written for an opera," he said, raising his own eyes, "it must be the strangest sort of opera ever seen."

Haydn nodded. "I can understand something of Kaspar's skepticism now. Even the most untrained eye can see these are songs in five voices. A chorus or two might be written in that manner, but no opera features chorus after chorus."

He thumbed through the pages he held. "Where are the recitatives that carry the plot forward, the arias that burst forth at the most intense emotional moments? What character sings a lament in five parts?"

Johann turned to the title page of the work he was holding and peered down at it. "Madrigals masquerading as operas," he said. "The title page suggests an opera, but the works indicate otherwise. Mine purports to be *Proserpina Rapita*."

Haydn thumbed back to the title page of the music in his hands. "*L'Arianna*," he read. "It does include Ariadne's famous lament, but written for five voices."

Johann's eyes drifted toward the stack of madrigals by his side. The great master had published no less than nine volumes of his madrigals, and his brother had borrowed them all from His Serene Highness's collection.

"If I mistake not, that particular lament is included in the sixth volume." He glanced down at the music. "I see some of the same features—the odd repetitions that break the poetic line, for instance—that you noted in the *L'Orfeo* Her Majesty purchased." He paused. "Could it be. . .?"

His younger brother did not have to finish the question. The selfsame notion had entered Haydn's mind. "It was at the request of a gentleman in Venice that Monteverdi re-wrote *Ariadne's Lament* in five parts," he said softly, still perusing the music. "Who is to say the same gentleman may not have requested a similar transformation of all seven of the great master's operas, in their entirety?"

The thought was breathtaking. If it were true. . .

"These works may be far more valuable than we imagined. And they would be valuable enough if they were merely handwritten copies of his published madrigals—painstakingly written in his own hand, perhaps." Haydn looked up. "Whoever is trying to steal Kaspar's bequest must suspect the scores are polyphonic re-workings of the operas."

"It should be a simple enough matter to establish," Johann said, patting the volumes stacked beside him on the narrow carriage seat. "The madrigals written for the singers of Venice must differ quite substantially from those written for Duke Gonzaga's singers."

"They do." Johann's comment had reminded the Kapellmeister of the hours he had spent studying the differences between the Mantuan and

Venetian madrigals for his perpetually irascible old teacher, Nicola Porpora.

The wise composer always keeps his singers' abilities in mind. The words had fallen like a constant refrain from his old master's impatient lips. *And his patron's tastes. Only a blockhead ignores the one. And it is at peril of his job that any musician disregards the other. Resist the temptation to be a blockhead, Sepperl.*

"The Duke favored sopranos," Haydn said, remembering the differences he had so meticulously enumerated. "The range of the canto part in the Mantuan madrigals speaks for itself. And the tenor part is quite extraordinary, making frequent use as it does of Francesco Rasi's astounding capabilities."

Johann nodded. "As I recall it, the alto part itself goes as high as the canto in some works."

"And as low as the tenor in others," Haydn affirmed. He leaned forward, warming to his subject. "In the Venetian madrigals, however, the range of the alto part is nothing out of the ordinary. Monteverdi himself lamented the lack of good contraltos in the city. But the Venetian basses. Why, the great master was quite in awe of the depths they could achieve!"

He placed the bundle of scores back in the chest, thankful for the lessons his crotchety old teacher had enforced on him. Who could have foretold that Porpora's instruction would lend itself to such divers uses? "If these madrigals are truly re-workings of his operatic works, the evidence will speak for itself."

"Is your cousin sure of this?" Rosalie asked. They had walked on in silence for a few minutes after Greta's revelation about Madame Chapeau's millinery.

But Greta knew what she was referring to. She drew her head back and regarded Rosalie for a moment.

"Otto has never tried taking any stolen items to Madame Chapeau, if that is what you are asking? But there's no smoke without fire, mark my words. If there's talk all over town, there is good reason for it. Besides, isn't that where Frau Dichtler went?"

"Yes, I merely meant. . ." Rosalie hoped her cheeks weren't turning red. Greta had a sharp eye, and she didn't want her friend to know... Oh, she mustn't be so stupid! There was nothing really for Greta to know.

But Greta had apparently not noticed anything. "I know what you meant. We shall have to look into it before we start hurling accusations. Did you see the necklace?"

Rosalie shook her head. "But I think Madame Chapeau gave Frau Dichtler some money." She recounted what she had seen and heard.

Greta pursed her lips. "She may have owed Frau Dichtler money, but it is hardly likely. And what else would she be paying her for?"

Rosalie nodded, thinking hard. The necklace must somehow have been conveyed to the milliner. But how? It had been stolen, and... "The ragamuffin!" She turned toward Greta. "If Frau Dichtler arranged for him to steal the necklace—"

"She may also have instructed him to deliver it to Madame Chapeau," Greta finished for her. She looked squarely at Rosalie. "You will have to find a way to get into that cellar. It is our only hope."

Rosalie felt her cheeks flaming. "I should've brazened it out this afternoon."

"It is a good thing you didn't. Sabina may not have said anything in Gerhard's presence, but she would know your being there was no coincidence. And if Frau Dichtler gets wind of this. . ."

Rosalie shuddered. "I know. It will be our jobs not Frau Schwann's that Sabina will be coming to take. I'm certain that was the arrangement Madame Chapeau was referring to."

"Of course it was," Greta agreed. "No matter what Frau Dichtler tries to say. Frau Schwann is the only person that dratted woman has been desperately trying to get rid of. And from the way Sabina was carping at the work we had her do, she wasn't expecting to be a mere kitchen maid."

"No, she was not," Rosalie said quietly.

They had just turned onto Wallnerstrasse, and she could see Gerhard's covered rack wagon parked outside the wine cellar. She would feel silly asking him to take her back to the milliner's cellar. But it was for Frau Schwann's sake, she told herself. And since she wasn't actually going to buy anything, she would owe him no more than the favor of a ride.

Greta must have sensed some of her misgivings, for she squeezed her hand as they entered the palace gates and made their way to the servant's entrance. "Your going may be as much of a favor to him. Sabina must direct some custom his way in return for any clients he refers to her."

CHAPTER TWENTY-TWO

The carriage conveying the Kapellmeister and his brother turned onto a busy thoroughfare and halted just past a milliner's establishment.

The name on the sign caught Haydn's eye as he stepped out, and he stopped, arrested by its pretentiousness.

Madame Chapeau.

"Madame Hat? Whoever calls themselves that?" he remarked, turning to smile at Johann. "But at least her designs show some flair." He indicated the jewelry displayed in the shop window.

"Paste, judging by the prices." Johann dutifully inspected the wares on display. "But beautiful, nonetheless." He took in his surroundings. "Where is Herr Moserle's establishment?"

Haydn pointed. "In that narrow alley up ahead, I believe."

The sign of a black hearse hanging from one of the buildings was barely visible from where they stood. The alley itself was too narrow to admit a carriage. The three- and four-story buildings on either side of the cobblestone-paved lane leaned precariously forward, almost meeting at its center.

Haydn reached within the carriage for the ivory-inlaid chest that held Kaspar's bequest. He lifted it off the seat and swung around, raising it high above his head to avoid hitting the passersby who crowded between Johann and himself.

"His Serene Highness's madrigals are safe enough in the carriage, but these—" he leaned back as two burly men jostled past him but felt a vicious elbow digging into his ribs, nevertheless.

"I beg your pardon, sir!" In the Vienna of his youth, such rudeness would have been unthinkable. But unless Eisenstadt had made him too much of a country gentleman, it was becoming all too common in the city these days. "Do you not see my brother and myself standing by the carriage?"

The men, swarthy-featured, ill-humored brutes, turned back and stared up and down the Kapellmeister's form, clad in blue-and-gold livery.

"We saw you standin' all right?" the taller of the two growled, inching closer to Haydn. "Right in the middle of busy folks' way. Did you not see us passin' by? And did you think to move out of our way, then?" He moved even closer, his voice sounding slurred. "No, you didn't, did you?"

"The carriage is parked at the edge of the street," Haydn pointed out in as even a tone as he could manage. A strong whiff of stale beer assailed his nostrils. Two other bearded men, artisans by the look of them and reeking just as strongly, pressed in on either side of the first two.

Under the circumstances, neither anger nor indignation would serve their purpose. Best to defuse the situation as quickly as he could. Already the commotion was beginning to attract a mob.

"There is room aplenty on the other side of the carriage," Johann was beginning to say when Haydn felt the chest being wrenched out of his arms.

He tugged back as forcefully as he could, but a few more ruffians had gathered close and were now pushing him back against the carriage.

"What's this, then? A chest full of precious jewels? Or is it money you carry so close to yourself?" a harsh voice taunted. "Give it here, then! Give it here!"

Haydn could barely see who it was jeering at him. A sea of outstretched arms sought to snatch the chest from his grasp.

Once he caught a glimpse of his brother, trying in vain to push the men between them out of the way. "Call for help, Johann!" he shouted. "Call—"

He heard a sharp thwack. His head felt as though it was split in two. A streak of blood ran down his forehead and over his eye. *Had someone hit him*? He staggered forward, feeling the chest fall open as it was yanked out of his arms.

He tried to grab at the scores as they floated toward the muddy water pooling at the edge of the street. But a hard fist made contact with his gut, the pain nearly making him retch. Another caught him in the eye as he bent forward from the force of the first blow.

"Herr Haydn! Herr Haydn! Brother!" He heard the chorus of voices coming closer at the same time as a female voice exploded: "For shame!"

"The music," he gagged. He was beginning to sink to his knees.

"It is safe." A pair of strong arms caught hold of him. "It is safe, Herr Haydn." Albrecht supported him under the armpits.

He could feel his eye swelling up and closing over, but through its narrow slit he discerned a slender elderly form batting her reticule, like an agitated crow, at the few passersby who still lingered on the scene. "There is nothing to see here. Off you go! For shame! Would you watch while an innocent man is attacked?"

"The music?" Haydn asked again. God forbid, they should have lost it!

"I have it here, brother." Johann extended the stack of scores out toward him. "Herr Moserle's pistol startled your attackers away."

Pistol? That must have been the explosion he had heard.

"One of the men who first confronted us made off with the chest," Johann went on. "But Albrecht's fist delivered such a masterful punch to the other's nose, he was forced to relinquish his hold on the music."

Haydn was about to reply when he felt something sharp scraping at his wrist. A small wrinkled hand was attached to his wrist. "If it is a chest you need, I have one for you. It is old and worn and not half as nice as the one I gave Kaspar, but it will do."

Rosalie hung back a few paces. Gerhard had finished unloading the crates of wine bottles meant for the Esterházy cellar and now sat on the wagon, eating a bit of bread and pickled mushrooms. The horses lazily munched the hay he had thrown down for them. She might have stood there forever had Gerhard not turned around.

"What is it, lass?" He tipped his head at the palace gates down the street. "Is more wine required? I have a few crates to spare, if that is the case."

Rosalie shook her head, feeling more tongue-tied than ever. She approached the wagon, picking her steps with care. "It is just—" she began hoarsely, then cleared her throat. "I should like to get Greta something for her name day. A brooch or a small locket. Perhaps, even a necklace." She smoothed down her apron. "Greta is uncommonly fond of necklaces," she added.

It would look most odd if, having decided to buy a locket or chain, she picked out a fancy necklace.

"Why, lass, you had your chance today! Sabina has every kind of trinket a girl could want, and yet you bolted as though the devil were at your heels!" Gerhard's blue eyes narrowed as he studied her features. "You have some other reason for wanting to go back there, don't you? What is it? What harebrained notion has taken hold of your mind now?"

Rosalie clutched the edges of her apron. This was going much worse than even she could have imagined. If only Gerhard had not chosen this very moment to suspect her motives. It was her own fault, she supposed. Her opposition to meeting Sabina had been so great that now her eagerness to return to the milliner's establishment must seem suspicious.

She swallowed. "I have obtained some—"

"You have not stolen anything from His Serene Highness's household, have you?" Gerhard put his meal away and climbed down from his perch. "You had better return it. No matter what you may have heard, Madame Chapeau does not traffic in stolen goods."

"I have not stolen anything." Rosalie's chin came up. Goodness gracious! What kind of person did he take her for? "I had no money to spare this morning, but Frau Dichtler just gave Greta and me a gold gulden to share between us. . ."

She spread her hands wide and lifted her shoulders in a small shrug. It was such a small lie, surely she had no need to even mention it in the confessional.

"No money! Why, didn't you say so at the time, lass?" Gerhard's blue eyes had such a depth of kindness in them as he gazed down at her, Rosalie felt tears welling up in her own eyes. She looked hastily down.

"Too proud to mention, it were you?" Gerhard laid a kindly hand on her shoulder, it's warmth seeping through the fabric of her thin blouse. "I suppose I can respect that. Well now, when would you like to go, then?"

"In a day or two, or whenever it is convenient for you," Rosalie said, raising her head. It could not be today for all that she still had an hour left of her half-day.

Why the thought hadn't occurred to her before, she didn't know, but she had only the vaguest idea of what the necklace looked like. She would need to learn its design from Frau Schwann first. And who knew whether the lady's maid would even approve of the plan she and Greta had concocted for its recovery?

"You are fortunate to be alive, Herr Haydn." Herr Moserle, the undertaker, clucked to himself as he dressed the wound on Haydn's head.

Haydn grimaced under the former barber-surgeon's ministrations. The cooling salve Herr Moserle had applied had done much to dull the initial sharp dagger-thrusts of pain. The pale pink parlor walls and the fine Rococo furniture had ceased to swim around him in a dizzying circle, but his head still throbbed. He attempted to make light of the matter, however. "It was just the one blow. It cannot be that bad, can it?"

He looked toward his brother, but the ashen color in Johann's face and the wide, staring eyes with which he gaped at the wound suggested that his brother had feared the worst.

"Your wig must have protected you from the worst of it. But the gash in your head is, nevertheless, quite deep—"

"There is no need to describe it, Johann." Haydn attempted a smile. But the image his brother's words had called up was causing such havoc in his stomach, he was in danger of losing the small meal he had eaten at the palace. He forced himself to swallow, grimacing at the sour aftertaste of soup and boiled beef .

Herr Moserle was still clucking to himself. "What can the world be coming to when thieves brazenly attack good men in the middle of the day? Your attacker either did not wish to do more than injure you or misjudged the force of his blow. A little harder, a little deeper. . ."

"That is quite enough!" Kaspar's aunt entered the parlor with a steaming bowl in her hands. "Can you not see the effect your gruesome imaginings have on these poor men? They have suffered enough. There is no need to agitate them any further."

She set the bowl before Haydn and patted his arm. "Take no notice of the man, Herr Haydn. He is more used to ministering to the dead than to the living and takes no thought of our sensibilities." She patted his arm again. "This is a potion of my own brewing. It will help the wound heal."

The slender, gray-haired widow turned toward Johann. "And a small glass of wine for you, perhaps, Master Johann. It will ease the shock." She hurried out of the parlor without waiting for a response.

"It was not to alarm you that I spoke," Herr Moserle said quietly when Kaspar's aunt had left the room. "In truth, it was a blow such as the one you suffered today that caused poor Wilhelm Kaspar's death. There were several such lacerations on his head. Quite unusual."

"How so?" Haydn swallowed a spoonful of the potion from the steaming bowl and nearly gagged. He had never tasted anything quite so wretched.

"Hold still!" The undertaker pursed his lips as he put a few more stitches in the Kapellmeister's head. "It was the same type of blow. Made by the same kind of weapon. A truncheon, I would wager."

"The same weapon," Haydn repeated. He forced himself to swallow another spoonful of the wretched concoction. Could the attack on him have been deliberate? And if it was the same weapon that had struck him, could it have been the same person?

His mind turned unbidden to Kaspar's widow and the stranger he had seen with her. The sour expression on Amelie's pinched features when he had taken the scores had grieved him more than he cared to admit at the time. Now he found himself angered by it. He had made Kaspar a promise, and nothing would prevent him from abiding by it.

CHAPTER TWENTY-THREE

"Wilhelm Dietrich was fond of his riddles," the old merchant's widow declared some hours later. She withdrew a worm-eaten casket from a hidden recess behind the bookcase.

But for its chipped ivory inlay and the small holes that pockmarked the dark walnut surface, it looked very like the chest Haydn had lost in the fray outside the widow's home. "And he seemed to get fonder of them as he grew older."

She turned toward the Kapellmeister and his brother. "It is old and worn"—she held out the chest—"but it should suffice."

Haydn was about to attempt a nod but thought better of it. The throbbing in his head had yet to subside despite Herr Moserle's ministrations. He was loath to make it any worse than it already was.

The undertaker had long left, but Kaspar's aunt had insisted he and Johann rest awhile. Haydn had gladly acquiesced. The very thought of rising still made his head swim. He made a feeble attempt at it all the same to accept the casket but was stayed by his younger brother's restraining hand.

Johann rose from his seat and took the chest, old but still sturdy, from the widow's slender hands. "It will do very nicely, Frau Dorfmeister." He set it on the long low table before him and opened the lid.

"There are some papers here, and a leather book," he announced as he peered within.

"Nothing important, I assure you." The widow pushed up the false volume in the bookcase that gave access to the secret recess. The volume rose to a vertical position and slid smoothly along its hinges, clicking into

151

place between two other volumes on either side of it. The portion of the bookcase which until now had stood open swung shut.

"The book and the papers are in excellent condition for being housed in such a receptacle." Mingled notes of surprise and awe tinged Johann's voice. "They appear quite old." He carefully set them on the table. "Who knows, but they may be of some value."

The thought of a book—an old one at that—had piqued Haydn's interest. He picked up the volume, rubbing his finger over the soft burgundy cover, scuffed and marked, but strong and exceedingly fine, nevertheless. Opening the book, he glanced down at the title page.

"It is the *Merchant of Venice*," he said softly. "William Shakespeare's *Merchant of Venice*."

"You may keep it." Kaspar's aunt, the widow Dorfmeister, sounded amused. "I see you share my poor husband's love of all things old and useless."

But Haydn barely heard her. His skin was tingling. Ever since his English friend Charles Burney had introduced him to the works of the great sixteenth-century bard, Haydn had sought every opportunity to add to his growing collection. But the plays were not easily available in Austria. Herr Burney had sent him all the tragedies, but Haydn had a greater interest in the comedies.

He flipped through the pages, recalling the very little Herr Burney had told him about this particular comedy. "A libretto based on a plot as ingenious as this would make for a most entertaining opera," he murmured.

"I suppose it would." The widow's eyes twinkled. The creases in her old face deepened as her lips stretched into a wide smile. She tipped her chin at the book. "It was a tale Wilhelm Dietrich so greatly loved, Herr Haydn, that he couldn't resist making it part of his riddle."

The remark caught Haydn's attention. "What riddle?" he wanted to know. Johann had been engaged in placing Kaspar's scores in the chest, but even he ceased his task.

Kaspar's aunt uttered a low laugh. "I see you find little mysteries of this sort as entertaining as my husband." She indicated the bookcase behind her. "The lever you saw me use a little while ago is made to look like a copy of the play you hold in your hands. Why, Dietrich couldn't resist making reference to it in his will."

She went toward a small rosewood secretary at the corner of the room and withdrew a document from within it. "He insisted on keeping a sealed copy of it in the house. I opened it after Herr Anwalt had read the one Dietrich entrusted to him." She turned over a few pages. "Here—" she handed one of the sheets to Haydn. "Read it for yourself."

"*Behind the Shakespeare lies a great treasure*," Haydn read.

"The hiding place Kaspar mentioned to us in his letter." Johann looked over his shoulder. "A clever reference to the lever." He turned back to the widow. "But I suppose you knew which volume it was."

"Not at the time," she replied. "But it was an easy enough riddle to solve. My husband kept all his volumes of Shakespeare on a single shelf. But the *Merchant of Venice* was the play he most loved, and there was only one copy of it. I tugged on the book and. . ." She spread her hands out, lifting her shoulders in a slight shrug.

Haydn smiled as he continued to pore over the will. "He seems not to have been able to resist a second reference to it. Here in his advice to Kaspar: *But remember, my son, it is what lies within that gives the vessel value.*"

"Yes, the story of the three caskets in the play. It was the part that appealed most to Dietrich."

Haydn's smile widened. "At least he did not make Kaspar choose one of several caskets."

Kaspar's aunt smiled back. "There would have been no point. The least intelligent person could see which casket was meant. The one Master Johann has now was covered in dust and cobwebs. I had it cleaned soon after we discovered it. I should have thrown it away, but it was from Dietrich's travels in Italy. . ."

Her voice caught, and she blinked rapidly several times.

Her faded blue eyes were still glistening when she spoke again. "The one that was stolen from you today, Herr Haydn, was a replica of it." She cleared her throat. "He had it made some years back. It must have been when he saw how old and worm-eaten this one had become."

"And to save the music he meant to bequeath to Kaspar, no doubt," Johann said gently. He turned toward his older brother.

But Haydn's attention had wandered again. He had put the play down and was now sifting through the papers from the old chest.

What he saw made his skin prickle. There was no doubt now that

Kaspar's uncle had been in possession of the great master's operas. But where were they?

———∾∾∾———

"You look as though you had seen a ghost, brother." Johann's voice aroused Haydn from his thoughts.

He slowly raised his head from the documents he had been absorbed in. The widow Dorfmeister had left the room.

"These are scenari, Johann." He had begun in a hushed pianissimo, but his voice started to crescendo. "These old papers left to languish in Wilhelm Dietrich's worm-eaten casket are scenari."

He stopped abruptly. What had he said to make his younger brother stare at him like that? Johann's gaze drifted upward, lingering on his bandaged head, before he finally glanced down at the papers in the Kapellmeister's hands.

"You are still thinking of the opera season at Eszterháza, I suppose." Johann tipped his chin at the documents. "Marco Coltellini will have no trouble creating librettos from the scenari if the synopses they contain are sufficiently detailed. And if he is preoccupied with matters at court, Carlo Goldoni—"

"No, no." The steady avalanche of the enormous cushion behind Haydn—forcing him yet again toward the edge of the rosewood chaise— lent his voice a sharper edge.

He braced his feet firmly on the ground, determined to prevail against the wretched thing. The widow had insisted he prop himself against it, but its cover of Tyrian purple satin was so treacherously slippery, he was continually sliding forward.

Tired of battling with the thing, he thrust it to one side. "You do not understand," he continued once he was comfortably settled within the chaise. "These are no ordinary scenari. They are synopses of the great master's operas. The very—"

He frowned, holding up a hand. Was that the front door opening? His ear caught the muffled sound of an unfamiliar voice. Kaspar's aunt must have guests. "Quick! Put these away and let us be on our way."

He thrust the papers into the bottom of the chest. "Kaspar and his aunt are so surrounded by vultures, there is no telling whom we can trust."

He rose, determined to take his leave, but the widow Dorfmeister clearly had other plans.

"Such good fortune, Herr Haydn." She marched into the parlor with a young man at her heels. "I was hoping you would be able to make Fabrizzio's acquaintance, and here he is. He is a music scholar. Trained in Italy, no less. The son of an old business acquaintance of Dietrich."

She laid an affectionate hand on the young man's ruffled sleeve. "Perchance we may prevail upon him to render an opinion on our Kaspar's music."

The scholar, far too young to receive such an appellation, bowed his head. "It would be an honor." A smile played upon his lips. "I offered my services to Wilhelm Kaspar on more than one occasion, but. . ." His shoulders lifted in a brief shrug.

"Kaspar did speak of you." Haydn's eyes flickered briefly toward Johann as he spoke. His eyes roved with some curiosity on the other's person. What had Kaspar seen in the man to distrust him so?

There was nothing out of the ordinary in his brown hair, although his waistcoat of blue satin and his white silk shirt with its ruffles might seem ostentatious to some. But the lips—smirking, a little too red, thrust out sensuously—

A man smugly secure, Haydn thought, *in the expectation that women will fawn over him.* What man of sense could bring himself to like such a man, much less trust him? *Even so . . .*

The Kapellmeister was about to dismiss Kaspar's suspicions when he noticed the other's dark eyes darting every so often toward the walnut chest.

"That is it—yes?" Fabrizzio moved a little closer toward it. "The bequest we have heard so much about?"

Before Haydn could stop him, the young man had opened the casket and taken out the loosely bound manuscripts that lay on top.

"*Madrigals?*" The sheaf of papers in Fabrizzio's hands visibly quivered. He had perused them for no longer than a moment. His fingers dug into the sheets as he wrenched the next few pages aside. "These are but madrigals. In five voices." His voice, already low, thickened—vocal cords caught in the intensity of some emotion.

Haydn had barely time to register what it was when Fabrizzio's tense features relaxed, and the corners of his mouth twitched. "I see my help may not be needed after all." He laid the documents back in the casket. "Poor Kaspar!"

There was no mistaking the mocking tone, although no one else appeared to have noticed it. Haydn himself might have thought he had imagined it but for the smirk that played about the man's mouth.

"You have heard the news, then?" Kaspar's aunt cried. "How the poor man was set upon by ruffians?"

"I uh—" The news appeared to have struck the young scholar immobile. Only his dark eyes darted, now here, now there. "He fares well, I trust?"

Fabrizzio looked at no one in particular as he asked the question.

"Unfortunately not," Johann said. "The attack killed him."

"Killed?" The color drained from Fabrizzio's cheeks. "That ca— How? To what end?"

"For his bequest, it would appear," Johann continued.

Fabrizzio's eyes drifted toward the chest. "For that?" His voice had risen. "Those scores. . .?"

"There can be no question of it," Haydn responded to the unspoken question. "His keys were stolen. His home broken into—"

"Broken into?" Fabrizzio's head came up. "What was taken?"

"Nothing, fortunately. Although it is quite clear what the thieves were after." Haydn indicated the chest.

"Herr Haydn and his brother were attacked as well, Fabrizzio. The rascals made off with the chest, but fortunately the music was saved. If it were not for Albrecht—"

"Albrecht." Fabrizzio echoed the name. "He—"

"Is a friend of Kaspar's," Johann put in. "From the Hofburg. It was he who prevented the theft of the music."

Fabrizzio swallowed hard as he attempted a nod. His eyes zigzagged wildly around the parlor.

Haydn ignored him as he took his leave of the widow. "We are indebted to you for your hospitality, Frau Dorfmeister, but we must be on our way."

The widow escorted them to the door, but Fabrizzio seemed oblivious to their departure. Haydn had just followed Johann out of the parlor when he felt a tug on his sleeve. He turned around.

Fabrizzio shut the parlor door behind them.

"It was a set of operas that Wilhelm Kaspar was supposed to receive, Herr Haydn." He glanced around as though afraid of being overheard. His voice lowered to a whisper. "The operatic works of the great Claudio Monteverdi." He took a deep breath. "Have they been found, do you know?"

He paused, but began to speak again before Haydn could respond. "Is it possible they even exist?"

Haydn regarded him for a space. "If they do, they will be found, no doubt," he said.

Fabrizzio searched his features, but Haydn kept them deliberately impassive.

"No doubt." The scholar quietly acknowledged the point before returning to the parlor.

CHAPTER TWENTY-FOUR

The better part of the journey had been spent in silence, filled only by the muted sounds of the city's traffic and the horses' steady clip-clop against the cobblestones. But now Johann broke in upon the Kapellmeister's thoughts.

"This chest appears to be quite sound." He rapped his knuckles against the worm-eaten wood. It rang clear, producing a warm, robust tone. "I would not have expected it, the entire surface is so ridden with holes."

"It is most fortunate," Haydn replied, rousing himself with difficulty. His thoughts were still on the music scholar they had met. The questions Fabrizzio had put to him had been most strange. What could he possibly have meant by them?

His mind turned on the question as he watched Johann examine the old casket. His younger brother was twisting the box around as he slowly ran his finger down its surface from the top to the decorative brass edges that capped the corners at the bottom.

"Not a square-inch of space has been spared. Yet the wood sounds so resonant, few luthiers would hesitate to fashion an instrument from it."

But when the Kapellmeister did no more than murmur a response, Johann twisted his head sharply to regard his brother. "You seem rather preoccupied. What is it?"

Haydn drew in his lower lip and began chewing on it. Was his mind running away with nonsensical imaginings? There had been a time—not too long ago—when he would have given the strange behavior he had encountered that afternoon no more than a moment's consideration.

He had ceased to be quite so blind. But was he now guilty of reading too much into every insignificant happening?

He tapped out a rapid rhythm on the carriage seat as he felt his way to a response. "I was wondering whether Fabrizzio might have had an opportunity to inspect Kaspar's bequest prior to this afternoon. He seemed so—" Haydn paused.

Unsurprised, he had been about to say. Although now that he thought about it, that was not true. There had been a flash—a very brief flash of . . . shock, astonishment? Something of the kind, coupled with . . . *anger*? But the young man had recovered almost instantly.

"Ready to accept what the bequest consisted of," he finished, aware of his brother's eyes on him.

He held his breath as Johann tilted his head to regard him, eyes narrowed, brows drawn together. But he had misread the look, apparently, for when his brother spoke, it was only to say: "Are you thinking Amelie might have shown it to him? Kaspar did not. He was quite adamant on the subject?"

Haydn pursed his lips. "No, Kaspar did not. And Amelie could not," he quietly added.

Johann's eyes opened wide at that. He expelled a breath, the air trapped in his throat coming out in a rush. "No. No, of course not. She did not even know Kaspar had hidden it. How then—You cannot think he broke into the house? Not last night, surely? The evidence—"

"Not last night, perhaps," Haydn agreed. "But the night Kaspar was killed." His mind returned to the marks around the lock on Kaspar's bureau. It was safe to say Kaspar had not ventured out without his keys.

Nor left his bureau unlocked.

"The Countess of Kuenberg saw a man going up—a young man, from the sound of it. What if she was mistaken about the night on which she saw him? She is old and no doubt forgetful, but she is not completely in her dotage."

Johann stroked his chin. "And Kaspar's keys were taken, but"—he turned toward Haydn, eyes opened to their fullest extent—"I thought you said the note was—"

"It was not in Herr Anwalt's hand," Haydn interrupted quietly. "I had an opportunity of seeing it on some documents that lay on his desk. Kaspar's lawyer knows more than he was willing to reveal. But it was not he who lured Kaspar to his death."

"But Fabrizzio's surprise seemed genuine enough."

"Feigned, I have no doubt of it." Haydn's expression as he turned to Johann was grim. He had met the man who had orchestrated his friend's death and seen no more than a young popinjay. How could he have been so blind? "It must have been he who staged the initial robbery. And I, like a fool, suspected Herr Anwalt."

"But what could Fabrizzio want with Kaspar's bequest? He seems to know nothing of the value of the madrigals. And he was at pains, Kaspar said, to point out that any operas the bequest might contain were quite possibly not even authentic."

Haydn drummed his fingers on the carriage seat. "He is after the operas. I know not why other than that they are valuable." He stared at the brocade draperies on the carriage window. "He seems quite certain they exist, which means that they must. But he has not found them. That is to our advantage."

He glanced down at the casket on Johann's knees. "I was wondering why Wilhelm Dietrich had chosen to keep that old worm-eaten thing, much less store his scenari in them," he remarked.

Johann's eyes followed the Kapellmeister's gaze. "Are you sure it is wise to take these to Papa Keller's house, brother. If you are right about Fabrizzio, it was he who arranged for those ruffians to attack us. Who knows what he might be capable of."

A smile hovered on Haydn's lips. "Ah, but he has no clue where the operas are. And coxcomb that he is, it will never occur to him where they are hidden."

—————

"There you are, husband! Where have you and brother-in-law been this entire day?"

Maria Anna herded the Kapellmeister and Johann across the courtyard, flapping her hands in the direction of her father's house as though she were rounding up a flock of restless fowl. She opened the door. "Come in, then. Come in. We have no time to dally."

"But what is amiss, Maria Anna?" Haydn could not prevent an aggrieved note entering his voice. He had been set upon by scoundrels and nearly killed, but his wife had taken no more notice of his bandaged head than she did his music.

She led them into the kitchen and turned around. "What have you been doing to yourself, husband?" she said with a frown, her eyes going toward his injured head.

"Brother was attacked and most grievously injured," Johann replied. "The thieves were attempting to make off with Kaspar's bequest." He set the casket on the table.

Maria Anna merely grunted. Her gaze moved to the worm-eaten casket. "Is that what that thing is? Kaspar did not think very much of his bequest, did he? Let it remain in the kitchen." She raised her eyes toward Haydn. "If that is woodworm, you must know the infestation spreads to everything."

Something stirred in Haydn's head as she spoke, but the thought was gone before he could catch hold of it. "We shall have to get the scores and scenari out of that chest before long," he murmured to Johann. Although for some reason he did not believe the documents were unsafe there.

"You may do it later," Maria Anna's tone had sharpened. "More urgent business awaits you at the moment. The music you left on your night-table, husband?"

"What of it?"

Fear clenched at Haydn's heart. His wife was referring to the *L'Orfeo* Her Majesty had purchased. He had made the mistake of leaving it on his bedside table.

God forbid that Maria Anna should have used the paper to curl her hair or for some other such preposterous business! No amount of money, even if he had it, would be adequate recompense for its loss.

"It is safe, I hope."

Maria Anna, as was her wont, ignored the question to ask one of her own. "Where did you come by it? Therese was quite beside herself when she saw it."

Haydn's head swam. Had the opera been stolen? From the convent no less? His gaze flickered toward his brother.

"It is a work Her Majesty recently purchased, sister-in-law," Johann replied, but his voice was filled with misgiving. "She requires that brother examine it and authenticate it for her. Why do you ask?"

Maria Anna stared at them both.

"It is the paper that Therese noticed." She paused. "It appears to be the very same that was stolen from the convent."

"Did Her Majesty tell you whom she had purchased the music from, Joseph?"

Therese's face looked white and drawn. Her sapphire-blue eyes flitted back and forth, like a pair of frightened starlings, between Haydn's visage and Johann's. The Empress's vellum-bound score of *L'Orfeo* lay on her lap.

"It was a gentleman from Italy. A physician. Dr. Goretti." Haydn's voice faltered as he volunteered the information. "He seeks a position at court," he added, not quite knowing why. It could make no difference surely.

"An Italian! From the imperial court. Oh dear God! Would that it were merely a coincidence."

Therese's head sank into her slender white hands. Haydn's gaze rested on her fingers, long and beautiful, as they massaged the smooth white skin between her eyebrows.

She raised her head a few minutes later. "The scribe we hired—the man sent to us from the Hofburg—was an Italian. A well-dressed gentleman with a neat beard."

"An Italian?" Haydn repeated with a glance at Johann.

They had not met the physician, and the reason for it returned to his mind. *For a man who seeks a position at the imperial court, he spends very little time here,* Baron van Swieten had said.

Therese nodded. She sat on the very edge of her chair like a bird poised for flight. "The documents we had him copy for Her Majesty included letters from Mantua—"

"From the Gonzaga court?" Haydn was stunned, but the last vestiges of doubt as to the identity of the scribe were beginning to vanish. Who else could it be but Goretti?

But Therese was speaking again. "The letters were to our foundress, the Empress Eleonora. She was from Gonzaga, the daughter of Duke Vincenzo."

"Monteverdi's patron," Johann said. "Were there letters from the great master as well?"

Therese nodded again. "Letters from Venice, seeking the Empress Eleonora's support for a position in Vienna." She turned to Haydn. "But the letters from Mantua were from Alessandro Striggio, the Duke's secretary. When her husband, the Emperor Ferdinand, sacked Mantua, Eleonora sought to bring as many of the Gonzaga musicians and as much of the music as she could to Vienna."

"The essence of the story Baron van Swieten told us was true then," Haydn remarked to Johann. "It must have been during the siege that the music owned by the Gonzagas made its way to Vienna."

His eyes fell on the scores on Therese's lap. "The *L'Orfeo*, I suppose, belongs, to the convent." He had had his misgivings about it, for all that it looked authentic. "One of the documents the scribe copied?"

Therese's face, already pale, turned white. "It was not something he was meant to. But he must have. From the printed score the convent has. I recognized the diamond-shaped notes of the printed scores from the time."

Haydn's eyes widened. How could he have failed to notice the significance of that? He had noticed the oddly shaped noteheads. The madrigals he had borrowed from the Prince's library had similarly shaped noteheads as well. "Dr. Goretti sold them to Her Majesty as manuscript scores in the great master's. I thought it unlikely, but . . ."

"It is not just the shape of the noteheads. The paper itself"—she held it up to the light—"has not the knots and clumps of older paper."

"No, it does not," Haydn said quietly. The paper was smoother, with the ribbed pattern so common to modern paper. How had he not noticed that either? "And the vellum—"

"The same soft vellum we keep at the convent. The ink all fresh and new."

"And there is his hand, too, do not forget," Maria Anna put in.

"It was his hand that confirmed my suspicions," Therese said. "For all the care he puts into copying his exemplar, he cannot disguise it entirely. He has an odd way of forming his n's—with a little circle on the top left. It is a habit he seems unable to rid himself of.

"Why, we saw those selfsame n's on that scrap of paper Maria Anna found in your pocket."

"The scrap of paper—" Haydn turned wildly toward his wife. Was Therese referring to the note found on poor Kaspar's body?

CHAPTER TWENTY-FIVE

Maria Anna reached into her pocket and drew forth a fragment of paper. "How came you to know Therese's scribe, husband? You were introduced to him at court, I suppose."

A knot of sickness was beginning to swell within Haydn's stomach—whether from the effects of the blow he had received to the area or the news he had just heard, he knew not. He took the scrap and stared at it.

Maria Anna repeated her question, a little more impatiently this time.

"No, no, we have not met him yet," Haydn said, still staring down at the shred of paper. It was bad enough to discover that the physician was a forger but that he was a murderer as well . . . What would Her Majesty say to that?

"Oh, Joseph!" Therese wrung her hands. "What if he was sent by the Emperor, just as we have suspected all along?"

But Haydn was too intent on calling to mind all the small scraps of information he had received to reassure his sister-in-law on the subject. He saw now that he had been too hasty in condemning the music scholar. Fabrizzio's shock at the news of Kaspar's death must have been genuine after all.

It was Johann who answered Therese: "I doubt the Emperor had any hand in the man's doings, Sister Josepha. Dr. Goretti's reasons were his own."

"To what end? What can he possibly have against Therese's convent?" Maria Anna demanded gruffly.

"Nothing at all," Johann replied. "The convent is merely unfortunate in being drawn into the affair for its connection—albeit remote—to a Mantuan composer the Empress is interested in."

"*Claudio Monteverdi.*" Therese's voice was hushed. "But other than the *L'Orfeo* and his madrigals, the convent has none of his music. And even the *L'Orfeo* survives only because it was printed to commemorate the occasion. They were stolen, I believe. The Gonzaga court had no copies, and consequently none came into our hands."

"He means to pass off his own works as those of the great master's," Haydn roused himself to speak.

"His own works?" Therese repeated, brow wrinkled, but Haydn's words were clearly beginning to make sense. Her eyes opened wider. "Sister Mariana's music—Of course! The care he took to simulate her hand plainly tells the tale!"

The realization that the convent was in no danger of being closed down seemed to bring with it a great sense of relief, for she was able to smile. "Although why he thought anyone outside the convent—"

"He did not," Haydn interrupted abruptly. "It was merely a test of his skills. He could not have known it would make its way back to St. Nikolai. The works of Monteverdi were all he was interested in. It would be a simple matter, he knew, to authenticate the *L'Orfeo*. After that, who would look too closely at anything else he brought?

"And, therefore, his great interest in acquiring Kaspar's works," he said more to himself than to anyone else.

The physician so desirous of obtaining Kaspar's bequest, he had offered his services in exchange for it. It could be none other than the Italian charlatan who had insinuated himself into the Empress's good favors.

And if he had penned the message that took Kaspar out on that fatal night, it would explain his knowledge of Kaspar's death before anyone had even been informed of the matter.

But Haydn would need more than mere supposition to convince Her Majesty. He turned to Therese.

"We have not met the man, but I know where he may be found."

"Her Serene Highness's necklace?"

Clara Schwann put down the gown she was mending as soon as Rosalie and Greta broached the subject.

"Oh, it was the most beautiful thing you ever saw! Tiny flowers with petals made of pearls clustered around an emerald center. The pendant, an emerald in the shape of a teardrop, set in a gold frame studded with diamonds."

Greta's mouth fell open. Her voice dropped to a throaty whisper. "Why, even a paste replica of the thing would be quite magnificent!"

"And, so it is," Frau Schwann replied, taking up her mending again. "But what of it? It is worthless compared to the real thing." Her needle flew in and out of the soft rose satin folds. "And Lord knows where that may be!"

She let out a heavy sigh. The sound seemed to fill the servants' hall, empty save for the three women sitting by the fading light that filtered through the eastern window.

Rosalie glanced over at Greta. She would wager every kreutzer of the gold gulden Frau Dichtler had given them that the necklace was in Madame Chapeau's warehouse. But would it be wise to get Frau Schwann's hopes up before they had even succeeded in retrieving it?

But clearly no such scruples troubled Greta, for she had no sooner caught Rosalie's eye than she blurted out: "Never fear, Frau Schwann! We know where it is."

The lady's maid raised her head.

"You know where it is? But how? Where did you find it?"

She turned from Greta to Rosalie, studying each girl's features intently.

"Where is it now?"

It was Rosalie's turn to sigh. If only Greta weren't so impetuous! She reached over and gently placed her hand over Frau Schwann's soft, plump palm. "We haven't found it. Not yet, at any rate. But we think Frau Dichtler must have taken—"

"You think she took the necklace?" The lady's maid drew back, startled. "Why, that is quite an accusation!" But it was clear she did not find the insinuation quite so dreadful.

Her surprise had already fled, replaced by a watchful curiosity.

"I am sure of it," Rosalie declared. She began to recount the details of the frayed rope, their fruitless search, and the theft of the necklace in Leopoldsdorf.

"I never mixed a packet of sleeping powder in my decoction of valerian tea!" Frau Schwann indignantly interrupted the narrative. "Why should I do such a thing?"

"Well, that is what Frau Dichtler said," Greta informed her.

"And the rope couldn't have been frayed when we set out for Leopoldsdorf," Rosalie added.

"It most certainly was not." Frau Schwann sat upright, her lips tightly pursed. "I always see to such things."

"Then it is just as I suspected." Rosalie turned toward Greta. "She sent us off on a wild goose chase and used the opportunity to steal the necklace. Only she didn't know it was a replica."

"Well, she found out soon enough," Frau Schwann said gloomily. "The Princess told her everything. And after that, the wretched woman kept on at Her Serene Highness to have another replica made.

"Let me take it to Madame Chapeau, she says. Madame can make a replica twice as quick as one of the jewelers in the Kohlmarkt, and at a third of the cost."

"Madame Chapeau!" Rosalie gasped. "She wanted you to go to Madame Chapeau? Why that is where I followed her this afternoon. It was Madame's assistant who came here, thinking to take your position."

"Of course, she had no idea you were still here. Madame was quite furious with Frau Dichtler when she found out."

"My position! Why, what have I done to hurt the wretched woman that she is after my position?" Frau Schwann shook her head. "Well, of course, Her Serene Highness would hear nothing of it. Whoever has heard of Madame Chapeau?" The lady's maid concluded with a sniff.

"And very wise of her it was, not to send you," Greta agreed. "You would've come back with two replicas if she had. Madame Chapeau deals in stolen goods. She is the only fence in the city who takes items of such great value. That's what my cousin Otto says, and he should know."

Rosalie nodded. "But what happened, then? Was it Frau Dichtler who suggested the necklace be taken to the bank for safekeeping?"

"No, but she insisted upon accompanying me to the bank. Wouldn't let the necklace case out of her sight. Wouldn't even trust me with it for the few minutes it took her to get her reticule from her room. But when we left the palace grounds. Why, then, she couldn't get rid of it fast enough!"

"So, that was when she exchanged the necklaces," Rosalie said. "Before you left the palace." She looked at Frau Schwann and Greta. "The little urchin who accosted you didn't have time enough to do it. She must have found a way to hand the necklace to him or to . . ."

She wrinkled her nose. Could even such a woman as Frau Dichtler persuade a police guard to join in her skullduggery?

A few moments of silence followed. Then the lady's maid spoke.

"But if the necklace is with Madame Chapeau, how will you get it back?" she wanted to know. "She is hardly likely to give it to you. And it will cost a pretty penny to buy it back, I can tell you that much."

Rosalie exchanged a small smile with Greta. "Oh, I have a plan. If all goes well, we shall have it back tomorrow."

"The idea is preposterous!" Therese said. She drew herself back and stared up at Haydn as though suspecting him of having gone quite mad. "It would never work." She turned toward Johann. "Would it?"

The movement and the question irritated Haydn more than he cared to admit. The Therese of old would have fallen in with his plan instantly. Might even have commended him for his resourcefulness. Yet now she looked toward Johann as though *he* were the elder brother!

Johann glanced briefly at him before replying. "If brother thinks it would . . ." he began stalwartly, but Haydn had caught the momentary hesitation before Johann voiced his opinion.

"It is not one of your better ideas, you must admit, husband." Maria Anna's glance roved toward the Kapellmeister's bandaged head. "Some of your brains must have fallen out when you received that blow."

His wife's last words, muttered under her breath, and her support of Therese's opinion irritated Haydn all the more.

"It must be made to work. It is the only way," he insisted. "I cannot approach Her Majesty with mere speculation. Surely, you can see that."

Therese sighed, the long-drawn, heavy sigh of a weary mother dealing with a fractious child. "How Joseph? If Reverend Mother Catherine were to find out—" The thought made her shudder.

Her slender fingers kneaded her forehead. "The convent is all I have known these ten years. It is all I have."

"There is a striking resemblance between sister-in-law and you," Johann pointed out. "In figure and form you are almost alike. And with a wimple covering her hair, who knows, but we may yet. . ."

Therese raised her head. "There is the matter of our voices. My duties include singing with the choir, sometimes taking the solo part." She looked over at Maria Anna, plucking nervously all the while at the embroidered cover on the armrest. "I beg your pardon, sister, but—"

Maria Anna brushed aside her words with a wave of her hand. "Our voices would give us away. Try as I would, I could never sing like my younger sister, brother-in-law. I crow like a jackdaw, or so husband puts it," she ended gruffly.

There must have been something in her eyes, for she repeatedly dabbed at the corners with her handkerchief.

"Is that your sole objection to the plan?" Haydn asked, although he had not until this moment considered it. It was true Maria Anna's singing—*Was that a tear glistening in his wife's eye?*

But he had never meant to hurt her with his words. He only spoke the truth about her failings as she did of his. *Surely—*

But Therese had begun to speak, and he turned his mind to attend to her.

"My dispensation to be out in the world is almost come to an end. Reverend Mother Catherine would grant an extension if I needed it to complete the task she has entrusted me with. But to attend a funeral. . ."

She wrinkled her nose. "If the Emperor were to hear of it somehow. You know how he walks about among the people like a common citizen."

Haydn nodded. He had heard quite enough of the Emperor's odd ways from his father-in-law. And even the Prince had let fall a word or two here and there.

"If His Majesty were to see anything, he would but see my wife at a funeral. Why should that seem strange?"

"But then, there is the matter of the Reverend Mother. There is no deceiving her?"

"Can you not have developed a sore throat?" The notion had just entered Haydn's head, and he blurted it out.

"What!" Therese and Maria Anna spoke at the same time.

"A severe hoarseness that prevents singing of any kind for an indefinite period," Haydn elaborated on his plan. "Maria Anna will be able to simulate that, won't you?" He turned toward his wife. "You may even develop a pain in your joints that prevents you from playing the keyboard."

The sisters looked at each other.

"I suppose it would work," Therese conceded. She glanced up at Haydn. "Are you sure this physician of yours will be at Kaspar's funeral? It will be a waste of our effort if he is not?"

"I am quite certain of it," Haydn replied grimly. "As long as you are certain you will recognize your scribe when you see him."

CHAPTER TWENTY-SIX

"What an unusual chest this is," Papa Keller commented, reaching out to touch the walnut wood chest Kaspar's widowed aunt had sent home with Haydn. "So full of holes, to be sure! What are they for, Joseph?"

"It is simply an old worm-eaten casket, Papa," Maria Anna replied somewhat testily.

It was the custom in Papa Keller's home to linger at the kitchen table long after the evening meal had been eaten. Maria Anna had voiced her displeasure on the subject, albeit in a more subdued fashion than was her wont, but Papa Keller had insisted Haydn and Johann remain with him at the table. Therese had retired for the night.

"I wish you would get rid of it, husband," Maria Anna continued as she bustled about the kitchen, putting pots and pans away. "Haven't I told you, the infestation spreads to everything?"

"Woodworm? Nonsense." Papa Keller burst out before either Haydn or Johann could respond. "That chest is not infested with woodworm." He tapped at the wood with his pipe. "Listen to that! The wood is still sound."

Haydn exchanged a glance with Johann. "How can you tell, Papa?" he asked.

For an old worm-eaten thing, the chest was much sturdier than either of them had expected it to be. He would have agreed with his father-in-law. Yet the tiny holes that pricked the surface of the walnut wood were evidence to the contrary.

"Why, you have only to look at the holes!"

Papa Keller tapped his pipe against the chest again. "Each one the same size and shape, about an eighth of an inch to a whole inch from its neighbor. What worm could make holes like that? And the wood so solid all over!"

He turned the casket around, knocking his knuckles on every side.

Haydn drew the chest closer to himself and peered at it. "I do believe you're right. These holes are so finely shaped, the worm in question must have been apprenticed to a carpenter!"

"And where there are holes the wood is always soft and rotted through," Johann said. "I should've remembered that. It is what Father always said, although I confess my mind was usually too lost in my music to pay much attention to anything he said about how he selected the wood for his hubs and wheels. We none of us intended to follow in his trade after all."

"No, we did not," Haydn quietly agreed.

He had caught the sadness in his brother's voice. Their father had no illusions about his sons' ambitions but had, nevertheless, sought to impart some of his own rough wisdom through the mundane tools of the wheelwright's trade.

"*Ach!* Children never mind their parents. Until it is too late, of course." Papa Keller brushed their remarks aside. He took a deep draught of his pipe. "Now, why did the old merchant want those holes in his casket, I wonder?"

Haydn's head jerked up at the question. "That question is quite easily answered, I believe," he said softly.

———

"It was to make us think the chest was worm-eaten."

"Nonsense!" Papa Keller's hand and the pipe it held swept the air in a peremptory dismissal of Haydn's suggestion. "Only a fool would be deceived by those holes." He brought his pipe back to his mouth and drew deeply from it. The wisps of smoke hung in the air before finally dissipating.

"Only a fool who had never worked with wood." Haydn's lips twitched at Papa Keller's gruff repudiation of anyone who had the temerity to think otherwise. "I ought to have known it as soon as we discovered the contents of the chest. But the presence of the holes, so like worm-eaten wood, made a fool of me."

He smiled at Johann. "Had we attended more closely to Father's lessons, we might have seen through old Wilhelm Dietrich's ruse."

"Yes, but what was the point of it all, husband? What treasure does that chest contain?" Maria Anna sounded impatient, but did not bother to glance up from the stove she was rubbing down. "Surely not the operas the old merchant claimed to own?"

"Always in his cups, as I mentioned to you, daughter," Papa Keller interjected before Haydn could respond. "There was never a drink that didn't fill the old man's sails to bursting."

"It may not have been mere talk," Johann replied as he opened the chest. He carefully brought out the madrigals Kaspar had inherited and then lifted out the scenari and the old leather volume Haydn had thrust at the bottom.

"More old papers," Maria Anna sniffed. How she could have known what they were without troubling to look around, Haydn did not know.

He held up the leather volume Johann had set next to him. "*The Merchant of Venice*. A play by Shakespeare, an English playwright, not more than a few years older than the Italian master, Claudio Monteverdi. It was a play that Wilhelm Dietrich so loved, he called attention to it in his will."

"Not something he would keep in an old, rotten chest, I'll warrant." Papa Keller pulled the pipe from his mouth.

"And he had no other copy in his library," Johann added. "The one on his shelves was in reality a lever made to look like a book."

"And what was the point of that?" Maria Anna demanded gruffly. "Merely an old man's tomfoolery, I'll wager."

Haydn rolled his eyes. The subtleties of the situation were lost on a woman like his wife. But then Maria Anna's interest in theatre was as deep as her interest in music.

"It was a reference to the play, Maria Anna. Only a man of character would look beyond the casket's appearance to its contents."

Maria Anna turned around. "Only a fool would look twice at an old, worm-eaten chest, husband."

"But it is not worm-eaten, daughter!" Papa Keller objected again. He indicated the leather volume in Haydn's hands with his pipe. "Are there worm-eaten chests in that play, then?"

Haydn's face broke into a wide smile. "No, the chests in this play are not worm-eaten, but the ruse it employs is just as clever."

He turned the pages to the scene in question.

"Portia is a wealthy young woman, all alone in the world. Her father, fearing that after his death men may seek her hand solely for the sake of her wealth, seeks to protect her."

"So, he sets a task for any suitor who comes to court her," Johann took up the story. "Any man who wishes to marry Portia must choose one of three caskets. The first is made of gold, the second of silver, and the third of lead."

Papa Keller took his pipe out of his mouth. "Gold, of course. It is the purest of the metals."

"Ah, yes!" Haydn responded. "But it is not the casket itself that we are concerned with. It is what lies within. The playwright tells us to look beyond the outward appearance of men to the inner being."

"*Ach so!* The leaden casket, then, I suppose." Papa Keller jabbed his pipe in the direction of the chest Haydn had brought home. "And that is it, I take it?"

Haydn nodded. "I am convinced it holds the key to Kaspar's bequest."

Maria Anna snorted. "Then, it is fortunate, no one thought to throw the thing away."

Haydn turned his head to look at her. "Wilhelm Dietrich's widow could not bear to throw it away. It was one of her most cherished memories of him." His own wife, he supposed, would hasten to discard all he owned after his death.

Maria Anna sniffed again, but continued to polish the ceramic tiles on the stove. "It will not bring her husband back. Still, if it contains the operas you spoke of, it cannot be a bad thing. Amelie has need of money, I am sure."

"It does not contain the operas, sister-in-law. We—"

Maria Anna whipped around. "It does not contain the operas? Then of what use is it?"

"It does not contain them so much as conceal them," Haydn explained.

———✦———

"Oh, you speak in riddles, husband!" Maria Anna threw her hands up in the air. "I thought you said the operas were not in that casket."

"They are not," Haydn repeated quietly. "Not where anyone would find them, at any rate." He ignored Maria Anna's snort and gently pulled the scenari toward himself. The paper was thick and strong still, but was nevertheless too old and too precious—for his purposes, at any rate— to bear rough handling. "Here is the proof that the old merchant was not lying when he claimed to possess all the operas of Monteverdi."

"What is it, then?" Maria Anna wanted to know. Her eyes shifted curiously toward Papa Keller, who had reached across the table for the casket and was beginning to poke and prod at it as he swiveled it around.

"Each of these is a scenario—"

"Scenario?" Maria Anna demanded.

"A brief account of the opera." It was Johann who volunteered the information. "They were printed specially for the audience to allow them to follow the story."

"*Ach so!*" Maria Anna nodded. "Well, it is an excellent notion, in my opinion. Who can be expected to understand anything when the actors insist upon singing in Italian?"

"The audience, it so happens, was Italian as well, Maria Anna," Haydn pointed out. His cheeks ached from the effort of holding in his laughter. But it would never do to highlight his wife's ignorance. He saw Maria Anna squinting down at him and restrained himself still further.

She came closer to the table, sponge in hand, still squinting suspiciously at her husband. "Well, well, and so what if they were? They are all cold in their graves now. Although why anyone would trouble to keep one of those, I don't see. Once you have seen the opera, what need would you have of the story?"

She motioned toward the scenarios with her wet sponge. The wide spatter of soapy droplets she cast around her fell perilously close to the sheets on the kitchen table. But Maria Anna, careless as always, seemed oblivious to the damage that might be caused.

Haydn drew the papers closer to himself and covered them with both hands. "No need at all, if you were an operagoer of the time, perhaps. Although, of course, some people must have kept them or these would not have survived. But that Wilhelm Dietrich preserved them, and in a chest he must have intended for Kaspar, is quite significant, I think."

"Why?" Maria Anna returned to the sink to wash out her sponge.

"Because they can be used to authenticate the scores, sister-in-law,"

Johann explained. "The scenarios were printed so close to the time of the performance, they incorporate details of the opera that would be in the score, but not in the libretto. In the great master's case, he changed the text of his librettos to such an extent that only the scenario could be reliably compared to the score."

"And Wilhelm Dietrich would have been aware of that, I am sure," Haydn added. "These scenarios contain the date of the first performance of each opera. Monteverdi's name is printed on them as well. An added inducement to attend the performance, no doubt. After all, who could resist his music? Wilhelm Dietrich must have realized Kaspar would need to prove the scores were genuine before he could sell them."

Maria Anna harrumphed. "He would need to find the scores first. I thought you said you had yet to find the operas. Where are they?"

"A false bottom!" Papa Keller's voice burst in upon their conversation. He pulled a long draught from his pipe and then tapped on the casket with its stem. "This chest has a false bottom. I am convinced of it. I have examined it very closely. It is not as deep inside as it is outside."

Haydn's lips broadened into a smile. "I did think that might be the case," he said. "That must be where the operas are concealed."

CHAPTER TWENTY-SEVEN

The night was pleasantly warm, the soft cherry-scented breeze carrying the promise of summer's arrival in Vienna. Haydn crossed the small courtyard of the Keller home to the barn that lined the back perimeter of the property. Johann followed him, carrying the old merchant's chest.

Papa Keller had spent the better part of the evening prying and prodding at the thing. But try as he might, he had not been able to unlock the secret compartment he was sure the chest concealed. He had retired for the night, defeated, and Maria Anna, not entirely convinced the chest was not worm-infested, had insisted Haydn keep it in the barn.

"Let us examine it once more," Haydn suggested as he laid his palm flat against the barn door and pushed. It opened with a small creak of protest. The lamp he carried aloft threw a bright glare over his surroundings—a large square space crammed with odds and ends.

In Eisenstadt a barn of this size might have been used for horses, cows, or other farm animals. Papa Keller, like any other city-dweller, used his to store three-legged chairs, cabinets with missing doors, and other broken bits of household furniture he had long meant to restore.

Haydn set his lamp at one end of the table that stood in the middle of the room and cleared a space for the chest by moving a rusty hammer, a box of nails, and a pair of wooden hand-planes out of the way. "Here! Set it down here, Johann."

Johann lowered the chest onto the dusty table with a grunt. "I cannot believe we will be successful where Papa Keller has failed, brother, but I don't suppose there can be any harm in trying."

He wiped down the table as best he could with a kerchief, but the dust had lain so long upon it, it seemed to have welded itself to the wooden surface. "I trust we shall be doing no damage to these old papers by letting them rest here," he said as he began to empty the chest of its contents.

Johann had no sooner taken the last of the pages out of the chest than the Kapellmeister drew it toward himself and began to feel the interior. The silk lining at the bottom of the chest had begun to fray, and Haydn could feel the rough threads cutting into his fingers as he gently probed the bottom. He frowned as his fingers encountered an obstruction.

"There are hard knobs at each of the four corners, Johann," he said after a while. "I wonder what they can be? They feel like buttons of some sort."

Haydn's fingers slid over the edge. The lining, a stiff mat of silk, was not glued to the bottom. Had his fingers been slimmer, he could have lifted the edges to touch the bottom. He had just begun to force his finger over the edge, tugging slightly, when the entire rectangular lining lifted out.

"Buttoned on," he said in some surprise, as he peered into the interior. He lifted it out.

"And look, there is a small notch carved into left wall. It must contain a lever of some sort." His finger, probing again, found a small square set in relief from its surroundings. He was pushing on it when suddenly the wooden bottom of the chest began receding from the center.

"You have found it, brother!" Astonishment and admiration co-mingled on Johann's features. "Well done."

A leather notebook rested on top of a sheaf of neatly folded papers in the space that was revealed. "A diary of some sort," Haydn remarked as he flipped through the pages of the notebook. "An account of the old merchant's travels, no doubt."

His attention turned toward the papers lying beneath the notebook. But even without lifting them out, he could distinguish the chain pattern on the sheets.

"These are not the operas," he said. He withdrew them from the recess and unfolded them, a heavy, sinking feeling erupting within his guts as he scanned them. There was not a single note on any of the pages, not even so much as a treble clef.

"Letters," he announced to Johann. "These are nothing more than letters. Where can the operas be?"

———— ∽∽ ————

Kaspar's funeral was to take place in the early hours of dawn. The city was still shrouded in broad swathes of watery rose and violet when Haydn set out from the Keller home that morning.

The poultice Maria Anna had applied to his wound felt pleasantly cool against his forehead, mitigating to some extent the pulsating pain that kept up its steady thrumming behind his temples.

It was far too early for very many people to be abroad and the roads were largely deserted. Even the street cleaners had yet to begin their work. Haydn glanced down at his silver timepiece. The final hours of the vigil had begun. That Kaspar's soul had spent it unaccompanied by family or friends nagged at his conscience.

His own injuries, the undertaker had pointed out, did not permit that he spend the entire night in watchfulness. And Amelie, after the shock she had sustained, was certainly in no better condition to spend the night watching over the dead.

The vigil had been kept instead by Herr Moserle, the elderly nuns from the Civic Hospital who had washed Kaspar's body and sewn it into its linen burial shroud, and Rudi, Kaspar's aged servant.

Haydn glanced at his timepiece again. He would, at least, be at the undertaker's establishment in time to end the vigil with the small group.

A servant ushered him into the small room where Kaspar's body lay in its narrow wooden coffin. That it was a coffin surprised the Kapellmeister. What need was there of a coffin when Kaspar's body would simply be lowered into the crypt kept for him at St. Michael's? But this was no time for questions.

The nuns sat with their heads bowed and hands folded in prayer. Rudi's tear-filled gaze swept over him in gratitude, then returned to his master's body, prepared now for burial. Only the undertaker gave Haydn a brief nod as he silently walked in and took his place by the wooden bier on which the coffin rested.

The minutes slowly passed. Where was Amelie, he wondered. Surely, it was not too much to expect that she spend the final hours of the vigil with her husband? The faint sounds of carriage wheels and horses' hooves penetrated the room, carried by the still morning air.

But it was not Amelie. Only Johann with Therese, dressed in Maria Anna's gown and looking remarkably like her sister, on his arm.

Johann caught the Kapellmeister's eye and inclined his head. Haydn's plan had been successfully executed. Maria Anna, dressed in her sister's habit, was now on Singerstrasse, in the convent of St. Nikolai. Therese would accompany them to St. Michael's Church where Kaspar had worked and where, after a short mass, he would rest until the end of time.

Amelie, Haydn hoped, would at least attend the service and interment. Her new friend, the bearded stranger he had encountered the day before, would, he was quite certain, be present as well.

"And I will eat my wig if the man is not the elusive Dr. Goretti," he muttered to himself. "He must think wooing the widow is as good a means of getting his hands on the music as an outright offer to purchase it!"

The somber tolling of bells sounded. "It is from the Karlskirche," one of the nuns said with a smile. "Pfarrer August will conduct the mass and then we shall accompany the body to its resting place in the Karlsfriedhof."

"The Karlsfriedhof!" Haydn rose from his seat, not caring to temper the anger that rang loudly through his voice. "But Kaspar is to be interred in a crypt in the Michaelerkirche. It is where he worked. Why should he be buried beyond the city walls? By whose orders, Herr Moserle?"

The undertaker stood up as well. "Your friend died without receiving extreme unction—"

"Through no fault of his own," Johann pointed out in a gentle tone. "He was killed. He could hardly have known it was to be his last day upon earth."

An expression of unease flitted over the undertaker's features. "Be that as it may. The crypt can only be used by those who confess their sins and repent. An untimely death, even one at the hands of another. . ."

One of the elderly nuns came up to Haydn and laid a gnarled hand on his arm. "The soul is filled with sin, and without confession, without repentance—"

"Not to mention the question of disease," Herr Moserle, who had been punctuating the nun's words with emphatic nods, now interjected.

"Disease?" Johann's gaze shifted toward the coffin before returning to the undertaker's features. "Kaspar died of no disease, unless murder can be called a disease."

The undertaker sighed. "His body was found abandoned in the streets. The Emperor advises burial beyond the city walls in such cases even when the cause of death is known. An added precaution against disease, according to His Majesty."

"We are to adopt the ways of the Lutherans, then?" The undertaker flinched at Haydn's words. But the Kapellmeister cared not. "What next? A surreptitious burial in the dark hours of the night?"

Papa Keller was right. The Emperor's officious ways seemed to know no bounds. It was small wonder His Majesty had not seen fit to dictate the precise number of guldens and kreutzer that could be spent upon the funeral!

But what had the poor nuns or the undertaker to do with any of this? With the thought came a measure of calm and his ill-humor subsided.

He forced his lips into a gracious smile. "If His Majesty advises it, what can we do but follow? At any rate, Kaspar will not be the only musician in the Karlsfriedhof. It is where the Italian composer, Antonio Vivaldi, is buried as well."

He turned toward Johann, his smile more genuine now. "We choirboys were to have sung at the funeral, but Kapellmeister Reutter was ever a stickler for the rules. The omission of the six-gulden fee for an unaccompanied funeral song was, in his opinion, too great an offence to be ignored."

———

The coffin touched the ground at the same time as Pfarrer August's choirboys finished their a cappella rendition of *Der Grimmige Tod*.

The song, beautiful in its simplicity, unaccompanied by instrumentation of any kind, had taken Haydn back to his own days as a choirboy at St. Stephen's. He blinked back his tears as he stepped away from the edge of the grave.

His work as pallbearer done, he could now look around him at the group that had attended Kaspar on his last journey. Kaspar's fellow musicians from St. Michael's Church and his colleagues from the Hofburg were gathered around the grave, heads bowed, listening gravely to the words Pfarrer August recited.

Herr Anwalt, the lawyer, stood by Rudi. They had all attended the funeral mass and then joined in the solemn procession to the gravesite. Haydn had even caught a glimpse of Fabrizzio, the young music scholar.

Johann and Luigi, pallbearers as well, stood opposite him. His eyes moved beyond them to where Amelie stood, pale-faced and tearless, under the shade of a beech tree, a handkerchief pressed to her nose. She was standing so far from the grave, one might have mistaken her for a stranger who had joined in the procession rather than the dead man's widow!

The bearded stranger who had passed Haydn on her stairs yesterday stood by her side, an arm wound loosely around her waist. The attitude of familiarity infuriated Haydn at the same time as it recalled him to their purpose.

"Have you seen your scribe yet?" He gave Therese a gentle nudge as he whispered the words. She had stood by him, head bowed, but had barely spoken a word.

Therese shook her head. "I thought I saw him, but I cannot be sure now."

"Look toward the tree behind Johann. Amelie stands under it."

"It has been ten years, but despite the careworn aspect her face now wears, I would know her anywhere."

"And the man who stands next to her?" Haydn probed. "He is Italian like your scribe. Dressed impeccably."

The sun's rays filtering through the leaves of the beech behind the couple obscured his vision, but unless he was mistaken the navy waistcoat the bearded Italian was wearing was made of velvet. His black coat and breeches were of the finest silk.

Therese turned her head with a swift, graceful movement and dutifully studied the man. "He has something of the same look. The beard, neatly trimmed. An elegant figure just like the man who came to us." She turned toward Haydn. "But I don't think it is he, Joseph."

"Are you quite certain?" The sun was in his eyes. How could it not affect her vision as well? "The man is so far off. Perhaps a closer look will aid your memory."

"It might." Therese inclined her head and folded her hands in front of her waist. Pfarrer August had begun another prayer as the last mounds of loose earth covered the coffin.

Haydn's gaze flickered toward his sister-in-law, resting briefly on her slender neck and the tendrils of golden curls that framed her face. Was she really in agreement with him or had she merely uttered the words to keep him quiet?

The funeral was soon over, and they were about to make their way back to Kaspar's aunt's house within the city walls when Amelie and her friend began to approach them.

"It is not him, Joseph," Therese said in a firm voice. "He is not our scribe, I am quite sure of it. And now it is time for me to return to the convent."

Not their scribe! How was that possible? But before Haydn could voice a protest, his sister-in-law had moved over to Johann's side. And the two of them joined the departing throng.

CHAPTER TWENTY-EIGHT

"Was that Maria Anna, Joseph?" Amelie's smile, affectionate yet full of regret, held the memory of bygone times. "The years have yet to set their mark upon her. If anything, she looks more beautiful. More radiant. And more and more, dare I say it"—she turned shyly toward Joseph—"like her younger sister."

"It was," Haydn assured her, glad now that Therese had hastened away.

He doubted the similarity between the sisters would have held under closer inspection. Amelie knew them both too well for that.

"She regrets not being able to stay. She is eager to visit Therese at the convent. Her younger sister is not at all well, and Maria Anna has a way with herbs as you may recall."

God forgive him for the lie, but what else was he to say? He looked pointedly at the bearded stranger who stood a short distance behind Amelie. "I don't believe I am acquainted with your friend, Amelie."

He had thought to embarrass Amelie, but his friend's widow did not so much as blush at his remark. "It is Kaspar's friend, in truth," she said, reaching for the stranger's arm and drawing him forward with an easy familiarity that set Haydn's teeth on edge. "Dr. Goretti. Kaspar may have mentioned him to you."

Ah! So, the source of Her Majesty's operas was also known to Kaspar. Had he not suspected as much?

"Kaspar did make mention of a physician who was greatly interested in his bequest," he began carefully. "But it was at the imperial court that I first heard your name." Was it his imagination or had the physician's olive complexion turned several shades lighter?

"Er, yes, yes, of course. I am indeed known to Her Majesty. Some of the medicaments I have provided have fortunately served her well. . ."

Haydn allowed a smile to flit over his features. "It was in connection with the operas you provided that she mentioned you."

"Yes, of course. The operas," Goretti said, inclining his head, but not before Haydn had noticed his nostrils flaring in quietly suppressed anger.

Did the good doctor fear he would be discovered in his treachery, Haydn wondered. Or had he never intended to let Amelie know of the Empress's interest in the great master's music?

The physician turned toward Amelie. "You see, my dear, what a fortune you could make with the music your husband received! If they are indeed operas. We shall have to examine them. Her Majesty seems to have developed quite a taste for old Italian works in the genre. Madrigals, on the other hand, are unlikely to find favor."

"Joseph here has been examining the works," Amelie hastened to assure him. "He is quite capable."

"I trust he can distinguish between madrigals and operas, then," the doctor responded. He took a small snuff box out of his pocket and pried open the lid. "It would be a pity indeed if you found yourself saddled with a parcel of madrigals. Those have no value at all."

Haydn saw no reason to acknowledge the barb. He might have countered with a rejoinder of his own, but the gold snuff box drove every thought away. It belonged, he was quite certain, to Kaspar. How had it come into Goretti's hands?

"A remarkable piece of work," he said, tilting his chin at the tiny golden case. "May I ask where you obtained it?"

"What? This snuff box?" Goretti attempted a laugh. "It is from my father's collection."

"Indeed! I was not aware your father knew my Prince." Haydn allowed his eyes to bore into the other's. The engraving of the winged griffin carrying a sword in one hand and three roses in the other was unmistakable. It knelt at the feet of the double-headed eagle that represented the house of Habsburg.

Only on one occasion had His Serene Highness thought to include both the Habsburg emblem and his own on his snuff boxes. Kaspar was one of the few persons besides Haydn himself and Luigi to have received one such.

"You are mistaken, Herr Haydn. My father received this from a noble patron in Venice." Goretti's fingers curled over the case. He quickly slipped it back into his pocket. "The mourners have all left. We should follow them, no?" He strode away without waiting to see if either of his companions would follow.

Haydn's jaw tightened. Therese was mistaken. Here before him stood his friend's killer, and there was nothing he could do about it. Not now. Not with Amelie watching him so closely.

He offered his arm to her. "Come, let us be on our way. It would be unseemly if you were not seen to preside over the funeral reception."

"Ready?" Gerhard lifted the reins and looked down at Rosalie. When she nodded, he gently tugged the reins. The nag bestirred herself and the rack wagon moved slowly forward.

Rosalie braced herself against its narrow seat with one hand and nervously fingered the folded sheet of paper in her pocket with the other. It contained a rough drawing in Frau Schwann's hand of the stolen necklace, but she didn't dare take it out.

She cast a surreptitious glance up at Gerhard, lowering her eyes before she could be detected. What would he think if he knew she was looking for a necklace of a specific design? Pearl petals clustered around an emerald center. The pendant made of gold and encrusted with diamonds.

"What kind of trinket do you mean to buy for Greta?" Gerhard enquired, never taking his eyes off the road as he concentrated on steering the wagon through the morning crowd.

Rosalie took a deep breath. "Something fashioned out of pearly white beads," she began, fingers closing over the rough wooden edge of the seat. The coarse fibers chafed against her skin and the sharp edges of a nail dug into her palm, making her wince. "And bits of green glass, perhaps, made to look like emeralds. Greta will like that."

Gerhard let out a deep throaty laugh. "Has fancy tastes, does she, our Greta? Well, Madame Chapeau has more designs than you can conceive of." His eyes flickered toward her, warm with concern. "I only hope we have time enough to pick out something you like."

They would be arriving a full hour before Madame Chapeau's establishment opened for business at eleven. To give Sabina time to attend to their needs, Gerhard had said. Madame herself was unlikely to bring herself down at that hour, being more likely to be ensconced in her room with a cup of chocolate like the fashionable ladies she hoped to serve.

"It will, I am sure." Rosalie forced herself to smile. *It would have to suffice.* She clutched the seat a little harder. She had but one chance to retrieve Her Serene Highness's necklace. And to prove Frau Schwann's innocence.

It was but a short walk from Karlsfriedhof where poor Wilhelm Kaspar now rested to his uncle Wilhelm Dietrich's home within the city walls. The house stood a few yards to the left of the Carinthian Gate, so close to the cemetery the merchant's widow had insisted upon its use for her nephew's funeral reception.

Haydn ushered Amelie into the parlor where the mourners were now assembled, giving the room a cursory glance as he pulled the door shut behind them. The pale pink furnishings he recalled from the previous day had been replaced with a more subdued black. And Kaspar's colleagues from St. Michael's were all in attendance.

There were even a number of musicians from the Hofburg. Kapellmeister Reutter had apparently not begrudged them the few hours away from their duties at the imperial palace.

He had no sooner settled Amelie into an armchair when Kaspar's widowed aunt bore down upon him.

"Herr Haydn! Your injuries heal well, I trust." She took both of his hands in her own gnarled brown ones. "You will have a glass of wine, won't you?" She turned to beckon to a round-featured maid bearing a silver tray laden with glasses of fine red Blaufränkisch.

Haydn was about to accept when the widow whipped around. "Or better still, a glass of the healing concoction I prepared for you yesterday. It will ease any discomfort that remains. Adelita here"—the maid had by now reached their side—"can boil up the herbs."

To his alarm, she turned toward Adelita, ready to instruct the maid on its preparation.

"There is no discomfort at all, Madam. The wound is quite healed," Haydn hastened to assure the widow, shuddering at the thought of having to endure yet another cup of the revolting brew. That he had tasted it once was misfortune enough. He was determined not to repeat the unfortunate incident.

To his relief, a few more guests arrived, recalling the widow to her duties. He reached for a glass of wine from the tray the maid held out to him. He would have taken another for Amelie, but Kaspar's colleagues and their wives thronged around her, wishing no doubt to pay their respects and offer words of condolence.

Dr. Goretti appeared to have assumed charge of the entire proceedings. It galled Haydn no end to see him standing guard over Amelie. The men who had come to mourn Kaspar's untimely passing had all known him far longer than the upstart physician.

Yet here was Goretti, a mere guest himself, beckoning this guest forward and drawing that one away from the widow.

Fabrizzio, dressed today in a fine suit of black silk, approached Amelie's chair and bent down to speak a few words. His eyes collided with Haydn's as soon as he looked up, and he turned swiftly around.

"That is the music scholar, I suppose." Luigi's voice rang as loud as a gunshot in Haydn's startled ears.

He had been so intent on watching Fabrizzio retreat rapidly to the other end of the parlor, he had failed to notice his Konzertmeister come up beside him. Johann, he was glad to see, was not far behind.

"Fabrizzio," Haydn responded with a nod. "The son apparently of an old friend of Wilhelm Dietrich's. From Italy." He turned to his younger brother. "Maria Anna was able to escape the confines of St. Nikolai without mishap, I hope."

"More easily than anyone could have expected." Johann smiled. "We were no sooner there than Reverend Mother Catherine insisted we take 'Sister Josepha' home. Ostensibly to bring her investigation to a close, but she hustled us out so quickly, it was quite evident that was not her only reason.

"I am afraid the sore throat sister-in-law feigned may have alarmed the nuns into fearing the infection might spread to the rest of the convent, and so bring to naught their preparations for the Sunday service."

Haydn smiled broadly, momentarily diverted by the news. For the sake of music, any convent in the city could be persuaded to bend the rules. St. Nikolai was no exception. He had used the knowledge to his own advantage to snatch a few precious hours with his Therese when she first entered the convent.

But that was before he had agreed to take Maria Anna as his wife. Before Therese had banished him forever from her presence. The memory recalled him to the gravity of their current circumstances.

"Therese was unable to recognize Dr. Goretti as the scribe the convent hired. I feel sure she is mistaken. But the fact remains: we have nothing more than our suspicions now that he is indeed our man."

It was evident from Johann's face that Therese had already acquainted him with their brief disagreement at the cemetery. "Sister Josepha said as much. She was quite adamant that she was not mistaken."

"Could it not be that young jackanapes?" Luigi, eagerly following the interchange, now broke in upon the conversation.

Haydn followed his gaze to where Fabrizzio stood near the parlor door, deep in conference with Dr. Goretti. Haydn's eyes narrowed. Did the two men know each other?

"He is Italian," Luigi went on, "just like our Goretti. And I have never seen a man more ostentatiously dressed. Only observe how his jacket flares out behind him. And the extravagant frills of that lace cravat! In a woman's eyes, I suppose, that might pass for elegance."

Haydn regarded the music scholar speculatively. Luigi's idea was not without its merits. He was still considering it when Johann spoke. "It is a likely possibility, brother. You yourself surmised he may have broken into Kaspar's apartment the night he was murdered."

"If that is the case," Luigi pressed his point, "that is our man, Joseph. Who else but his killer could have gained access to Kaspar's keys?"

Haydn stared at the two foreigners still engaged in conversation. Therese's description of the scribe the convent had hired would have fit either man, although the physician seemed to be the older of the two by several years. Had his initial impression of Fabrizzio been correct?

On the other hand, the man who had penned the note luring Kaspar out—the very same who had copied the convent's manuscripts—must also have killed him. How could that man not be Dr. Goretti? *Moreover...*

"Who else could have stolen his snuff box?" His softly muttered words had the effect of jolting both his Konzertmeister and his brother.

"What! How can you know who took it?" The words erupted out of

Luigi's mouth, entwining themselves in a discordant counterpoint with Johann's stunned: "You cannot mean Kaspar's snuff box?"

"You recall the snuff boxes His Serene Highness ordered some years back, don't you, Luigi?" Haydn turned toward his Konzertmeister. "The lid showed the Esterházy griffin kneeling at the claws of the Habsburg eagle?"

"Made for the Empress." Luigi nodded. "And a few of us musicians received one as well. Kaspar was fiddling with his that night at the Seizerkeller. It was taken from him when he was killed."

"And is now in Dr. Goretti's possession," Haydn quietly informed them.

CHAPTER TWENTY-NINE

"He was foolish enough to show it to you?" Disbelief colored the rising tones of Johann's voice.

"I doubt he knows what the emblem on it represents," Haydn replied. "When I tasked him on the matter, he insisted the snuff box was from his father's collection. A gift from a noble patron in Venice, apparently."

"With the same coat of arms as both His Serene Highness and Her Majesty?" Johann turned toward Luigi. "Surely, that is not possible."

Haydn's gaze followed his brother's, resting expectantly upon his Konzertmeister's features.

Years ago, Luigi, a mere valet at the time, had been sent by His Serene Highness's older brother to Italy to develop his mastery of the violin. His long travels there had made him familiar with most of the noble families and their crests. If anyone could shed light on the matter, it would be him.

The corners of Luigi's hazel eyes crinkled as he considered the question. "I can think of only one emblem that comes even close to the Esterházy griffin. A lion with a divided tail."

"The Gonzaga lion," Haydn said at once. "It is the watermark used on the convent's paper," he explained when Luigi looked at him in surprise. "To honor their foundress, the Empress Eleonora, who hailed from the house of Gonzaga."

"If you have seen it, you know the two emblems are nothing like each other," Luigi replied.

"The doctor is clearly unfamiliar with the griffin, then," Johann remarked to Haydn. "Or what it represents. He would hardly have attempted to deceive you had he realized its significance."

"Is it Dr. Goretti you speak of?" Albrecht, who had been hovering nearby, drew closer.

"His inability to acknowledge his own ignorance on certain matters," Haydn explained with a smile.

How much of their conversation Albrecht had overheard, he knew not. But there was little point in arousing his curiosity any further by denying the subject of their discussion. Their eyes, fixed on the doctor, as they spoke of him told the tale plainly enough. And who knew, it might elicit some gossip from the young violinist.

"You still find him admirable, I suppose?" Luigi, quick as always to follow the Kapellmeister's lead, asked in a teasing tone.

"W-well, I know nothing of medicine, gentlemen," Albrecht faltered. "But in matters of music"—he cast a surreptitious glance around the room and lowered his voice—"it would appear the good doctor is not as well-versed as he lets on."

"Whatever do you mean?" Johann asked.

"You see the young man leaving his side?"

"The music scholar, Fabrizzio," Haydn said. "What of him?"

"Well," Albrecht continued, clearly relishing the older men's interest in the tidbit he had to offer. "He is something of a pretentious know-it-all, if you want my opinion. But he demonstrated quite clearly the good doctor's musical insufficiencies."

"Why, what did he do?" Luigi impatiently pressed the younger man.

"It was at the Seizerkeller, and in the good doctor's defense, he had consumed more wine than was good for him. It must have gone to his head for he started discoursing at length on the fine marks of style that distinguish one composer from another. Fabrizzio would have it the music of the past, unlike modern music, is all of a piece."

"By which assertion he only succeeded in showing up his own ignorance," Haydn commented softly.

The remark elicited a puzzled stare from Albrecht, but at Haydn's brief nod of encouragement, he resumed his account.

"To prove his point, Fabrizzio brought out a sheet of music, laying a wager Dr. Goretti would not be able to tell whether it was by Bach or Vivaldi."

"Indeed!" Johann raised an eyebrow. "What happened then?"

"The doctor perused the work and identified it positively as a concerto grosso by Vivaldi." Albrecht stared wide-eyed at his listeners.

"And it was not, I take it?" Haydn was beginning to tire of the young man's unnecessarily dramatic style.

"It was a violin concerto. Inspired by the seasons, or so the title would have us believe."

"He mistook a concerto for a concerto grosso?" It appeared to take Luigi an effort to keep his voice low. His lips twitched. "Not even a child would make that mistake."

Albrecht seemed about to smile as well, but restrained himself. "If it were only as bad as that!"

"You mean it was actually a Bach concerto? With a title from one of Vivaldi's works?" An impish grin spread over Luigi's lean dark features. "I do believe I begin to like the man."

"*Ach* no!" Albrecht shook his head vigorously. "It was by neither composer. Just something Fabrizzio himself had penned. An exercise in contrapuntal style with several errors that he painstakingly pointed out after he owned to writing the piece."

"He is only a physician," Johann pointed out gently as Luigi began to chortle. "How can he be expected to know anything of counterpoint?"

The Konzertmeister, seeming somewhat ashamed of his outburst, curbed his amusement. "There is that, I suppose." He turned toward Haydn, but the Kapellmeister was lost in his own thoughts.

"If he understands so little of music, how could he have known Kaspar's bequest was valuable?" Haydn said so softly, he seemed to be speaking to himself.

"He had no opportunity to see it," Johann reminded him, evidently having heard the words. "It can have been nothing more than a surmise."

"A surmise on which he was willing to gamble a substantial amount of money." Haydn turned to face his brother. "And I would like to know why," he added grimly as he surveyed the parlor.

But most of the mourners had left, and neither the physician nor the music scholar were among the few that still remained.

———— ❦ ————

The Carinthian Gate came into view as Gerhard's rack wagon made its turn onto the street where Madame Chapeau's millinery was located. They were still a half-mile from their destination, but Rosalie could discern the glass doors and fancy awning of the establishment.

A single mote of light reflecting from the glass panes flashed in her eyes. It disappeared, replaced by a familiar bristle-haired, stocky figure swinging a truncheon.

Poldi!

Rosalie grabbed hold of Gerhard's arm, unconsciously driving her nails into the flesh. His sudden yelp of pain made her release her hold on him. The rack wagon lurched to a halt.

"I didn't mean to. . ." she faltered, but then saw the police guard headed their way. She laid hold of Gerhard's arm again. "Quick! Turn into the next alley."

"Why?" Gerhard regarded her, baffled. He held the reins aloft, but made no move to prod his nag forward.

"Please, just do it." With a swift motion of her chin, the maid indicated the police guard advancing toward them.

"Scared of police guards, are you?" Gerhard sounded amused, but he began nevertheless to slowly guide the rack wagon into the alley. "It is just Madame Chapeau's brother. He has a rough, blustering manner about him, but I doubt he means any harm."

"Her brother!" If Poldi was Madame Chapeau's brother, then. . .

Rosalie cast a quick glance behind her, turning her face away just as Poldi came into view. If he had troubled to look their way, he would have seen no more than a few straggling curls of her hair framing a sliver of cheek, but he strode out of sight, never once looking into the alley.

So Poldi was Madame Chapeau's brother. Rosalie twisted her head all the way around to the front and regarded the narrow cobblestone alley. There was something deeply oppressive about the dingy buildings looming over them on either side, and she was glad when Gerhard turned the rack wagon around.

"Your face is as white as a sheet, lass!" Gerhard's words penetrated through the fog that surrounded her mind. "You have not done anything to—"

"Of course not!" Rosalie swallowed. It would never do to tell Gerhard about the necklace. He would never believe Poldi had anything to do with it. But some explanation was necessary. She cast about in her mind for it when something Master Luigi had said returned to her consciousness.

"He came to the palace, Poldi did," she said, turning to face Gerhard. "To inform Master Luigi about a friend of his who was beaten and left to die in front of the Seizerkeller." She forced herself to imagine the gruesome sight to lend some credence to the lie.

"And seeing him reminded you of the awful incident, no doubt." Concern and sympathy commingled on Gerhard's features.

Rosalie had never felt worse about deceiving a man. She nodded, neck feeling stiff and rigid.

Gerhard brought the wagon to a halt and dropped the reins. "There is nothing amiss here and nothing to fear, lass," he said, clasping Rosalie's hands in his own strong, warm palms. "Poldi must simply have been visiting his sister."

He let go of her hands and took up the reins again. "Come! The warehouse is but a minute away. Sabina's trinkets will divert your thoughts." He smiled down at her. "Can't have a young lass such as yourself imagining death on a summer morning now, can I?"

<hr />

The carriage sped eastward across the city toward the Danube Canal. The charitable hospital run by the Brothers of Mercy where Dr. Goretti was frequently to be found was on the other side of it.

"I trust he will still be there," Luigi muttered through clenched teeth. His fingers curled around the edge of the window in a tight grasp. Even the springs on their fine Hungarian carriage could not sufficiently protect them against the wild jolts and swaying they were forced to endure as they hurtled forward.

"He intends to return to Schönbrunn after," Haydn said, repeating the information Albrecht had given them. He winced as a particularly brutal lurch hurled his shoulder against the side of the carriage. Every bone in his body seemed to be rattling. "We will follow him there, if we have to."

He ignored the pained expression on his younger brother's face. The Empress's summer palace was on the other side of town, nearly sixteen miles to the west of the charitable hospital on 16 Taborstrasse.

As the carriage drove past Singerstrasse, he caught a glimpse of the towers of St. Nikolai. "I wonder if the operas—the great master's operas, that is to say—are concealed within the walls of the convent." If they had to chase Goretti back to the summer palace, perhaps there would be time for a brief stop at the cloister.

"I doubt it. Sister Josepha said the convent had none but the printed copy of *L'Orfeo* in its possession," Johann responded.

"So she did." Haydn had quite forgotten that she had. He stared at his brother and Luigi in turn. "Where then can Goretti have hoped to obtain the operas he purported to have? I doubt he has the ability to compose a single minuet, let alone write an opera in the style of Monteverdi."

He warmed to his subject. "If the convent had the scores, he could copy them in his own hand and pass them off as works in the great master's own hand."

"If the convent had the scores, Joseph, he would not be so desperate to acquire the music left to Kaspar." Luigi's grip on the window tightened as the carriage rounded a sharp curve.

"No, I suppose not." Haydn stroked his chin as he slowly nodded. "But then there remains the question of how he knew Kaspar's bequest was of any value. If the man cannot tell a concerto from a concerto grosso, I doubt he can distinguish between a madrigal and an opera."

"What are you suggesting, brother"—Johann leaned forward as he asked the question—"that someone gave him the information?"

"Someone must have," Haydn replied. "The only question is who? I have no doubt it was he who arranged for that band of ruffians to hold up Kaspar's carriage the very evening he received his bequest."

CHAPTER THIRTY

The carriage drew up at last outside a building the color of a heavily overcast sky. Slabs of a darker gray granite skirted the edge of the facade in a narrow wainscot some six inches high. A brother of the order dressed in a black cassock tied loosely around the waist was hurrying toward one of the doors under a large sign marked *Spital*.

He had almost reached it when Haydn flung himself out of the carriage, not waiting for it to roll to a stop. He heard Luigi's heavy footfall and Johann's lighter tread behind him as he ran to catch up with the friar.

"Whoever you are, let go!" the religious said when Haydn stopped him, fingers closing over the other's wrist in a firm clasp. "A man lies dying in one of the beds within. I must go." He was about to wriggle free when Luigi laid a heavy hand on his arm. The friar looked up, indignant.

"We require but a moment," Johann hastened to assure him before he could utter a word in protest. "The Italian physician who volunteers his services at your order, is he within?"

The friar wrinkled his nose, his hand still pressed against the black door. "We have no need of Italian medicine, gentlemen. And the only physicians here are brothers of the Order of Johannes von Gott.

"But a foreigner does come often to our apothecary. You may find him there." He gestured to the sign at the end of the building to the right. "The entrance is around the corner past the sign."

Brushing Haydn's hand off his arm, he thrust open the door and dashed inside before either the Kapellmeister or his companions could ask any further questions.

"We have but wasted our time coming here." Luigi was still breathing heavily from his exertions. "Are you sure of your information?"

Haydn hesitated. Albrecht had seemed quite certain of his facts. Could Goretti have lied to the young violinist about frequenting the hospital run by the Brothers of Mercy?

"It does us no harm to go to the apothecary," he suggested. "How many Italians can there be who frequent this place?"

"Then let me, at least, go to Schönbrunn, Joseph. It is on the other side of town, and I have no doubt Goretti will rid himself of that snuff box when he realizes its significance. If he has it"—Luigi's lips tightened—"I would like to see it for myself. He will not find me quite so easy to fob off."

———

The granite slab wainscoting continued around the corner, but the light gray facade of the convent and hospital run by the Brothers of Mercy gave way to patches of dingy yellow that had yet to be replaced. Scaffolding clung to the sides of the building and clouds of paint dust hung in the air.

Johann clapped a kerchief to his nose as soon as they rounded the corner, and after swallowing a mouthful of dust, Haydn decided to follow suit. The only entrance on this side of the building stood under a black pomegranate-shaped globe. A black plate on the wall beside the glass-fronted door indicated they were at the *Apotheke*.

Inside, another brother in a black linen cassock stood behind a counter busily dispensing bottles of medicaments and packets of powder. Haydn and Johann waited, admiring the paintings on the low vaulted ceiling and the head of Christ above the wooden shelves behind the counter.

"Prescription, please." The friar approached them at last. "The prescription that the brother doctor gave you," he repeated when Haydn stared uncomprehendingly at him.

"*Ach* no!" Haydn said, understanding at last. "It is not medicaments we are here for, but information. We were told an Italian physician by the name of Goretti frequents the apothecary. Was he here today?"

"A while ago. Is he really a physician?" The friar stared at them in avid curiosity.

Haydn exchanged a glance with his brother. "So we were given to believe. He was recommended as being an expert in problems of the womb." He supposed Amelie's ailments could be categorized under that broad rubric.

"He cannot be much of an expert, then," the friar replied with a smile. "His own wife suffers from a number of ailments. He himself suspected child-bed fever due to her frequent miscarriages. But then he says the cold baths at Baden have provided great relief."

"What does she ail from then?" Haydn asked. Kaspar had spoken of Amelie's frequent fevers. He knew nothing of medicine, but if it were child-bed fever, surely a warm bath would be better than a cold one. Oil of almond or a spoonful of poppy syrup, perhaps.

"Most likely a wandering womb. We recommended a tincture of chamomile to soothe the irritability and a vigorous massage. The latter is best performed by a husband rather than a maid. The brothers instructed him as best they could."

"Why?" Johann wanted to know. "Surely, a maid could achieve the very same results."

"I rather doubt it," Haydn said hastily. The intricacies of the female womb were not matters he wished to discuss with his younger brother.

Small wonder, Amelie had looked so bright and rejuvenated after her husband's death. What expense might Kaspar have saved himself had he but known. "Where did the good doctor go, do you know?"

———

Rosalie had to resist a strong urge to hide behind Gerhard as he rapped his knuckles on the ancient door at the millinery's side entrance.

After what seemed like an interminable period, the uneven rattling of a bolt being pried open came to their ears. The door creaked open, drawn back with some difficulty, and Sabina's long, narrow features peered out at them.

"You!" she cried, staring straight into Rosalie's eyes. "What are you doing here?"

An indignant flush suffused the thin cheeks of the milliner's shop assistant. Her eyes roved past Rosalie as she spoke and stopped inches above her head. Her mouth stayed open, but the next words remained unsaid.

"You know her?" Gerhard exclaimed. He twisted his head around to face Rosalie. His eyes narrowed and his brow furrowed as he stared down at her. It seemed like an eternity before he turned away.

Rosalie felt more than ever like cowering behind him when she caught sight of a hint of a smile on Sabina's features. The shop assistant regarded Rosalie with a malicious glint in her dark eyes, then swept her lashes up at the tavern keeper. "She looks familiar, like—"

"Oh, I do recall you!" Rosalie straightened her shoulders, determined not to let the woman best her. "You came to the Esterházy Palace, didn't you? Was it yesterday?"

She didn't think Sabina could have any suspicion she had been followed the previous day. And as to the events at the palace, they showed the milliner's assistant in a much worse light than they did her.

The smile was gone from Sabina's features, and her lips puckered into a thin line. "I'm sure I don't know what you're on about. I have never been to the palace."

She looked down her long nose at Rosalie and sniffed. "I merely mistook you for one of the many maids who come here with jewelry pilfered from their mistress, thinking Madame Chapeau will aid in their misbegotten activities."

Rosalie twisted the corners of her apron, aware of Gerhard's eyes on her again. Sabina's spiteful remark had aroused his suspicions again, and she had barely allayed them.

Not that she could blame him. What else was the poor man to think? She'd been lurking outside the milliner's premises just yesterday. And been so apprehensive at the mere sight of Poldi this morning.

"Well, it is not Madame Chapeau she has come to see, Sabina," Gerhard said firmly. "The lass is here to look at your wares. You had not forgotten, had you?"

"Of course not." A veil of civility had by this time descended upon Sabina's face. She glanced down her nose at Rosalie again. "So, this is the girl. Captured your fancy, has she?" she muttered, loud enough for Rosalie to hear, although there was no telling whether Gerhard had heard the remark or not.

"Well, come on then." Sabina spun around. "I don't have all day." She led the way down a narrow flight of steep stairs, still speaking, "Madame Chapeau expects the shop to be ready at precisely eleven o' clock. That is when we open.

"Here we are." She stepped into a dimly-lighted cellar overflowing with goods and swept a satin-sheathed arm around the room as Rosalie and Gerhard followed her into it.

Trunks with drawers fitted into their sides were thrown open revealing lacy gloves, stockings, and scarves. Hats, the most elaborate affairs Rosalie had ever seen, hung upon pegs.

The lids on some of the hat boxes stacked beneath were left ajar. Bolts of colorful silks, satins, and printed linens lined a long row of shelves near a second shorter flight of steps leading up to the shop. Gerhard had already stepped over that way and was examining the fabric.

But where was the jewelry? And where could Her Serene Highness's necklace be?

"Have you no earrings?" Rosalie asked. "Or pretty bracelets or even a necklace?" She took a deep breath. "Gerhard—Herr Heindl—says Madame Chapeau's paste jewels are as beautiful as anything you could buy at one of those fashionable jeweler's in the Kohlmarkt."

Sabina tugged at her earlobe. Her eyes flickered to where Gerhard stood by the hat boxes.

"Earrings, you say?" She seemed to be having some trouble taking her eyes off the tavern keeper, who was now bending down to examine a quantity of rose satin.

"We have some of those. But wouldn't you rather look at some dresses instead?"

The assistant indicated a number of outfits neatly hanging from a row of pegs attached to a cross-piece in the ceiling. "Something like mine"— she ran her hand down her outfit—"would cost you next to nothing."

Small wonder, for who would wear a dress like that? Rosalie thought, eyeing the garment. It was, if anything, even more outrageous than the hat Sabina had worn the day before.

The skirt fashioned of wide strips of pink and red satin; the bodice all red; and the sleeves pink and all puffed up near the shoulder, but wrapping the arm tightly below the elbow.

She was still trying to frame a response when the tavern keeper intervened.

"She has set her heart on a piece of jewelry," Gerhard said, managing to knock the lid off one of the hat boxes as he straightened up. He was about to pick it up when Sabina scooped it up from the floor and jammed it back on the box.

"Do be careful!" she snapped. "Those are Madame's latest designs."

"A present for a friend," Rosalie added, watching Sabina. "Greta is—"

"Full-figured?" Sabina adjusted the mound of hat boxes. "I don't suppose a dress will do, then."

"No, but a hat might." Rosalie took a few paces toward the milliner's assistant. She was beginning to have an idea where in this vast room, brimming with all sorts of merchandise, the necklace might be hidden.

CHAPTER THIRTY-ONE

"I think you had better content yourself with looking at the jewelry." Sabina withdrew a pile of flat, round boxes from a shelf behind the hat boxes.

She arranged them into a tall stack and shoved them into Rosalie's unprepared arms."I doubt Madame's hats will suit your budget even at my rates."

"Madame's hats cost more than her dresses?" Rosalie gasped, reeling back. The boxes were light enough, but Madame Chapeau's assistant had rammed them against her chest with enough force to crack a rib, and she felt winded.

She would've fallen had Gerhard not caught hold of her arm and steadied her. "Easy now, Sabina!" he said as the milliner's assistant began to retrieve another pile of boxes from the shelf. "The lass can barely carry these

"Here"—he cleared some lengths of fabric cut into strange shapes off a small worktable and drew it closer to Rosalie—"set those down."

Rosalie did so, watching the milliner's assistant with some interest. Gerhard's mild admonition seemed to have displeased her no end. She doubted it had anything to do with her own interest in Madame Chapeau's hats.

"I would think a mere kitchen maid would be robust enough for anything," Sabina muttered as she thrust the jewelry boxes back and swirled around. Her eyes fell on the lengths of fabric Gerhard had cleared off the table.

"My sleeves!" She glided across the room in a single swift motion, snatched the fabric pieces off the chair, and placed them on a second worktable lined with ribbons in various shades of pink and purple.

"I did not think you would want them mixed up with your ribbons," Gerhard said simply, apparently as much at a loss to explain Sabina's behavior as Rosalie herself. Sabina's narrow features appeared more pinched than ever and a splotch of angry red burned in each pale cheek.

"Why does Madame Chapeau charge more for her hats?" Rosalie asked again.

"Because she manufactures them for ladies of fashion," Sabina snapped, turning toward her. "Pearls, emeralds, and other costly gems are sewn onto the ribbons."

"*Oh!*" Rosalie's heart sank within her as she glanced up at the hats on display. So *that* was how Madame Chapeau disposed of the stolen items that found their way into her shop.

She could only hope Madame had left Her Serene Highness's necklace intact. It would be impossible to track down each pearl, emerald, and diamond that had gone into its making.

Gerhard must have mistaken her sigh for disappointment, for he turned to Sabina with a determined air.

"They cannot all have precious gems. Surely, there are some with paste jewels. It'll be an extra crate of wine for you, if you let the lass have one of your cheaper hats."

———

"Herr Tomasini went that way." The footman Haydn had accosted with his enquiries threw open the garden doors and pointed a gloved hand out over the terrace.

Haydn stepped through the doors. The soft summer air caressed his features, flushed from the long drive to Schönbrunn. They had made excellent time, if Luigi, despite having a head start of ten minutes, had only just arrived at the imperial summer palace.

A vista of marble statues, neatly trimmed hedges, and areas of soft verdant lawn stretched out before him. The faint breeze was fragrant with the scent of a myriad flowers. He took a deep breath and, aware of Johann's anxious eyes on him, reluctantly returned his attention to the matter at hand.

"The Italian physician is within, I take it?" He turned in the direction the footman had indicated.

A small section of yellow was visible through the trees in the sunken

Privy Garden. The Cavalier Wing, he supposed. It had been built to accommodate members of the imperial staff. Although he doubted the physician was deserving of that honor.

"Her Majesty must esteem him greatly." Johann softly voiced the thought in Haydn's mind.

"He himself would have preferred a suite in the Belvedere," the footman confided, his voice low.

"With Count Kaunitz, the Imperial Chancellor?" Haydn turned to stare at the man, startled by the temerity of Goretti's hopes.

But the footman, made aware of the impropriety of his remarks, glanced away. "You will find the Herr Doktor on the first floor of the building that faces the Kastaniensaal," he said, his features impassive.

"Very well." Haydn pressed a gulden into the servant's hand and strode across the terrace, with Johann close behind, to the steps that led down to the Privy Garden.

They had but emerged from the grassy verge onto the road fronting the Cavalier Wing when a heavyset, panting form nearly collided with them.

"Haydn!" Kapellmeister Georg Reutter peered up at his former pupil, his heavy jowls quivering. "Is that you? What brings you here, my boy? And with your brother, too!" His penetrating blue eyes turned from Haydn to Johann. "Has this anything to do with that parcel of scores the Italian persuaded Her Majesty to buy?"

Haydn exchanged an uneasy glance with Johann. "I am afraid it is much worse than that."

"Worse? What do you mean, worse? Well, don't just stand there like a blockhead, boy! Speak."

Haydn exchanged another glance with Johann. He was Kapellmeister to the most powerful noble family in the Empire, but here in the presence of his former teacher's glaring eyes and furious features, he was reduced to a mere schoolboy. Johann gave him an imperceptible nod. It would be as well to take the older man into his confidence.

"Kaspar—the violinist who was recently killed—"

"I do know who he was, boy! I am not entirely a dolt," Reutter broke in impatiently. "What about him? Get on with it."

"Have you heard of his bequest?" Johann asked softly.

"The operas his uncle supposedly left him?" Reutter's eyes narrowed as he nodded. "That young turkey, Albrecht, gabbed on about it endlessly. I imagine the entire world knows by now."

Haydn turned to his brother. "Then, that must be how Dr. Goretti learned of the bequest." He turned back to his former teacher. "He has pursued it relentlessly."

"Why should he not?" Reutter demanded. "I knew that nincompoop had nothing other than the *L'Orfeo* he sold Her Majesty. And that was no doubt copied from the printed copy in the imperial library. I could tell from the diamond-shaped notes."

"The imperial library has a copy of the printed score?" Haydn could scarcely credit his ears. "Was Her Majesty not aware of it? Or His Lordship, Baron Gottfried, for that matter?"

"I could've informed her of it had she cared to seek my opinion. But no, Her Majesty is so taken up with this foreign nuisance, she takes no heed of those who have served her well for countless years before this nobody showed his face." Reutter's eyes bore into Haydn's. "I trust you were able to see through the deception, my boy?"

"Yes, yes, indeed." Haydn hoped his nut-brown complexion would prevent Reutter from detecting the color rising in his neck and cheeks. He should have detected the deception the moment he set eyes on the score.

"If Goretti copied the score from the imperial library—" Johann began.

"Then, Therese was right. He is not the scribe," Haydn completed the thought. "It is merely another matter that appears to be tangled up with this," he explained in response to Reutter's enquiring glance.

"But what of his n's?" he murmured, recalling the scribe's strange writing. "Are you certain you have seen the printed score in the library, Herr Chormeister?"

"Well, not with my own two eyes. But it must be there. Where else could he have obtained the score? Do you suppose he composed the music himself?"

"Oh, we are well aware of his abilities in that direction," Johann said with a smile. He went on to recount the anecdote Albrecht had regaled them with earlier.

"To be fair, anyone could've been fooled," Reutter acknowledged gruffly. "I myself considered it to be a work by Vivaldi with errors introduced perhaps by an inept copyist. Or by Fabrizzio himself."

"And what convinced you otherwise?" Haydn pressed his case close to his stomach. The notion that had just entered his head was causing a discomfiting heaviness to swirl around in his abdomen.

"He wrote something similar in my presence," Reutter replied. "I challenged him to it when he insisted he had written the work he showed Goretti that night at the wine tavern."

Haydn drew in a heavy breath. Dear God, surely they had not followed the wrong man? If only he had listened to Therese. "His n's, Herr Chormeister"—he pulled out a sheet of paper from his case and formed an inverted u, then drew a large circle on the left arm—"were they anything like this?"

Rosalie's fingers itched to examine the hatboxes. The hats within those were unfinished, Sabina had said, sweeping them aside to clear a path to the flat round containers in which Madame Chapeau's establishment stocked its jewelry.

She absently fingered a pair of earrings she had withdrawn from one of the boxes open on the worktable before her. At any other time, she would have marveled at the design: blue forget-me-nots with gold-tipped petals surrounding a tiny gold center.

She curved her finger around the long gold hook on the back of the ornament, twirling it as she pretended to inspect the hats.

There was not one without a gem of some kind affixed to its crown or to the ribbons wound around it. All precious, according to Sabina. Yet she had exhibited no unease at their inspecting one of those.

"This white one with the flowers is nice enough," Gerhard said, plucking it gently off its hook and extending it to Rosalie.

"Greta might like that." Rosalie glanced down at the carnation pink flowers that were embroidered around the wide brim of the hat. Were the pink sapphires on the pink ribbon genuine? She reached out to touch them.

"Sabina will take those off, never fear," Gerhard reminded her.

Rosalie nodded. Why had Sabina agreed to all that work? It must have required fine workmanship to attach the gems to the hat. Would it not be even more difficult to remove them without damaging the delicate fabric?

Her gaze shifted to the hatboxes. Sabina had been strangely reluctant that they should inspect them, yet the lids still sat ajar. The white-and-green hatbox Gerhard had accidentally bumped into was all the way at the back now.

Rosalie reached for the hat in Gerhard's hands and inspected the flowers on it. Sabina had spent the last half-hour trudging up and down the stairs, carrying hats, jewelry boxes, and dresses up to the store.

But she had not returned after the last time she'd gone up, and Rosalie had heard the dry swish of a broom. And now the wet thump of a mop being applied to the floor and dragged across. If only she could rid herself of Gerhard's presence for a few minutes—just long enough to examine the hatbox Sabina had set out of reach.

"It is a pretty hat," she said, turning her face up to Gerhard with a smile. "But"—she cast her eyes ruefully down—"it doesn't go with these blue earrings. If Sabina has some blue flowers to attach to the hat, perhaps. . ." Rosalie let her voice fade away, as though fearful the milliner's assistant would cavil at the additional work.

Gerhard took the bait. "It is but a question of asking her, lass," he said briskly, and taking the hat from her, he bounded up the stairs.

Rosalie waited until he was out of sight, then whipped across to the pile of hatboxes. Stretching over the mound, she reached across to the green-and-white one and pulled the lid toward her. It was surprisingly heavy.

Heart thumping with apprehension, she turned it over. She was no seamstress, but her sharp eye detected a bulge within the lining. She pressed her fingers lightly along the interior.

Yes, there was undoubtedly something concealed within the lining. She ran her finger along the inner edge. The bumps, small, hard, and uneven, continued all the way around. A necklace?

She felt around the circumference again, trying to ease up the lining. Sabina's voice rising in annoyance and the wet thump of a mop being set down startled her and she nearly dropped the lid.

Rosalie raised her eyes anxiously up to the ceiling, hoping Gerhard could keep Sabina grousing about the alterations a little while longer. But the sound of footsteps crossing the floor above suggested the tavern keeper and the milliner's assistant were about to descend the stairs to the cellar.

She cast her eyes down, searching feverishly for some kind of opening, and found it at last. A loose thread in the hem around the lining. She looked around for a pin or needle, but finding nothing of the kind, used her fingernail to pry the stitches up.

A light footfall was followed by a heavy creaking. Sabina had set foot on the top step. Rosalie had just time to slide the necklace out and shove it into her pocket when she heard Gerhard's heavier footstep.

Another creak. And a third. Growing steadily louder and closer.

Was there a paste necklace she could push into the open lining? She had been alone long enough for Sabina to accuse her of theft if the lid was discovered to have been deprived of its contents.

The sharp tap of Sabina's heels and the heavy thumping of Gerhard's boots rained down from above, interspersed with the loud groans of the wooden steps flexing. She cast her eye around in desperate search of inspiration.

CHAPTER THIRTY-TWO

"You scoundrel, you!" Luigi's angry snarl was clearly audible through the heavy paneled door of Goretti's bedchamber. The loud thud Haydn heard next as of a body being slammed against a wall quickened his pace. "Do you still say that snuff box is yours?"

Haydn burst through the door. Luigi's right hand was around Goretti's throat, his face inches from the other man's. "For shame, man! Would you kill a man and rob him, too?"

For a brief moment, the Kapellmeister found himself unable to move. Then the choking sounds emanating from the physician's throat and his bloodshot, bulging eyes galvanized him to action.

He rushed toward Luigi, gripped him by the waist, and pulled hard. "Let him go!" he panted. "It was not he who killed Kaspar."

"No? How came Kaspar's snuff box into his possession, then?" But Luigi's fingers had already loosened their grip. The physician shook himself free and coughed deeply just as Kapellmeister Reutter puffed in through the door, breathing noisily in short, heavy gasps. Johann waited behind him.

The crisis averted, Haydn leant heavily against a chair standing conveniently awry in the middle of the room. The rapid fluttering of his heart slowed, and his mind took in the disarray of their surroundings. The chair on which he rested belonged to the heavy oak desk that stood by the window.

Kaspar's golden snuff box balanced precariously on its side on the edge of the carpet, close to where the tussle had taken place on the other side of the window. Haydn retrieved it, then searched the floor for the lid with its twin emblems. He found it facing upward under the desk, partially concealed behind the front leg.

"Even if Kaspar's name were not etched into the underside of the lid," he said, approaching the armchair in which Goretti sat huddled, "there can be no doubt it belongs to him." He held the lid out to the physician, but the other's eyes remained stubbornly lowered, his head sinking deeper into his chest.

"There are only a handful of these in all of Vienna, commissioned by His Serene Highness, Prince Nikolaus Esterházy. Few people in the Empire would fail to recognize the double-headed Habsburg eagle or His Serene Highness's griffin."

Haydn paused. "Kaspar was never without his snuff box. It was on him the night he was murdered. What do you know of his death?"

Goretti emitted a hoarse sound, then cleared his throat. "I know nothing about it," he croaked. He cleared his throat again and raised his head at last. "You have manhandled a visitor to the imperial court. Her Majesty will hear of it, never fear!"

"Will she now?" Reutter strode into the room and took a menacing stance over the physician's armchair.

Goretti sank deeper into his armchair looking for all the world like a fox cornered by a pack of hounds. But his eyes continued to blaze defiantly up at them, and the corners of his mouth began to twitch into a sly grin.

The thought of his hunting gun flashed into Haydn's mind, and his grip on the snuff box hardened. "I doubt Her Majesty will have much concern to spare when she learns she was deceived into buying a copy of a printed score from her own library."

The physician's cheeks turned gray. "The *L'Orfeo* is not from her library, I swear it. That at least is authentic." His eyes desperately surveyed them

"I do believe he speaks the truth, gentlemen," Johann spoke softly. "Or thinks he does."

<center>~~~</center>

Rosalie wiped her clammy hands on her apron just as Sabina's heels clattered onto the cellar floor. The curls at the nape of her neck felt damp and limp; a slow trickle of perspiration made its way down her neck.

She reached up to wipe it as Sabina approached the worktable, a baleful glare on her face. Gerhard was close behind her.

"She has blue flowers of a kind, lass." The tavern keeper's voice boomed through the cellar. "See, if they will do."

"They are purple hyacinths, and they had better do." The hat in Sabina's hands made a dull thump as it landed on the worktable. She walked over to the second worktable, her heels tapping sharply, and tugged open one of its drawers. "It is all I have at the moment."

She returned to the first worktable with a fistful of the satin flowers and scattered them over its surface. "It will take me a good half hour or more to remove all the gems and to replace every flower with these," she grumbled. "And all for a few gulden—"

Rosalie let out the breath she had unconsciously been holding. She had thought Sabina was eyeing her suspiciously, but the milliner's assistant appeared to have noticed nothing amiss. Her plan might work after all.

"There is no need—" she began.

"No need!" Sabina sputtered, hands on her hips. "No need for what?"

"I meant that there is no need to make any alterations," Rosalie amended hastily. "The purple flowers don't go with the earrings any more than the red flowers. But"—she pointed to the hat rack—"the straw hat with the tiny green leaves and the white edelweiss will go beautifully with this paste necklace and earring set." Rosalie lifted the case up.

Sabina stared down at the earrings of green paste and the necklace with its pearl petals and emerald pendant. Her nostrils seemed more pinched than ever. Her face appeared whiter than a meadow of edelweiss.

"*That* necklace and earring set?" Her head twisted around toward the hatboxes behind her.

Rosalie held her breath. But the lids all sat properly askew, as though weighted down at one end. Gerhard was peering into the case in her hand.

His soft whistle of admiration startled both women.

"Madame Chapeau has outdone herself this time. I have never seen beads that looked more like pearls, and the emeralds are not half-bad either. They look genuine enough for all that they are paste, don't they lass?"

He tilted his head up toward Sabina. "You can keep the additional gulden I promised you for the alterations. The necklace alone is worth it."

Kapellmeister Reutter hauled an armchair over the carpet toward Goretti's seat and dropped into its cushioned interior with a muffled thud. "You had best tell us all, man," he grunted.

"I know not about the *Proserpina*, but the *L'Orfeo* is by Monteverdi. That is indisputable." Goretti sat up straighter, his face still ashen. "Even I know the music."

Haydn frowned. Once the *L'Orfeo* had proven to be a mere copy, he had not thought to more closely examine the *Proserpina*. There had been no need. The paper, the vellum, and the ink told the tale. Could the convent, unbeknownst to itself, have the score for *Proserpina* as well? His pulse quickened at the thought.

His attention returned to the physician. "Where did you obtain the scores?"

"You had best tell us all you know or you will get another taste of my fist," Luigi growled. He thrust his face menacingly close to Goretti's.

The physician drew back, wincing. "It was at the bookseller. The one on Singerstrasse."

"Surely not Herr Dahl?" Johann turned to Haydn. "He would not knowingly foist a copy on an unsuspecting stranger. The scribe must have deceived him as well."

"Scribe? What scribe?" Goretti stared up at Haydn, half-rising in his eagerness to receive an answer. He collapsed back into his armchair when Luigi growled at him: "Never you mind what scribe!"

"Was it Herr Dahl who sold you the score?" Johann asked at the same time as Haydn said: "How many more such scores did he claim to have?"

Goretti gaped first at Johann, then at Haydn, looking as though he was trying to decipher the score of an unfamiliar piece of music.

"Well, speak up man!" Kapellmeister Reutter bellowed.

The physician swallowed. His cheeks appeared more ashen then before. "It was not Herr Dahl. Not the bookseller himself, I mean, although I assumed at the time he was the source of the scores.

"The man I met at Herr Dahl's claimed to have purchased some old music retrieved from a convent that wished to rid themselves of the scores. The *L'Orfeo* and the *Proserpina* were among them. The only two operas in the lot."

Haydn's eyes narrowed. "If he had just purchased the scores, why was he so eager to sell them?" Tired of standing, he drew a chair close to Goretti and sat down.

"What other reason could there be to procure such music?" The physician appeared genuinely puzzled. "The operas had been reputed to be lost, and the man was quite certain of being able to interest some wealthy nobleman in the music.

"Of course being a newcomer to Vienna, he had no contacts. When he heard me mention Her Majesty to Herr Dahl, he approached me to ask if I would present him at the imperial court."

"And you offered to buy the scores instead?" Luigi's mouth twitched, then widened into a grin.

Haydn could scarcely restrain his own amusement. It would appear the scribe had studied his mark well. The physician, learning of Her Majesty's interest in the operas, must have been making his own enquiries at the bookseller. He exchanged a smile with Johann and noticed his old teacher Reutter's shoulders shaking with suppressed mirth as well.

Goretti glared up at them, chin jutting out in an attitude of defiance. "I hoped to make a profit on the transaction, yes. Why shouldn't I? He had procured the operas for mere kreutzers. I paid him fifty gulden."

"Then turned around and charged Her Majesty ten times as much, I'll warrant." Luigi emitted a disgusted snort.

"She was willing to pay it," the physician responded simply as though the matter required no further explanation.

"And so you made a rash promise to procure the remaining operas?" Haydn was so certain he was right, his voice barely rose above the tonic as he phrased the question.

"Not a rash promise, no." The physician shook his head emphatically. "I was given to understand they had been discovered as well, but when I returned to Herr Dahl's establishment later, it was to learn that all he had was a parcel of worthless scores from a Sister Mariana.

"Stolen apparently from the convent down the road. He neither knew nor cared by whom. The parcel had been delivered by an errand boy who received no payment other than a few kreutzers for his trouble."

"St. Nikolai," Haydn said softly, marveling at the scribe's forethought in arranging for an errand boy to deliver the music to Herr Dahl's establishment. Although he very much doubted the bookseller would have troubled to notice the man himself had he chosen to deliver the scores in person.

"And then, quite fortuitously, you heard of Kaspar's bequest, I suppose," Luigi said.

"It was shortly thereafter. One of the musicians at the Seizerkeller mentioned an unusual bequest his fellow had received. I would have taken no notice, dismissing it as drunken braggadocio, had Fabrizzio—the man—"

"We know," Johann interrupted gently. "It was he who sold you the *L'Orfeo* and the *Proserpina*, was it not?"

Goretti nodded, an aggrieved expression on his face. "He was happy enough with the fifty gulden I paid him until he heard—from those gossiping musicians, no doubt—the value the Empress set upon those operas."

As he spoke, the physician glared balefully at Kapellmeister Reutter as though the older man were responsible for his troubles. "At which point, the young ruffian demanded his share of the profit, refusing to sell me the remaining operas at anything less than the price Her Majesty had paid for the first two!"

Luigi's grin widened. "I suppose that was fair enough. And that prompted the little trick he played on you at the Seizerkeller, I'll warrant."

"The doctor brought it upon himself," Kapellmeister Reutter gruffly interjected before Goretti could reply. "He said at the Seizerkeller that if Haydn knew anything at all of music, it would take him minutes rather than days to determine the composer of a work of music. Fabrizzio merely put his claim to the test."

The physician's features darkened, and he drew himself up. "It was a rude trick. Most uncalled for. But it exposed him for what he is, a mere forger." He looked up at Haydn, the picture of indignant wrath.

"Either that," Haydn agreed, "or he has found the operas and merely copied them." Although that would not explain the music scholar's reaction—a mixture of anger and fear—upon the discovery that Kaspar's bequest was comprised of madrigals. Nor could it entirely explain his determined pursuit of the bequest.

After all Fabrizzio had killed Kaspar for it. And attacked—and nearly killed—Haydn himself. The recollection chilled and infuriated him at the same time. Every muscle in his body seemed to tauten as he twisted his neck to gaze down at the physician.

"Was it Fabrizzio who attacked Kaspar? Do not attempt to lie," he barked sharply as Goretti began shaking his head. "You watched Kaspar being beaten to death. Then you stole from his dead body. How can you presume to call yourself a physician?"

"There is no need for insults, Herr Haydn. Yes, I saw it all. What would you have me do? Confront a posse of thugs, all armed with truncheons?"

"Was Fabrizzio among the attackers?" Haydn wanted to know, although the answer was obvious enough.

CHAPTER THIRTY-THREE

"**A**rmed with truncheons?" Kapellmeister Reutter sounded skeptical. The words had caught Haydn's attention as well, but he had no trouble believing them. Or that Fabrizzio had not been present at the scene.

A faint rustling from the balcony beyond came to his ears, but he ignored it. A servant going about her chores, he thought, slowly stroking his chin as he contemplated the disclosures they had coaxed out of the physician.

"That at least is the truth, Herr Chormeister," he heard Johann explain. "Herr Moserle, the undertaker, divined as much when he examined Kaspar. The wounds on his body recounted the brutal tale only too well."

"And it was a truncheon that caused Joseph's injuries yesterday, wasn't it?" Luigi added, looking toward Haydn for confirmation.

Haydn nodded, glad he had not been too squeamish to attend to Herr Moserle's vivid musings on Kaspar's injuries and his own. Fabrizzio had not been present at the scene of either attack. Why should he be, if he had orchestrated both?

But it was not above an hour after the attempt that the music scholar had made an appearance.

Was it because the attempt on Haydn's person had yielded nothing? Albrecht had after all saved the music itself.

"What were you doing outside the Seizerkeller so late?" Luigi asked Goretti the question a bare second after it had occurred to Haydn.

"I had just left the tavern," the physician responded with as much dignity as he could muster. "There were no carriages to be had at that hour, so rather than return to the palace, I decided to walk to my lodgings in the city. The rooms are still paid for, although I have had little enough occasion to use them since arriving here."

"And it was then that you saw Kaspar being attacked?" Johann gently steered the conversation away from the physician's nocturnal routine.

"But never thought to seek help or call a police guard to the poor man's aid." Luigi sounded disgusted.

"I rushed to his side as soon as the ruffians left. What good could I have done while they were still beating him? They would have turned upon me with as little provocation."

The doctor twisted in his seat. "They were still raining blows upon him while one of the thugs rifled through his purse and flung it to the ground. A good stout purse of fine leather. It made no sense to me that the thieves should discard it."

"After his keys, no doubt," Haydn said softly, recalling the damage around the lock on Kaspar's bureau. The murderers had broken in that very night, then. The thought sickened him.

"And what little money he had." Goretti nodded. "The purse was empty when I examined it. Then I went up to Wilhelm Kaspar." His fingers encircled the ends of the armrests, the knuckles a grayish-white. "He was beyond help that much was plain to see. No pulse. The body beaten to a pulp."

The mere memory of the sight seemed to have caused the bile to rise up in the physician's throat. He swallowed convulsively.

Haydn waited patiently. "And the snuff box?" he enquired after a few minutes. He held it out for the physician to see.

"It had been flung to the side of the road during the skirmish, no doubt. I was about to flee the scene—"

Luigi snorted at the words, and Goretti turned toward him, stung to the quick.

"What would you have had me do? Had the police guards found me—a foreigner—hovering over the body of a dead man, do you suppose they would have hesitated to impute the crime to me?"

"I suppose not." the Konzertmeister made the admission grudgingly. His features darkened. "I have yet to encounter a more worthless bunch of scoundrels."

He turned to Haydn "Do you know what one of them—a bristle-haired dolt with the manners of an ass—said to me? That Kaspar must in a drunken rage have provoked the attack upon himself!"

Haydn's lips tightened, but he said nothing.

"And that dummkopf Pergen tells us his police guards keep the city safe," he heard Kapellmeister Reutter mutter behind him. "Worse still, the Emperor will hear no complaints against him or his precious men."

Haydn's nostrils flared at the revelation, but he forced himself to keep his mind on the matter at hand. "The snuff box," he said again through clenched teeth.

"I picked it up out of mere curiosity. I had scarcely begun to examine it when I felt a loud thwack against my head." The doctor's hands reached up to probe the area under his wig. "I still have the bump to prove it, if you—"

"There is no need," Johann said hastily. "What happened then?"

"I imagine the scoundrel who hit me made off with the purse. It was gone when I regained consciousness the next morning. But there the dead man lay right next to me." Goretti shuddered. "Naturally, I had no desire to be found in such close proximity to a murdered man.

"I staggered to my feet, making haste to leave before anyone could see me. Dawn was just breaking, and the streets were fortunately deserted. It was only when I reached my lodgings that I realized I was still clutching the snuff box."

"Did it never occur to you to return it to his widow or to tell his friends what you saw?" Luigi stood up and paced slowly around the physician's chair, his hazel eyes fixed on the other's person.

"Would you have believed a word I said?" Goretti retorted. "He would still be alive now if you"—he thrust his chin out at Haydn—"had allowed him to sell his bequest to me"

A scorpion lashing out in fury could not have stung Haydn more deeply than the physician's words. His chest tightened, the sensation flaring across his ribcage until he could barely breathe. The throbbing in his head deepened.

Through a haze of pain he heard Kapellmeister Reutter speak. "What will you tell the Empress, Haydn? She must be informed at once."

Haydn stared at the massive figure of his teacher. "There is no time for that," he said at last. "Fabrizzio must be found."

It was late afternoon when Luigi led Haydn to an oak door set within a low, pale cream wall on Singerstrasse.

"Fabrizzio lodges with Signora Padrona, I'll warrant." He lifted the heavy brass ring on the door up high before letting it fall. It struck the oak panels with a loud, ringing sound. "Any Italian who wishes to be comfortably lodged within the city"—Luigi took hold of the brass ring again—"comes here, for all that it costs twice as much as an entire apartment in the suburbs."

"A likely enough assumption," Haydn agreed. "He would have had to lodge nearby to study Goretti so closely and to frequent the convent while he worked there as a scribe."

He could only hope they had come to the right place. Goretti had professed to knowing nothing of his compatriot's whereabouts. And Kaspar's aunt dwelt too far for them to avail of any information she might have.

He studied the area while they waited for the Signora.

Set back from the wall, Signora Padrona's house stood considerably lower than its neighbors. Haydn could just make out the red shingles covering the twin gable roofs that peeked over the wall. St. Nikolai, his sister-in-law's convent, was a few doors to his right.

Across the street, on a diagonal from where he and Luigi waited, the glass-fronted doors of Herr Dahl's bookstore glinted in the late afternoon sun.

The Kapellmeister sighed. The Signora must be hard of hearing, it was taking her so long to respond. His mind turned to another matter. "I trust Her Majesty will not take exception to hearing of the affair from Johann."

It had been the only way with his old teacher insisting the Empress be informed of the matter at once.

Luigi, about to knock for the third time, glanced over his shoulder at Haydn. "I am sure she will understand that pursuing the villain responsible for the affair was more important than staying behind to apprise her of the details. Besides, Johann is likely to handle the situation with far greater delicacy than you, Joseph."

True enough, Haydn thought, beginning to smile when the door opened. A tall, slender woman, slightly above middle age, dressed all in black emerged from within. There was something so familiar about her almond-shaped, dark, hooded eyes and long face, Haydn could only stare.

"If it is lodgings you want—" she began when Luigi interrupted.

"We wish to meet a lodger of yours. A music scholar recently arrived from Italy. Fabrizzio."

"He is within," Signora Padrona said. She opened the door wider, stepping aside to let them in. "In the cottage behind the garden. Next time, come through the back. The gate is kept open during the day for my lodgers and any visitors they may wish to receive."

She led the way down a cobblestone path that ran through the middle of the profusion of vines and flowers that formed her garden to a tiny whitewashed cottage at the back. The blue door stood ajar, and after a brief knock, she pushed it open and set foot within.

"He will be in the parlor," she informed them, briskly crossing the narrow hallway to open the parlor door. Haydn was still wondering where he might have seen her when the Signora uttered a muffled scream and reeled back against him, hands clapped to her mouth.

"What is it?" Haydn asked, startled. But the Signora could only point wildly toward the open parlor door. He edged into the room with the middle-aged woman still clinging to his arm and nearly staggered back himself.

Fabrizzio lay sprawled on the floor, eyes staring lifelessly up at the ceiling. A small pool of blood stained the white nap of the carpet beneath his head. Haydn took in his matted hair, the bruises on his arms and chest, the forehead severely indented, and felt his stomach roil.

Sheets of music surrounded the young man's still form and were scattered all over the desk. Ink dripped in a slow stream from a silver inkwell tipped onto its side.

Luigi knelt beside the young man and clasped his limp wrist between his palms. "His body is still warm to the touch." His gaze drifted to the door—inexplicably open—at the rear end of the room. "It cannot have been too long ago that he was—" he swallowed, unable to continue. "Did you hear nothing?" he enquired of the Signora.

Fabrizzio's landlady shook her head mutely. "My maid and I were at the market. We had just returned when you and your friend arrived."

"I cannot understand it. Why—?" Haydn ran his fingers through his wig. The only man who could have wanted to kill the music scholar had been at Schönbrunn in their presence. His gaze fell on the desk. Had

Fabrizzio somehow discovered the lost operas? But that would mean someone other than Goretti and Fabrizzio himself had been after them as well.

"Beaten. With a truncheon just like Kaspar," Luigi said in a low voice. His eyes flickered briefly toward Signora Padrona. But she seemed too much in a daze to attend to her visitors' speculations.

Haydn nodded, turning his head to inspect the desk again. A ring of keys sat carelessly atop the sheaf of papers next to a leather pouch.

"Kaspar's purse and keys," Luigi said grimly, having risen to his feet. He set the silver inkwell upright. His eyes remained fixed on the dead man.

"I would say he has earned his just deserts. Kaspar would still be here were it not for him."

CHAPTER THIRTY-FOUR

The late afternoon sun blazed into the servant's hall at the Esterházy Palace on Wallnerstrasse. Rosalie sat at the table with Clara Schwann and Greta, basking in its golden glow.

"A gulden?" Greta said, peering down into the shallow depths of a round jewelry case. "Is that all Gerhard paid for Her Serene Highness's necklace?"

"And a crate or two of wine." Rosalie's lips twitched, then broke into a broad smile. The expression on Sabina's face when Gerhard had made the arrangements had been priceless. "It is the real thing, isn't it, Frau Schwann?"

The lady's maid nodded. "It is indeed!" She drew the necklace carefully out of its case, gently feeling the pearls and touching the pendant. "I still can't believe you managed to get it back. I would not have thought it possible!"

"But how could *you* know where it would be?" Greta pushed herself forward, her pudgy hands gripping the table on either side of her rounded bosom.

"It was because Sabina kept turning her head to look at the hatboxes." Rosalie smiled at her friend. Greta's mouth hung open ever so slightly, her blue eyes round with avid curiosity. "Sanyi and I would do the same when we hid Mama's things to tease her."

Rosalie's smile faded, the memory was so vivid.

She could still hear Mama's scolding tone in her head and feel Sanyi's small fist pressing into her palm as he stood by her side, cackling hard. A dry lump arose in her throat. She swallowed it.

"Mama always found us out because of that."

Her eyes filled with tears, but she brushed them aside. Sanyi was gone. Had been these six months. And there was nothing anybody could do about it. She felt the weight of Mama's letter in her pocket. Gerhard had handed it to her on the ride back from Madame Chapeau's millinery.

"It was sent to Eisenstadt," he said, looking closely at her. "I meant to give it to you yesterday, but what with one thing and another . . ."

Rosalie had taken the letter and dropped it unread in her pocket. She supposed she should have said something to Mama about being in Vienna, but . . .

Greta's warm, plump hand closed over one of hers.

"A guilty conscience does give itself away." Frau Schwann tightly squeezed the other, head bobbing sagely up and down. They sat in silence for a while.

Then Greta pointed to the necklace. "I'd have liked to see Sabina's face when Gerhard offered her a gulden for that." A cheeky grin spread over her face.

"But what if she had looked in the hatbox and accused you of stealing it?" The corners of Frau Schwann's mouth drooped at the thought. "And she could still do it, you know!" Her hand flew to her mouth.

"Oh, she can look in the lining of the lid all she likes," Rosalie assured her. "She'll find nothing." To think she had outfoxed the woman at her own game! She sat up a little straighter, the very notion going a long way toward restoring her spirits.

"Nothing but a paste necklace, that is to say. With beads made to look like pearls and paste emeralds. It was a bit of luck finding it, it was so like Her Serene Highness's necklace. I'd barely retrieved that and pushed the other into the lining in its place when she returned to the cellar."

"She'd have a lot more explaining to do if she tried to hurl accusations at our Rosalie." Greta thrust her chin out. "How she got her mittens on the Princess's necklace for one thing. Never mind, hiding jewelry in the lining of a hatbox lid for another."

"And it is Her Serene Highness's necklace, there's no denying it." Frau Schwann seized upon the explanation. "The design is the only one of its kind as her jeweler will attest. But—" She looked crestfallen again, and this time pressed both hands to her cheeks in dismay.

"What are we to tell Her Serene Highness when she asks how we recovered it? She'll never believe Frau Dichtler had anything to do with it. That dratted woman can do no wrong in her eyes."

"And what's worse, Poldi was in on the whole affair, most likely." Rosalie's features drooped as well as she recalled the police guard's presence at the millinery that morning. How could she have forgotten it? "Gerhard says he is Madame Chapeau's brother."

"Well, we have to do something," Greta burst out. "Do you think she's going to be content with letting the necklace slip out of her fingers so easily?"

"I did not think to find him dead," Haydn said, walking slowly around the parlor where the music scholar still lay supine by the desk.

They had settled Fabrizzio's widowed landlady in her own cottage. A glass of wine had done much to calm her nerves, and she had agreed to allow them to search her lodger's rooms before calling for the police guards.

What he expected to find, Haydn knew not. The operas, perhaps, or some evidence that the scholar had succeeded in retrieving them. At any rate, it had seemed imperative to scour Fabrizzio's rooms before the police guards arrived to remove the body.

Luigi stood by the desk, sifting through the papers on it. "It is hardly surprising, given the company he kept," he responded. "He must have been at work here—doctoring another 'Monteverdi,' I imagine—when he was attacked. There is an unfinished *Ariadne* here. The ink is barely dry."

He held the score out behind him. Haydn, crossing the parlor in no more than three strides, plucked the sheets from his Konzertmeister's fingers. "He mixes modes where even Monteverdi would not," he commented after a brief perusal of the music.

The great master had worked in a period of transition when the system of modes was giving way to a newer harmony. And although Artusi, the crotchety old monk, had taken exception to Monteverdi's experimentation with the old rules, there had nevertheless been a method to his madness.

"It is supposed to be the lament, is it not?" Luigi asked. "All he had to do was simplify the five-part madrigal. Why go to all the trouble of composing a new lament?"

"He may not have known quite as much about the great master's music as he claimed to." Haydn returned the score to the pile on the desk. The body lay barely inches from his feet, but he had no need to look down at it. The image of it was etched into his brain.

"I still cannot understand why he was killed? Deliberately, it would seem." He twisted his head to regard the door in the rear wall, still ajar. "The police guards will say no doubt that the thieves are grown even more bold, forcing their way into homes in broad daylight. But this seems too brutal for . . ." He expelled a breath, frustrated.

Luigi harrumphed. "The guards will say anything to shirk their duty. The ruffians he hired must have returned for their money. He either did not have it or refused to pay it, and they set upon him as well. That is all that happened here, Joseph."

"But they rifled through his belongings."

"In search of something valuable, no doubt."

"And yet their search seems to have concentrated upon his scores." Haydn opened the drawer on the left.

A ream of paper, such as had been stolen from the convent, was stacked within. Beneath it was a slim roll of bills. He fished it out.

"How could they have failed to notice this? It is not a lot of money, but it is nothing to sneeze at either."

Luigi was quiet. "If he hired them to procure Kaspar's bequest, they must have realized the scores were of some value," he ventured eventually.

Haydn considered the remark. The hired ruffians may have been rough, ill-educated brutes, but it would be a mistake to suppose they were entirely devoid of any kind of intelligence. He inclined his head.

This brief show of agreement appeared to encourage Luigi, who continued in a stronger voice: "Well then, is it not possible he offered to recompense them for their services with some of the items they had stolen?"

"I suppose it is," Haydn conceded the point. "He may have had the means to take lodgings at a comfortable establishment such as this but still not have commanded the resources needed to—" An image of Kaspar's bruised, raw flesh surfaced in his mind, and he found himself unable to complete the thought.

"I cannot tell how much money it would take," Luigi took up the thread of the argument, "but I doubt the fifty gulden he managed to squeeze out of Goretti would suffice for the purpose."

"And so they returned to extract their dues." Haydn stroked his chin. It was a sufficiently plausible argument. He scanned the room and then turned to look at Luigi. "The question is did they find what they were looking for?"

"The chest they managed to wrest from your arms yesterday is not here."

"No, it is not." Haydn glanced around the room again. Had the old merchant transferred the contents of his Italian chest to the one designed to replace it, then? "The chest Kaspar's aunt gave us—a shabby affair that originally contained the music—had a false bottom. I was quite sure. . ." He scratched his head.

"He must have had a false bottom made in the new chest," Luigi concluded. "Fabrizzio may have surmised that to be the case when he saw the scores in your hand."

"Then the operas are lost?" Somehow Haydn did not think that was possible. Why make such extensive references to Shakespeare's King Lear if not to direct their attention to the dusty, shabby, apparently worm-eaten case? He said as much to Luigi.

"The old merchant may never have possessed the operas," Luigi replied. "The madrigals would be valuable enough to anyone who recognized them for what they were. And the scenari you discovered in the older chest would serve to eliminate any doubts on the matter."

Haydn nodded, but the explanation did not satisfy him. The keys and the leather pouch on the desk caught his attention again. Had the thieves left them where they were or had Fabrizzio been examining them when he was interrupted? Why had he even kept them?

"It is fortunate that he retained them." Luigi must have divined his thoughts, for he pointed to the items on the desk. "There can be no doubt who killed Kaspar. And, in his death, some manner of justice has been served."

"I suppose so." Haydn's tone was resigned. He reached forward and drew the items toward himself. "We had best remove them and all the paper stolen from the convent before the guards arrive. I cannot imagine their presence will lead those men to any other conclusion then the one they're most likely to arrive at."

"I knew you would be able to help, husband," Maria Anna declared as Haydn and Johann delivered a quantity of vellum and paper into Therese's astonished arms.

The Kapellmeister and his brother had returned so late, Maria Anna had been forced to put the evening meal back nearly an hour. But she had not uttered a word of recrimination, mollified, no doubt, by the recovery of the convent's supplies.

"All recovered from the scribe, I suppose." Therese lurched unsteadily on one foot but managed to hold herself firm. "I was mistaken, then, about the man we saw with Amelie?" She lowered the stack onto the parlor table and turned toward Haydn.

Her eyes, a brilliant sapphire, seemed to plumb the depths of Haydn's soul before turning their gaze toward his younger brother.

"What man?" Maria Anna asked.

"The doctor I was telling you about," Haydn replied quietly. "It was I who was mistaken about him. He was not the scribe, but he knew who the man was."

Therese took both his hands in her own. "I should have had more faith in your abilities, Joseph." Her gaze included Johann in her next remarks. "Reverend Mother Catherine and the entire convent of St. Nikolai will be in your debt forever."

"The man should be punished severely. But I suppose the convent will want to keep the entire affair discreet," Maria Anna said.

"His role as a forger has been exposed," Johann replied. "I explained the matter to Her Majesty. But as to punishment. . ." he shrugged. "He seems to have received the harshest punishment possible. Brother found him at his lodgings, beaten to death."

"Beaten to death!" Maria Anna and Therese cried out in chorus. "By whom?" Therese's question mingled with her sister's: "Whatever for?"

"Those are questions I have yet to answer," Haydn said with a resigned sigh.

They continued to preoccupy him long after the evening meal was over and the rest of the household had retired for the night. He sat with Johann in one of the rickety chairs in Papa Keller's barn pondering the matter.

There had been something amiss about the scene he and Luigi had discovered that afternoon. If only he could lay his finger on what it was.

"His death should resolve the entire affair," he muttered. "Yet it seems to complicate matters still further."

The steady creaking of Johann's chair ceased. He raised his eyes from the pages of the journal they had discovered the night before in Wilhelm Dietrich's worm-eaten Italian chest.

"How so?" he enquired in so direct and forthright a manner, Haydn found himself floundering about for a response.

His chair teetered dangerously as he shifted uncomfortably in it. He braced his feet hard against the floor to steady himself.

"Fabrizzio was so savagely beaten," he said when his chair eventually stopped rocking. "I cannot believe a mere falling out with the company he kept could have caused such brutality."

"A more deep-seated grudge against the man, then?" Johann regarded Haydn, head tilted to one side. "I suppose it is possible. If it was money they were after, they had only to intimidate him."

"Moreover, there was a thick roll of notes in the drawer in his desk. Concealed under some papers to be sure. But it could quite easily have been discovered. Why not take that?"

"The only reason not to would have been if they were interrupted in the midst of their crime. But that seems not to have been the case."

Haydn shook his head. There had been no signs of a hasty departure although the music scholar had not long been dead when they had found him. "I am sure we would have heard something had the scoundrels still been within when we arrived."

"Is that what is troubling you, brother?" Johann set the leather notebook face down on the table between them. "The disarray suggests the thieves combed through Fabrizzio's study quite thoroughly. And yet even the most cursory search should have easily yielded the money he kept hidden."

"It felt staged," Haydn said, but the words did not adequately express what he felt. He hunched forward, chin cupped in his hands, elbows digging into his thighs, and gazed into his brother's eyes. "I have the same sense of unease His Serene Highness experiences when he hears a false reprise or a deceptive cadence in a piece of music."

"As though there is more to come." Johann seemed to comprehend the sentiment. "Do you fear that it is not over, then?"

Haydn straightened up, placing his palms flat on his thighs. "I fear someone wishes us to think that it is," he said quietly.

CHAPTER THIRTY-FIVE

Echoes of Haydn's comment, uttered so softly it might have been whispered, lingered in the still, warm air within the Keller barn. "But what more could take place?" Johann's voice, rising to a puzzled mezzo forte, penetrated the thick silence that surrounded them. "You have retrieved the quantities of vellum and handmade paper Fabrizzio stole from the convent and divined his reason for doing so. It was he who killed Kaspar. That is clear enough—"

"Is it?" Haydn interrupted. "Or are we being led by the nose to think that it is? To look no further. To accept the illusion presented to us."

"It was his hand on the note that took Kaspar out on the night of his murder," Johann pointed out. "And was it not at his lodgings that you found Kaspar's keys and purse?"

Haydn inclined his head, retrieving a ring of brass keys and a leather pouch, somewhat the worse for wear, out of his jacket pocket. He set the pouch on the table but let the keys hang from his forefinger. They twirled around, revealing a tiny gold key in their midst.

"Kaspar's bureau key," he said, indicating it with a quick tip of his chin. It sparkled and glinted in the flare of light the lantern spread around them. A stray beam struck Haydn's eye, piercing the dense fog clouding his mind.

He raised his eyes, meeting Johann's steady gaze. "Kaspar's keys hung from his belt. But the gold bureau key was always in his purse."

Johann frowned, clearly not seeing the significance of the remark. "Fabrizzio must simply have put them on the ring with the other keys."

"But the ruffians had already emptied the purse and discarded it when Goretti found it."

Johann's frowned deepened. "Yes, of course. It must have been with

231

the intent of seizing his keys that they attacked Kaspar."

"At Fabrizzio's instructions, or so it would appear."

"Yes— *Oh*! I see what you mean now. There was no reason for Fabrizzio to have been at the scene at all. He was quite sure of receiving the key, if he trusted his henchmen to do the job properly."

Haydn nodded. "Not only that. There was no reason for him to steal an empty purse. Nor any good reason for his stooges to return to the scene of the crime for it. They already had what they wanted."

"Yet he stole the purse. That much is clear, for you found it in his lodgings. He must have thought the bureau key would be in it."

Haydn could not but agree. "So he took advantage of its owner being incapacitated—" A memory interjected. "I could swear he had no conception Kaspar was killed in the encounter when we gave him the news."

He leaned forward, oblivious to the unsteady wobbling the motion set off in his chair. "Fabrizzio must have intended to meet with him, Johann. That is why he was at the scene."

"Why then did he sign his note with Herr Anwalt's name?"

"Someone set him up to it, I fear. Someone who is on the hunt for those operas; who took Kaspar's keys and thought nothing of planting them in poor Fabrizzio's lodgings.

"He must still be looking for the music. Unless"— Haydn's fingers tensed into a fist as he recalled Luigi's words—"he has already found it in the chest stolen from us. But I fail to see how. . ."

His eyes drifted toward the battered old Italian chest Kaspar's aunt had given them. Would a man who professed a fondness for *The Merchant of Venice* be likely to move his most precious belongings into a newly made chest? From the little Haydn had learned of the old merchant, Wilhelm Dietrich, he thought not.

His gaze wandered around the barn and fell on the old merchant's journal. He picked it up. "It is too much, I suppose, to expect that he recorded anything about the operas here." He gave Johann a feeble smile.

"I have read nothing of greater interest than his torrid dealings with the women he met on his trips to Italy." Johann pursed his lips. "He seems to have given no thought to his wife ever discovering his guilty secret."

"I suppose it was only natural for a man whose business took him abroad so much." Haydn turned the journal over and perused the script that sprawled carelessly over its stiff, yellowing pages.

"A woman in Cremona seems to have caught his fancy more permanently," he said.

"Yes, he bought her a house there," Johann said, his lips still pursed in distaste.

Haydn nodded, his eyes skimming over the entry in question. He flipped over a few more pages, deciphering their contents as quickly as the untidy hand would allow.

"And she—" His eyes were halfway through the next sentence before the words he had read sank in. His startled gaze collided with his younger brother's steady gray eyes.

"She bore him a child, Johann."

———

The evening's entertainment over, Luigi dismissed the musicians and hurried up to the Music Room. The violin concerto he had begun composing shortly before Kaspar's death awaited his attentions, and he was eager to return to it.

It had been a harrowing day. The sight of Fabrizzio's lifeless corpse, beaten and bruised, had brought back disturbingly vivid memories of poor Kaspar's body. But the satisfaction of seeing Kaspar's murderer brought to the same fate had somewhat eased his distress.

The guards, when they eventually arrived, had thought no more of the situation than that the music scholar was an unfortunate victim of the thieving bandits that plagued the city.

"The cutthroats grow more brazen with each passing day," one of them commented as he helped remove the body from Signora Padrona's cottage.

"Not much we can do about something like this," another one grunted in response to the Signora's frantic questions. "Keep your gates and your doors locked. It is the only way to keep your lodgers safe."

It was evident Fabrizzio's murder would receive as little attention as Kaspar's had.

"Just as well," Luigi thought as he sank into Haydn's chair and drew his sheets of music toward himself. The young jackanapes deserved no better.

He dipped his pen into the silver inkwell and tapped it against the sides to let the excess drip back into the receptacle. "Besides, the Emperor is more concerned with cutting the nobility down to size than with pursuing thieves and murderers."

Many an errant nobleman had been forced to sweep the streets along with petty thieves and other miscreants, His Majesty delighting in setting an example of his peers in this manner. The only exceptions were the assassins whose attempt on the Empress's life Haydn had fobbed this past winter.

They had been publicly executed.

"But the rest of us, mere mortals that we are, could be murdered in our beds, and His Majesty would think nothing of it."

He was about to write down a phrase when a hesitant knock sounded. The door opened to reveal a pretty, heart-shaped face framed with dark curls.

"Rosalie." Luigi gave the maid a feeble smile. The room needed to be put in order, he supposed. The candles snuffed out. "I will not be long," he assured her. "And I can put the candles out when I leave."

"It is not that, Master Luigi."

"No?" A droplet of ink made a splotch on Luigi's paper. He replaced the pen in its stand. Rosalie stood before him, twisting her apron. He waited expectantly.

"It is Frau Dichtler." Rosalie cleared her throat. "We felt Herr Haydn ought to know."

"What has she done now?" The Konzertmeister sank back into the cushioned depths of his chair. He ought to have known his troubles were not over. How could they be when La Dichtler was near?

———∿∿∿———

In Papa Keller's barn, the revelation from the merchant Wilhelm Dietrich's journal had driven all thoughts of sleep from its occupants' minds. The candles in the lantern burned low, flames sputtering dangerously close to the wax that was pooling around the wick.

But neither the Kapellmeister nor his brother took any notice.

"If there is a child, Johann," Haydn said, jabbing his thumb into the binding of the leather notebook, "a child that Wilhelm Dietrich wanted nothing to do with, as seems evident from these pages—"

"Then possibly it was he, not Fabrizzio, who was behind the assault against Kaspar and yourself." Johann gently prized the notebook out of Haydn's fingers as he finished his brother's thoughts.

He swiftly skimmed a few pages. "Wilhelm Dietrich's steadfast repudiation of his own child would be reason enough, I suppose, for the child to lash out against anyone his father appeared to favor."

Haydn nodded. What kind of man had the merchant been to reject his own offspring? His own long-suppressed yearning for a child, doomed never to be fulfilled, swelled within his chest, clenching his heart and lungs. Surely a childless man would seize upon any opportunity, any child . . .

"Wilhelm Dietrich's mistress was apparently not content to remain husband-less," Johann's voice checked his brooding thoughts. "She seems to have demanded that he marry her."

"A demand he naturally could not meet, having a wife already." Haydn gazed sightlessly at the lantern as he reeled his mind in. He was vaguely aware of the flames from the guttering candles dancing before his eyes but was too preoccupied to bestir himself.

"His mistress appears to have been well aware of his predicament when she entered into the arrangement with him." He sat with his chin cupped in his hand, fingers slowly stroking it in a broad, pensive sweep. "He cannot have fobbed her off with mere words."

"Money might have kept her quiet," Johann suggested. Drops of wax sizzling against the glass surface of the lantern caught his attention. He reached for a pair of fresh candles from a shelf behind him.

"It might have," Haydn agreed. He watched as his brother carefully held the new candles against the flare of the old before snuffing out the dying flames. "It would have to be a substantial amount given her demands."

"Do you suppose his lawyer handled the details?" Johann raised his head from his task.

"It is possible. It would have been the only prudent course of action under the circumstances."

Innumerable questions blazed through Haydn's brain all at once. The implications of Wilhelm Dietrich having a son had still to sink in.

At their last meeting, he had received a strong impression that Herr Anwalt was concealing some aspect of the matter from them. Was it this unsavory fact revealed to him quite by chance?

Had the payments to his mistress put such a dent in the merchant's estate, he could leave Kaspar nothing more than his most prized possession? Or had Wilhelm Dietrich so resented having to support a child he eschewed, he was determined to keep his music, at least, from his mistress and her son?

If so, it would account for his meticulous preservation of his scores. But had the old merchant's collection included Monteverdi's operas? The will, as he recalled it, had specified neither genre nor composer.

As the thought passed through his mind, his gaze fell on Johann sifting through the packet of letters, all written in a graceful, flowing hand, retrieved along with the leather journal.

One in particular seemed to seize his younger brother's attention. He smoothed it out and brought it closer to his eyes.

"She refers to a collection of operas here, brother." Johann proffered the sheet of paper to the Kapellmeister.

"*The legacy of Cremona,*" Haydn read the words aloud. "*And rightfully belonging to my son.*" That settled the question, then. The operas did exist. "But where are they concealed?" he wondered.

A most disquieting thought took hold of his mind. "Is it possible my assailants were after the chest and not the madrigals it contained? They let go of the scores all too easily, I thought."

"After a bigger prize, you think?" Johann's features' reflected his own unease. "If Wilhelm Dietrich concealed the operas somewhere in that chest, they are lost forever."

"Or until we find his son," Haydn said softly, beginning to have a notion who the man might be. There had only been three people after the bequest, and two of them were quite easily eliminated.

"Trying to get Clara Schwann dismissed, is she?" Luigi repeated Rosalie's words. He recalled the dustup about a necklace.

La Dichtler, he supposed, had acquired a bee in her bonnet that poor Clara was the culprit. That didn't surprise him at all. A more meddlesome woman he had yet to see.

His eyes, clear, hazel, rested on Rosalie's features. "Surely Her Serene Highness doesn't believe that nonsense?"

He had come out just in time to see her rousting the idiot Poldi out of the palace. Her manner as she swept him out could not have been more masterful, in the Konzertmeister's opinion.

"No-o." Rosalie bit her lip. "But nothing will persuade her that it was Frau Dichtler who stole her necklace."

"*What*?" Luigi's back stiffened. "Are you certain? How do you know?"

It was not news Haydn would enjoy receiving. The Dichtlers, husband and wife, had joined the opera troupe against the Kapellmeister's wishes. In vain had he remonstrated, Luigi adding his own voice to Haydn's protests on the subject. The Prince, however, had been adamant.

He returned his attention to the maid.

"I followed her to Madame Chapeau's millinery," Rosalie was saying. "She has a reputation for being a fence."

"Madame Chapeau?" Luigi frowned. The name sounded familiar. Hadn't Haydn been attacked in the vicinity of an establishment with a ridiculous name like that? "Is it near the Carinthian Gate?"

"Yes. And Sabina is Madame's assistant."

"Sabina?" Who was the girl referring to now?

"The girl who came here insisting she was the new lady's maid Frau Dichtler had sent for. Frau Dichtler insisted it was all a mistake. But it was not." Rosalie shook her head emphatically.

"No?" The softly uttered monosyllable seemed to spur the maid on. Luigi settled back in his chair as she plunged headlong into her narrative.

"So, Frau Dichtler knows a fence, does she?" He said when Rosalie, at last, paused to take breath. A soft smile played around his mouth. The news had troubled him at first. But the more he thought about it, the more it seemed like a heaven-sent opportunity.

What better means than this to rid themselves of the wretched Dichtler and her feckless husband? His Serene Highness could hardly be persuaded to keep on a thief.

"It was the necklace Her Serene Highness received for her name day, was it not?" he asked.

Rosalie nodded. "So expensive, Her Serene Highness had a paste replica made and only wore the real necklace on very special occasions. Had Gerhard—Herr Heindl, that is—not driven me there this morning, it might have been lost forever. Madame Chapeau takes out the jewels and attaches them to the hats she makes."

"*Ach so!*" Luigi said, liking the girl's gumption. "You have found a way of returning it, I hope." When Rosalie nodded again, he continued: "But you'll need Frau Dichtler out of the way when you do it? That is no trouble at all. I can find some means to keep her occupied."

And he would enjoy doing it, he thought.

Rosalie took a deep breath, then let it out. "But if Frau Dichtler were to find out—and I am sure she will. If Sabina doesn't come here to tell her about it, Her Serene Highness will. And then. . ."

"And then that idiot Poldi can earn his keep and take Frau Dichtler away," Luigi said. "The facts speak for themselves. Even Her Serene Highness cannot refute them. . ."

He had raised his voice, drowning out her objections, but something she said caught his ear.

"But Poldi is Madame Chapeau's brother, Master Luigi."

CHAPTER THIRTY-SIX

Luigi wrenched his head aside as a stout, dark truncheon, swinging from a hairy wrist, whirled through the air, landing with a bone-crunching crack upon the fragile bones of a face.

Who was the poor soul? Kaspar? Or Fabrizzio?

The sudden pounding in his head told him it was own skull being attacked.

He had barely registered the fact when his eyes flew open, encountering the still darkness of his bedchamber. *A dream. It had been but a dream. Nothing more, God be thanked.* He sat up against his pillows, gasping for breath.

When his ragged, uneven respiration slowed to a steady pace, Luigi allowed himself to return to the images his slumbering mind had conjured.

One in particular wavered before his eyes.

Armed with truncheons? Kapellmeister Reutter's skeptical tone echoed in his ears as he examined the hairy wrist that had haunted his dreams. A leather thong, secured to a truncheon, was twisted around it.

A police guard? Luigi frowned. They were the only men in the city so armed. His mind's eye wandered up from the hairy wrist to a coarse-featured man with dark, bristly spikes of hair. *Poldi.*

The thought caused Luigi to sit upright. His eyes widened. Had the brigands who attacked Kaspar been led by Poldi? Small wonder the police guards were helpless against their onslaught on the city.

It would be easy enough for Poldi! The wretched man was related to a notorious fence. As a police guard, he could force any petty criminal to join his murderous pack. Gossip about inheritances or expensive items being transported reached his ears quite easily no doubt, fueling his

239

illegal trade.

And Poldi was acquainted with La Dichtler.

The woman who had stolen Haydn's newspaper; who had persuaded Rahier to purchase Kaspar's bequest; whose own husband seemed to bear an unusual interest in the music. Had Haydn not caught a glimpse of Fritz loitering about near Herr Anwalt's chambers?

The thoughts dislodged a few more uneasy, half-forgotten memories from Luigi's brain. Frau Dichtler had been at the Seizerkeller the night Kaspar was murdered. It was a memory he had consigned to oblivion, his day with her had been so traumatic.

He recalled her passing by his table, a bottle half-full of wine in her hand. He had flinched at her touch and the sound of her wine-animated laughter. Had his own glass been a little fuller after that brief encounter?

He knew his mind had been quickly befogged after it. Never before had he been so drunk. If La Dichtler had drugged Clara Schwann's tisane, could she not have drugged his wine?

Luigi pressed his fingers to his forehead. His head was beginning to throb. How could the wretched Dichtler woman, or her husband for that matter, have heard of Kaspar's bequest? They had all been in Eisenstadt when the will was read.

From Fabrizzio? His father had known the merchant Wilhelm Dietrich, had he not?

But how had Fabrizzio, a stranger to the city, fallen in with Poldi and his gang?

Dawn had scarcely broken, bathing Vienna in a warm rust-orange glow, when Luigi hurried out of his apartment. He had almost neared the Kohlmarkt when his mind took note of the early hour.

He stopped uncertainly, glancing up. The sun hovered low in the red-tinged horizon. No time to be barging in on anyone unannounced, let alone the Countess of Kuenberg. Best to wait a while, he thought.

He paced around the fountain, fists clenched. Once; twice. Could Her Grace, ancient and wizened, be counted on to remember anything at all? He had wasted his time if the couple she claimed to have seen going up to Kaspar's apartment were simply an invention of her fancy.

Luigi circled the fountain a third time. Then, unable to contain his impatience any longer, he strode into the building, determined not to be turned away. The Countess no doubt habitually rose as early as he had this morning. She would receive him, he insisted to himself.

The raspy voice when he set foot on the landing took him entirely by surprise.

"Come to woo the widow, have you? And her husband dead no more than a week. You should be ashamed of yourself."

The Countess's door stood wide open. Her Grace herself sat in a wheeled chair before a table set with the remnants of a half-eaten breakfast.

"It is not her I am here for," Luigi said, stepping across the threshold. "Her husband was a good friend of mine. I was hoping, in fact, to meet you, if Your Grace can spare me a moment or two. "

The Countess tipped her chin at his uniform. "After another position, are you? Well, I have no money to spare. Even if I did, I could not pay you as well as Esterházy does."

"It is information I am after, Your Grace. And I could think of no better person to approach. It was just the other day that Haydn was commending your faculties. It would be a wonder if anything escaped the Countess of Kuenberg, he said."

Haydn had in truth called her a nosy, gossiping harridan, but Luigi saw no need to be too exact.

The small flattery had its desired effect. The Countess's shriveled cheeks spread into a wrinkled smile. "Katherl says I imagine things, but my mind is still as keen as ever," she said proudly.

"Haydn said you saw a man and a woman climbing furtively up the stairs. Was it on the night poor Kaspar was killed?" It must have been the very night his keys were stolen. The locks had been changed shortly after.

But the Countess seemed puzzled by the question. "A man and a woman?" she repeated.

"Your Grace has no memory of the incident?" Luigi's hopes, barely afloat, sank heavily. It had been a mistake to come.

"I have not forgotten it," she snapped, offended by the mere suggestion. "I was merely trying to recall which night it was. They all seem the same to me now."

She pondered the matter a few minutes more, then said: "I suppose it could have been on that night. Or not long after it. It was certainly not before it. Things were quiet then."

"What did they look like?" Luigi leaned forward eagerly, oblivious to the bald phrasing of his words.

"It was late evening! Do you think I saw enough to paint you a portrait? A silhouette against the glass panes on the door, that is all. The woman seemed like a brazen hussy, that much I can tell you."

"Indeed." Luigi held his breath. Anyone who saw Frau Dichtler might be tempted to characterize her as such.

"Her bodice provided so little cover for her bosom, it was entirely inadequate for the job." The Countess pursed her lips. "I suppose a man like yourself would find it attractive. Men always do, dumb fools that they are."

"Dressed provocatively was she?" Luigi grinned. That seemed like La Dichtler all right. "And her companion?"

"A stout man. Like a porcupine." The Countess seemed to have tired of the conversation.

But Luigi persisted. "A porcupine?"

"His head"—the Countess's shriveled hand circled the air irritably—"a big block with short, stiff spikes rising from it in every direction. The nose like a bulbous snout."

"*Ach so!*" Luigi murmured softly. He would wager every last kreutzer it was Poldi Her Grace had seen. The stubby bristles on his head were the first thing one noticed about him. Besides, there could not be two men in Vienna quite so grotesque as that vile police guard.

The lawyer fingered a gold pen on his desk. "Yes, Dietrich did have a son. I know not who he is. Or where." He raised his head, staring resignedly at the three men who sat before him. "He appears to have inherited his mother's grasping nature."

A single word penetrated Haydn's consciousness and sat uneasily within it. *Where?*

"What demands has he made?" he enquired, puzzled. "And how can you fulfill them if you know not where he is?"

The same word must have caught Luigi's attention as well, for his voice mingled with Haydn's: "Where would he be but Cremona? It is where he was born, is it not?"

The Konzertmeister had been making his way to the lawyer's chambers when Haydn's carriage rolled to a stop before it. Haydn himself had been too preoccupied to see anything more than the freshly washed cobblestones of the Graben, but Johann had espied Luigi approaching.

"There you are, Joseph," Luigi had said, hurrying over, the relief on his features unmistakable. But the confidences he wished to share had been forgotten in the revelation of Wilhelm Dietrich's closely guarded secret.

Now as he sat within the lawyer's comfortable chambers, Haydn threw his Konzertmeister a quick glance. What urgent matter, he wondered, had caused Luigi to venture out so early in the morning without his wig?

The lawyer had been speaking, and a single phrase arrested the Kapellmeister's wandering mind and reined it in.

"*Vienna*?" he repeated. "The boy was raised in Vienna? How can that be?"

Herr Anwalt sighed. His hand went up to his forehead, fingers massaging the sagging skin between his firmly drawn eyebrows. "She followed him to Vienna. Years ago when Dietrich abandoned her, she followed him, bringing her son with her.

"She threatened to go to his wife and reveal all unless he set her up within the city, with a monthly stipend for herself and the boy."

"*Ach so!*" Johann said. "Wilhelm Dietrich made all the arrangements himself, then. Brother and I were of the opinion that, being a cautious man, he would have used your services."

"So, he did"—the lawyer dipped his head in acknowledgement of the fact—"but being ever the cautious man, he had me deposit the payments into a bank account. In his name, but she had access to it."

Haydn leaned forward, grasping the edge of the table. "Do the payments continue now that he is gone?"

The lawyer nodded. "They are to continue during her lifetime. Almost all of Dietrich's estate is tied up in this affair. His widow fortunately takes no interest in matters of business and seems to have accepted the view that her husband's once-flourishing business has steadily dwindled."

"Surely, then, it would have been a simple matter to discover her identity and her whereabouts? She must go herself to the bank or send someone she trusts."

"Wilhelm Dietrich was my client, Herr Haydn. He trusted me not to pry into his affairs against his express wishes." A telltale vibration in the lawyer's voice suggested it cost him an effort to keep his tone even. "Nothing would persuade me to break that trust."

"Of course not," Johann interjected as always to smooth things over. "Brother only meant that it could be done now that Wilhelm Dietrich is no more. Surely his debt to her has been paid many times over. And if her son—"

"I fear her son might be a more dangerous man than anyone can conceive." Herr Anwalt grasped the edge of his desk, the wrinkled skin on his hands beginning to stretch tautly over his bony knuckles. "I have always feared—"

"We know," Haydn gently interrupted. "It is why we think he needs to be stopped before he does more harm."

CHAPTER THIRTY-SEVEN

"Has a young man by the name of Fritz Dichtler ever come by your chambers?" he continued briskly.

The sudden turn in the conversation caught the lawyer by surprise. He blinked rapidly, shaking his head as though clearing cobwebs out of his mind before responding. "He has indeed. You know him?"

"He is one of my musicians. A member of the opera troupe."

"Oh! He said he was representing a man of great wealth. I cannot say I believed him. Had I known he had come on behalf of His Serene Highness. . ." Seeing Haydn shake his head vigorously, he faltered.

"His reticence on the subject put my guard up, I am afraid." A hot flush of mortification suffused the lawyer's cheeks.

"And so you sought a substantial surety to allow his patron to examine the bequest?" Johann's voice drew the lawyer's attention.

"No, of course not. I merely stipulated any examination take place in my presence. Surely—"

"Fritz Dichtler was not sent by His Serene Highness, Herr Anwalt." Luigi's quiet voice sounded insistently over the low rumble of the lawyer's tone.

The color had drained from the Konzertmeister's cheeks, leaving them ashen. "You think Fritz is Dietrich's son, do you not, Joseph? I fear you may be right."

⸺⸺

"What can Fritz have done to arouse your suspicions, Luigi?" The question erupted from Haydn's lips the moment they emerged from Herr Anwalt's chambers. He steered his Konzertmeister toward the carriage waiting for them.

It would be better than talking in the street. Wagons rumbled down the Graben now; maids and housewives jostled past.

"It is not Fritz, but his wife," Luigi responded as soon as they had settled into the comfortable seats of the carriage. The coachman prodded the horses into a slow walk.

"I thought at first we had simply been deceived into harboring a thief. But it is far worse than that." Luigi began to recount the details of the soprano's attempts at theft.

"A bristle-haired individual, you say?" Haydn asked when Luigi mentioned the police guard Poldi. "I recall him. He was most eager to take charge of Kaspar's chest. Not something I would have allowed, naturally."

"He had only to bide his time, however," Johann pointed out. "We made no secret of the fact that we were bound for the undertaker's."

"I could not think where or how Fabrizzio could have chanced upon La Dichtler and her police guard," Luigi continued. "But it all makes sense now. If Fabrizzio's father really was old Dietrich's friend, he must have known who Fritz was."

"And sought, if I mistake not," Haydn continued grimly, "to take advantage of his knowledge. It has cost him his life, unfortunately. The only question is, does he have the operas?"

"We could have the maids—" Johann began, but Haydn had already begun shaking his head.

"It would be best if they were not involved. Fritz has proven himself to be a most dangerous man. There is no knowing what he might do if he thinks they are after his precious chest."

"What is to be done then?" Luigi stared earnestly at the brothers.

A small smile flickered at the corners of Haydn's mouth. "Perhaps an opportunity to steal them will entice him. Unless, of course, the operas are already in his possession."

"I know just how to do it." Luigi grinned.

He pulled a timepiece out of his jacket pocket and gave it a quick glance. "We had best hurry. In a few hours more, I shall have to keep La Dichtler close by my side while Rosalie returns Her Serene Highness's necklace."

"Where is Clara?" Her Serene Highness gazed curiously up at Rosalie. The frantic ringing of her bell had impelled Rosalie to climb hurriedly up, two steps at a time, to the Princess's bedchamber.

"In the kitchen," Rosalie panted out the words, hoping Master Luigi had arrived at last.

It was noon, past the hour when Her Serene Highness usually arose. Her bell had rung faintly once before, but Rosalie had persuaded Frau Schwann to ignore it. The return of the necklace required the Princess's presence in her toilette boudoir. And it was best done at a time when Frau Dichtler was not free to sweep in, unannounced.

"In the kitchen? What is she doing there?"

Her Serene Highness thrust aside the olive green drapes around her bed and swung her legs in a graceful sweep onto the polished parquet floor. The movement caused her hair, still dark despite her years, to uncoil itself. It tumbled down in glossy curls, cascading past her shoulder onto her white nightclothes.

"Making the cup of hot chocolate you requested, Your Serene Highness," Rosalie replied, hoping the excuse would suffice. The Princess had made no such request that morning. Or the night before. Her frown suggested she had trouble recollecting it, but she accepted the statement without remark.

"She asked me to help you into the toilette boudoir."

"She must have great confidence in your abilities." The Princess pushed herself to her feet and led the way into the boudoir. "You are one of the kitchen maids, are you not?"

She glanced over her shoulder at the maid and at Rosalie's nod continued: "Unable to make a good cup of chocolate, are you?"

"No, Frau Schwann merely thought . ." Rosalie faltered, feeling foolish.

Frau Schwann could just as easily have returned the necklace. But Her Serene Highness's fledgling suspicions would only be strengthened if the stolen necklace were miraculously discovered by the very person suspected of stealing it.

The Princess glided toward the marble-topped dressing table.

"You may dress me," she said, sinking into the upholstered bench standing in front of it. "But I will not have any hands beside Clara's attend to my hair, do you understand?"

She gazed into the tall, gilt-framed mirror above the dressing table. Her blue eyes, kind and shrewd, held a hint of humor as they met Rosalie's violet orbs in the polished glass.

"Yes, Your Serene Highness." Rosalie was glad to be spared the task. An uncomfortable flush spread over her cheeks as the Princess continued to regard her in the mirror. Had she divined something was amiss?

Rosalie's own gaze shifted toward the door. When would Frau Schwann arrive? Despite the instructions the lady's maid had issued, Rosalie was not sure she was quite up to the task of dressing the Princess.

"My gowns are in the closet." The Princess waved a graceful hand in the direction of the white double doors in the wall behind Rosalie. "Behind you," she said again when Rosalie wavered.

Rosalie smoothed down her apron and slowly turned around, aware of Her Serene Highness's eyes on her. The necklace she had retrieved from Madame Chapeau's establishment felt heavy in her pocket, weighing her entire body down.

She forced herself to walk to the closet and open the doors. A dazzling array of gowns in expensive silks and satins hung before her.

"Has Clara told you which gown I am to wear?" The Princess's musical alto startled her. "It would be most remiss of her if she has not. But Clara is nearly as old as I am, and quite forgetful besides."

"It is the peacock-colored dress," Rosalie replied, made nearly breathless by the spectacular swell of rich purples, gorgeous crimsons, and brilliant blues; all barely contained within the closet.

"There it is!" Her Serene Highness's voice, ringing out behind her, made her flinch.

It took Rosalie a moment to see it, tucked between an emerald-green silk and a rose-hued satin. She reached a tentative hand up, fingers brushing against the rich folds of fabric. Her other hand drifted toward her pocket. Was Her Serene Highness still looking at her? She cast a quick glance at the mirror.

Her gaze collided with the Princess's

"Yes, that is the one. Bring it down!"

If only Her Serene Highness would look away. Rosalie hardly knew how to retrieve the necklace from her pocket without being caught in the act. Where could Frau Schwann be? Without her, the plan they had devised was sure to fail. And unless the necklace was returned this morning, Frau Dichtler would soon get wind of its recovery . . .

An annoyed furrow creased the Princess's forehead, and she opened her mouth to speak when a soft knock sounded on the door.

Frau Schwann entered the room bearing a tray with a silver pot and a ceramic cup.

"Here is your chocolate, Your Serene Highness. *Oh dear!*" Her round features proclaimed her alarm. "I didn't think you would still be undressed." She hurried over to the dressing table, set her tray down, and bustled over to the closet.

"Here let me bring that down." Frau Schwann reached for the peacock-colored silk gown, her ample hip nudging Rosalie unceremoniously out of the way and into the closet. A soft thud followed. The sound of metal hitting the parquet floor.

"What was that?" The Princess swept across the room.

"Your Serene Highness's necklace!" Frau Schwann cried, feigning astonishment. "How did it get there?"

Rosalie bent down to pick up the piece of jewelry she had dropped. "It must have been caught up in the dress." She held her palm out as she straightened up.

"This is not the paste replica, Clara!" Her Serene Highness's eyes when she looked up were startled. "It is the necklace you lost on the way to the bank."

Frau Schwann's hand flew to her mouth. "I must have taken the paste necklace to the bank and forgotten that one here with your dress."

Her Serene Highness frowned. "But I thought—"

"That is exactly what must have happened, Frau Schwann," Rosalie hastily interjected. Best that the Princess didn't recall the incident in Leopoldsdorf. There was no explaining that away. Although her quick mind had already divined a method to remedy the problem.

"Well, I am glad it is found," Frau Schwann declared. "But come, Your Serene Highness. Let us get you dressed."

"I would like it taken to the bank, Clara. At once. Ring for Elsa."

"No!" Rosalie cried sharply. "I m-mean," she stuttered as the Princess's head jerked up in her direction. "I mean that Master Luigi said they were on no account to be disturbed. Frau Dichtler is with him, preparing for the evening's entertainment."

She clutched at the corners of her apron, hoping that at least was true.

The Princess sighed. "Then, I suppose I shall have to do it myself. Have the carriage prepared as soon as I am dressed, Clara."

"You have somewhere to be, Frau Dichtler?" Luigi enquired, his tone all innocence. He sat, fingers poised above the harpsichord in the Music Room, ready to play the same phrase that had occupied their entire practice.

"Not at all. I am entirely at your disposal this morning, Herr Tomasini," the soprano said sweetly enough, although the Konzertmeister thought he heard an irritated sigh as she twisted her head back from the door and gazed down at him.

"Shall we sing the phrase again?" Luigi suppressed the twitching of his mouth. The appoggiatura, he had known, would trip La Dichtler up. The woman could barely read music. "The first note must be sung on the beat. It is part of the melody."

"Then why not write it as such instead of as a small note," the singer grumbled. "One naturally treats those as incidental, and of no significance at all."

But she dutifully sang the phrase again, although her eyes kept wandering, he noticed, to the wooden chest on Haydn's desk. Luigi had found it in Papa Keller's barn, Haydn being loath to part with either the chest Dietrich had brought back from his travels in Italy or the madrigals the merchant had left his nephew.

"I am still inclined to believe it conceals the operas," the Kapellmeister had said. "It would be a mistake to allow Fritz to get his hands on it."

It had taken the better part of an hour, but with Frau Haydn and her sister, the nun, lending a hand to the effort, they had succeeded in copying a substantial number of them.

The changes made had been sufficient for the scores to hold up to a cursory inspection. Frau Haydn's sister had even offered up some of the paper he and Haydn had retrieved from Fabrizzio's lodgings.

"They will lend the deception greater credence," she had said with a twinkle in her lovely blue eyes.

"Continue, please." Luigi motioned with his head as La Dichtler came to the end of the phrase. Her voice warbled and wavered, then grasped the next note.

"Excellent!" he said when the piece had come to a close. "Now, if we could add some emotion—"

"I am tired, Herr Tomasini. And my voice is dry. Won't you be a dear and—"

"I will ring for some water." Luigi smiled broadly. She would not be rid of him quite so easily. It was not yet time for the trap to be sprung.

He strode easily to the bell pull near the door and gave it a quick tug. When he returned, it was not to the harpsichord but to the chair by Haydn's desk. He sank into it and stretched his legs out.

La Dichtler had already made herself comfortable in the chaise between the instrument and the desk. Her eyes, he noticed, were riveted on the chest.

"Opera scores," he explained, drawing the chest toward himself and brushing off some of the dust that still clung to it. "There seems to be a renewed interest in the works of a composer by the name of Monteverdi."

"I have heard of him, Herr Konzertmeister." The soprano sounded annoyed. "I am an opera singer after all."

"Yes, of course. And you sang his *Lament of Ariadne* the other night. A remarkable performance. His Serene Highness called me aside himself to commend me on it." The Prince had done no such thing, but it was a small lie.

It caught La Dichtler's attention, however. Her gaze shifted toward him, eyes narrowed enough to cause a small frown to appear between her delicately drawn eyebrows. She said nothing, and Luigi continued, barely pausing to take a breath.

"His Serene Highness was keen to know whether we had any plans to perform the opera itself—"

"How could we, when it is lost? Along with most of his other works." But La Dichtler's eyes had widened with ill-concealed interest.

Luigi's lips broadened involuntarily into a smile. "They appear to have been found." He patted the chest. "The music is old. Ill-suited to modern ears, perhaps. Haydn has asked me to peruse the scores—"

"All of them?" La Dichtler interrupted, appearing to have trouble withdrawing her eyes from the chest. "They are all there?" She tipped her chin toward Luigi's desk, sounding breathless.

"I believe so." Luigi lifted the rusted hasp and brought out a sheaf of the papers, holding them out toward the soprano. She peered at them, sitting perilously close to the edge of her own chair, mouth parted.

Luigi replaced the scores in the chest. "Haydn will be by tomorrow to discuss the changes necessary. The tempo will undoubtedly have to be quickened. As for the ornaments—"

"You don't mean to make the changes on the score, do you?" Luigi could have sworn the woman seemed stricken with horror.

"Where else would we make them?" he asked, his tone as guileless as he could make it.

Naturally, neither he nor Haydn would dream of writing on scores purported to be in the great master's hand. Any more than they would consider painting over the Auerbach that hung in His Serene Highness's receiving chamber.

No need for La Dichtler to know that, however.

"I may even begin some of the work now unless. . ." He made a reluctant gesture toward the harpsichord.

She rose at once. "I think we had better rehearse that piece again, Herr Tomasini. Especially if you would like me to sing it this evening."

CHAPTER THIRTY-EIGHT

"They are valuable at least. That is some comfort." Haydn returned the madrigals to the apparently worm-eaten chest that had concealed evidence of the old merchant's sordid liaisons and his illegitimate offspring.

After Luigi's departure that morning, he and Johann had spent the day poring closely over the scores from Kaspar's bequest.

It was plain to see the great master had been attempting a set of madrigals that were derived directly from the operas written for the Mantuan court.

"I saw no reason to raise Her Majesty's hopes yesterday regarding the discovery of the operas," Johann replied, handing over the scenari they had used to put the madrigals in some kind of order.

"But it is likely those"—he motioned toward the scores with his head—"will restore her spirits greatly."

"And soothe the Mantuans too, I hope," Haydn said, recalling the details Baron van Swieten had shared with them. "Although they will undoubtedly carp at the fact that the collection excludes his last three operas."

"The three Venetian operas? They must have been so well known to audiences in the city, he saw little reason to replicate the material."

Haydn nodded. That might well have been the case. Unlike the Mantuan operas intended for a private ducal audience, *Poppea*, *Ulisse* and *Nozze d'Enea* had been written for the public opera houses.

"Or he was too infirm to attempt anything of the sort," he suggested. They had been written, after all, barely three years before the great master's passing.

Whatever the case, he doubted the madrigal versions of the three

Venetian operas were missing. Far more likely they had never existed. Wilhelm Dietrich's possession of the scenari for those operas as well could only mean one thing.

They had been intended to aid in the authentication of the operas. Not the madrigals. His pulse quickened as he closed the lid, snapping the hasp into place.

"Although I doubt any sense of infirmity would prevent him beginning the work." Therese's dulcet tones interrupted his thoughts. She stood smiling by the door, a case in her hand.

"He seems to always complain of ill-health in his letters," she explained with a smile when the brothers glanced up at her.

"Will Reverend Mother Catherine allow your return?" Johann inclined his chin at the valise of plain brown leather in the nun's hands as he rose from his seat.

Her brow crinkled, then cleared as memory returned. "Ah, the cold sister feigned on my behalf yesterday!" Therese's smile widened. "My return to health can hardly be surprising. Sister's healing potions have been known to do their work in a day."

"And the Reverend Mother will be in need of your voice and not ask too many questions, I imagine." The small jest allowed Haydn to forget the strange awkwardness that afflicted him.

He stifled a strong desire to shuffle his feet. A decade earlier their parting had been rife with recriminations. He had felt betrayed, then. But now. . . He scarcely knew what to feel.

The silvery tinkle of her laughter dissolved all traces of tension. "No, she will not." She came into the room and, more sober now, grasped both him and Johann warmly by the hand.

"I cannot thank you sufficiently for what you have done. There have been rumblings of the Emperor's discontent with the convents and monasteries. We serve no purpose, His Majesty says. The slightest hint of any impropriety. . ."

"There is little to fear as long as Her Majesty is alive, Therese," Haydn assured her, his ability to do so placing him on a firmer footing. "I will let her know that were it not for one of the nuns of St. Nikolai, the deception Fabrizzio perpetrated on Goretti and herself would have eluded discovery."

Her sapphire eyes held his. "That is kind of you." She stretched her hand out to him, fingers lightly brushing the gold embroidery on his jacket.

"I hope you find your operas, Joseph. If they are to be found, that is," she added with a gentle smile.

———

Maria Anna poked her head around the door before he could respond. "The carriage is here, husband!" His look of surprise propelled her hands onto her hips. "Surely, you were not thinking of letting her go alone."

"No, of course not," Haydn said hastily before further recriminations could follow. He allowed himself to be bustled out of the parlor like a stray hen.

He had no objection to escorting his sister-in-law back to St. Nikolai. Although, since she had come from the convent without his help, he could not fathom why she should need it to return.

Her last words to him, and the skeptical tone in which they had been uttered, chafed Haydn no end. There was no doubt the operas existed. How could they not after all the mayhem the bequest had caused?

Besides, all the rigmarole with the English play and the caskets must mean something, he muttered to himself.

"We will find out soon enough where they are, brother." Johann's quiet voice penetrated his consciousness. "Fritz would not be after them if they did not exist."

"No, he would not." Haydn squinted against the bright sunlight that blazed uncomfortably into his eyes as he stepped out onto the courtyard. But he was beginning to doubt the operas were in the casket the young tenor had stolen from him.

Why else had Wilhelm Dietrich taken such pains to make the chest he had acquired on his travels appear worm-eaten? It could not merely have been to prevent his wife peering within and detecting his secret. Yet the false bottom had contained nothing but a packet of letters and the old merchant's journal.

"And the reference to them in his mother's letters to the old merchant"—Johann's voice interrupted the Kapellmeister's reverie again—"could not have been clearer."

Haydn nodded. "Unless"—the thought brought a smile to his lips—

"she is anything like our Frau Dichtler and managed to mistake a parcel of madrigals for a set of operas."

He watched as Maria Anna opened the gate and peered out. There were no signs of a carriage outside, and her muttered grumblings told him it had yet to arrive. His wife, as usual, had exaggerated, hustling them out of the comfort of the parlor before the need arose. He was too preoccupied, however, to be irked by it.

Another thought occurred to him, and he glanced over his shoulder at his brother. "The bank Herr Anwalt mentioned. It is on Singerstrasse, is it not?"

"What business have you at the bank, husband?" Maria Anna's voice cut in sharply just as Johann nodded. They had been speaking in such low tones, Haydn had not thought it likely that his wife, still standing by the gate, could overhear their conversation.

"It is where Wilhelm Dietrich's mistress goes to collect her payments," he explained. "The bank manager—"

Maria Anna uttered a snort. "I doubt the bank manager will reveal her whereabouts to you so easily, husband. I have heard he hoards information as though it were gold. Besides, Wilhelm Dietrich will have enjoined him to be discreet."

"Signora Padrona might have more information, Joseph," Therese chimed in, stepping quickly back as Maria Anna closed the gate with a loud clang. "And be more willing to help. She has dwelt in the vicinity twenty years or more. It is more than likely the woman you seek lodged with the Signora when she first arrived."

"*Padrona.*" Maria Anna sniffed again as she turned around. "An assumed name, if ever I heard one. It means 'mistress,' I believe."

At Haydn's stare of surprise, she went on: "It is the only bit of Italian I recall from the lessons we had from some singer or other Papa hired for us. He was convinced we needed Italian to succeed at the task."

But the Kapellmeister had already ceased to listen.

The iron gate that led into the ancient stone walls of St. Nikolai clanged firmly behind Therese. The nun who had responded to their knock allowing them only the briefest farewell before nudging Therese in and drawing the gate shut.

Haydn blinked as it swung past his nose but took no offence at this abrasive dismissal. It would be most unseemly for a nun to be seen lounging by the gate in conversation with two strangers. Besides after Maria Anna's strange suggestion, he was curious to renew his acquaintance with Signora Padrona.

They had no sooner turned their steps toward the lady's cream-colored dwelling with its twin gable roofs when Johann, discerning the Kapellmeister's thoughts with his usual perspicacity, asked: "Do you suppose sister-in-law was right?"

Haydn considered the question, merely raising his head slightly as an indication of having heard it. Thanks to Porpora, his Italian was sufficiently up to the task of setting an entire opera to music. But he had never needed it for more than that, and the nuances of daily speech still eluded him.

"I cannot tell. Whoever she is, she has bested old Wilhelm Dietrich and could certainly be called mistress of the situation," he began slowly after they had walked a few paces down the narrow street. "And a woman who runs an inn or provides lodgings as does the Signora could also be called *padrona*.

"But a man's lover, a kept woman, is more commonly referred to as a *mantenuta*."

"It is not a name any woman would wish to assume," Johann said, his rejection of the idea quick and emphatic.

"No," Haydn agreed. No woman he knew would care to degrade herself so in the eyes of the world.

"I fear it was merely Maria Anna's prejudice speaking," he said after a while. "Besides, it would be too much of a coincidence that the first Italian woman we have encountered in the city should turn out to be Wilhelm Dietrich's mistress."

But he had no sooner voiced the thought than he saw a familiar satin-clad form sweeping into a waiting carriage.

"Elsa Dichtler!" Johann's voice seemed explosively loud to his ears. "What business could she have here on Singerstrasse?"

"It is what I would dearly like to find out," the Kapellmeister replied, his voice grim. His eyes took in their surroundings. They were but a few steps away, he realized, from their destination. Signora Padrona's house—low, set back from the street—was not easily visible even from a distance of a few paces.

"I imagine she came to visit her mother-in-law." He gazed after the soprano's departing carriage; Maria Anna's supposition beginning to take deeper hold of his mind now.

———

"What is it now?" Anger lent a harsh edge to Signora Padrona's voice. She wrenched open the oak door, then took a step back in surprise at the sight of the Kapellmeister and his brother.

Her hooded eyes opened a little wider and her features, roughened with irritation, smoothed themselves out. "I beg your pardon. I thought you were—"

"Frau Dichtler," Haydn interjected without hesitation. "You appear not to like her."

If the Signora was surprised by the Kapellmeister's ready conjecture, she showed no signs of it.

"How could I?" she replied in a matter-of-fact tone. "There is little enough to like about that one."

"Your son might disagree," Johann pointed out, although Fritz exhibited no more signs of marital fidelity than did his wife.

"He sees through her well enough now," Signora Padrona said sharply as soon as he had finished, then glanced up in open curiosity. "You know him?"

At Johann's nod, she went on: "I would ask how you made his acquaintance. But you are musicians as well, so it is no surprise."

She opened the door a little wider, turning her nearly lidless dark eyes up to Haydn at the same time. "What brings you here again?"

"The need for some information." Haydn followed her into the courtyard. "About a fellow compatriot of yours," he elaborated as her brow lifted up, revealing some more of the lustrous pupils that usually hid behind them.

"Who is it?" she asked, leading them past a row of densely flowering shrubs that separated her cottage from the lodgings she let out at the back.

"A woman who arrived in the city some twenty years ago." Johann paused briefly to admire the pink blooms of Alpine rose that covered the shrubs.

"I have been here as long as that." She threw them a quick glance over her shoulder as she stepped across the threshold of her cottage. "But people come and go. I cannot claim to know every Italian who comes into the city."

"No, of course not," Haydn began, then stopped short, his eyes arrested by the chest that stood in full view directly across the room. "What is that?" he asked, having trouble uttering the words.

It was plain to see what it was, but he had not expected to see it displayed quite so brazenly in the Signora's parlor.

"Was it Fabrizzio who brought that here?" He heard Johann ask the question, and almost wished that was the case. If not, it would mean. . .

The Signora looked past them to see what had attracted their attention. "That chest? It belongs to my son. It has nothing to do with Fabrizzio." She planted herself before them. "Now what was it you wanted to know? This Italian woman you mentioned?"

"I believe we have found her." Haydn's head swiveled slowly toward the Signora's long, narrow face. "You were involved, were you not, with the merchant Wilhelm Dietrich?"

The Signora regarded him, her eyes cold as stone. "I have no husband to defend my honor, Herr Haydn. But surely the misfortune of widowhood does not merit such a scurrilous attack on my person? In my own home at that!"

Haydn was momentarily stunned. He had failed to notice her widow's weeds. Could he be mistaken, then? But his gaze fell on the chest again, stolen from him only two days ago. By the Signora's own admission, her son was guilty of the deed.

"A small portrait, strongly resembling you, was found among the merchant's belongings."

It was a lie, but the nearly imperceptible flicker of the Signora's eyelashes suggested he had hit his mark, and he pressed his point. "Your letters to him remain intact. A comparison of those against your hand would reveal the truth quite easily. Do you still deny you were his mistress?"

The Signora's features tightened. "And what if I was? What has that to do with you or my lodger's untimely death?"

"Everything if it was your son who killed him."

The Signora flinched hard as though he had slapped her across the face with the back of his hand. "My son has killed no one. He has no reason—"

"No reason?" Haydn cut through the Signora's increasingly shrill voice. "Rejected by his father, his birthright given to another. I would say he had every reason to kill anyone who stood in his way."

"And his cousin Kaspar stood in his way, did he not?" Johann softly added.

The widow did not deign to give him a glance. Her arms hung straight down by her side; her fingers twisted the folds of her gown, bundling the plain black fabric into a wrinkled ball.

"You have no proof of it," she said at last.

Her lips stretched into a thin, icy smile.

"And without it"—she gave a tiny shrug—"well, you have seen how little the police guards care whether one lives or dies in this city."

CHAPTER THIRTY-NINE

"She all but confessed her son's guilt to us!" Johann stared at the Signora's door, implacably closed now to their inquiries.

"She all but threatened us," Haydn reminded his brother. He had thought it best to leave after the Signora's last remark, having no desire to match cudgels with the likes of a ruffian such as Poldi.

It was not cowardice that had sent him away, although the Signora's sly smile as she watched them depart left no doubt as to her own opinion on the matter.

Johann was too frail to hold his own in a brawl. And without a weapon, Haydn, although more sturdily built, would soon succumb to any attack. Their death would serve no purpose at all. Besides, the police guards and the marauding band they controlled were a matter for the Emperor to deal with.

He said as much to Johann. "And while we are there, we may as well let Her Majesty have the madrigals. They are bound to be safer at the imperial palace than in Papa Keller's house."

He only wished he had not dismissed the carriage Maria Anna had hired for them.

Before he could express his regret on the matter, a hackney coach passed by, slowing down as it neared them. Johann hailed it and, giving the coachman their destination, climbed in after Haydn.

"If Signora Padrona considered her son to be in danger, she would do anything to protect him I imagine," Johann took up the thread of their conversation once the coach was underway.

"Or, if she had a hand in the affair herself," Haydn replied. His eyes, when he turned to his brother, were worried. "She had as much cause as her son. In abandoning her and evading her demands, Wilhelm Dietrich slighted her no less than he did his son."

"Do you suppose it was she who ordered Fabrizzio's death?"

Haydn considered the matter. "She seemed genuinely shocked by it," he said after a while. "I begin to wonder, however, if it was her word that sent Kaspar to his death."

"She seemed to know something of the matter," Johann agreed.

Haydn recalled the Signora's unnatural stillness the moment Kaspar's name had fallen from his younger brother's lips. She had seemed to him like a cornered animal, desperate and afraid, but nevertheless unwilling to give up.

"She must have had no thought her son would be suspected of the crime."

"I can scarcely see why not," Johann countered. "It would be far easier to suspect a man—even one as vapid and vacuous as Fritz—than a woman, however embittered."

"But that is just it, Johann. How could a man of Fritz Dichtler's meager intelligence mastermind a crime of this nature? It is impossible to believe."

"Appearances are often deceptive, brother. His habitual vacant demeanor must be deliberately cultivated, concealing a mind of great cunning and malice. The chest, wrested from your arms and brought to her house, is evidence of the fact."

The Kapellmeister considered Fritz Dichtler. He had never thought much of the tenor. His singing was merely passable. And as for his acting, if what his brother said was true, Fritz was clearly in possession of a far greater talent than he had been willing to display for either the Opera Director or himself.

"It would appear so," he said at last. "He has successfully deceived us all."

But his voice held more than a hint of skepticism, and it must have been evident to his younger brother, for Johann pressed on: "It can be no coincidence that his wife was at the Signora's door this afternoon. What could have brought her there other than the news Luigi must have delivered?"

Haydn remained quiet, unable to either deny the coincidence of Frau Dichtler's presence or dispute that it had been caused by news of the supposed discovery of the operas. Still, the niggling doubts in his mind remained.

Another tenuous possibility named itself, but it seemed so implausible, he thrust it away almost as soon as it surfaced.

They were almost at the River Wien when he spoke again. "Fritz looks nothing like his mother, does he?"

———

The late afternoon sun streamed into the Princess's sitting room, transforming the yellow damask furnishings to a warm gold; burnishing the mahogany armrests and backs of the Rococo chairs with a coppery hue. Rosalie cast her head aside to avoid its glare as she followed Clara Schwann into the room with a tray of refreshments.

"The necklace has been recovered, Elsa," Her Serene Highness was saying to Frau Dichtler. "There is nothing more to say on the subject." The Princess turned her head to smile at Rosalie.

Convinced Rosalie had ambitions of someday rising to the position of lady's maid, the Princess had insisted upon her attendance in the sitting room that afternoon. "How else will you learn, my dear, if not by observing Clara at work?"

Rosalie had consented readily enough when she realized Frau Dichtler would be present as well.

"I am glad to see you here, my dear," the Princess now said, accepting a cup of coffee and selecting a small piece of ginger-spiced *lebkuchen* from the plate Frau Schwann held out to her.

But Frau Dichtler was clearly in no mood to allow the matter to rest.

"If it has been recovered, it is only because the person who stole it chose to return it." The words came out in an irritable snap that clearly caught the Princess by surprise, although she made no comment on the soprano's ill humor.

"I have already told you, Elsa, it was never stolen," she responded calmly. "Clara merely forgot to put it away."

"Then what was stolen when we were on our way to the bank?"

The Princess took a sip of her coffee before replying. "Nothing apparently. The police guard whose help you sought evidently warded off the theft." She took another sip of her coffee. "Although, it appears he only prevented the theft of a paste replica."

"And the theft in Leopoldsdorf?" The soprano watched the Princess carefully. It was a question Rosalie had been waiting for. She was about to utter a cough to draw attention to herself when the Princess spoke.

"Theft!" Her Serene Highness repeated, puzzled. "But I thought a few small items merely fell off the carriage." She looked toward Rosalie, who nodded.

"Frau Dichtler found the rope frayed," she explained.

"Be that as it may." The soprano brushed aside the matter with an irritable wave of her hand. "How did the items in question find their way back to the palace, then?" Frau Dichtler nearly hissed out the question.

Rosalie was prepared for it. "They didn't," she said, suppressing a strong urge to giggle. "I'm afraid it was your enamel case that fell off the wagon. They look so alike, one of the maids mistakenly put Her Serene Highness's jewelry case in your luggage, while yours was simply tied in place with the hatboxes.

"Your maid discovered the error shortly after our arrival and returned Her Serene Highness's case with the paste necklace in it to Frau Schwann."

"Indeed!" Frau Dichtler's eyes narrowed.

But it was not a story her maid would refute. Rosalie had taken care of that.

The hat she had purchased from Sabina had won the girl over completely. Rosalie and Greta had been allowed into the soprano's bedchamber in her absence that afternoon and had combed the room in search of the case.

It had taken a while, but they had eventually found it, tossed into a corner of the closet with some old silk scarves.

"I hope you had nothing valuable in it, Elsa." Her Serene Highness looked concerned. "As for the case itself, it should be a simple matter to have another just like it fashioned."

The Emperor was seated at his desk when Haydn and Johann followed Her Majesty into the Walnut Room. It was not an encounter the Kapellmeister was looking forward to, but the Empress had insisted he repeat his story to her son and co-regent.

"Haydn has some information on the prowlers and footpads who have been dogging the city, Joseph," she said without preamble as soon as she entered the lavishly furnished walnut-paneled chamber.

She walked briskly in and sank heavily into one of the gilded, damask-covered chairs set against the wall.

"Information?" The Emperor raised his head and turned around.

His pale blue eyes fastened themselves upon the Kapellmeister and then swiveled toward Johann.

"What kind of information might you have, gentlemen?" He motioned toward the chairs at the edge of the carpet.

"Information that might help you apprehend the thieves, Your Majesty," Haydn said, swallowing the irritation that had risen like bile at the Emperor's sardonic tone. He lowered himself into the crimson damask seat of the chair His Majesty had indicated.

"Indeed!" The Emperor arched a perfectly shaped eyebrow. "Becoming quite the detective, are we?"

"He would have no need to take on the job if your Count Pergen and his police guards were quite as capable as you consider them, Joseph," Her Majesty retorted. "Did you know the ruffians have already killed one musician—one of our own?"

"Not to mention breaking into a house nearby in broad daylight to kill a foreigner, a visitor to the city," Johann added, speaking for the first time.

The Emperor frowned. "I had heard of the first incident. The man was left abandoned in the streets. The second incident—"

"Was not reported to you, I suppose." The Empress uttered a loud snort, making her jowls quiver.

His Majesty ignored his mother's remark. "How did you come by the news?" he demanded.

"The man in question," Haydn responded, "was the one responsible for the deception perpetrated on Her Majesty.

"It was Dr. Goretti who led us to him. But when we went to his lodgings, we found him already dead. Brutally murdered. The matter was reported to the police guards, but I fear nothing will come of it."

"And why is that?"

Haydn paused. His suspicions were based on such tenuous evidence, he doubted His Majesty would find them very compelling. "It would appear that one of the police guards himself is involved."

"On what grounds do you make this accusation, Haydn?"

"Both men were attacked in the same manner, Your Majesty. As was my brother." It was Johann who volunteered the information. "With a truncheon.

"Whether the barber-surgeon involved in the first case detected the instrument that caused the wounds, we do not know. It was the undertaker, trained as a barber-surgeon himself, who made the observation."

"The implications under the circumstances," Haydn began but the Emperor held out a palm to silence him; the gesture so brusque, it had the stinging sensation of a hard slap.

"I am quite aware of the implications, Haydn." His Majesty said. "I am not quite the fool you imagine me to be."

"There is more, Your Majesty." Haydn swallowed his ire, forcing himself to speak. "The police guard in question, Poldi, has a sister who operates as a fence. Her establishment is near the Carinthian Gate."

The Emperor sat so still, Haydn wondered whether he had even heard him. His Majesty's face was an expressionless mask, the widening of his eyes the only indication he had not been struck suddenly deaf.

The Kapellmeister shuffled his feet. The Emperor continued to stare at him as though he were a prisoner who had omitted to provide all the facts. But what else was he expected to say?

The silence was growing uncomfortable when Johann spoke, having fortunately divined the Emperor's unasked question.

"We discovered the connection quite by accident, Your Majesty, when Her Serene Highness's necklace was stolen and subsequently recovered from Madame Chapeau's establishment." Johann briefly recounted the circumstances. "Were it not for a maid's suspicions of Frau Dichtler—"

"Elsa Dichtler!" His Majesty echoed, surprise animating his features. "I would not have taken her for a thief."

"No, you would have merely taken her to your bed," his mother muttered. It was all Haydn could do not to gape at the Empress, her words were so unexpected.

He similarly resisted the urge to glance at his brother, but His Majesty seemed quite unfazed by the remark.

"A man has needs, Mother. And Elsa fulfilled them admirably. For a time."

"And then you insisted Esterházy give her a position in his orchestra."

"His wife was only too happy to take in a *fallen woman*. She wanted to reform Elsa, an act in which you, I believe, encouraged her."

Ach so! It was thanks to the Emperor, then, that La Dichtler had been foisted upon him. This time Haydn did allow his gaze to shift toward his brother's face.

"Well, clearly the woman is quite beyond reform, Joseph," the Empress burst out, apparently at the end of her tether. "Esterházy ought to have her arrested."

"On what grounds, Mother?" enquired the Emperor coldly. "The necklace has already been recovered without anyone having the slightest suspicion it was ever stolen. No one saw Elsa deliver it to the fence in question.

"And rather than tell the truth, the maid herself seems to have aided in the elaborate deception that the damned thing was merely misplaced."

Haydn sighed, unable to refute His Majesty's argument. "Rosalie had no choice in the matter, Your Majesty. It would take more than a mere maid's word for Her Serene Highness to accept that Frau Dichtler is a common thief."

"Then I shall have a word with Princess Marie Elisabeth myself," the Empress declared.

"There may be a better way, Your Majesty," Haydn said with a smile.

"Indeed!" The Emperor stared down his imperious nose at the Kapellmeister, the contempt in his eyes so evident, Haydn felt his smile freeze and all but disappear. He marshaled his thoughts.

"If the Police Inspector himself along with a few of his most trusted men were to pay Madame Chapeau's millinery a visit, they would find sufficient evidence of her misdoings to arrest her and close down her establishment."

"The thieves cannot operate without a fence, Your Majesties," Johann hastily added before the Emperor, who was looking increasingly skeptical, could object to his older brother's proposition. Unable to refute the truth of this, His Majesty merely harrumphed.

"And Madame Chapeau may, perhaps, be prevailed upon to disclose the names of her associates," Johann continued.

"As for Frau Dichtler," Haydn said, more confident now. "If she cannot be arrested for theft, she can, I am convinced, be apprehended for murder."

CHAPTER FORTY

"Nonsense!" the Emperor dismissed the notion. "Who could Elsa possibly have murdered? You let your imagination go too far, Haydn."

Even Her Majesty seemed startled. "I can well believe that the woman might steal a few trinkets. But to kill someone? Surely you are mistaken. Is Esterházy aware of your suspicions?"

Haydn was silent. He had never intended to bring the matter to Her Majesty's attention. But the words had erupted out of his mouth in the heat of the moment, and there was no taking them back. Now he regretted having spoken at all.

He threw his younger brother a glance of desperation, but Johann seemed just as disconcerted as he himself. In the growing silence, Haydn was uncomfortably aware of Her Majesty's warm gaze settling on his features. It remained there, waiting for an answer.

"I have not yet had occasion to speak with His Serene Highness on the matter." He allowed his eyes to meet hers at last. "It is only recently that I have become aware of Frau Dichtler's possible involvement in the matter."

"And the person she is suspected of killing?" Her Majesty enquired, although her son snorted his contempt. "Must you encourage him in his ravings, Mother?"

Haydn swallowed. It took an effort not to allow his eyes to stray toward the Emperor. "Kaspar, Your Majesty, the musician who was found killed in front of the Seizerkeller. I believe the ruffians who attacked him, did so at the behest of Frau Dichtler and her husband."

"When did Elsa acquire a husband?" the Emperor exclaimed.

"She has had one ever since she joined the Esterházy troupe," Johann explained at the same time that the Empress hissed: "Shh Joseph . . . Let the man speak."

"When his uncle died," Haydn began, "Kaspar inherited a casket of scores that the old merchant had acquired during his travels in Italy. The bequest apparently consisted of the entire operatic works of Monteverdi."

The name caught Her Majesty's attention. "Where are the scores now?" she enquired, tilting her bulk forward. Even the Emperor seemed suitably impressed.

Haydn hesitated again. "We have yet to find the operas, I am afraid, although I feel quite sure they exist. The madrigals the casket contained, however, are quite valuable in and of themselves."

With Johann's help, he explained the situation as succinctly as he could.

"Kaspar left a widow, Your Majesty," Haydn finished as he handed over the scores. "In ill health and impoverished. His bequest is the only provision he left for her."

The Empress's fingers closed around the thick bundle of music. She perused the sheets carefully. Her lips widened into a slow smile of satisfaction.

"Haydn, I do believe you have done it again!" She held the scores out to her son. "These will appease the Mantuans just as well as the operas. Although," she continued turning back to Haydn, "if the operas can be found. . ."

"I will do my best, Your Majesty. It is only a matter of deciphering the workings of old Wilhelm Dietrich's mind."

The Empress nodded, glancing down at the scores again. "I would prefer to keep the madrigals for the imperial library.

"As for the other matter." Her smile disappeared, her lips thrusting out in suppressed anger. "You were wise to come to us. The Police Inspector—"

"Cannot arrest anyone on the mere suspicion of murder, Mother," the Emperor cut in irritably. "And as for the Countess Kuenberg's imaginings, the woman was ever a notorious gossip. If she were to be believed, half of Vienna would be in prison! Haydn will have to—"

"Brother already has a plan Your Majesties," Johann interjected, his voice and manner so mild, they mitigated the rudeness of the interruption.

He elaborated on the trap they had set for the Dichtlers.

"You would agree, would you not, that anyone who wishes to steal Kaspar's bequest must have sought to kill him as well?"

"If that were the case, one would be forced to, I suppose," the Emperor reluctantly conceded the matter.

"But what will you do when they make the attempt, Haydn?" Her Majesty asked anxiously. "If you are right, Elsa is involved with a dangerous band of criminals. They have already killed twice."

Haydn nodded. "All we ask is that someone entrusted with your authority accompany us. If only to witness the crime."

"Take van Swieten. And"—Her Majesty glared at her son—"the Police Inspector must be ordered to lie in wait with his men as well, Joseph."

The Emperor drummed his fingers on the polished walnut armrest of his chair, then sighed. "Very well. Although I will likely look a fool, wasting the city's resources on every tenuous thread of suspicion brought to us."

"That we tolerate these ruffians at all makes us look like fools, Joseph," his mother countered sharply.

She held out a note toward the Kapellmeister.

"Have van Swieten pay you for the madrigals from the privy purse. The first sum is for you. The second for the poor widow. We will secure her a yearly pension as well."

The sight of a familiar rack wagon parked at the corner of Wallnerstrasse and Haarhof brought Rosalie to a sudden halt. For one inexplicable moment, her heart seemed to cease. Then a warm tingle prickled at the nape of her neck.

What was Gerhard doing here? Surely the Esterházy Cellar was not in need of any more wine?

She inched into the alley, forcing her suddenly leaden feet to step forward.

"There you are, lass!" Gerhard's voice boomed out behind her. "I have been waiting here for you."

"Oh." Rosalie swiveled around, shoving her hands deep into her apron pockets. What could Gerhard possibly want with her? Did it have anything to do with Madame Chapeau?

From the way he was looking at her, it didn't seem likely. A discomfiting warmth suffused her cheeks.

"I leave for Eisenstadt today. I thought I would see if you wanted me to carry a letter for you. To your mother," he explained when she stared expressionlessly at him. "Rohrau is not far out of my way."

"Oh." Rosalie said again. Her eyes shifted down to the dusty brown cobblestones. She had forgotten all about Mama's letter. It was still in her apron pocket. Unopened.

Her fingers closed around it now.

She sighed and glanced up. "It is kind of you to offer, but I have nothing to send her. I am sure Mama has no wish to hear from me."

"Why would she write to you, then?" Gerhard's deep blue eyes gazed down into hers with an intensity that made her look away. "She has lost a son. She must cling even more to the children that are left to her."

"She holds me responsible for his death." Rosalie's gaze swung up toward Gerhard's face. "She has never said it in so many words. But it is as clear as day in every letter she writes."

She felt Gerhard's warm hand upon her shoulder. "Perhaps it is her grief that makes her lash out so."

"Perhaps." A tear rolled down her cheek. "I never saw it until it was too late, but he was lost to us long before it happened." She glanced up at him. "I often wonder what became of the little boy he used to be. Why didn't I see him drift away?"

"No one does, lass." Gerhard's tone was somber. Rosalie wondered if he was thinking of Marlene, the woman he had lost. His fingers dug into her shoulder blades for the briefest moment. "Your mother asks herself the same question, no doubt."

Rosalie stared at him. It was not a consideration that had ever occurred to her. Did Mama merely need to know she was not the only person who'd failed to see what Sanyi had become?

She brought out the letter and tore it open.

"You are angry with me, Rosalie. How can I blame you? I have held you at fault for giving in to Sanyi's whims. As though it was his music that led him astray. I only wish I knew what did.

"I bore your father but one son, and now he is lost to us forever."

"One son may be lost. But another may be gained." Gerhard's quiet voice intruded upon Rosalie's thoughts.

What? She raised her eyes, unaware she'd been mouthing the words out loud.

"I can take care of your parents as well as I do my widowed mother, lass. If you will have me, that is to say."

"But. . ." Rosalie scarcely knew what to say.

"Think on it, lass. I don't need your answer right away."

What of Marlene? she wondered, but was too dazed to voice the thought. She scribbled a hasty note on a scrap of paper and watched him leave, her question still unanswered.

Had Gerhard really just asked her to marry him? What would Greta say about that? It was some minutes before she remembered the Blaufränkisch she had been sent out to fetch.

It was far too late to return to Landstrasse to Papa Keller's home. The Kapellmeister and his brother repaired instead to Wallnerstrasse and walked toward the Grüner Baum, a small inn down the street from the Esterházy Palace.

Soft strains of music emanated from within its quiet tavern.

"It is one of your quartets, brother," Johann said, turning to the Kapellmeister with a smile. "Shall we go in?"

Haydn listened for a moment, his head cocked. One of the violins was ever so slightly out of tune, but there was such emotion in the way the performers played the lyrical minuet section of the quartet, one hardly noticed it.

"It is an excellent performance," he remarked, making his way to the old oaken door, weathered and warped from long use. He pushed it open, wincing at the sound of the loudly creaking hinges.

The tavern's patrons, crowded around the four bearded performers, turned their heads at the noise and glared. Haydn, looking as contrite as he could manage, hurried quietly in toward a table in a dark corner.

They had no sooner seated themselves when the innkeeper approached them, a bottle of wine, some glasses, and a dish of pickled mushrooms on his tray.

"You are new here, gentlemen?" It was phrased more as a statement than a question, but Haydn nodded in response.

"A word of advice, then," the innkeeper continued as he poured out their wine. "Next time, wait until the players have finished a movement before opening the door."

"The performers are much sought after, I suppose?" Haydn pushed one of the wine glasses toward Johann and drew another toward himself.

"It is the composer who is popular, gentlemen," the innkeeper replied. "You may have heard of him, Joseph Haydn."

"We are familiar with the name," Johann said, suppressing a smile.

Few people expected the great Haydn to be a small fellow, no different from themselves, with brown pock-marked features and a humorous light in his eyes. Small wonder the innkeeper had failed to recognize the Kapellmeister.

"His music is decent enough," Haydn agreed.

The lukewarm words would have to suffice. He could hardly praise his own music. And to express his pleasure at the reception of his works would only serve to disclose his identity.

Not something he was keen to do, given the nature of their mission.

The innkeeper was outraged. "Decent enough!" he exploded. "He who cannot appreciate Haydn's works can know nothing at all of music. Decent enough, indeed!" He left the table, still muttering under his breath.

There was little to do but wait, and the Kapellmeister and his brother settled down to it. The musicians took up a quartet by Dittersdorf, then played one of Jommelli's trio sonatas transcribed for four strings.

By the time Haydn and Johann had ordered the evening meal—a simple beef gulasch served with noodles and potatoes—the tavern had attracted a few more customers. But no one paid any attention to the two men sitting quietly at a table in the corner.

At the appointed hour, Haydn settled his bill, leaving ten gulden for the musicians.

"The music was superb and the musicians excellent," he explained to the astonished innkeeper.

He and Johann strode out into the cool night air, making their way toward the Kaiserhaus. The palace—once the property of the Empress's deceased husband, Franz Stephen—stood directly opposite the Esterházy Palace.

The portico over its front entrance afforded such an excellent view of the Music Room, they had arranged to meet Baron van Swieten under it to await the events of the night.

His Lordship was already there when they arrived.

"Are you quite sure the thieves will strike tonight?" he asked in a low voice when the brothers joined him.

"If Luigi has fed them the bait correctly, I have every expectation they will, Your Lordship," Haydn replied.

"There is a police guard patrolling the streets. He has stopped before the palace several times."

"It will be Poldi, no doubt," Johann said. "Was he a stout man with hair that stood up on his head like the bristles of a porcupine?"

The Baron nodded. "The same. But never fear, we shall bring the matter to an end tonight. There are two men posted near the inn down the street and the Police Inspector himself along with a fourth man at the other end, near the Kohlmarkt. All at the Emperor's orders."

Haydn peered up at the Music Room window. Luigi would be concealed within, but he doubted the Dichtlers would be foolish enough to keep the stolen music in the castle. Most likely, Poldi would deliver the music to Fritz's mother at Singerstrasse.

"Then, it is just a matter of time," he said.

CHAPTER FORTY-ONE

Luigi shifted his weight from one foot to the other. He had been standing within the coat closet for so long, his legs felt stiff and a soreness had crept into his knees. Rosalie had long since snuffed out the candles in the Music Room, but the room was not entirely bereft of light.

Through the partially open window, the full moon cast a dull golden glow that illuminated Haydn's desk and the chest containing the scores he had tempted La Dichtler with. The rest of the room remained in obscurity, but the Konzertmeister found himself able to see well enough.

The streets would be more brightly illuminated despite the clouds that flitted briefly across the moon. Haydn and Johann, he hoped, would have had the forethought to take up a discreet position opposite the Esterházy Palace.

The quiet of the night was broken only by the steady clip-clop of a solitary police guard's boots on the street outside interspersed every now and then with the calling of the hour. Luigi heard the harsh cry once again and wondered if it was Poldi patrolling Wallnerstrasse and the surrounding streets.

When would La Dichtler come? He shifted his weight yet again, flinching at the sound of his joints snapping, the sound eerily explosive in the stillness of the night. He was about to move once more when he heard the soft murmur of voices and the muffled sound of footsteps.

He pressed himself against the rear wall of the closet, scarcely daring to breathe. The door to the Music Room opened just a crack. Then a little more. La Dichtler crept into the room, the candle in her hand illuminating her features. But even without it, Luigi would have recognized the tall, voluptuous figure of the soprano.

Fritz sauntered in behind her. "Where is it?" he asked, looking around the room.

The soprano whipped around. "Shh!" she hissed. "The maids may still be up."

"At this hour?" Fritz sounded skeptical, but he lowered his voice nevertheless.

La Dichtler had reached the desk now and was fumbling with the hasp on the old chest. "I cannot understand why he wants the chest as well. It would be much easier to simply take the scores and leave this old thing behind."

He? Luigi leaned closer to the closet door, pressing his ear against the tiny crack between the door and the jamb. Was La Dichtler referring to Poldi? What could Poldi possibly want with the chest?

"We had better take it, then, Elsa. Here let me." Fritz reached for the hasp and after some wiggling managed to lift it up.

"There is no need to inspect them, Fritz. They are all within," the soprano hissed impatiently. "Let us be on our way."

For once Luigi found himself in agreement with her. The scores would not hold up to a very close inspection, and he doubted even a man as vapid as Fritz would be entirely deceived.

But Fritz had already brought out several sheets and was peering at them, head lowered. He moved his candle slowly over the sheet. A blob of molten wax dripped onto the edge of the paper, eliciting a sharp cry from his wife.

"Now, look what you've done!" She attempted to grab hold of the papers, but Fritz moved them out of her reach. "Put them back, Fritz."

"These look nothing like operas, Elsa."

Luigi cursed the young man under his breath. But La Dichtler merely snorted.

"What can you know of the matter? Of course, they are operas. That's what Herr Tomasini said they were."

"In five voices?" Fritz continued to scan the sheets in his hand.

"You must be looking at a chorus. Now put them back, and let us be on our way."

For the first time since his acquaintance with the soprano, Luigi found himself thankful for her supreme ignorance. Fritz, too weak-minded to argue with his wife, obediently returned the scores to the chest.

But his next words were so odd, Luigi hardly knew what to make of them.

"I still think we should keep a few of these for ourselves," Fritz said as he hoisted the chest up and made his way to the door.

Keep the music for ourselves.

The words echoed in Luigi's mind. He was vaguely aware of the door clicking shut as the Dichtlers left the Music Room. But the Konzertmeister remained within the dark closet, too preoccupied to move.

Who was Fritz stealing the music for, if not for himself? And who else but Fritz would want anything to do with the chest that contained the scores?

———※———

Luigi found Haydn and the Baron van Swieten waiting for him under the portico that loomed over the enormous wooden entrance of the Kaiserhaus. He had barely time to wonder where Johann was, or what the Baron was doing there, when the Kapellmeister grabbed hold of his arm.

"That way!" Haydn whispered urgently, hustling Luigi along in the direction of the Kohlmarkt. "I sent Johann after Fritz and his wife, but that bristle-haired scoundrel of a police guard is with them—" he shuddered, not wishing to complete the thought.

He had seen Poldi walk past several times as they waited, his truncheon swinging from his hairy wrist. He hurried on, sickened by the thought of what a blow from such a weapon could do to his younger brother's frail form.

"Never fear, Herr Haydn," the Baron panted after them. "Master Johann will not have to deal with the ruffian by himself. The police guards stationed near the Kohlmarkt will have begun to follow him and have been instructed to intervene at the slightest hint of trouble."

Haydn merely nodded. "Her Majesty suggested His Grace accompany us," he explained to Luigi. He had noticed his Konzertmeister glancing over his shoulder at the Baron in a bewildered way.

"*Ach so!* But how will we find Johann?"

"The Baron was kind enough to supply Johann with some kuchen. The trail of pieces he lets fall to the ground will guide us." It had seemed a silly idea at the time, but Haydn was grateful the Baron had thought of it.

They were at the Kohlmarkt now, but Johann was nowhere to be seen. Haydn turned left, carefully scanning the ground for the white pieces of kuchen. He walked a few more paces, close to the Graben now. But there was still no sight of the marzipan-covered pieces Johann had promised to let fall.

He was beginning to grow desperate when the Baron called to him in a low voice.

"They turned right, Herr Haydn."

Haydn spun around. "*Right*? But that is the wrong way. Signora Padrona's house is on Singerstrasse. They ought to have turned left."

"They appear to be headed for the Michaelerplatz," Luigi remarked.

"What reason could they have to go there?"

"Perhaps they intend to meet someone other than Signora Padrona." Luigi recounted the conversation he had overheard.

"Perhaps," Haydn agreed.

But quite another alternative had suggested itself to him.

What buyer, after all, would want the chest as well as the scores? There were only two people in all of Vienna who could have any interest in the old merchant's chest. One of them was Signora Padrona. And nothing in her manner had suggested the casket in her possession was not the one she sought.

The other could only be. . .

He recalled the Signora's dark, hooded eyes and her features, vaguely familiar to him. Fritz looked nothing like her. And, but for his interest in the bequest, Haydn would have sworn the boy had not a trace of Italian blood in his veins. Was it possible that Fritz was not the Signora's son, after all?

But in that case, who was?

⁓

The trail of kuchen crumbs Johann had left behind came to an abrupt end at St. Michael's Square.

Haydn paused near St. Michael's Church at the corner, hugging its shadows as he craned his head to inspect the enormous square. The Hofburg rose before him, the greenish patina of its copper dome illuminated by the light of the full moon.

He heard Luigi's firm tread and the Baron's heavy footfall behind him, the sounds seeming to ring out in the quiet of the night. Where could Johann possibly have gone?

The palaces of the nobility lined Herrengasse on the left, while the imperial palace continued on to the right of the square. There was no telling where his younger brother had turned.

A dark figure moving under the church portico caught his eye as he twisted his head around. He was about to draw back when it raised an arm, frantically motioning him forward.

"It is Johann," Luigi whispered in his ear.

"What can he be doing there?" the Baron huffed. "Would to God, he has not lost trace of the thieves!"

Haydn made no reply to this, determined not to consider the possibility at all. It was enough that his brother was safe. Still hugging the shadows, the men inched forward, circling around the church facade until they reached its entrance. Johann emerged from the portico.

"Whoever they are meeting is within the church, brother," he said in a low voice as he gestured within. "Waiting near the door that leads into the crypt. The police guards are already within."

Haydn grasped his brother's arm, too overcome with emotion to say a word. Had anything happened to Johann. . .

His fingers dug deeply into his younger brother's shoulder. Then noticing the faint grimace of pain in his features, the Kapellmeister hastily released his hold and slid forward.

The door leading into the nave had been left ajar, allowing a small pyramid of moonlight to fall on the square tiles of stone just beyond it. The men crept inside, taking care to avoid the patch of light falling down the center of the floor.

Haydn, leading the way, made a wide arc to the left. The pillars reaching up to the vaulted ceiling separated the pews from an aisle that flared out into a circular area containing the Barnabite chapel.

It was within this chapel that the singers of the north choir stood during service, close by the door leading down into the crypt.

A low growl of anger reached them as their neared it, causing Haydn to stop.

"Where are the operas, then? I warn you, it will not go well for you if you have attempted to purloin them from me."

Not wishing to be seen, the Kapellmeister hastily stepped within the chapel dedicated to St. Anthony and beckoned to the others to follow him in. In the Barnabite chapel on the other side of the wall, the argument continued on unabated.

"You hold them in your hands, you fool! All the scores you asked for." Fury appeared to have rendered Frau Dichtler's normally shrill voice hoarse.

"And the chest you wanted as well, who knows for what reason." Fritz's light tenor rose in indignation. "Do you think Elsa would have taken the trouble to inform your mother of this unexpected development if we intended to dupe you?"

"*Your mother!*" Johann echoed, his voice barely above a whisper. "Fritz cannot be Signora Padrona's son, then."

"No." Haydn shook his head, straining his ear against the stone wall.

The resounding whoosh of a sheaf of papers hitting the stone floor echoed through the walls of the church just then, startling him into biting his tongue. The pain nearly caused him to cry out, but he forced himself to stay still.

"The chest that I asked for?" The words were uttered in an angry snarl. "You call this the chest I asked for? This moth-eaten bit of worthless driftwood should be destined for the garbage. And as for these scores—"

The sound of a shoe grinding into the papers on the floor filled the Kapellmeister's eardrums.

"Careful! By the arrangement we had with you, half of those belong to us," said someone in a much deeper, menacing tone. Poldi, no doubt, Haydn thought.

"The arrangement called for opera scores, not for a parcel of worthless madrigals." A loud crack was heard, the sound of a fist landing squarely against someone's jaw.

Then a thwack.

Haydn stiffened. Poldi had begun to wield his truncheon. His opponent, whoever he was, stood no chance unless he was similarly equipped. Alarmed, the Kapellmeister swung around, but the Baron was already signaling to the Police Inspector and his guards.

Armed with lanterns, stout ropes, and truncheons, they raced toward the Barnabite Chapel.

"Halt! In the name of the Emperor, halt!" Haydn heard the Police Inspector call out.

A brief commotion followed, but by the time he followed the Baron into the choir, the Dichtlers and Poldi had been restrained, their hands tied behind their backs, a strip of cloth roughly tied around their mouths to prevent them from crying out.

Haydn's gaze drifted past to the tall man who stood next to them, similarly restrained. His eyes roved over the other's dark hair and hooded eyelids, thunderstruck.

"*Albrecht!*" he rasped out, then cleared his throat.

This, then, was the old merchant's bastard son; the man who had killed Kaspar. How had he not . . .?

Innumerable memories shuffled themselves inside his mind as he sought to make sense of this revelation. The man before him was the spitting image of Signora Padrona. Yet he had failed to see it.

Worse still—

The thought remained unvoiced in his mind as Luigi swept past him. The Konzertmeister drew his arm over his left shoulder, then swung back to strike Albrecht across the face with the back of his broad palm.

"I could kill you with my bare hands for what you did to Kaspar, you ungrateful cur! He was a good man. He trusted you and called you his friend."

Albrecht's gag had slid down to his chin, leaving his mouth exposed. He hawked, expelling a gob of spittle that barely missed Luigi.

"He stole my inheritance." His eyes glittered in a baleful glare at the group. "He deserved to die."

Luigi raised his arm again, but the Baron drew him aside.

"That is enough, my friend. Rest assured, the man will not go unpunished."

CHAPTER FORTY-TWO

The events of the night had left Haydn exhausted, and he was glad to avail himself of the rooms reserved for him at the Esterházy Palace. Another note had been despatched to Maria Anna to inform her of the fact.

He climbed into the soft feather bed and pulled the covers up. His head sank into the depths of his pillow; his eyes closed. But he found himself too troubled by the revelations of the night to drift easily into sleep.

Had there ever been cause to suspect Albrecht, he wondered. Or had he simply been blind to the truth? His mind pored uneasily over every detail that had come to his attention since Kaspar first sought his help.

He had considered the lawyer's involvement in the first attempt to rob Kaspar of his bequest. But that Albrecht might be involved. . .

It had never once occurred to Haydn to question the young man's friendship. He had, he supposed, seen the man through Kaspar's eyes. Even so, Albrecht had quite cleverly managed their impressions of him.

A man, aware of an impending attack, might be expected to arm himself. But Albrecht had traveled unarmed. Even taken a bullet in the course of the robbery. Only a man trained in the habitual deviousness of criminals could have suspected his motives. Haydn certainly had not.

That one gesture of trust had clouded his mind entirely. Albrecht had never been regarded as a suspect.

He recalled the suspicious break-in at Kaspar's house the very night the locks had been changed. It was Albrecht, he remembered now, who had suggested changing them; Albrecht who had gone to the trouble of locating a locksmith for the purpose.

How easy it would have been for him to have a second set of keys made for his own use.

He had even returned the very next day, curious perhaps to see how the break-in had been regarded. Or, more likely, to con poor Amelie into entrusting the chest to him. But Haydn himself had fortunately been present to take charge of the bequest.

His eyes flew open, all thought of sleep gone.

Small wonder he had been attacked. *And Albrecht*—Haydn sat up now—*had made a point of saving the music, allowing the ruffians who attacked him to escape with the casket.*

"The casket", Haydn whispered into the darkness, his mind turning to the worm-eaten chest Kaspar's aunt had lent them. The operas were concealed somewhere within it, he would warrant.

Wilhelm Dietrich may have wanted nothing to do with his son, but he had been astute enough to realize the wretched boy would be deceived by outward appearances.

"Albrecht must have taken care to befriend Kaspar," Haydn said softly to himself.

The two musicians must have met at the Hofburg, the younger man gaining Kaspar's trust. When the old merchant fell ill, Albrecht had no doubt made himself indispensable to Kaspar. Conveying medicaments and other healing substances to the old man.

Kaspar, his hands full with an ailing wife, would have welcomed the assistance.

"But old Wilhelm Dietrich was wily, too." Haydn smiled in the darkness. "He would never have been able to confide in his wife, but he had made arrangements to secure Kaspar's inheritance."

The bequest that had cost poor Kaspar his life.

Haydn's smile faded. Would to God, the old merchant had dispensed with his prejudice and allowed his son the satisfaction of besting him. An innocent man had been caught in the crossfire, and another had lost his life as well.

Fabrizzio, realizing that Albrecht had murdered his cousin, had apparently sought payment for his own silence. A foolish move, Haydn thought, shaking his head. Nothing good ever came of greed. Or a desire to profit from another's sins.

He slid down under the covers again. If anyone could find the hidden compartment, it was Papa Keller. He would send for his father-in-law as soon as dawn broke. Maria Anna. . .

His mind drifted into oblivion before he could complete the thought.

———

Papa Keller, sitting astraddle one of the cushioned chairs in the Music Room, tilted his head to regard the chest on the table before them.

"The outer dimensions of the box, Sepperl," he said, using Haydn's boyhood name, "are far larger than would be required given the space contained within."

"That would suggest the presence of an inner compartment, would it not?" Luigi leaned closer to the chest, hazel eyes bright with excitement.

The Kapellmeister had shared his nighttime ponderings on the subject with him, and they left no doubt as to the existence of the operas. Somewhere within this chest were the entire operatic works composed by the great Monteverdi.

Luigi's feverish anticipation touched Haydn as well. He could almost feel the thick, old, handmade paper in his hands; smell its musty odor. His heart seemed to be executing a never-ending rapid trill.

But the memory of the compartment he and Johann had discovered dimmed his eagerness, tingeing it with frustration.

"The one Johann and I found"—he drew up the lining that concealed the compartment—"had nothing save for some letters and a journal Wilhelm Dietrich kept."

"Of his numerous conquests, I have no doubt," Papa Keller snorted.

The comment startled Haydn. He stared at Papa Keller, wondering how much his father-in-law knew of Wilhelm Dietrich's various dalliances. He had not supposed the news to be so widely known.

Papa Keller, if he noticed Haydn's astonishment, chose to ignore it. He continued instead to regard the chest, rubbing his forefinger pensively across his chin.

Haydn slid back in his chair, swallowing his curiosity. Most likely, the old merchant had bragged about his amorous affairs as well. His younger brother, had he been present, might have tactfully elicited an explanation from Papa Keller.

But Johann had set out at the stroke of dawn in search of a tenor and a soprano to replace the Dichtlers who, along with Poldi and Albrecht, were detained in the Alte Burg. There under the watchful eye of the Swiss palace guards, they awaited the Emperor's justice.

Johann had not been gone above a half hour when the carriage Haydn had sent for his father-in-law and Maria Anna had arrived.

The prospect of spending an entire day browsing the delightful wares within the expensive establishments on the Kohlmarkt had persuaded Maria Anna to forgo breakfast, and she had deposited her father outside the palace and set off.

"There must be another compartment," Papa Keller said at last. "The outer dimensions of the box are much larger than would be warranted by even the one you discovered, Sepperl."

"Another false bottom, perhaps," Luigi said, stuffing the last of the sweet rolls into his mouth. He wiped his fingers on his breeches and drew the chest toward himself.

Reaching within, he rummaged around for some time. "I can find nothing," he said, pushing the chest toward Haydn.

"Where could it be, I wonder." Haydn set it on his lap and slowly rotated it, surveying the casket from top to bottom. Small brass plates decorated the corners at the top.

He let his forefinger slide back and forth on the smooth, cold surface.

His eyes turned toward the brass legs at the bottom. They were quite extraordinary: ornate, angled pieces that looked rather like wings. Each affixed to the bottom corner of the casket.

Something stirred in his brain. He might know nothing of carpentry, but even he knew that an angled piece could serve as a lever.

He pressed a forefinger and thumb on either side of one of the pieces. To no avail.

"The bottom drops out, I'll warrant!" Papa Keller cried. "But the carpenter will have fashioned four levers. Here"—he reached out—"let me hold it up for you. Put your other thumb and finger at the opposite end. There! Now twist hard, Sepperl."

Haydn pushed, grunting with the effort. He could feel the pieces slowly move, but they had not been oiled in a long time and it took all of his strength to twist them away from the box. Luigi reached up and began pushing the brass pieces at the third and fourth corners.

They had barely managed to pry open the last lever when, with a small crash, the bottom dropped down. Four slim wooden pipes extended down from the middle of the box to the deep receptacle that had dropped out.

"There are papers in there," Papa Keller's voice was hushed. "A thick stack of yellowing pages. Are those your operas, Sepperl?"

"Set the chest on the table here, Joseph," Luigi advised, beginning to draw the box down.

Haydn could barely draw breath. The pages were face down within the container. What if they were not. . .

———∽∽∽———

A hard rapping on the door nearly made him bite his tongue. The door opened, revealing His Serene Highness, Prince Nikolaus Esterházy.

For a moment he stood in the doorway, his eyes fixed upon the chest standing as it were on stilts. Then he strode into the room, letting the door swing shut behind him.

"You have found the lost operas, I see."

Before Haydn could say a word, His Serene Highness bent down and plucked the stack of papers from within the lower receptacle.

He cast his eye over the page on top. "It would appear the old gentleman knew who amongst his nephew's acquaintances was willing to kill for these works."

He handed the page down to Haydn who spread it on the table before them.

"Beware of whom you befriend, my boy," Dietrich's unsteady hand had scrawled the warning across the page. "If you have found these, for God's sake, keep them safe from Albrecht. He means you no good."

"If only we had found these in time." Haydn's voice was tinged with regret.

If only he had taken possession of the scores the very night he had arrived in Vienna. But news of the Empress's acquisition had only convinced him Kaspar's bequest was nothing valuable.

"Her Majesty will be most pleased to add these to her collection, Haydn," the Prince said as he took a vacant chair between Papa Keller and Luigi. He set the stack of scores down. "It would be as well to examine them, however, before we get her hopes up."

Haydn nodded. He glanced down at the pages. Even if it were not for the name inscribed at the top, he would have recognized the loops that graced the stems of Monteverdi's notes.

He had noticed the characteristic in a letter the composer had written to the Empress Eleonora, daughter of the Duke of Gonzaga.

Her Majesty had shown it to him the previous day, having requested the entire correspondence between the great composer and her great-great-grandfather's second wife be sent to her from St. Nikolai. It was to the nuns of the convent she had founded that the Empress Eleonora had entrusted her papers and her most precious possessions.

"It may help you recognize his hand when you see it, Haydn," Her Majesty had said.

"If it will set your mind at rest," the Prince's deep voice interrupted his thoughts, "the Emperor has ordered Albrecht and the wretched police guard be publicly executed."

Publicly executed! Haydn looked up, too stunned to speak.

It was a harsh punishment, reserved only for the worst traitors. One of his violinists had met his death thus not more than five months ago for a heinous act of treason.

But the relentless and brutal murder of Vienna's citizens were an act of treason as well, he supposed.

"Was there no trial?" Papa Keller enquired.

There had been some rumors of judgment being passed and punishments being meted out to supposed criminals without the benefit of a trial. It was said these were men who tended to be too outspoken in their criticism of His Majesty.

Haydn supposed it was true, the Emperor not being one to brook opposition lightly.

"He saw no reason for one, and for once I agreed with him," the Prince replied. His nostrils flared in distaste. "I have met few men so hardened in their crime, they showed no remorse for their deeds.

"The ape Poldi bragged to all who could hear of the gang of thieves he had spearheaded to terrorize the city. And Albrecht was no better, crowing about having led the great Haydn by the nose."

"He said that?" Luigi's voice vibrated with a quiet menace.

"He was well aware the music scholar had duped Goretti and that the man was in desperate need of the scores he had promised to procure for Her Majesty. Once his attempt at a robbery failed, he casually let drop news of the bequest."

"Kapellmeister Reutter surmised as such," Haydn said. "We all thought the young man was naïve, too prone to gossip. I suppose he hoped initially the physician would be able to purchase the bequest."

"Or that the music scholar might," the Prince added with a nod. "In either case, it would be easy enough to procure the chest. He was never interested in the madrigals they contained, foolishly imagining them to be of no value."

"Wilhelm Dietrich counted on him to be just so stupid," Haydn said with some satisfaction.

In so many other ways, however, Albrecht had proven himself to be quite devious. He recalled the palpable fear Fabrizzio had exhibited upon hearing of Kaspar's demise.

"I suppose he deliberately led Fabrizzio into sending Kaspar the note that took him to his death."

"Not deliberately, although the consequences could not have been more fortuitous, Haydn. Your attention was so consumed by the physician and the scholar who had both expressed such an interest in the bequest—"

"That I considered no one else," Haydn admitted ruefully, glad Maria Anna was not present to hear of his shortsightedness. "When I learned Wilhelm Dietrich had a son he had repudiated, I felt a strange pity for the young man, whoever he was."

"I doubt that fact alone accounts for his evil nature," Papa Keller said wisely.

"Nor can it excuse it." Luigi's voice was hard. "I am glad there was no trial. Those scoundrels deserved none."

"And what of Goretti?" Haydn enquired. "What do Their Majesties intend to do with him."

"He will be cleaning the streets every morning and afternoon with the other prisoners of the city," the Prince commented dryly. "For a month. It is a punishment the Emperor is quite fond of meting out. But for their part in the thefts around the city, he would have dispensed it to the Dichtlers as well.

"But that reminds me."

He dug into his ample pockets and brought out a small leather pouch.

"A small token of my appreciation, Haydn," he said as he handed the bulging pouch to his Kapellmeister. "I never thought we should be rid of that infernal woman."

He reached within his pockets again. "The occasion demands even greater generosity, in fact."

He pulled out two more bulging pouches, handing one to Luigi and the other to Papa Keller, whose eyes grew round with astonishment.

Haydn was about to enquire after the fate that awaited the Dichtlers when the Prince spoke again.

"I know not what His Majesty intends to do with that couple after they have completed their term of imprisonment, but suffice it to say there is no likelihood of their ever infesting us with their presence again."

The Prince rose. "I trust Master Johann will have hired two new singers by the end of the day," he said, staring down at Haydn.

"I imagine that is not entirely impossible." Haydn hastened to his feet.

"Excellent! Then we may prepare to return to Eisenstadt within the next day or two. The city makes my skin crawl," he muttered as he left the room.

It was a sentiment Haydn discovered himself ready to agree with. After the horrendous events of the past few days, Eisenstadt, quiet and still as a pond on a windless day, beckoned to him.

He was even ready to remove to Eszterháza and the dreadful prospect of consuming paprika-spiced stews.

The End

YOUR BONUS STORY: WHIFF OF MURDER

Haydn is glad to return to the quiet backwaters of Eisenstadt in Royal Hungary. Better still, the dreaded trip to Eszterháza has to be postponed. The opera house at His Serene Highness's former hunting lodge is not complete. But things don't remain quiet for too long. Before long the baker's wife goes missing, and when Haydn finds a bloodstained mattress in her bedchamber, he wonders if she is the victim. Or the absconding murderess.

Get another taste of murder and Haydn's sleuthing skills with this complimentary story, "**Whiff of Murder.**"

Download Your Free Copy at:

NTUSTIN.COM/TASTEOFMURDER

NOTE FROM THE AUTHOR

Claudio Monteverdi (1567-1643) was an Italian composer widely renowned, even in his own time, for his operas and theatrical works. We're less likely to remember that he also wrote and published several volumes of madrigals—that uniquely Renaissance genre of secular song written for four or five voices.

Like Joseph Haydn (1732-1809), the protagonist of my mysteries, Monteverdi was a prolific composer, a man recognized to be at the vanguard of musical development. If Haydn is regarded as the father of such modern forms as the string quartet and the symphony, Monteverdi was hailed even in his own time as the master of opera.

Working in a period of musical transition, Monteverdi represents not just a transition from Renaissance to Baroque music, but a development away from modal harmony toward tonal harmony. Later composers like Haydn would have been familiar with the modal system through church music and, in Haydn's case, through his study of Johann Joseph Fux's text on counterpoint, *Gradus ad Parnassum*.

Fux's exercises—still in use today—assume a familiarity with basic modal harmony, which is sufficiently different from the tonal harmony familiar to us all as to seem almost like Greek. The differences are far too complex to elaborate upon here. Suffice it to say that Renaissance music is as different from later music as that itself is different from twentieth-century atonal or chromatic works.

But tonal harmony was not fully developed in Monteverdi's time, and when criticized for breaking the rules of modal harmony, all Monteverdi could do was to assert that there was a musical sense behind his harmony. That he wasn't breaking the rules at random. In the introduction to his *Fifth Book of Madrigals*, he promises to articulate a theory of the new system, but he never got around to it.

What inspired *Aria to Death*?

The plot of *Aria to Death* was inspired by two tidbits I learned when I first started researching the Haydn Mysteries. First, in 1613, Monteverdi was the victim of a curious attack. On the road from Mantua, where he had until then worked at the Duke of Mantua's court, to Venice, where he would assume the position of Kapellmeister at St. Mark's Basilica, his carriage was waylaid by bandits, who proceeded to rob from the party at gunpoint.

All that was stolen was a new serge coat Monteverdi had bought for the journey, but the accompanying courier's strange behavior led the composer to suspect he was in some way involved.

To a mystery writer, a deliberately staged robbery needed to have a much greater motive than the theft of a serge coat. The second Monteverdi fact helped me here.

Musicologists have long puzzled over the loss of seven of the ten operas Monteverdi wrote, and it seemed not implausible to speculate that the theft of his works—so radically different that they deeply offended men like the secular monk Giovanni Maria Artusi—might have been the motive.

And who better to have orchestrated the attack and theft than Artusi himself? Artusi, of course, had died in August of the year of the robbery, but, nevertheless, this seemed like too excellent a connection to ignore.

The Haydn-Monteverdi Connections

And what of Haydn? How does he managed to get embroiled in a theft that took place over a hundred years ago? The connections—when I found them—between Haydn and Monteverdi, Vienna and Mantua, were so startling as to take my breath away.

Monteverdi's patron at the Mantuan court, Vincenzo Gonzaga, was the father of Eleonora, who married the Habsburg Emperor Ferdinand II. She was his second wife, and while they had no children, she was instrumental in influencing the artistic and musical currents at the Habsburg Court.

There are several letters from Monteverdi to both the Emperor and the Empress, seeking a position in Vienna. Monteverdi even dedicated a volume of madrigals to the Habsburgs. His desire for a position at the Viennese court never came to fruition, but it's tempting to think that the composer may have sent along the scores for some of his operatic works to the royal couple.

Years later, the scores for Monteverdi's *Il Ritorno D'Ulisses*, one of three operas to have survived, were discovered in the Habsburg Library. When her husband sacked Mantua, Eleonora made a herculean effort to save the music and the musicians at her father's court.

Later, she arranged for her niece, also an Eleonora, to marry her stepson, Emperor Ferdinand III. The younger Eleonora was the Emperor's third wife and, therefore, stepmother to Emperor Leopold, the Empress Maria Theresa's grandfather.

Both Eleonoras were devout women and founded convents in Vienna. One of these happened to be St. Nikolai, the convent that Haydn's first love, Therese Keller, entered. Readers familiar with my blog (**ntustin.com/blog**) will know that Haydn went on to marry Therese's sister, Maria Anna—not a match made in heaven, although my characterization of them suggests there was some fondness between the two despite the surface acrimony of their daily interactions.

Authenticating Musical Works

For the sake of simplicity, I have assumed that Haydn was as familiar with Monteverdi, his life and his letters, as the modern reader. That the Habsburg library, the collection of his own patron, Prince Nikolaus, and the convent of St. Nikolai would provide him with the letters and documents he needed to authenticate the great master's operas.

Monteverdi was a copious correspondent, and the survival of his letters have ensured that his music lives on even when the actual scores are unavailable.

ABOUT THE AUTHOR

A former journalist, Nupur Tustin relies upon a Ph.D. in Communication and an M.A. in English to orchestrate fictional mayhem. The Haydn mysteries are a result of her life-long passion for classical music and its history. Childhood piano lessons and a 1903 Weber Upright share equal blame for her original compositions, available on **ntustin.musicaneo.com**.

Her writing includes work for Reuters and CNBC, short stories and freelance articles, and research published in peer-reviewed academic journals. She lives in Southern California with her husband, three rambunctious children, and a pit bull.

For details on the Haydn series and monthly blog posts on the great composer, visit the official **Haydn Mystery web site:** NTUSTIN.COM.

Sign up for the Haydn Mystery Newsletter at <u>ntustin.com</u>
Subscribe to the Haydn Blog at <u>ntustin.com/blog</u>

Made in the USA
Coppell, TX
23 February 2020